DARE
TO
DREAM

Also by Gemma Jackson

Through Streets Broad and Narrow
Ha'penny Chance
The Ha'penny Place
Ha'penny Schemes
Impossible Dream

Published by Poolbeg

DARE
TO
DREAM

GEMMA JACKSON

POOLBEG

Published 2019
by Poolbeg Press Ltd.
123 Grange Hill, Baldoyle,
Dublin 13, Ireland
Email: poolbeg@poolbeg.com

A catalogue record for this book is available from the British Library.

ISBN 978178199-805-2

Printed and bound by Liberduplex, Barcelona

www.poolbeg.com

About the Author

Gemma Jackson was born in the tenements of Dublin. She is the fifth child of Rose and Paddy Jackson.

Gemma has travelled extensively and experienced life from a viewpoint of wealth as well as extreme poverty. She freely admits she preferred being wealthy.

She grew up listening to and being fascinated by storytellers. The radio was a large part of her growing-up years – back in the days of the dinosaurs – when stories were read aloud on the radio to the delight of millions.

She has never lost her love of stories. To open a book and escape into an unknown world still delights her. To be able to share her world with her readers is a great joy.

Acknowledgements

I want to thank all of the readers who have taken the time to comment on my books. It is such a thrill to know that my world is enjoyed by many.

I have to thank my daughter for putting up with me – and the dog for forcing me to walk and look at the world around me.

My number one fan and friend Jewell Gore – I misspelled her name last time – which she was quick to point out. She little knows she is about to become one of my experts for my research!

The many people who work in libraries around the world. They are amazing – the ones I've met and all of those I haven't met. Libraries are such wonderful places and the people who work in them always seem to greet you with a smile.

The people at Poolbeg Press for allowing me to share my world with readers. My editor Gaye Shortland, who surely must be up for sainthood by now. She makes my words shine. Paula Campbell who devotes her time and energy to promote writers like me.

It has all been a wonderful dream – thank you.

Dedication

For my daughter Astrid as always for the back rubs – food – and of course the constant supply of hot tea. Where would I be without you?.

Chapter 1

East Hinsdale
Queens County
New York

December 1898

"Caleb, thank you so much for coming." Eleanor Foster held the door of her home open.

"My dear Eleanor, look at you." Caleb Anderson stepped over the wooden threshold and into the tiny vestibule. "Nathan would not be happy to see you looking so worn, my dear. You must take better care of yourself."

Eleanor ignored his words. "You may leave your outer clothing there." She pointed to a freestanding mahogany coat stand and stepped into the second of the rooms leading off the hallway – the room imprinted on her mind now as 'the sick room'.

She looked at the tall handsome man of colour standing over her husband Nathan's still form. "Samuel, I wish to have a private conversation with Mr Anderson – would you make sure we are not disturbed?" The almost constant stream of visitors to her home since they had brought her husband home to die was irritating.

"Yes, ma'am." Samuel Johnson, after stoking and adding fuel to the fire, left the room to take up position at the front door.

1

"Eleanor –"

"Take a seat, Caleb." Eleanor waved to a tall-back wooden chair pulled close to one side of the narrow bed. She took a matching chair on the other side and picked up and kissed her husband's unresponsive hand. "He is not long for this world." She shook her head sadly – she knew her beloved husband's spirit was just waiting for her permission to leave his body. She could not explain how she knew but know she did.

"What can I do for you, Eleanor?" Caleb didn't know what to do or say in this situation. That something like this should happen to a couple so happy in each other's company was tragic. Never had he seen a love such as these two shared. "You sent for me."

"Yes," Eleanor sighed. "I have a proposition to put to you, my very dear friend." She stared across her husband's body at the man who had been her friend since childhood. He was so very handsome with his tall upright body, thick blue-black hair and the bluest eyes she had ever seen. If a man could be beautiful, Caleb Anderson was. "I must make plans for my future." She had spent hours grieving for her husband while frantically trying to find a way through the uncertain future before her.

"My dear, this is surely not the time to upset yourself." Caleb felt it was wrong to have a discussion about the future while seated over the form of a man who quite obviously had none.

She smiled sadly as she rubbed her cheek against her husband's hand. "I defied my mother by marrying Nathan as you know, Caleb. I will not return to her home now as a poor relation. My mother would delight in making my life intolerable."

2

"Did Nathan make no plans for your future security?" Caleb stared down at the man his dear friend had given up everything for – surely he had made some provision for her if ever anything happened to him? He had risked his life to save strangers, jumping onto the railway tracks to release a jammed signal – without his brave action two trains would have rammed into each other. Nathan himself hadn't been so fortunate – one of the trains had hit him, knocking him from the tracks onto nearby waste ground. He was being hailed as a hero but, as many a man knew, that would not put food on the table or a roof over your head.

"My darling Nathan believed that if anything ever happened to him my mother would welcome me back with open arms. He was so very trusting. He thought the best of everyone he met." She pressed a kiss into the hand she held while fighting the tears that wanted to flood from her eyes. She couldn't cry now – she feared if she cried she would never stop. "I have never understood how a man with such an enquiring mind believed so fervently in the goodness of his fellow man." She looked with love at the figure lying so still upon the bed. "We fought about it constantly, did we not, my love?"

The silence that greeted her words to her husband was painful.

Eleanor squeezed her husband's hand so tightly that if the man had been responsive he would have winced. "I have been selfish holding my darling Nathan to this life. I am convinced he is but waiting for me to let him go." The tears she had been fighting began to flow from her eyes. "It has been ten days since they carried his broken body in to me. The railway doctor gave him only hours to live

3

when they placed him here." She sobbed into the limp flesh she held. Soon he would be cold and her heart would break.

"My dear!" Caleb couldn't bear to see the pain on her beautiful face. How could she bear it?

"Caleb," Eleanor wiped her face with her handkerchief, "I must protect myself. That has been made very clear to me. While Nathan has been lying here I have been visited by many hairy-fisted men uttering polite phrases of sympathy while undressing me with their eyes. You know I don't exaggerate." She tightened her fingers on Nathan's hand. "I could not bear to have another man touch me. That these railway men are only waiting until my beloved breathes his last to come courting is painfully obvious to me. I simply cannot bear it."

"It was your choice to live almost in isolation – just you and Nathan. Without him by your side you leave yourself open to opportunists." He tried not to criticise the man lying so gravely injured. "Do you wish to remain here?" Caleb could not see the joy in remaining in this remote area, surrounded only by Mother Nature. He preferred the lights of his beloved New York City.

"This is my home – the house Nathan brought me to when we married seven years ago. I have no wish to return to New York society. I have had the freedom to be myself here."

Caleb watched and waited. He didn't understand his friend's thoughts – he only knew she was up to something. Behind that stunningly beautiful face was a brain to rival any of the Titans of industry he bargained with daily. He almost held his breath as he waited for her to speak again.

"I want you to marry me." Eleanor put it bluntly. She had no time to dance around the social niceties so beloved by New York society. She watched the colour leave his face.

4

"I know, Caleb." She allowed him no time to find the words he so obviously searched for. "I know – Nathan explained it to me. He opened my eyes to so much in the world around me – I was blind for so long. Nathan was more than my husband and lover, Caleb. He was my friend, my mentor and my educator. Nathan had no fear of intelligent women."

There was a stunned silence for what seemed to Eleanor a very long time.

Caleb finally reacted. "What did he explain?" He stood up, shocked by her words, unable to find a way to respond to her comments. He crossed to a window that looked out on only darkness, seeing the room at his back reflected in its glass.

"I do not judge you, Caleb. You are my friend and so you shall always remain, even if you deny me." Eleanor looked at her husband's flaccid face. It looked wrong. Nathan had always been so alive. She brushed his blond hair from his face with a hand that trembled, knowing that he was somewhere listening to her and supporting her as he always had. "I know you prefer the company of men. That does not shock me. I am glad you will have no desire for my body. But you are five years older than me, almost thirty years old, Caleb. You will not be able to deny the matchmaking mamas of New York for very much longer. Not without drawing attention to yourself. They will force you to marry. You know I speak truth."

"What you suggest is outrageous. Your husband isn't even dead yet," he bit out. His preferences were a matter of disgust for all good-thinking men. How could she claim to be different?

"I have thought about this while I sat here watching my darling die inch by inch." Eleanor didn't turn to look at him. She watched her husband's chest struggle to rise. "It is early days yet, but I believe I am with child. Nathan knew this. It is a comfort to me that a part of him will live on. I want you to be a father to this child – a protector." Her body shook with the effort to suppress her sobs. "You are a rich eligible man, Caleb. You need an heir."

"Eleanor, your grief has turned your mind." He returned to the seat across the bed from her.

"No," she shook her head, "I need to survive. I need to protect the life that I carry. I will not allow any child of mine to be raised as I was – male or female, this child will be free of the constraints put upon you and me."

"Many would claim we were raised in luxury."

"We were not allowed to broaden our horizons – never allowed to form our own opinions. I was stifled. You were there – you know I am right."

"You should have been born male," Caleb said softly.

"I am happy with my gender." Eleanor offered her hand. It was important to her that he realise his preferences did not affect their friendship. "So what do you think – will you marry me?"

"It is madness." Caleb was sorely tempted. To have a wife and child tucked away in the country. To live a life without having to lie – without watching every word out of his mouth – how wonderful that would be.

"It is perfection. We already share a sincere friendship. I will remain in this house. We will set Samuel up as caretaker for the empty house next door – a man such as he has no business living in a shed at the bottom of my garden – already people comment about his being here alone with me. We can put it about that I stay here because the fog of New York affects my breathing. I live here for my health. I would be available to visit you in your 5th Avenue home whenever society demanded it. You could visit me – and Samuel – without anyone passing remark on your comings and goings."

"You always did see too much." Caleb glanced down at the figure on the bed. What would Nathan have thought of all of this?

"You and Samuel have not been as careful as you believe." She waited with bated breath. He had to agree to marry her. It was the solution to a great many problems. "So, will you marry me?"

"Should I agree to this madness, what do you want?" Caleb was in no doubt that she had worked out a list of demands. Eleanor had never been one for allowing life to happen to her. She was frighteningly clear-sighted for all that some accused her of being 'fey'.

"I want you to purchase my house and the one next door. I want the deeds to both houses and the land surrounding them put in my name." She and Nathan had discussed buying the two houses sitting in front of the fire of an evening. Nathan insisted the land surrounding the two houses would form a perfect homestead – providing enough food and wood for their needs. Samuel had the practical knowledge and had offered to help them for a share of the produce.

"I am in need of a cash injection – Nathan worked on the railway, we had a small income but not enough to purchase this house." She moistened her lips. "I want a small sum of money deposited into my bank account monthly. I want a telephone installed in this house. The post office has had one installed and it is a marvel." She shook her head, angry at herself for allowing her thoughts

7

to stray from the subject. "I am in need of a horse and carriage. These houses and this land will be my child's inheritance. The child will be raised knowing society through its connection with you and the wonders of the countryside from its birthplace. If this child should want to remain on the outskirts of New York life, I want it to have options available to it. I cannot see the future. I have to make a life for myself and my child. That is my motivation and I know too that the thought of being once more in the control of my mother scares me rigid."

"Have you thought that your mother may well welcome you back into the fold? She is getting older as we all are."

"My mother is a social-climbing harridan and well you know it. She has tried to use me to advance her status all of my life. I will not allow it. The woman is on her third husband for heaven's sake! The latest is ready to cock up his toes. She is on the lookout for number four. I do not want to have any part of that life again." Her mother married old men with fortunes to leave to their grieving widows. She cared nothing for the heirs left without their inheritance because of her greed. She had as many enemies as she had dollars in the bank.

"Nathan," Caleb took a shaking breath before addressing the still figure on the bed, "I promise to protect this amazing woman that we both love to the best of my ability and, should there be a child, I will love him or her all the days of my life."

"Thank you." Eleanor put her aching head on her beloved husband's chest and whispered, "I will be alright now, my love. You can go." Her heartbroken sobs shook the still figure on the bed, giving an imitation of life, but she knew he had gone. She would have to forge her own path now.

Chapter 2

Percy Place
Dublin
Ireland

January 1899

Georgina Corrigan-Whitmore wrapped her red woollen dressing gown tightly around her and ran on bedsock-covered feet up the stairs from her second-floor bedroom to the third.

"Ladies, what in the name of goodness is causing all of this noise?"

"Madam!" Bridget, one of Georgina's three convent orphan maids almost ran over to her mistress. "Sorry – we've been moving this chest around." She dropped her voice to a whisper, looking around. "The Dowager Duchess of Westbrooke sent it on ahead of the new woman – she had one of her men deliver it to the back door this morning."

The house in Percy Place Dublin had recently been set up as a form of halfway house for women in need, under the auspices of the BOB. The organization BOB – Brides Of Breeding – was set up originally to entertain bored society women but had soon become a force of good in the protection of women. BOB helped gentlewomen in dire situations escape. Percy Place not only sheltered some of these women but was training them to find employment and become self-supporting.

Now two such women were leaving to take up enviable positions as secretaries to society ladies.

"The chest carries the Dowager's coat of arms and she wants it to be returned to her – she suggested Miss Ermatrude could use it when she leaves," Bridget said in a normal tone of voice. "So I'm taking the items belonging to the new woman out of the chest and putting them in this bedroom." The rooms on the third floor had been turned into dormitories for the women who would pass through the house.

"It is just as well this occurred." Verity Watson stepped out of the open door of the bedroom Bridget had gestured towards. "It was only while changing chests that we discovered Erma intended to leave all the new clothing Sarah has made for her behind." She shook her head in sorrow at this short-sightedness on the other woman's part.

"I shall have no need for fancy gowns." Ermatrude Willowbee appeared in the doorway behind Verity. The stout little woman was scowling. "I am to be a servant." She put plump little hands on her hips and glared.

"You are to be employed as secretary to the Dowager Duchess of Westbrooke – not the village fishmonger!" Verity wanted to shake the smaller woman until her teeth rattled. Had she learned nothing in the months that they had lived in this house? "You must start as you mean to go on, Erma." She did take the woman by the shoulders then and shake her gently. "You will have working hours and time free," *shake*, "you must not fade into the background," *shake*, "you will perhaps be invited to social occasions by the other employees," *shake*, "you must be prepared for anything!"

"But –" Erma tried to object.

"Verity is right." The door across the corridor had opened and two women pushing and pulling a large chest between them stepped out. "I, for one, have no intention of disappearing into the furniture," said Octavia White-Gershwin, a pretty strawberry blonde. "This is a new beginning for all of us and it is up to us to make the best of it."

"As if you disappearing into the furniture were ever a possibility!" Euphemia Locke-Statton said, laughing at her roommate's comments.

"I too will be taking up a position as social secretary to a titled lady. I am sure Lady Sutton will be agreeable to us meeting up in our free time." Tavi stood holding a hand to her back. That chest was heavy. "Perhaps you and I will have the opportunity to go to the theatre some evening, Erma. I will expect you to be dressed to impress – no more little brown mouse." Tavi had thought that she would be forced to go into service. She had collected an assortment of drab clothing with this purpose in mind. It was only when she came to this house that a world of opportunity had opened before her. She had passed all of the drab clothing on to Erma to be adjusted by the talented young Sarah. The woman did love her greys and browns.

Georgina stood watching the women she had come to think of as her students.

"We need to get these chests organised." Felicia Hyde-Richards, a statuesque blonde, stepped from the bedroom she shared with Verity. "The carriages will be here before we know it."

"I am going to dress to meet the day." Georgina turned

11

away. "We'll meet up for breakfast, ladies," she said over her shoulder. "I'll send Billy and his men up for the chests. Bridget, hurry the ladies along." Billy Flint and his men were a blessing that came into her life after her husband had left her practically penniless.

Captain Charles Whitmore had planned to sail away leaving his young wife without servants and with no income to support the house that was her only possession. His plans had backfired on him rather brutally – nonetheless Georgina had been forced to find a way to survive.

"Yes, madam." Bridget continued emptying the chest while whispered arguments went on between the others.

"Good morning, Cook," Georgina said as she pushed open the door from the stairs leading into the kitchen. "Liam, run down the garden and fetch Billy Flint," she ordered the bootboy, stepping fully into the kitchen. Billy Flint and his men occupied the carriage house at the rear of the Percy Place property.

"Are that lot about ready to eat, do you think?" Betty Powell, or 'Cook' as she was called, turned from her coal-fired black-leaded range. "I've the breakfast meat cooked and warming but I need to see the whites of their eyes before I cook the eggs."

Ruth and Sarah hadn't stopped in their work when their mistress entered the kitchen.

"I'm about to have Billy move them along." Georgina stepped over to the long work table that ran along the middle of the kitchen. "I'd kill for a cup of tea."

"I'll join you," Lily Chambers said, walking into the kitchen.

"Lily, I thought you'd still be sleeping." Georgina

12

turned to greet her long-time housekeeper and friend with a smile. She'd hoped that at least one of her old retainers would have the chance for a rest. Betty and Lily – both women in their sixties – should be taking it easy – but what would she do without them? She was less than half their age and was finding the pace of life exhausting.

"How could anyone sleep with the noise that lot are making?" Lily looked around and had to remind herself not to sigh in despair. The absence of the master had brought peace to this house, but she would never adjust to the lack of trained servants.

"Ruth!" Lily called to the dark-haired young maid. "Serve Miss Georgina and me a pot of tea at the alcove table." It was coming to something when the mistress of the house and the housekeeper sat in the alcove off the kitchen for a pot of tea. Gone were the days when they had servants aplenty. "Sarah, run upstairs and give Bridget a hand. There was more talking than working on that landing when I came down."

"*Tell that lot to hurry up or I'm giving their breakfast to the pigs!*" Cook shouted at the disappearing back of the maid. "Ruth, the arse is boiled out of the kettle. I'll have a cup of tea and all." She walked over to join the two women at the table pushed into the alcove. "If we're having this much trouble with only two of them leaving, what will it be like when the next lot leave?" She sat on one of the wooden chairs pulled close to the table.

"Erma is the problem." Georgina surveyed the two women fondly. When her husband showed his disdain of her to all of Dublin by passing his mistress off as his common-law wife, what would she have done without them by her side?

"Never!" Cook and Lily said together in mock astonishment.

"Yes, she's trying to leave behind the clothes Sarah made for her."

"What a waste! Who does she think those clothes will fit?" Lily shook her head. "Honest to goodness. It was sheer good fortune that those bodices fit her. Sarah had only to refashion the skirts."

Sarah Brown, one of the convent orphans sent to this house to be trained as a maid, had proven to be an excellent seamstress. The young girl had spent almost all of her time bent over a sewing machine refashioning the out-of-date garments found in the attics of the house and those that the women themselves had brought with them.

"It will feel strange without them. Well, at least these two are not going far." Georgina watched Ruth place a heavy teapot in the middle of the table. The girl then placed delicate china cups and saucers before each woman – sugar and milk were placed close to hand. It still felt strange to her to be served in this simple fashion – had she been spoiled with the abundance of servants that had surrounded her all of her life?

"Do we have any new information on when the rest of the students will be leaving?" Lily Chambers was feeling her age this morning.

"Billy Flint has been making enquiries for us," Georgina told the other two women. "The many sailors on the Dublin docks have information they shared with him about the docks of New York." She picked up her cup and sipped. "I feel responsible for the women who have been placed in our care. I want to know more of what they might expect when they reach America."

"If the docks in New York are anything like our own here in Dublin, you'd be taking your life in your hands if you didn't know where you were going or what you were doing," Betty Powell said.

"That is my fear," Georgina said. "The American branch of the BOBs will be responsible for the girls when they arrive in New York – but you have seen the docks here – it's worse than a cattle market – how will they ever be able to find each other in such crowds? I simply can't imagine it. I travelled in the company of my parents always. We had servants to take care of matters. My father had an agent who advised him about travel. We do not have such a luxury." Betty was right: the docks were a dangerous place for unwary travellers. Billy Flint had told her of men and women who preyed on young people who arrived bewildered onto the docks seeking new lives – the young people disappeared never to be seen again – many sold into houses of ill-repute. How could she safeguard the young women she was being paid to train for a new life in America?

"Might Richard Wilson not be able to advise us?" Lily mentioned Georgina's friend and business advisor.

"I am afraid America is outside Richard's area of knowledge," said Georgina, sipping her tea. "Lady Sutton appears to be the one in the know about America." Lady Sutton was a member of BOBs, as was the Dowager Duchess of Westbrooke.

"That woman appears to have a great deal of knowledge about a great many things," Lily agreed.

"Can she help you arrange something for the three getting ready to leave us?" Betty Powell had grown fond of the women, who had been willing to turn their hand to anything since they had arrived all of a flutter to this house.

"Arabella, Lady Sutton, has an acquaintance in an area adjacent to New York. The woman has been approached about meeting the women from the ship and helping them adjust – for a fee of course." Georgina looked around to be sure no one could overhear what she wished to share with these two women who had been servants to her family since before her birth. "The woman has recently lost her husband – an accident on the railway – I believe."

"Poor thing!" Lily shook her head in sympathy for a woman left alone to manage her own affairs.

"The money offered might be welcome to the poor thing." Betty too felt sympathy for the unknown woman.

"Yes, well, I'm afraid that is not the case . . ." Georgina again checked the area. "This woman – her husband wasn't even cold when she remarried – to a wealthy man prominent in New York society."

There were gasps of delighted shock as each woman leaned in to enjoy what promised to be titillating gossip.

"It seems," Georgina paused delicately, "the man in question had been a friend to both the husband and wife. He was a much sought-after prize on the New York marriage market – many people despise this woman for catching this man in her coils."

"*No!*" Lily gasped.

"*Well!*" said Betty.

"It seems the marriage was a matter of some urgency according to Lady Sutton's informant."

"*No!*" gasped Lily and Betty together.

"Indeed. They offered each other solace of a personal nature." She ignored the no's that greeted this titbit.

"There may well be a child from their actions – hence the hasty wedding ceremony."

"Well, I never!" Betty Powell blushed to think of it.

"Is this the kind of woman we want to advise our ladies?" Lily asked. "Besides, if this woman has made such an advantageous marriage would she still be willing to help our girls settle in? Surely she would have no need of the money on offer?"

Ruth looked over at the whispering women in the alcove, wondering if she should ask them if they had need of more tea but reluctant to interrupt.

"The women who came to us came to learn to live an independent life," Georgina said with a laugh. "If this woman wants to take them on, I for one would be glad of it. This is obviously a woman who knows how to look after her own interests. Something women like me need to learn."

"Well, I never!" Betty Powell stood to fetch fresh tea. She didn't know what to think of this latest development.

"The world as we know it is certainly changing," Lily said.

"We are all being forced to learn new ways of doing things." Georgina had been shocked when Arabella told her of this woman. But who knew what had caused the woman to behave in such a fashion? *Judge not lest ye be judged*, she thought.

Chapter 3

"With the best will in the world, Cook, I cannot eat a large breakfast this morning." Octavia White-Gershwin looked around at the women and one young boy who shared the servant's dining room with her. She remembered how angry she had been the first time she'd been expected to dine with servants. "I am looking forward to starting work for Lady Sutton, but – the butterflies in my stomach – they are whirling in a most disturbing way. I fear anything I might eat would make a swift reappearance."

"Have a slice of toast with your tea, Tavi." Cook, watching Ruth pour tea from an enormous teapot, advised. "See how that settles."

"We were sick with nerves when we found out we were coming to this house." Bridget pointed to her friends Sarah and Ruth. The three orphans had been given no choice in the matter. One day they were in the orphanage – the next in service. That was their lot in life and they accepted it. However, having come to this house and

18

listened to what these women had been taught here – well, that had changed everything – for Bridget at least.

"You must be sure to remember all that you have learned here, Tavi," Verity Watson said. "It will be difficult for you at first. You will be neither fish nor fowl." She well knew, having spent ten years as an unpaid secretary to her distant relative the Dowager Duchess of Westbrooke. "The upper servants will try to dominate you – put you in your place." She laughed gently. "I can't see you allowing such a thing, Tavi, but you will need to make friends among the servants. You cannot walk through life alone."

"You must be sure to leave the house in your free time," Lily Chambers said. "If you remain on the premises there is always some little chore that can be found for you to do."

"I will have nowhere to go." Ermatrude Willowbee was already sick with nerves at the thought of leaving this house. What would she do when left to her own devices?

"Nonsense!" Euphemia Locke-Statton was heartily sick of the constant moaning Erma indulged in – everyone else almost drowned the woman in sympathy. She was on her own – as they all were – time and past she began to take charge of her own life. They had been fortunate enough to be given the tools to survive in this house. It was now up to each of them to apply what they had learned to their own lives. "You will be based in Dublin for heaven's sake. There are museums, galleries, theatres, lending libraries and a host of other entertainments that you can visit. There is no need for you to sit alone in your room and wail at the world."

"You will be employed by a duchess, Erma." Felicia

Hyde-Richards felt a great deal of sympathy for the poor little mouse of a woman. "I don't suggest you abuse that privilege but surely you realise that you will be employed by a woman of great distinction, a leading light in Dublin society? That will reflect on you – you need to be prepared to step out of the shadows." They had been telling the woman the same thing for months.

Georgina exchanged glances with Cook and Lily. They had done their best by this group – the first of its kind – it was now up to the women to make the best of what they had been given.

Liam the bootboy shoved food into his mouth, wondering what all the fuss was about – you made the best you could with whatever came at yeh – they should know that – they were older than him.

The tears flowed freely when it became time for Octavia and Ermatrude to leave. Two carriages stood in the street outside the house on Percy Place. There were frantic squeals as last-minute items were sought. The carriage drivers were anxious to get their charges inside the vehicles. They didn't like to keep the horses standing.

Promises were extracted to keep in touch. Erma had assured the women that she would be delighted to become their postmistress. She would receive and send on news from all of them. They would keep up to date with each other.

The remaining group – mistress, servants and students alike – stood on the tall granite steps leading up from the Percy Place garden and waved as the carriages carrying the first two graduates of this strange school into their new lives took off with a whisper of the whip from the carriage drivers. They stood watching until the carriages disappeared from sight.

"Come – we have much to do." Georgina waved her hands to encourage the drooping women back into the house.

They were still staring down the empty road.

"Ladies, please!" Georgina clapped her hands loudly. "Let us get inside and stop filling the neighbours' mouths." The goings-on in this house had become a subject of gossip to the other residents of this terrace of houses. There was no need to supply additional ammunition. She marshalled her troops ahead of her into the beautifully tiled, long hallway of the house.

"Madam, if I might have a word?" Billy Flint, the young man who was becoming a vital member of this strange household, appeared in the open doorway at the top of the stairs leading down to the basement.

"Certainly." She took a moment to lock the door at her back and watched while the others passed Billy Flint and one of his men as they stepped out into the hallway to allow the women to return to the basement.

"What can I do for you, Billy?" Georgina was making a mental list of the chores she needed to complete this day.

"The Dowager sent this fella," Billy jerked his chin at the strange-looking young man who had been sent along with the chest that morning. The man hadn't removed his hat even indoors. Billy was tempted to pull it off himself but hadn't yet. The fella didn't even tip his hat to the ladies – rude. He'd received written instructions to hide him until the two women had left the house. Well, he'd done that. What happened next was up to the mistress. "I'll leave him with you." Billy turned and stepped into the stairwell. He pulled the door closed at his back and made more noise than strictly necessary running down the stairs.

"Hello, Georgina – it has been a very long time, my friend." A soft feminine voice came from the man standing with his back pressed to the closed door.

"Dear God!" Georgina had to grab at the nearby hallstand. "Is that you, Eugenie?" She had been expecting her childhood friend – but could this possibly be her? It was difficult to make out the figure, wrapped up as it was in workman's clothing.

"*C'est moi*. I am sorry – it has been a very long time since I spoke in English. I am finding it surprisingly difficult to remember words."

"Eugenie, I can't believe it, where have you been?" Georgina suddenly came to life, almost leaping at her friend and pulling her into a close embrace as the tears began to flow. She rocked her from side to side, sobbing all the while.

"Perhaps we could go somewhere I can change back into being me?" Eugenie pushed her friend gently away from her. She didn't know how or what to feel. It had been so long since she had been in the company of anyone who truly knew her.

"Some clothes were delivered here this morning. Yours, apparently." Georgina tried to pull herself together. She took her friend by the elbow and began to tow her towards the stairs.

She allowed herself to be pulled along. "Yes, the Dowager thought it would be better for me to arrive here in disguise. Georgie, I know we have much to talk about, but do you think I might have a bath before we indulge in long conversation? I am afraid I am tired and dirty." She had been given a mug of tea and a thick sandwich by the men in the carriage house. The food had been strange but very welcome.

"Of course – but, Eugenie, what you are doing here?" Georgina wanted to demand answers from her friend. It was folly for her to be here at this time. "I couldn't believe it when the BOBs told me you were coming."

"I am going to be a Harvey Girl." She half smiled as she said it.

"In the Name of God!" Georgina almost fell down the stairs. What an absurd idea! She wanted to tear her own hair out. This was madness.

"Please, Georgie, help me become a female again. We can talk later. There is time – is there not?" She had thought about this meeting in the days and weeks of travelling. Now that she was here, she was simply too tired to indulge in the many conversations she had imagined.

"In here . . ." Georgina opened the door to the bedroom recently vacated by Ermatrude Willowbee. It was fortunate that Erma hadn't shared this room with anyone. Trying to explain Eugenie's strange appearance to anyone would be beyond her at this moment in time. She cast a quick glance around the room before turning to face her friend.

She gasped. "Eugenie, dear God above, what happened?"

She stared at her friend's head of silver hair. What had happened to her riot of jet-black curls?

"I had almost forgotten." Eugenie stood with the hat she had removed in her hand. The door was closed at her

23

back. She reached up and touched the hair that fell loose around her shoulders. "My hair has been this colour for a very long time." Her hair had to be shaved in order to treat her injuries many years ago. It had grown back this silver colour. She'd grown used to it. "I need to change," she said, changing the subject.

"You will need a robe, towel and soap for your bath." Georgina tried to force her eyes away from her friend. She looked so different to her memory of her. She had grown taller if she wasn't mistaken. Her features had thinned down, losing their youthful plumpness, and her sad blue eyes looked ancient. "I had a bathhouse set up in the outside boiler house. I had to handle the requirements of all of the women in the house." She was babbling but she didn't know what to say to this familiar stranger.

"It's alright, Georgie." She knew how her friend was feeling. She was confused herself. "Tell me what has been going on in your life. I was very surprised when told you were now running a home for the BOBs." She began to peel the men's garments from her body. She had travelled in them and was desperate to remove them and have a long hot bath. She searched for the items Georgie said she needed from the articles placed neatly on one of the two unmade beds in the room.

"You kept in touch with the BOBs?" Stupid question, Georgie, she admonished herself. Obviously she had. "They refused to tell me anything about you – no matter how much I begged."

"Madam!" a girl's voice called from the corridor outside. "Madam, are you up here, Madam?" The sound of doors being opened and closed could be heard.

It was Bridget.

Georgina looked at Eugenie in shock. The other woman was still half-dressed in men's clothing. Georgina stepped quickly towards the door and, with a last glance over her shoulder, stepped into the corridor.

"What is it, Bridget?" Dear Lord, this had all the ingredients of a farce.

"Cook sent me to find you," Bridget said with a smile. "She said you hadn't eaten very much breakfast and it would soon be lunch."

"Thank Cook for me. Tell her there will be one extra for lunch and could you have one of the Smiths light the fire under the copper and prepare the bathhouse, please?"

"Yes, ma'am." Bridget bent a knee in a quick bob before turning back the way she had come. She wondered who the extra person was? Was the new woman about to arrive? And was she the one who would need a bath?

Georgina watched and waited until Bridget had reached the hall below. That young madam was insatiably curious. There was a great deal to be decided before she brought her old friend downstairs to join the company. When she was sure the coast was clear, she stepped back into the bedroom.

Eugenie stood in the middle of the room, the wrist cuffs of her robe pressed to her mouth. "Was that my daughter? Was she so close?" She fell to her knees, trying to muffle her heartbroken sobs in the folds of material. To be so near and yet not able to claim her child – had this all been a mistake?

"Oh, my dear!" Georgina joined her friend on the floor and pulled the sobbing woman into her arms. "Why have you decided to come here? Why put yourself through so much pain?"

Chapter 4

"I wanted to see her," Eugenie hiccupped. "When I heard she was in your home – it seemed a sign – I long to see her – even if only once."

"Eugenie –"

"I go by Jenny now." The name Eugenie sounded foreign to her ears. It had been a long time since she had been that person.

"Jenny then." Georgina didn't know what to do or say. She had longed to see her dear friend but for her to arrive at such a time – it was insanity. "You do you know that Clive Henderson the Earl of Castlewellan is here in Dublin? The man is still your lawful husband, your daughter Bridget's father. He is here in Dublin and shows no sign of leaving."

"I knew they had called her Bridget." She couldn't allow herself to think about the man she had married. She wanted only to see her child. The pain in her breast would last a lifetime but in this she was determined – she would see her daughter.

"Did you hear what I said?" Georgina gently shook the thin shoulders. "Clive Henderson is in Dublin."

"I know." Jenny pulled away and on shaking limbs stood. "Look at me!" She held out thin arms and turned slowly. "I have changed so much – do you really think that man would recognise me? Could he possibly see the woman I was in the woman I've become?"

"Oh, Eu … Jenny," Georgina too stood, "I fear for your safety. The man was enthralled by you." That was a polite way to describe the brutal obsession the man had held for her friend. She was lucky to have escaped his clutches with her life.

"I am not the person he knew." Jenny walked over to look out the window.

"Come away from there, for goodness' sake. That window overlooks the street." Georgina pulled her friend back. "Who knows who may be out there?"

"Really, you …"

"Jenny –" yes, it was easy to address this familiar stranger as Jenny, "I don't know what you've been told about the situation in this house but my husband is determined to make my life as difficult as he can. I have reporters and nosy neighbours checking out my every move."

"This is all so very different from the life we planned when we were young girls, isn't it? We talked so bravely of having life choices – remember? We talked of running away – we talked of making a life for ourselves outside of marriage – remember?" Jenny was exhausted. She had been travelling for what seemed like years instead of weeks. She walked over and sat on one of the stripped beds. The temptation to simply roll onto the bare mattress was immense. She fought it, wanting a bath and the chance to see her child before she slept.

"How I have wished over the years that we had been brave enough to follow our dream," Georgina said.

"We could not have known the nightmare that awaited us – they call it the institution of marriage – I would have chosen a mental institution over what awaited me with that man." Jenny had spent years suppressing the memory of her time as a wife to the Earl of Castlewellan.

"It does seem beyond the realms of fantasy that we should both have made such bad marriages," Georgina agreed. "If only we had been brave enough to take to our heels."

"Is that why you agreed to set up this school for runaways for the BOBs?" Jenny asked.

"That and the offer of an income – I am desperate for funds."

"Enough!" Jenny smiled as Georgie joined her on the bed, then whispered, "Tell me about my child – my daughter." Her child had been a secret she had kept close to her heart for so many years.

"Bridget?" Georgina almost laughed. "She is a delight to have around the house. It is as well Reverend Mother placed her with me – that child will never make an obedient servant. She has the greenest eyes that express her every opinion – fluently."

"Your Great-aunt Allie, or Reverend Mother as we must call her, was so kind to me." Jenny tried to stop the memories that wanted to escape her control. "Particularly since I am not Catholic."

"I thought that rather clever of the BOBs. Who would think to look for the Countess of Castlewellan in a convent?"

"Indeed." Jenny did not want to revisit old ground. There was something far more important on her mind. "Bridget – my child – tell me more of her, please."

"She looks a great deal like him – the man who fathered her." Georgie wondered if that would affect her friend's reaction to the child. "The nuns shave the orphans' heads, you know, but her hair is growing. It is that marvellous blonde-toffee colour, rich and thick. She has his green eyes but your smile. She is so bright, sharp enough to cut herself as my granny would say." She would not tell her friend that Bridget had been badly treated by the orphanage – trained to be a scrubbing woman. To condemn such a child to that life was obscene in Georgina's opinion. "You must be extra careful in your dealings with her. She questions everything."

"I kept her with me for as long as I could." Jenny remembered those precious months with her child. Sometimes she thought those memories were all that had kept her sane through the years. "I drew so many miniatures of her. I loved to paint her." The nuns had refused to allow her to keep the tiny drawings but she had the memories in her heart. They couldn't deny her those.

"You were always such a clever portraitist." Georgina had a collection of miniature paintings her friend had created. They were hidden away and it had been years since she had taken them out to view them.

"She showed no signs of her father's evil nature – has that changed?" Jenny asked the question that had kept her awake on many nights. Could the evil be passed from father to child?

"Oh, no." Georgina reached over and covered the hands that Jenny was twisting in her lap. "She is her own person but fundamentally she is a kind and loving girl."

"I worried," Jenny said simply.

"There is no need." Georgina stood and looked down on the silver head of her friend. How ironic – her child was golden. "I will take you to the bathhouse now. You will need to bring a change of clothing with you. You can dress there – it is warm. I will introduce you to Bridget and the rest of my strange household at lunch."

Jenny sank up to her chin in the hot water. She wasn't nervous about seeing her child – she was desperate. How would she bear to leave her? But she had to – she had no way of supporting them both. Life could be so cruel.

"You are being ridiculous," she whispered and prepared to wash her hair. "You haven't even seen the child yet and already you worry about leaving her. You must do better than this or all will be lost."

It had taken so much courage to give up the safe life she had made for herself in France. The smile on her face was ironic as she wondered, not for the first time, what her employers would have thought of having the Countess of Castlewellan as their under-housekeeper.

When she'd received the letter from Beatrice – Lady Constable – she had been shaken. The hand holding the letter had shook as if with fever. Could this opportunity in America be the first step to getting her child back in her life? America, it was so far away from Ireland – perhaps that too was a point in its favour. She didn't know, she only knew she was ready to take back control of her life.

"Enough of daydreaming." She stepped from the cooling water. She dried off swiftly and pulled a lawn chemise over her damp skin, then quickly dressed.

30

"Jenny!" A rap of knuckles on the outer door sounded. "Are you decent?"

"I am dressed." The black skirt and white blouse she wore had been part of her uniform but they would serve her now, she hoped.

She turned the key in the lock and pulled open the door.

"I've brought Bridget to help you restore order to the room." Georgina believed it would be better for mother and child to meet without being under the gaze of the rest of the household. "There is a trick to it, you see." She deliberately blocked Bridget's view into the bathhouse, giving Jenny a moment to gather herself.

"Bridget," she drew the young maid forward, "this is Jenny ..."

"Castle," Jenny supplied. Reverend Mother had a sense of humour giving her that name.

Georgina almost laughed aloud at the name. "Yes, of course, Jenny Castle – she will be joining the other women waiting to leave for America. I'll leave you to show Jenny how to empty the bath, Bridget."

"Yes, ma'am." Bridget stepped into the room, glad to be the first to see the latest woman to join the house.

She smiled at the pale woman standing as if frozen, before bustling about. She used a bucket to empty most of the water from the bath, all the time looking at this new resident out of the corner of her eye. The woman was just standing there, staring at her – how strange!

"If you would give me a hand, please," she said, gripping the head of the freestanding rolltop bath. It was a lot lighter now that most of the water had been removed. "There is a hole in the floor as you will have seen. If we tip the bath the rest of the water will flow away – clever, isn't it?"

"*Bien sur.*" Jenny hurried to join the girl, trying desperately not to trip over her own feet. She had to force herself to look away from the beautiful smiling face she wanted to cover in kisses. She wanted to grab her child and run – but where would they go?

"Oh, you're French!" Bridget smiled. "My friends Ruth and Sarah are going to learn to speak French. I wish I could."

"I am not French, little one." Jenny turned to look into the bright green eyes. "I have lived so long in France that I suppose I react in French. I must change that. If you like I can help you learn French while I am here and you can remind me of my English language."

"Thank you. I would like that."

"Bridget!" Ruth put her head into the room. "Cook is asking have you taken root out here – the food will be ruined."

"Coming!" Bridget took hold of the bathtub and, with the help of the stranger, tipped it over. When all of the water was gone she wiped the bath out before again asking for help to store it in the corner of the room until it was next required. "We must hurry. Cook doesn't like her food to be ruined. She takes great pride in what she serves us."

"I look forward to meeting her," Jenny said. "Tell me, Bridget, what do I do with my robe and soap? Do I leave them here?" She asked just to hear her child's voice.

"No, no," Bridget answered. "I put what I think are your belongings in an empty bedroom for the moment. You will be sharing a room with Mia, I suppose. If you like I can lend you a hand to move your belongings into that room. I hope you're tidy – it has been a chore to teach Mia to pick up after herself, I can tell you."

"I will leave my things upstairs and join you momentarily." Jenny had to get away before she lost control of herself and frightened the child.

"*I'll tell Cook!*" Bridget called after the fleeing figure. She didn't have to run that fast. Cook would understand.

Chapter 5

"Ladies," Georgina stood at the head of the table in the servant's dining room, her arm around Jenny's shoulders. She was hungry – breakfast had been a rushed affair – she was going to take her time over the midday meal and enjoy it. "Allow me to introduce you all to Jenny Castle. Jenny will be going with you ladies to America." She looked at Mia, Verity and Felicia. "We can all get to know Jenny over the next days. Right now Cook wants us to eat her good food."

"I don't know why I bother," Cook grumbled.

"Hello, Jenny – my name is Felicia. It must be difficult to join a group as the new girl." Felicia stared at the attractive woman who took the seat Georgina indicated. "You are very welcome."

"Thank you." Jenny wondered how she could get food past the lump in her throat. She was sitting directly across the table from her daughter. She silently thanked Georgie for her kindness.

"I am glad I am to have company." Mia smiled at the

new member of their group. "Verity and Felicia share a room and seem to have become close. I lost my companion this morning when she left to take up her new position."

"Oh." Jenny sat back and listened intently as the women at the table told her of the two members who had left that morning. She was free to stare under her lashes at Bridget. Her mother's heart didn't know whether to sing or weep.

"I hope you know how to peel a potato and boil a kettle, Jenny." Felicia smiled softly at the newcomer to their group. "We have been given lessons in the domestic arts, you know."

"Really?" Jenny forced her attention back to the group around her. "I did learn how to prepare vegetables but it has been a long time since I worked in a kitchen."

"Jenny!" Georgina gaped. "You can peel vegetables?"

"Georgina already knows something of my past." Jenny looked around the table. These people would be curious about her. She needed to give them some information about herself. "This is not the first time the BOBs have helped me." She waited to see if anyone would question her but they remained silent, giving her their attention. "I have been on the run with the BOBs' assistance for ten years." She deliberately lessened the time – she wanted to give no one room to question. "I was originally sent to France."

"You had such difficulty with the French language, Jenny," said Georgina. "Miss Auden quite despaired of you – how on earth did you manage?"

Jenny laughed.

"How long have you known each other?" Mia looked from one woman to the other.

35

"We grew up together." Georgina waved that away.

"It is amazing how quickly you can learn a language when nobody around you speaks a word of English." Jenny wouldn't tell them of her year in a French convent. The nuns had forced her back to life when she had given up. The loss of her child had seemed to her the final nail in her coffin. The gentle nuns had insisted that she need only put one foot in front of the other and survive each day. It had worked. "I began my life as an under-servant – as such I could be called upon to do any chore. I rose in the ranks to under-housekeeper."

"France!" Mia gave a deep sigh. "They have clothing of a superior nature, wine, chateaux, dashing Frenchmen – oh my!"

"Not when you are a servant." Jenny laughed. "I lived in a remote area of the French countryside. I worked in a manor house in the area around Aix-les-Bains. That is a spa town and much visited. The house was a holiday escape for a Parisian family and their friends." The house had felt more like a hotel than a home with visitors and their servants constantly coming and going. The family had been very generous with their friends. Jenny suspected there was a certain amount of prestige involved in loaning your holiday home to those in your social circle. It had been beautiful countryside winter and summer, but Jenny had missed city streets.

"Did the BOBs find you that position?" Verity wondered what this woman's life had been like before she'd been forced to flee. There was such incredible sadness in her eyes – even when she smiled.

"They did." Jenny looked at the curious faces around her. "I was grateful but it is very difficult to find yourself alone in a foreign country. It took me a long time to find my feet. I had to learn how to do the most basic chores." She had been trained by the nuns before she ever went into service. It would have been a disaster to send her directly into the home they had found for her: she had always given orders – never followed them. She sometimes wondered what the nuns had done with the jewellery she'd used to pay her way with them.

"You said you were under-housekeeper?" Felicia was curious.

"Yes, I worked hard and was promoted through the household." Jenny had nothing else in life but work.

"Yet you decided to leave France to become a Harvey Girl?" Mia said.

"I believed I would spend my life in service. Not something I ever aspired to." She gave a Gallic shrug. "When I heard there was a possibility to make a new life with this Mr Harvey, I jumped at the chance. I am at the upper end of the age limit Mr Harvey sets for his workers." Jenny was willing to explain her reasoning. "I am twenty-nine years old but may well have to shave a few years from my age. The advertisement Mr Harvey runs in American newspapers calls for women from eighteen to thirty. I may have to remain twenty-nine for a few years. Of course," she looked around the table, "you do know we are not guaranteed to be employed by Mr Harvey? It is my understanding there is a great number of women trying for the same positions."

"What have you heard?" Georgina leaned in to ask.

"Mr Harvey employs primarily French and German chefs." Jenny had heard of Harvey through the years without really paying too much attention. "I know of two chefs that have applied to work for him in America. In fact, I agreed to teach one such English – for a fee, of course. The man was an excellent chef whose family was employed in the household where I worked. He was successful in gaining employment with Mr Harvey. He wrote to his family of the crowds of women who turned up on the days the interviews were being held. I know no more than that, I'm afraid." She had never thought when she'd listened to those letters being read aloud to the servants that someday she herself would seek employment in America.

"It is frustrating to have so little information," Georgina said. "I worry about the risk we are asking women to take – to travel so far from home – with no guarantee of success."

"Do we know what we will do when we reach New York?" Jenny wondered about arriving in an unknown port.

"The BOBs have secured an American lady to meet you from the ship and offer her home and what assistance she can to you," Georgina said.

"This is the first time the BOBs have done something like this." Verity looked at Jenny. "I was secretary to the Dowager Duchess for many years and handled the paperwork for the BOBs. I know of the difficulties they have experienced in finding and making new lives for the women who seek their help. The Harvey Company may well be the answer for some – it will be up to us – the first – to lead the way and supply any information and assistance we can."

The three maids and Liam the bootboy listened while shoving food into their mouths. You never knew when you might hear something of interest.

"This lot have been learning to ride horses like a man," Cook put in.

"Really?" Jenny looked around the table, wondering when it would be polite to leave the company. She desperately needed sleep.

Georgina could see her friend's eyes practically close. "Bridget, if you have finished your meal, please take Jenny upstairs and help her make her bed. If I'm not mistaken it will be morning before the poor woman moves again."

"I am sorry. I don't wish to appear rude but I am exhausted." Jenny covered her yawn with her hand.

"I can take you now if you like." Bridget was uncomfortable with this new addition to the household. The servants had been encouraged to treat the women who passed through this house as equal to themselves. It had been difficult at first to ignore the teachings of the nuns but over time the household had fallen into a pattern. The departure of two women this morning and the addition of this woman had shaken things up again.

"Finish your meal," Jenny said. "I won't fall out of my chair – at least not yet."

"I'm done." Bridget swallowed the last drop of tea in her cup and stood.

"Thank you." Jenny glanced around the company. "I will see you all when I am more awake."

She followed Bridget from the servant's dining room, aware of the whispers at her back. She supposed the others were curious about her but with her daughter walking in front of her leading the way she couldn't care about their opinions. She hurried her steps to catch up with her child.

"Are you too learning to ride astride, Bridget?" she asked as they climbed the stairs.

"Yes, I am." Bridget turned a smile of such delight on her that Jenny was startled. "We three maids are being given a lot of opportunities in this house." She for one was delighted but her two friends worried about getting ideas 'above their station'.

"Everything we learn is useful." Jenny was almost panting as they continued to climb the stairs.

"So Reverend Mother always said." Bridget thought about putting her hand under the poor woman's elbow and giving her a boost but was afraid of being too familiar. "We are almost there – it won't take us long to make up a bed for you."

"Thank you." Jenny was at the end of her strength. The thought of having to make a bed was exhausting. She need not have worried. While she stripped to her lawn chemise Bridget had the bed made in what seemed a matter of moments. The bed linen had been laid ready for use on the bare mattress.

The last sight she saw before closing her burning eyes was her daughter smiling down at her as she pulled the bedclothes over her exhausted body.

Chapter 6

Georgina was surprised to receive a visit from her friend and advisor Richard Wilson that very afternoon. She took him into her private sitting room and, when both were comfortably seated on either side of the glowing fire, she awaited her chance to share her news with him.

Richard had stated on arrival he had a matter of some importance to discuss with her.

"I made bold to write to the steamship line in Liverpool, Georgie," he said after he had refused the refreshments she'd offered. "I presented myself as a man wishing to travel to New York. I hope you don't mind but I feel I have come to know the young women travelling so far from home. I am concerned for their safety."

"Well, I have had many sleepless nights worrying about their safety – nothing is guaranteed." Georgina would accept all the help she could get.

"For the investment of one pound I was able to ascertain that it is no longer necessary to purchase what was known as a sailing kit," he said. A great many people had made a business of selling 'sailing kits' to ship passengers. The kits contained a mattress, plate, fork, knife, spoon and tin mug to be used by the passenger on the ship – many sold vermin-infested and dented goods to the travellers at an exorbitant rate. The shipping companies now provided these items for their steerage passengers. "I was rather impressed with the shipping company's enterprise. The shipping agent demands the sum of one pound before any documentation or information will be supplied to people inquiring about sailing to America. This means the company does not incur the cost of posting heavy packets of documents to all who inquire. The pound paid is deducted from the price of the ticket when you book to sail with them.

"Yes, very clever." Georgina didn't know what else to say.

"In the early days of steerage passage –"

"Steerage! Dear God, I hadn't thought of them travelling in such a way."

"They have no money, Georgie." Richard understood her concern. There were many horror stories told of the voyage in steerage floating around the Dublin docks. "The BOBs must pay their passage and supply funds for their use when they reach their destination. Far better the difference in cost between steerage and second class – which is more than fifty per cent – should be in the pockets of our travellers. The journey from Queenstown," he named the busy port town in the south of the country, "to New York will take between seven and ten days depending on weather conditions. That is a vast improvement over days gone by."

"There is so much to be aware of." Georgina's head

was in a spin. "We will need to have a meeting with the women travelling to New York. The BOBs too need to be advised of any information we may gather."

"I have time now." Richard believed the women should be prepared for the journey ahead of them sooner rather than later.

"First, there are matters to be discussed between ourselves." Georgina took a deep breath, preparing to shock Richard as she had been shocked. "We have a new member of the household who will also be travelling to America."

"I am happy to hear it," Richard said. "It will serve the women much better to travel in pairs. It will be necessary, I believe, to always have someone at your back – that is easier to achieve in two's."

"The new woman …" Georgina couldn't allow herself to be distracted. Richard needed to be aware of the need for caution. "Richard, it is Eugenie Lewis," she almost sobbed.

"I beg your pardon?" Richard sat forward in his seat, staring at Georgina's pale face.

"Richard, our dear friend Eugenie has turned up. She is determined to travel to America and become a Harvey Girl."

"Dear God!" Richard stared, incapable of speech.

Georgina understood completely.

The two friends sat in silence for quite a while, each grappling with their memory of a friend they had not seen or heard from in many years.

"Where has she been?" Richard broke the silence that had fallen between them.

"France."

"My word, she was never very useful at the exercises set for her in that language as I remember – didn't her brothers tease her unmercifully about having a French name but unable to get her tongue around the language?" Richard bit back a curse. "Her brothers – Georgie – they are my friends – what shall we tell them? Dear Lord, her parents!"

"What can we tell them?" Georgina leaned forward and placed a hand on Richard's knee, shaking it gently. "The Earl of Castlewellan is in Dublin, Richard – word of Eugenie's presence in my home cannot be made known. The man is unstable. I have no wish to draw his attention, I do assure you. I have had dealings with him before. Because the friendship between Eugenie and me was well known I was questioned extensively when Eugenie disappeared."

"I didn't know," Richard replied absentmindedly. He was thinking of a family that had grieved for their lost child. How could he face them knowing that child was within reach? "Georgie, I can't …"

"Richard, there is a great deal you do not know about Eugenie's situation." Georgina wondered what she could share. Secrets – they were such a problem – trying to remember who knew what – and who was allowed to know what – was the very devil.

"Because you never told me," Richard had wondered what would make a well-raised girl run away from what was, on the surface, a very advantageous union.

"The Earl of Castlewellan," Georgina wanted to spit the man's name, "is a man of unhealthy appetites. You will be aware of this after his treatment of Clementine." The young girl had been sheltered in the house after the Earl – the man her parents wished her to marry – abused her dreadfully. Clementine had been the first girl to pass

44

through Georgina's hands – and the most difficult, she sometimes thought. "His behaviour towards Eugenie was worse – so much worse – he delighted in carving strips of flesh from her body."

"Surely not?"

"Yes, apparently to his ears Eugenie's screams were a delight of musical proportions." Georgina's great-aunt had told her of the scars she'd found all over Eugenie's body. The old nun had been horrified by the torture performed in the name of love. "Her voice, as he assured her over and over again while he sliced into her, was perfection. He has never stopped looking for her." The man was obsessed.

"I have never heard of such a thing." Richard was shocked to think that a man he had met socially could be such a monster.

"There is much in this world that we do not know." Georgina had had her eyes opened to a certain degree by the perversions and cruelty of her own husband – she was aware, however, that there was much she didn't know. She had to find the words to convince Richard that he could not reveal Eugenie's present whereabouts.

"There was a rumour at the time that Eugenie was with child," Richard mused. "Henderson – the Earl of Castlewellan – put it about that this had caused his wife's nervous disposition and eventual disappearance."

"Did he indeed?" Georgina was almost afraid to open her mouth. How much could she share? Richard was a dear friend – a man of modern ideas – but he was also a product of his environment. Would he be able to see past the fact that Eugenie had borne a child to her husband? No, she couldn't risk sharing that knowledge with Richard.

"Her family have long wondered if Eugenie is living somewhere – in dire need – with the heir to the Castlewellan fortune." Richard knew Georgie was hiding something from him. "Georgie, it isn't fair to leave them worrying and wondering about the whereabouts of their daughter and sister."

"Richard, Eugenie went to her family for help." She held up her hand when he looked as if he was about to speak. "I know this for a fact. They sent her away – told her she was a married woman – that suffering was a woman's lot in life. I consider they forfeited any right to know of Eugenie's whereabouts."

"You are being very harsh, Georgie. They could not have known the particulars. Where has Eugenie been all of these years? What if there is a child?"

"Eugenie prefers to go by the name of Jenny now." Georgina would make no mention of any child. "She has been a servant in a French household since her disappearance. I should warn you that her black hair has turned completely silver. There has been no mention of a child." If she should inform the family that the child had been a girl it would mean admitting she knew about the birth. Eugenie's family had married her off in style with a handsome dowry. It was a clever investment – any male child born would inherit its father's fortune and title – the child would be heir to a vast estate – thus increasing the social standing of Eugenie's birth family.

"Are you telling me the Countess of Castlewellan, our friend Eugenie, has been doing menial chores for some French family to earn a living?" Richard stared at Georgina, sure she was jesting. It beggared belief.

"Yes, indeed," Georgina replied. "It makes one

wonder how terrible her life must have been, does it not? That she would be willing to become a house servant to earn a crust. That she would travel to a country far from her own where she knew no one and had difficulties with the language – cutting off all ties with her family and friends – rather than live surrounded by every luxury." She wanted to reach across and box Richard's ears and shout at him to think!

"But what do I tell her family?" Richard's mind was reeling. He had spent time with the women in this house. He knew they were all seeking a better life for themselves. But surely Eugenie had no need of doing such a thing? She came from a wealthy well-situated family – had married a man of vast wealth. Why should she have found it necessary to flee as if for her very life?

"You can tell them nothing, Richard," Georgina snapped. "Jenny will be leaving here with the other women and taking a ship for America. Her family can know nothing of her circumstances."

"Eugenie is to travel steerage!" The horror in Richard's voice almost brought a smile to Georgina's lips.

"As will the others or so you have informed me."

"But … but … it is one thing to worry about women one has a passing acquaintance with – quite another when one has known the woman from birth!" Richard didn't know what to think or feel. The world had run mad. How could he keep such a secret from his friends? Should he?

"You cannot tell of Jenny's presence here." Georgina could almost read Richard's mind. The poor man had no knowledge of the world Jenny and people like her inhabited. He could not imagine the cruelties one man could visit on another. That was both a blessing and a curse.

"Georgie," Richard pushed his hands through his hair, "I have not mentioned – I have delayed discussing the subject – but I must tell you – you need to know. The steerage passengers on board ship – they are frequently used as amusement for the cabin-class passengers."

"I beg your pardon!" Georgina stared in open-mouthed shock.

"Not in the way I see by your face that you are thinking – there is no intimacy involved, I do assure you." He had been curious when he'd read an article in the newspapers about the custom – never thinking he might one day know someone who would be subjected to the practice. "No, the voyage is long and some passengers become bored. The cabin-class passengers stroll around above the steerage decks examining the people – discussing them as if at a live exhibition – I understand they sometimes throw them fruit or pennies." He had been horrified to think the women he knew could be subjected to something so foul. How much worse it was to think of sweet, innocent Eugenie having to endure such a practice!

"Surely you jest?"

"I'm afraid not, Georgie. But what if someone from society recognises Eugenie or any of the other women for that matter? We cannot obtain a list of cabin passengers in advance of the voyage."

"They will have to be warned about the custom, of course," Georgina said. "But, honestly, I wouldn't worry about any of these people recognising our ladies. Think about it a moment, Richard – these passengers are convinced of their superiority – they must be to subject their fellow man to such horror. They would never believe they knew anyone travelling in steerage – not even if their own mother stood before them. We know people like this, Richard. They see nothing they do not wish to see."

"I hope you are right, Georgie, but I will still worry." Richard briefly wondered if he should offer to pay the difference in fare. He closed his eyes in resignation. These women were starting out on a new life. They would have to survive as best they could. He would be doing them no favours in trying to hide them from the reality of their situation. Again, the money would be better served in their pockets rather than in the coffers of the shipping line. They were fortunate the journey only took seven days. In the not too distant past it had taken weeks.

"I think you should join us for breakfast tomorrow." Georgina wanted to change the subject. They could achieve nothing sitting here wondering and worrying. "The breakfast table has become our meeting place. We meet for breakfast and discuss what the day will bring – everyone will be there. It will be an ideal time for you to share what you have learned about the needs of a person travelling steerage." She stood. "It will not be long now until my ladies leave this house. I shall miss them but no doubt the BOBs will send me others to replace them."

Richard too stood. "I will have a great deal to discuss over breakfast then. I was sent a very full package of information along with forms that need to be filled out. I believe it is time to advise the BOBs to purchase the tickets for travel. If, as you insist, Eugenie is to remain hidden in this house – then, my dear Georgie – we must move her out as quickly as possible." It broke his heart to think of refusing a friend shelter but there was a very real danger if Georgina was discovered hiding a man's lawful wife. She could be imprisoned for that crime.

"It saddens me to agree," Georgina said. "I too worry about the evils that could befall us if any were to learn of her presence here. I was horrified when I saw her. She is my dearest friend but there can be no doubt but that she has brought a great deal of danger to my door." She was bitterly aware that a wife was simply one of her husband's possessions.

"We will have to help her all we can." Richard decided he would not visit his family estates until Eugenie had left the country. Her family estates ran alongside his own. He would be incapable of deceiving friends of such long standing. "I shall join you and your motley crew for breakfast tomorrow. I shall study the papers I was sent from the shipping company with due diligence in order to be ready to answer any questions that may be put to me."

"I'll inform Cook we'll have one extra for breakfast," Georgina said as she led the way out of her private sitting room. "We will see you bright and early tomorrow."

She gave him his hat and jacket and waited until he had pulled them on before opening the front door.

"I will use the rear entrance in the morning," Richard said softly. "I do not think it would do your reputation any good to have men arriving at your doorstep so early in the morning."

"I'll tell Billy to look out for you." Georgina stood watching the passing traffic while Richard ran down the granite steps to the ground. He waved before turning to head in the direction of his Dublin townhouse.

Georgina closed the door with a sigh. There was always so much to do and so little time to do it – or so it seemed to her.

Chapter 7

"*Rise and shine, ladies!*" A loud bang on the wood of the bedroom door shocked the sleeping women awake. It was still dark outside. "*Time to rise and greet the day!*"

"One of these days, Bridget, I'll pay you back!" Mia felt as if she had barely closed her eyes. She'd been looking forward to interrogating her new roommate but the woman had slept like the dead all night through.

"You have to get out of the bed first!" The sound of Bridget's laughter came through the door.

"Is it morning already?" Jenny couldn't think of anything that had ever pleased her more than having her child's face be the last thing she saw before sleeping and the sound of her laughter the first thing she heard in the morning – her personal idea of heaven. She jumped from her bed and stretched mightily – every bone in her body felt compressed. She leaned over to touch her toes, almost groaning as the tension in her body released. "Good morning," she said with a smile at the still snuggling Mia before turning to make her bed.

51

"*Nooooo!* "Mia groaned dramatically before pulling her pillow over her head. "Say it isn't so ... my new roommate is another one of those dashed people who like morning ... God couldn't be that cruel."

"*Stop your complaining!*" was shouted from the next room. "Bridget will be back soon and you know she won't be gentle shifting you." The sound of women's laughter carried into the room.

"This sounds like a happy house." Jenny used the po found under her bed to relieve herself. She poured cold water from the pitcher sitting on top of the dresser into the washbasin and washed her face, neck and hands. She emptied the dirty water from the washbasin into the po. She had her bed made and was busy brushing out her hair by the time Mia moved.

"I suppose we have to make the best of the situation we find ourselves in." Mia pulled her reluctant body from the bed. She turned to use her own po then restored order to her bed. When she turned around Jenny had her hair coiled around her head. "I could grow to heartily dislike you if you are always this quick to get ready in the morning." She yawned.

"I'll leave you to complete your toilette. I hope I can find my way to the dining room. I was so tired when I arrived here yesterday I'm not sure I noticed any details. I'll see you downstairs."

Jenny opened the bedroom door just as Bridget raised her hand to knock. Smiling, she stepped into the corridor. "Good morning, Bridget."

"Good morning, Jenny."

"Bridget, could you tell me please what to do with my night waste?"

"Don't worry, Jenny. Liam will pass through the house later with a bucket and empty the night waste."

"Thank you." She turned to go, longing to stay and listen to her child move the reluctant Mia along but afraid of attracting attention by lingering.

"Good morning, Jenny." Ruth smiled from her place behind the teapot and a row of blue-and-white enamel mugs. "We usually have a cup of tea and a slice of soda bread to start the day." She waved her hand over the sliced bread, butter and marmalade arranged on the long kitchen table.

"Tea – I had forgotten the Irish love for that beverage." Coffee had been the drink served in France. She began to butter a slice of bread. She ignored the marmalade, having never enjoyed the taste of the orange preserve.

"You're as bad as our Biddy," Ruth commented.

"I beg your pardon?" Jenny took the proffered mug of tea.

"I am sorry." Ruth almost kicked herself. She was falling into bad habits in this house. She knew better than to pass comment.

"No, it's perfectly alright." Jenny added a touch of fresh milk to her mug. "I just wondered why you said that?"

"You wrinkled your nose at the marmalade." Ruth was glad to see the other women enter the kitchen. "Biddy does the same thing." She turned to pour tea for everyone.

Jenny took her tea and slice of bread and stepped out of the way of the others. Imagine – she and her child shared a dislike of marmalade! She locked that little pearl of information away in her heart.

"Right, ladies." Bridget consulted her notes. "Mrs Chambers gave me my orders last night."

Jenny was astonished to see a junior housemaid order everyone about. Verity, seeing the look on Jenny's face, leaned in to explain.

"This is an unusual household. The rigid rules of polite society had to be thrown out the window while we established a new way of doing things. Bridget, by dint of being up with the larks, receives any important information to pass along to us in the morning. It is unusual, I grant you, but it works for us. If you can think of a way of improving the system we have put in place – please do say – we are all learning here." She turned her attention to Bridget.

"We will have to rush through our chores this morning," Bridget was saying. "Today is the day that Ruth and Sarah begin their intensive training." She smiled with obvious delight at her two friends. "Their escorts will be here at ten." She held up her hand when the women began to babble. "This morning we are to have male guests for breakfast. Mr Richard Wilson and Mr Billy Flint will be joining our group. They have information they wish to share." Again she held up her hand as the others began to question her. "It's no good peppering me with questions – I've told you all I know."

She grabbed a mug of tea and, upon noticing Jenny's plain bread and butter, asked her if she would like marmalade to go on her bread. When the offer was refused the women applied themselves to eating and drinking – there was work to be done.

"Good morning, ladies!" Richard Wilson with Billy Flint

close on his heels greeted the fresh-faced women and one bootboy gathered around the large table in the servant's dining room. "Thank you for allowing us to join you this morning."

"Well, would yez ever sit down out of the way!" Cook almost barked. Honestly, what was the world coming to – she had to be up early and have breakfast on the go – and to add insult to injury this morning they were having guests. "You're making the place look untidy."

"If you would please take a seat, gentlemen." Lily Chambers passed a quick eye over the two gents, delighted to see that Billy Flint more than matched the elegance of his companion. She was enjoying watching Billy turn from a street tough into an elegant gentleman. The lad would pass muster in any company these days when he made the effort to dress up.

"Richard, Billy, good morning." Georgina laughed from her place at the head of the table. "The rules of polite society do not apply here, I'm afraid." She waved to the chairs on either side of her. "Please, join me while Cook and her helpers organise our meal."

The two men stood by the indicated chairs after Richard had placed the fat folder he carried onto a nearby sideboard. Richard stood because he was uncomfortable being seated before the women sat, Billy because he was following Richard's example – he was determined to learn everything he could about gentlemanly behaviour.

"Jenny!" Georgina called. "If you could step forward a minute while I introduce you to our two guests."

The niceties taken care of, the business of serving breakfast continued.

When everybody had taken a seat after serving

themselves from the food supplied, Georgina looked around the room with a smile. "Richard, we do not stand on ceremony here. You have something to share with this group. If you have no need of notes," she waved to where the folder sat, "please begin."

Richard tore his eyes away from Eugenie. One could not be too careful. It would be best if he did not display his prior knowledge of her – although truthfully he would not have recognised her – the change in her appearance was shocking. He held himself under tight control. How had the sweet girl he had known come to this?

"I have been making enquiries about travel arrangements for those of you going to America," he began. "Unfortunately I must now speak to you about the matter of travelling steerage …"

He was interrupted by gasps of horror. Felicia grabbed Verity's hand. She was the youngest of the group and at times felt at a disadvantage because of this. Mia bit back a cry. Jenny simply prepared to listen.

"I am sorry but the cost of sending all four of you to America must come from the coffers of the BOBs."

"We should have realised." Verity looked around at the women who had become her friends. "Sorry, we won't interrupt again – I think – I can't promise."

"As I was saying," Richard smiled around the group, "when travelling in steerage different rules apply. There are documents you have to fill out before a ticket will be sold to you. I took the step of applying for a ticket in my own name, in order to investigate what you will be facing." He waved towards the documents sitting on the sideboard. "I was amazed by what I discovered." He took a deep breath. "The questions asked on the form appear rather intrusive to me. I've shown them to Billy." He nodded in Billy's direction. "I wanted his opinion."

"Me being one of the 'Great Unwashed'." Billy had travelled to England disguised as a gentleman of wealth. He had been mortified to realise the opinion of his class held by those in society. He had heard a man cast disparaging remarks on the 'Great Unwashed' and been horrified to realise he was one of them.

Richard ignored Billy's disparaging remark about himself. The man was working to change that. Look at him sitting at this table dressed as a true gentleman. "We will have to read through the questionnaire together and decide on the answers we will supply. A great part of the form deals with your reason for going to America, who you will visit – the name and address of that individual. They even dare to ask who paid for your ticket."

"I believe that is because a great many people travelling to America in steerage have had their tickets purchased for them in America," Billy said. He had been asking around for information. "Those who have gone before them work hard and save the money necessary to purchase tickets for their relatives. When would any of us be able to save the five-pound fare?"

"That may well be so," Richard said. "However, the fact remains, the forms must be filled out. We will have to decide how it is to be done." He was finding it difficult to eat and speak at the same time. "The tickets have to be purchased ahead of time and a deposit of one pound is required. You then send off the completed form and pay the rest of the fare to the shipping agent in port. The BOBs need to begin making those arrangements – the ship sails from Liverpool stopping off at Queenstown in County

Cork. I believe you have to be in port days ahead of the sailing, to process your paperwork and undergo physical examinations. I believe the shipping company provides hostelry for those wishing to travel steerage."

There were gasps around the table.

"The steerage passengers are tested for disease before they can travel to America." Richard grimaced in apology. He would make no mention of the delousing process – time enough to worry about that when the women were under way.

"This problem has arisen again and again with the BOBs." Verity put her knife and fork down to comment. "The society is a wonderful institution but it is run by ladies of privilege who have no idea of the constraints placed upon those with a low income."

"Isn't it lucky then that you have me?" Billy said.

"We'd never mock the aid you give to us, Mr Flint," Georgina said.

"We would be lost without you and your men, Mr Flint," Lily Chambers said with a smile.

The conversation became general with everyone questioning and wondering. The discussion continued until the food had been consumed, the table cleared, and a fresh pot of tea served.

The three young maids and Liam left the room to tend to their chores – Bridget reluctantly. She wanted to know everything there was to know about the process. But they would not be travelling so had no need for the information about to be shared.

Richard brought the file of information he'd amassed to the table and with a sigh passed the printed form to the first lady, with instructions to pass it along.

"Ever in prison, or an almshouse, or supported by charity?" Verity ran her nail under the question when it was her turn to read the form. "Do they really expect people to answer that question honestly?" She continued to read but said no more before pushing the form along the table.

"They ask how much money we have in our possession," Mia said. "How rude!" She finished reading the form and with a disgusted headshake passed it along.

"It even enquires if we can read and write – how do they suppose the form will be filled out by the illiterate?" Felicia was shocked by some of the details demanded.

"Well, I imagine many are illiterate," said Verity, "and need help to fill out the form."

"Whether a polygamist?" Jenny looked up from the form. "Really?"

"They are setting themselves up for a fall asking questions like that." Cook had things to do – she couldn't sit around all day. "Them forms will be myths and legends – you mark my words." She could be heard muttering as she left the room. "The cheek of it – imagine asking a woman how much she has in her purse – the very thought of it!"

"If you will excuse me, I've matters to attend to." Lily followed her old friend from the room. She needed to keep an eye on the youngsters. They couldn't be expected to know what needed doing. She sighed – she did wish for even one experienced maid.

Chapter 8

"I must take care of seeing Ruth and Sarah away safely." Georgina stood when the conversation had become repetitive. "I will want to inspect both of them before they leave the house. In their absence, ladies, if you would give Cook and Lily any help they need? Billy, do you have a spare Smith or Jones floating about the place?"

"I'm sure I can find one." All of Billy's men were introduced to this household as Smith or Jones. The faces changed but the names remained the same.

"If I might enquire?" Richard said as he watched the others file from the room. "Ruth and Sarah?"

Georgina stopped her forward motion to answer. "I have arranged for them to have additional training in their speciality. Ruth is to train two days a week under the Dowager Duchess of Westbrooke's French chef. Sarah will spend the same amount of time with Lady Sutton's French lady's maid, studying couture."

The two girls had already been trained to a high standard by the nuns. Lily Chambers had questioned why such skilled girls had been placed in this house. Girls with their skills were much in demand by the Big Houses. Georgina suspected it had a great deal to do with the girls' friendship with Bridget. When Georgina's great-aunt, the Reverend Mother, had decided to entrust Bridget to her the other two girls were sent along too. She was determined to see that the girls would not lose by this placement. The two girls had been offered the chance of advancement – a different way of life – but they had been horrified by the very thought of stepping out of the life planned for them from birth. All except Bridget – that one was game for anything.

"Are we sure they are French and not simply people calling themselves Henri or Claudette?" Richard asked.

"They are French and very snobby about it," Georgina said with a laugh. "Now, I must get on – I have a great deal to get done but I will return. This conversation is not over."

"I'll be back too." Billy went to follow.

"Georgie, if you could spare the new woman for a short while," Richard called after her. "I have some questions to put to her."

"It will be done, O Great One." Georgina was thrilled Richard had found a way to be alone with Jenny. They needed to speak in private.

"Hello, Richard." Jenny closed the door of the staff dining room at her back lest the noise of the people in the kitchen drown out their words.

"Eugenie, dear God, Eugenie!" Richard crossed the room swiftly, his arms outstretched. When he reached the woman he had not seen for many years he took both of her hands in his. "How has it come to this?"

61

"Let us sit." Jenny pulled her hands free. She sat in the chair at the head of the table furthest from the door leading into the kitchen.

Richard took the chair to her right and simply stared for a while.

"It has been a very long time, Richard. I am having trouble believing I am here."

"Eu …"

"I prefer to be called Jenny." She laughed. "It is how most Irish people pronounce my name anyway, when they are trying to give it the French pronunciation: *U-Jenny*."

"Jenny," Richard covered one of her hands with his, "I want to tell your family."

"No!" Jenny pulled her hand free and glared at him. "Absolutely not … I must remain dead to them."

"That is cruel."

"You have no idea of cruelty, Richard." Jenny felt years older than everyone around her. How could she feel so ancient and everyone else so fresh and full of hope? She would have to work on her attitude. "I must remain dead. They would be doing me an enormous favour if they applied to the courts to have me declared so."

"I have no idea how I could even approach such a subject." Richard tried to see the girl he knew in the woman she had become. "Do you not wish to know how your family has fared?"

"How are they?" Jenny had been fond of her two brothers. She had wondered about them from time to time. She wished them well but that part of her life was over – it had to be. She had no choice in the matter.

"Your parents are aging." Richard spent time with Eugenie's family but in all honesty he had seen more anger

62

than regret in her parents. "Both of your brothers have made good marriages –"

"That would be important to my parents." She tried not to let her bitterness show.

"Yes, but they have been fortunate," Richard leaned in to say. "I believe they learned from your situation. Both of your brothers chose women who suited them rather than their parents. They have each been blessed with two fine sons."

"So," Jenny said sadly. "I am an aunt four times over."

"Oh, my dear!" The sorrow in her eyes was breaking his heart.

"Don't, Richard. It is what it is. I have accepted this and you must too. I am dead to all who knew me. It was unfair of me to put Georgie in the position of concealing me. I wanted to see her and when I heard what she was doing here," she waved vaguely around the room, "I was curious and hopeful of improving my circumstances."

"Do you really mean to travel to America and become one of these Harvey Girls?"

"It is the best opportunity I have heard of for a woman to improve her lot in life." Jenny was determined. She wanted to be able to claim her child someday. She would have to wait until Bridget was older before approaching her, but it was this thought alone that had kept her going in her darkest days. She hoped and prayed that Bridget could forgive her.

"I am at a loss." Richard was forced to accept Jenny's decision. Since working with the women in this strange household his eyes had been opened to the many inequalities in the world. Who was he to stand in the way of Jenny improving her lot in life?

A knock on the dining room door interrupted them. At a "Come in!" from Richard, Bridget put her head inside the doorway.

"Cook wants to know if you would like a pot of coffee? She said Jenny didn't drink much tea."

"Come in a moment, Bridget." Richard waited until the maid walked over to where they sat. "Jenny, I don't know if you are aware of it but I am teaching money matters to the women in this house." At her shrug he continued. "Bridget has a very bright mind," he said to the young girl's delight. "I have been teaching the women about fractions and percentages. I am adamant that each woman will understand how to deal with money in this fashion. I consider it essential. Now, some people – and I do mean people, men and women alike – have difficulty understanding mathematics. Bridget, like me, is not one of those people. She can teach you what she has learned so far and, if you have any problems, you can ask me." He considered it a scandal that women were not better prepared to handle their finances.

"If Bridget can find the time, I would be delighted to learn from her." Jenny had to fight her face's inclination to beam. Time spent in her daughter's company – how marvellous! She had to be careful. It wouldn't do to allow Richard to suspect something.

"I'll discuss it with Georgie." Richard couldn't give orders in this house. "Thank you, Bridget."

"And the coffee?" Bridget asked.

"Thank Cook for me, Bridget," Jenny said. "I would appreciate a pot of coffee. It will take me some time to become re-accustomed to the Irish fashion of drinking tea."

"I'll tell her." Bridget departed after a quick bend of the knee.

Georgina, Mia, Verity, Felicia and Jenny, with Richard and Billy, sat around the table in the dining room discussing the upcoming travel details. Bridget served coffee and tea, wishing she could find a reason to linger in the room. She wanted to know every little detail of the life of a Harvey Girl and how to achieve it.

"Jenny," Richard said, "something I don't think has been mentioned – Billy and his men have been teaching the women to defend themselves." He remembered his shock when he discovered the women fighting with weapons while wearing divided skirts. "I believe you will need to catch up with these lessons."

"We will all help you," Mia offered. "It is very empowering to think you might be able to fight for your dignity." She made no mention of Georgina fighting off her own husband and his henchman. That discussion would be for another day.

"I believe those lessons may be more important than even I realised." Billy looked around at the women. "I have been talking to sailors and cabin crew around the docks." For the price of a pint most men would share what they knew. "I believe we will have to teach you to fight in close quarters. I have taught you to hit and run away but on a ship that will not always be possible." He looked at Richard, showing the disgust he felt at the actions of his fellow man. "It appears that there are people, men and women both, who lose all of their manners as soon as the ship has pulled away from port. It can sometimes come down to the survival of the fittest."

There was a shocked silence following his words as everyone tried to deal with this latest development. They exchanged glances – but really, what could be said?

"There is so much to do and think about." Georgina broke the uneasy silence. "The first order of business must be to send away for the tickets to sail." She looked around. "Does everyone agree?"

"Yes," said Richard. "It is vital we get those forms filled out and returned to the shipping agency."

"We will need to begin to prepare our trunks with travel in steerage in mind," Mia said.

"You *would* be the one to think of clothing!" Felicia laughed.

"The journey will take between seven and ten days depending on weather conditions," Billy said.

"We'll need to consult the committee of the BOBs. They should be involved in these matters. They have a need to know the particulars," Verity said.

"There is something else I need to mention." Billy was embarrassed but determined. "The people you are travelling with – the upper class may well refer to them as 'the Great Unwashed' and unfortunately it is very true. The people travelling steerage will not have had your advantages. I was astonished at how much hot water you ladies use. I don't know how the arse hasn't been boiled out of the copper boiler in the wash house. Your fellow travellers will truly be unwashed. Putting it frankly – they will stink. You might want to consult Granny Grunt about some form of pomander that you can use. A supply of Sassafras oil will be vital. Men can sleep on deck but women are not allowed."

"Dear Lord," Mia groaned. "There is so much to learn and consider."

"We are very fortunate that we have people willing to help and educate us, are we not?" Jenny said softly.

"I am sorry." Mia looked around, shamefaced. "I do not mean to moan constantly. I am rather overwhelmed by it all."

"We all are," Verity said. "But as Jenny said we have help and most importantly we have each other."

"That's a good attitude to have," said Billy.

The conversation continued in this fashion for some time until everyone was convinced they had milked all the information the men had to hand. It was time to take action.

"I will send a letter to my contact in the BOBs requesting a meeting." Georgina looked around to see if anyone had anything else to say. When they remained silent, she continued. "Richard, Billy, if at all possible I would like you both to be present when the ladies from the BOBs visit. You will be able to answer any questions they may have. There is a great deal to accomplish. It will be all hands on deck as they say. That seems rather appropriate in the circumstances, does it not?"

"I will make myself available to meet the ladies who come to call," Billy said. "I ask only that you give me fair warning so that I can put on me best bib and tucker."

"And very handsome you look too in your fancy attire." Felicia smiled at the man who was trying so hard to prepare them for their new life. Billy Flint had been a godsend to the ladies in distress of Percy Place. "If we are allowed to offer an opinion, kind sir."

"Always happy to receive a compliment." Billy tipped an imaginary hat.

67

Chapter 9

"My body aches in places I didn't know I had." Jenny smiled down at Bridget who was kneeling on the floor dusting the skirting board while Jenny concentrated on dusting doorframes.

"The exercises Billy Flint insists on will help with the aches," Bridget rested on her heels to say. "Eventually!" She laughed at the disgusted look on Jenny's face.

The journey to America had been delayed while the BOBs studied the documents and information available to them thanks to Richard Wilson and Billy Flint. Bridget was glad on the one hand – she'd be sad to see the ladies leave – on the other, she was uncomfortable with this latest addition to the household. Jenny seemed to spend a great deal of time staring at her. She seemed to want to know her every thought and feeling. It was strange for someone more accustomed to a box around the ears and a demand for silence.

"You are fortunate to be learning how to defend yourself at such a young age." Jenny had to force her eyes away from her child. She knew she was making the poor girl uncomfortable but it was such a precious gift to spend time in her company.

"The lessons Billy Flint and his men are giving us should be available to all." Bridget returned her attention to her work.

"Bridget, do you know about using your mind while involved in menial tasks?"

Jenny was trying to share her knowledge with her child – cram years of learning and motherly advice into weeks and days. Who knew how long she would have with her before she was forced to move on and once more leave her behind? The pain behind her breastbone was constant. She was so angry at the nuns. She had entrusted her daughter to their care – how dare they train her only as a scrubbing woman! Ruth and Sarah had been offered skills that would support them and increase their chances in life. In speaking to Bridget she had discovered her child, her precious darling, had been denied the few privileges available to orphans. It was a disgrace. She had paid the nuns very well for her care.

"I don't know what you mean." Bridget once more sat back on her heels. She tried not to sigh – at this rate they would never be finished cleaning the woodwork.

"This task we are involved in – it is mindless – you would agree?" Jenny waited for Bridget's nod before continuing. "I find when my hands are busy I can use my mind to learn."

"How?" Bridget returned to her dusting.

"Well, take what you are teaching me about percentages for example." Jenny continued to dust as she spoke. "I can count doors and work out what percentage of the house they represent. I can measure each door while I work and think about its design. It is divided in quarters so each panel is roughly twenty-five per cent of the door – do you see?"

"Oh, I think I do that already." Bridget continued to dust. "I've been repeating the French phrases you taught me as we've been going along. I'm trying to do my times tables in French too. It's not easy."

"*Bridget, Jenny, there is a pot of tea on the go in the kitchen!*" The sound of pounding feet and Liam's shout echoed up the stairwell. "Yez must be parched with all the dusting you're doing!" Liam's head appeared.

"In the Name of God, Liam, look at the state of yeh," Bridget gasped. "Don't touch anything, yer filthy."

"So would you be if you'd been cleaning out fires." Liam was indignant. "How am I supposed to remove ashes and rake out coals and remain clean, I ask yeh? The bedrooms are done and the halls swept. The other women have gone down. I'm off for a wash. I thought I'd tell yez there was a mug of tea available, but suit yerselves." He left in a huff.

"If we put a bit of elbow grease into it we can finish up here in no time." Jenny had been going slow enjoying Bridget's company but the pair had been inhaling dust for what felt like hours. A drink would be most welcome.

"Now," Granny Grunt settled back in the comfortable chair by the fire in what had once been the senior servant's living room. It was the evening of the same day and the women had gathered to discuss their needs for the upcoming sea voyage.

Bridget sat in an alcove to one side of the fire, praying

to go unnoticed. She'd been kicked out of the bedroom because Sarah and Ruth wanted to study in peace and quiet. They were sick of Bridget asking questions about their time away from the house.

"I don't know if yez are aware or not, but head lice hate dirty hair." She didn't wait for a response but continued. "What I think yez should do is have a bath and wash your hair the evening before you leave here. Yez can give each other a hand running the fine-tooth comb through yer hair. Then each apply a generous portion of Sassafras oil to yer hair before plaiting it tight. You would be wise to leave it like that for your travels."

"I'll have Billy's man keep the copper boiling." Georgina made a note to herself.

"I had a word with a woman who works on the ships." Granny noted how everyone leaned in to listen. They were all desperate for as much information as possible, poor lambs. "She works in cabin class and hadn't a good word to say about the unfortunates travelling steerage." Their conversation had fair put the wind up Granny. "It was more what she didn't say than what she did say that I took account of." She hoped that made sense to them. She'd had to sort the wheat from the chaff from all the woman's complaining. "Yez will have no hot water from the time yez leave here until yez arrive in America."

"Surely the hostel in Queenstown will have a water supply?" Georgina was horrified at the very thought. When she had travelled with her family they'd had all the comforts of home.

"There will be cold water but it is given out sparingly." Granny had questioned the woman about this very thing.

"We will have to plan our journey carefully." Jenny

looked around at the other women who would travel with her. "When I arrived here I wanted to tear the clothes from my body and burn them – I felt so soiled. But if we know what faces us and plan accordingly, surely we can survive?"

"I've made up pomanders and salves for yez to take with you," said Granny. "Something strong-smelling that yez can use how yez like." Billy Flint had told her what was needed.

"Surely we will be allowed sea water to wash, wouldn't you think?" Verity looked around her. The others looked as fearful as she felt.

"I don't know and that's the God's honest truth." Granny said. "It's better to be prepared for the worst and be pleased if things are better than you expected."

"That's always a good motto no matter what you face in life," Lily Chambers said quietly.

"According to the papers we got," Cook wouldn't want to face what this lot had in front of them, "you can leave a chest – clearly marked with your name – in storage on the ship. You need to pay close attention to what you plan to bring with yez into these here berths that them brochures talk about. You'll want to keep everything you might need close to hand." She shook her head and fought back tears. This wouldn't do. These women were to be the first of many. She couldn't cry over them all. "You'll be fed at least." She wondered how anyone catered to so many on the high seas. It was a skill she didn't have and never wanted thank you very much.

"We can only plan for so much," Felicia said. "We have no knowledge of what we face. It is lucky we are travelling in cold weather – as we can keep our money and such about our persons without too much effort." The shipping company had issued warnings in their literature about leaving valuables lying around. There was seemingly a great deal of theft aboard ship.

"One of us needs to keep a journal so that we can pass on any useful information we gain in this first American venture for the BOBs," Mia said and laughed when everyone looked at Verity. The woman was always scribbling.

"I can do that," Verity agreed. "We can discuss our findings each evening and I will take notes."

"We have done all we can for you." Georgina felt a headache coming on. How could they possibly plan for something none of them had any experience of? She was determined to learn all she could from this first venture. She would have the information they needed at the tip of her fingers for the groups that would follow this one, she promised herself – just not yet. She cast a prayer towards the heavens for the safety of this first group of brave women.

Chapter 10

Queenstown
Cork Harbour

"I think I have lost all feeling in my feet," Mia whispered into the dense smog that surrounded them.

The cheerless people waiting on the pier in Queenstown, to board the tender that would take them out to the ocean liner, paid no attention. The days spent in the shipping company's hostel had not been pleasant. Mia thanked God frequently for her three companions. There was an almost visible air of despair hanging around the pier where they waited. These people were leaving their home and loved ones – perhaps never to see them again. She gave herself a quick silent lecture. She would not descend into despair. She was escaping into a bright new future.

"Stamp your feet." Verity put words to action. It was perishing cold waiting here on the dock to board. The steerage passengers had to board at four o'clock in the morning – so as not to disturb what the shipping agent had called 'the important people'.

"Do you think they will really address us by number,

like Richard said?" Felicia looked at the gathering crowd of strangers. There appeared to be more than a few of the men and women the worse for wear even at this early hour of the morning – or perhaps it was the end of a night of drinking for some.

"I don't care what they call me." Jenny looked around at the people she could see in the fog. She wondered if her face wore the same expression of resigned acceptance. "It was a nice surprise to discover that our ticket included the train fare for the next part of our journey," she added for something to say.

They had been accompanied to County Cork by Richard, Georgina and Bridget. Those three had sensibly remained in bed at their hotel this morning. It would be a long time before the ship set sail. There was no point in them freezing while waiting to wave the travellers goodbye. Besides, they would not have been allowed onto this pier which was for people waiting to board the ship.

The four women stood huddled in a tight group around their luggage. They had their tickets, stamped with their passenger numbers and destination, in hand. After weeks of talking, planning, argument and discussion, they were finally on their way.

An official of the steamship company appeared out of the fog and began herding the shivering people, all clutching their worldly possessions in unwieldy bundles, onto the tender waiting to carry them out to the ship. No one spoke. They went where they were pushed. Those who found seats sat hugging their bundles or children and staring miserably around.

When they neared the ship it towered over them, a black bulwark dotted with portholes. With efficient movements a gangplank was lowered, a bugle sounded and a bevy of male and female stewards lined up to greet the passengers.

The four women stood with white-knuckled grips on their belongings and prepared to board the ship that would be their home for the next week and more.

Mia was the first of the group to step onto the deck. She was greeted by an official-looking man in a uniform she didn't recognise.

"Second cabin, madam?" he asked pleasantly.

"No, steerage please," she said and was shocked by the change in his attitude. He almost threw her from him into a crowd of bewildered milling people. She stood watching while her friends received the same treatment. "They are treating us like cattle," she muttered under her breath.

"Not at all, missus." A whiskered gent touched the brim of his cap and blew alcohol-laced breath over her. "They wouldn't treat the livestock like this." He tapped the side of his bulbous nose. "Been a cowman all me life. I know. They has to pay a penalty if any of the animals get injured – don't matter about the humans. If we break a leg or our fool necks it's our own lookout."

"Thank you." Mia wasn't sure how to respond under the circumstances. She moved away to join her friends.

The stewards ran around shouting and pushing, females and males were separated, children were cuffed around the ear and ordered to behave. The chests of those passengers who could afford them were pushed to one side to be put into storage for the voyage.

The steerage passengers were led towards a steep stairway that led down into what appeared to the untrained eye to be the bowels of the ship.

"Be sure to remind me to write to Mr Flint, expressing my gratitude for his forewarning," Verity said as they stood waiting for their turn to climb down the steep ladder.

Billy Flint had insisted they wear their divided skirts for this voyage. When they had complained that their strange clothes would attract attention he'd demanded to know if anyone on board had paid for their tickets. It was no one's business what they wore, he insisted. So it came about that all four women wore divided skirts, laced boots and a veritable pound of hatpins holding their hats to their hair. They were still forced to climb down using only one hand as they carried the bag they had packed for use in the cabin in the other hand. There were cries of fear and shouts of objection as women tried to navigate what was effectively a ladder attached to the wall.

A uniformed female herded the women in the direction she wanted them to go. She stopped from time to time to shove a group into what appeared to be a room. "*You, you, you, you!*" She ordered each group to wait for her return before continuing to herd the women in front of her.

As the crowd of women thinned she scanned the BOBs group with experienced eyes.

"You lot," she stared at their skirts, "are travelling together?" She barely waited for their nods before pushing another group of sobbing women towards a doorway. "I'll be back, wait for me – don't move."

They continued on in this fashion until only the four friends remained.

"This will be your cabin for the voyage," the woman said then. "You're lucky there are four of you. I'll allow you to choose your own bunk – keep everything tied down – the buckets on the wall are for sickness only – there are toilets and sluices along this hallway – use them – keep the area clean – empty vomit as soon as you can – the sour smell will have you tossing your guts. The females have a room for dining – meet me there when you have your stuff stored – I'll be giving instructions to all of you at the same time." She spun on her heel and left.

"Does anyone have a preference for the top or bottom bunk?" Verity eyed the cabin. The room was spotlessly clean, which was a point in its favour, but it was a very small space for four people. She kept her opinion behind her teeth.

"Since none of us have ever slept in bunk beds before, why don't we rotate and see how we get on." Jenny pushed the enamel tableware stacked on top of the bunk out of the way and felt the mattress.

"It's a donkey's breakfast." Felicia too was pushing on a mattress.

"Pardon?" said Mia.

"The mattress is hay-stuffed. It will not be very comfortable." Felicia removed the plate, cutlery and mug from the mattress and stood holding them in her hand. "We need to organise the cabin – tie things down as she said. We wouldn't want anything floating around the room if we hit heavy swells." This too was advice from Billy.

The foursome stood surrounded by their fellow passengers as the mammoth ship began to make its way from the harbour. They were searching the crowd for a last sight of Georgina, Richard and Bridget. They had promised to be on the dock to wave them off.

"*Look, there!*" Bridget's bright young voice carried on the wind.

Eyes searched frantically and finally spotted the group with Bridget jumping up and down, waving both arms. They waved until the ship carried them away from everything they had ever known.

It was a sombre group who stood in the dining room listening as the stewardess explained their way of life for the following week.

"My dear, let us leave this place." Richard was tempted to put his arm around Georgie's shoulders. She looked so unbearably sad.

"I hope and pray that they will thrive in their new life." Georgina looked out to sea as if she could still see the women.

"Come, there is nothing more we can do here." He wanted to remove her from the crowd of weeping and wailing people that surrounded them. He felt the cold to his bones and he was sure the females with him did too. It was time to move. He consulted his fob watch. "The train will not wait for us."

"Is it wrong to have enjoyed this break from the routine of Percy Place?" Georgina asked as they turned to make their way to the train station.

Richard had ordered their bags removed from the hotel and brought to the train station. They could go directly from the docks to the train.

They walked along chatting softly with Bridget bringing up the rear. She would have so much to tell her friends. They might well be learning French and all manner of new things, but she had been on a train, stayed in a hotel and she had seen an ocean liner. It had been a great adventure she would dream about for years. She'd been sad to see the four women leave but that was to be her life now it would appear. She would see women come and go to the Percy Place house but one day, *aahh,* one day it would be *her* travelling on a big ship off on an adventure. She stuck her chin in the air and with clenched fists marched along behind the couple in front. And with each beat of her shoes against the cobbles she repeated her vow – *one day.*

While Bridget was dreaming her dreams the four women were settling into their cabin. The cabin was in the bow of the ship and met every wave first, causing it to bounce in a very unsettling way.

Felicia was the first to feel the effect and dropped onto one of the lower bunk beds with a groan. Mia quickly passed her one of the buckets. Jenny too took to a bottom bunk.

Verity grabbed a bucket from Mia's hands and emptied her stomach of what little she had eaten. "How are you feeling, Mia?" she gasped.

"I'm finding it difficult to stand upright," Mia grabbed onto one of the bunk supports, "but otherwise I'm fine. However, I don't think that will continue with this stench." She pushed Verity down to join Jenny and ordered them to share a bucket while she set out to find the sluice.

"Make sure they drink plenty of water," the uniformed stewardess barked out to no one in particular. "It's going to be a bumpy voyage so people will become dehydrated – you must make sure they drink. The taps all hold sea water so you must get drinking water from one of the stewards." Grabbing her stomach, she disappeared into a W.C.

Mia returned to the cabin to find Verity on her feet and attending to the other two.

"I am feeling much improved." Verity passed Mia with a soiled bucket. "I think we should help the others into bed." The deck beneath their feet heaved. "The beds have rails – I didn't understand their purpose – I do now." She hurried from the cabin, fighting to keep her feet under her. The smell that swept around the deck challenged her delicate stomach but she fought off the desire to vomit.

"We need one of Granny's concoctions," Mia said as soon as Verity returned. "Do you remember which bag we put them in?"

"I have them." Verity hurried to unpack the pomanders Granny had made of goose fat and strong-smelling pleasant scents. She broke a piece off one and allowed the heat of her hand to soften it before attempting to rub it under her nose on her top lip, praying it would help settle her stomach. She hung the solid strong scented pomander from the rail of one of the two top bunks hoping it would hide the aroma of vomit that seemed to seep into and around the cabin.

The two women remained on duty, ministering to their friends as the ship danced and bucked under them. The groans from the two sufferers were pathetic.

The first full day of travel passed in this way with Mia and Verity carrying bottles of water to their friends and almost forcing them to swallow.

When darkness fell the two women climbed into the top bunks, praying their companions had nothing left in their stomachs that might make a reappearance.

Chapter 11

Castletown
County Louth

While the ladies of Percy Place were dealing with what life was throwing at them, another woman was making plans. In County Louth, on the east coast of Ireland, Flora Kilroy was kneading a giant mound of bread dough. The chore was one of her many punishments – along with milking the cow, making cheese and butter, feeding the chickens, gathering eggs, tending the garden. She had to be ever-cautious not to reveal how much she loved these chores.

She watched the couple she thought of as her gaolers. When they sat at the other end of the kitchen table, at the end of the day, they reminded her of a nursery rhyme. Tom Smith with his long lean body reminded her of Jack Spratt who could eat no fat. His short tubby wife Mary was a perfect complement, as the woman who could eat no lean.

There was a pile of open post on the kitchen table between the pair. There was never any post for her. Why should there be? She didn't exist. She recognised one of the envelopes and almost groaned aloud but she wouldn't give them the satisfaction. What task did he expect her to achieve now?

"The master is sending a piano," Tom Smith told his wife Mary. "It is being shipped over from England and will arrive in Greenore on the Ferry," he checked the letter in his hand, "today."

"How are we supposed to pick it up without a horse or cart?" Mary snapped.

"It is to be delivered tomorrow. I'm to unlock the gates."

"Does he expect her to learn to play with no teacher?" Mary Smith, as the woman was known here, ignored the comment about the gate. She could have worked that out for herself. "I can't teach her."

Flora wanted to snap that Mary had never taught her anything.

Tom consulted the letter. "He says she can learn to play using one of the books from the library." He was aware of their charge listening intently. She might keep those bewitching black eyes on her task but she didn't fool him.

"That must be a magical library," said Mary. "The master seems to think the ruddy room is the fountain of all knowledge."

Flora began to shape the dough into the loaves that would be left at the end of the long driveway after the Smiths had taken what they needed. The dole box on the gate was filled with the fresh loaves twice a week. It was one of her assignments to make the bread but she was not allowed to eat any. Bread was not part of the strict regime laid out for her.

She began to assemble the ingredients she needed to make the sweet bread her gaolers were so fond of – the raisins, nuts and cherries tempted her but she knew better than to try and taste them. She worked silently, hoping they would say more. She needed information. She was ready to leave this place and never return.

However, with a glance at his wife Tom Smith folded up the letter and placed it in the inner pocket of his jacket. Flora knew from experience that there was information in that letter which he would not mention in front of her. They turned to other trivial conversation and nothing more of importance was said.

At last the loaves were ready.

"Are you nearly finished?" Tom asked. "Some of us want to sleep this night."

"Yes." She placed the loaves on the heavy tray and carried them into the cold pantry. They would be left to rise overnight. She would be up early in the morning to put them into the large bread oven. She returned to the kitchen and washed her hands.

"I'll take her up." Mary stood up, holding out her hand for the key to lock the bedroom door.

"I'll bank the fire." Tom passed the heavy black key across the table. "Don't forget the buckets."

"Do I ever?" Mary snapped her fingers in Flora's direction.

Flora picked up the two buckets – one empty to be used for her body waste – the other almost full of clean water.

Tom sighed, watching the two women leave the room. He didn't know how much longer he and Mary could do this job. It had seemed such an easy chore when it had been offered to them.

Upstairs, Mary stood in the open doorway of Flora's

bedroom, her arms crossed over her ample bosom. "Your clothes," she said. "Hurry up, it's late and I want my bed."

Flora stripped to her skin. She passed her clothing to the other woman, grateful she kept her eyes raised somewhere over Flora's head. Her clothes would be returned to her in the morning when the door was unlocked.

When she heard the key turn in the lock Flora slammed home the bolts she'd demanded be placed on the inside of her bedroom door. It gave her a feeling of power to believe that she locked herself in – it was a simple pleasure – but she treasured it.

She pressed her ear to the door, listening for the heavy footsteps of the other woman as she moved away. She was smiling when she crossed to the cupboard built into the wall of her bedroom. She had discovered a great deal more in the library than they knew.

She placed a heavy wooden chair into the wardrobe and stepped up onto it. There was a shelf there at a convenient height. She folded her naked body onto the shelf while using her back to rock loose the top of the wardrobe. The bedroom she was locked into when he wasn't here was directly below the attics. She had found the design for this house in the library and studied it until she knew every nook and cranny. They might think they had her contained but she would get free. The scurrying of rats didn't bother her – the biggest vermin in this house walked on two feet. She pulled the old-fashioned groom's uniform she'd found in the attic over her chilled flesh. A drawer of black socks she had discovered had been a boon to her in her nightly wandering around the concealed servants' corridors. No one living remembered their existence. She pulled black socks over her hands and feet.

"We must have enough money saved for us to get out of here," the woman known as Mary Smith said to her husband while they prepared for bed. "I don't know how long I can stay here and remain sane."

"Would you want to be the one to tell the master we're leaving? And what would we do about *her*?" Tom Smith agreed with his wife. He'd have been away months ago but how could they leave that poor woman locked up while they slipped away? She'd never agree to remain here and wait for her Lord and Master – if he was the judge of anything. And he wasn't willing to take her with them. Those black eyes of hers gave him the willies.

"I can't be here if he comes to visit again." Mary was almost sobbing. "The sound of that poor girl's screams the last time he was here was enough to turn a body's hair grey. I almost cried when I saw her hair – imagine cutting it off like that with a knife. He threw that long braid in the fire. You could smell it. It's not right. And then to force the poor thing to make all of that bread – and her not allowed touch a slice. It's cruel – that's what it is – cruel."

"You know what happens to people who begin to feel sympathy for that one."

"They have unfortunate accidents." Mary sighed. "So he's giving her two weeks to learn to play the piano? But doesn't say when he's coming here. He usually visits after he sets her one of his 'little lessons' as he calls them."

Flora, stretched out on the floor of the servants' hidden passage, her ear pressed to the hole in the skirting board of the couple's bedroom, held her breath.

"He does. But we both know that with that man one never knows."

Flora crawled away from the room. She had heard everything she wanted to hear.

The following morning Flora was up and waiting. She had unbolted the door and stood with the buckets at her feet.

Mary Smith unlocked and opened the door. "Here," she said. She picked up the heavy clothing she'd left on a chair outside the door overnight. She had no idea why the girl had to wear such a heavy cumbersome outfit – but she followed orders. You had to, to survive in this house.

Flora pulled the clothes on over her shivering flesh. She picked up the buckets and without a word followed Mary.

The two women walked down to the kitchen. Flora went outside and emptied the buckets in the sluice, then returned to the kitchen and stoked the fire. She needed a very hot oven for the bread. Still without speaking, she left the house to tend to the cow.

She loved these early mornings when it was just her and the cow.

"It is time to go, Buttercup." Sitting on a three-legged stool she leaned her head into the cow's flanks, listening to the sound of rich milk falling into the bucket. "To be a prisoner for ten years is enough – is that not the truth?" She didn't expect the cow to answer but she needed to hear her own voice. She was speaking in Latin. It gave her a feeling of deep satisfaction to think she could speak a language 'the master' conversed in, sure she wouldn't understand. "Today we will go for a walk." She couldn't leave the cow behind to suffer. She had been laying her plans for years. She couldn't fail. She would never survive the punishment failure would bring. "I will put laudanum in the sugar and cherry ice on the sweet bread." She used the word 'ice' as she didn't know the Latin word for 'icing'. "They alone eat it – they devour it all with their tea every afternoon. When they fall asleep I will return for you. Wait for me." She rubbed the cow's ears then picked up the bucket.

She returned to the kitchen to bake her bread and put her plan into action.

Flora sat in the cold library waiting for Mary to come and order her to her room. The couple were creatures of habit, their life ruled by the instructions dictated by the master. Every minute of every day had to be accounted for. She had completed the lessons set out for her in quick order. She had learned to conceal her aptitude for the rather simple lessons the master demanded she complete in his absence. She wondered if she would miss this library. She had learned a great deal while trapped within its walls.

"Time for your nap."

In spite of waiting for this summons Flora jumped at the sound of the woman's voice.

She stood and walked from the room without objection. She wondered if the rapid pounding of her heart could be heard. She was committed to her task now. Today was the day. She knew from years of spying that the couple made a pot of tea and enjoyed the sweet bread before Tom piled the loaves onto a wheelbarrow to push to the estate gates. The time for the disposal of the bread was laid down by the master. Flora was convinced the bread was left in the kitchen until then to drive her almost insane with its tempting smell.

She hoped she hadn't put too much laudanum in the

icing. She had found the bottle of medication while on her travels around the empty rooms of this house. The stopper had not been breached. She had tested the liquid on the rats. She didn't want to harm her gaolers.

With the bedroom door locked Flora sprang into action. She was in the attic in minutes and pulling on the clothes she'd laid out. She'd discovered a great many discards over the years. She pulled a set of widow's weeds on, wrapping the long skirt tightly up around her belly before pulling on a dated suit of gent's clothing. She had practised – she should look like an overweight gent from a distance. The veiled black hat went inside the gent's shirt. She moved around to make the items fall into place. A pair of boy's sturdy black boots would finish the outfit. She didn't put the boots on but carried them by the laces. She could make no noise as she crept around.

"I am that tired." Mary Smith covered a yawn with her hand. "Honest to God, Tom. I can't keep this up. We will have to do something."

"I could do with a nap meself." Tom yawned. "That lot at the gate can bloody well wait for their bread. I'm sick and tired of this job, Mary, but I don't know how we can get out of it with our skins intact. I'll have to think on it." He yawned again.

Flora in the servant's hidden hallway outside the kitchen held her breath. If the pair decided to go to their room for a nap it would make her escape so much easier. She crossed her fingers and waited.

"Right, Buttercup, let's be havin' yeh!" Flora for the first time in years spoke in a normal tone of voice and in English to the cow. "That pair are in their room and snoring. You and me, Buttercup, are making a break for it." She attached a rope to the cow, picked up the handles of the wheelbarrow of loaves and began to push. She walked at speed, the cow having to trot to keep up. She had money she'd stolen through the years. She'd tied some of it in a handkerchief and it sat alongside the key to the estate gates in her trouser pocket. It wasn't a great deal of money but it would get her away from here.

"Here, who are you?" one of the women waiting by the dole box asked.

"What do you care, missus?" Flora forced her voice into a lower register.

She pushed the bread into the large square 'dole' box attached to the outside of the tall openwork iron gates – the box had a covered hole in the back to allow foodstuffs to be placed inside without opening the gates – an opening in the front of the box allowed people to remove whatever was to be found in it. She unlocked the heavy iron gates. She abandoned the wheelbarrow and pulled one side of the gate open enough to let her and the cow pass through. She slammed the gates closed at her back. She didn't relock them. She walked away from the crowd fighting over the bread and pulled the cow along with her. She knew these roads. She'd been born in one of the houses that were built for the estate workers. She intended to leave the cow at the last house in the row. The animal could feast on the weeds in that garden. Flora had to stop her feet from breaking into a fast run.

Chapter 12

Kilross Stud
Athy
County Kildare

Dorothy Lawler listened to her brother-in-law pontificate, a stiff non-expression on her face. She was forced to bite her tongue while her twin sons were subjected to the most outrageous dissertation on the evils of the female. She would not enter into argument with the pompous windbag – not while her husband lay breathing his last in the room over their heads. She knew the comments were directed towards her. Her brother-in-law considered her a jumped-up nobody. No mention was ever made of the fortune she had brought to this house. She had also brought fresh blood to their family line. Her twin sons were tall and strong, not chinless wonders like her husband and his brother. She fumed silently, concentrating on relaxing her grip on the silver cutlery in her hands. It wouldn't do to allow the man to know he was upsetting her.

"You need to get rid of this cook," Peregrine Lawler stated. "We are a family of means – a French chef is what you should have – none of this woman's rubbish." He pushed his plate away.

Dorothy noticed it was practically licked clean but refrained from commenting.

"I disapprove of the changes you have made in the family home, woman!" He beat his clenched fist on the table. "There will be changes made around here, you mark my words."

His beady black eyes in his red fleshy face glared hatred at the woman sitting at the head of the table – as if she belonged there – the hussy.

The meal continued in this fashion, while the three people whose home it truly was remained silent.

"Lean in close," Dorothy murmured to her twin sons.

They were in her husband's sickroom – the only room in the house where they could escape their interfering relative – the man let it be known in his loud fashion that he couldn't be around the sick. A fall from a horse was not an illness but his avoidance of this room was a blessing to the small family. The master of this house was taking a long time to die.

"Benedict, Zachariah, listen to me." Dorothy had spent years planning for her future. She had never thought her husband would make old bones. Her husband had insisted she be the one to draft his will. As soon as the will was lodged with the family lawyer, she'd begun to plan. She would not remain in this house under her brother-in-law's thumb.

"Mother?" Ben knew it was important when their mother used their full names.

"The doctor has told me your father will not again regain consciousness. He will not last out the week." There were no gasps of dismay as there would have been for a loved parent. "You two will be returning to your studies after the funeral ..."

"But, Mother . . ." Zach wouldn't think of leaving his mother at that man's mercy.

"I will not hear of either of you abandoning your education." She glared at them, her brown eyes determined. "You will have need of your studies."

"Do you know what state Father has left his affairs in?" Ben, the eldest by ten minutes, asked.

"Indeed I do." Dorothy had a fine business brain and it hadn't taken her long to realise the man she had married was a fool – an ineffective, charming wastrel. "This house and its contents will come to you, Benedict, on your twenty-fifth birthday. If anything is left after Peregrine has lived here for the next six years."

"*What?*" they gasped together.

"Oh yes, your father has named that man as your guardian."

"*Never!*" Ben went to stand but his mother grabbed hold of his hand, keeping him in place.

"*Stay,*" she hissed. "I have matters I wish to discuss. This is the only room in the house that is free from that man's interference."

"Sorry," Ben sighed.

"I have begun to remove my affairs from this house." Dorothy ignored their identical looks of horror. "I will not remain here while that man thinks to rule. I have taken steps to rent a room in Dublin – in the home of a gentlewoman who has fallen on hard times."

"*Mother!*" they objected together.

Dorothy ignored their attempted interruption. "Your father has gambled and whored away practically all of the

93

money I brought to this marriage. Your uncle will find that he has been handed a poisoned chalice. The money for your education was secured by my father – your grandfather. My husband was unable to touch those funds."

"What will you live on?" Zach, the more moderate of her twins, asked.

"My father made it a stipulation of the marriage agreement that my family firm should remain in my hands." She almost laughed at their surprised looks. "What do you two think we have been living on for the past ten years?"

"Obviously our uncle doesn't know this." Ben admired his mother greatly. She was not a pretty woman but the strength in her chiselled face was more attractive than prettiness in his eyes.

"No, but he will find out when the lawyer reads the will." She almost hated to miss her brother-in-law's horror when he discovered how little was being left to him. The man had been almost rubbing his hands in glee since his older brother took to his bed. "I will not be returning to this house after the funeral." Dorothy knew she had to remove herself from the house before her brother-in-law discovered the true state of affairs. "I will leave the churchyard alone and make my way by barge to Dublin. You two must appear shocked and horrified – broken-hearted at my desertion of you both in your hour of need."

"Mother, I don't like this," Ben said.

"We have no time to discuss finer feelings, I'm afraid. I have made my decisions. I have sold all of the horseflesh your father purchased – at a loss, I'm afraid – and I have

94

found work for our grooms and trainers. The Good Lord knows there is always work for skilled men in the stables of Kildare."

The plans she'd been making were put into effect as soon as her husband's body was carried into the house. She'd known – looking at his body – he'd broken his fool neck. It was a blessing he never woke after the accident. He would have been crippled from the neck down. He was not a man to bear such horror.

"I have closed down the family stud." She hated to see the sorrow on their faces. She'd had to move swiftly. There was no time to consult them. They were away from home for a great deal of the time these days. It made no sense to keep such an expensive business running under the careless control of her brother-in-law while waiting for the twins to mature. "I have opened a high-earning account in both your names with my broker. I used the money I made from the sale of goods from the estate. Ben, you will inherit the estate in time and you have always loved the stud. You will have a fund to start up the business again if that is your desire.

"I'm surprised old Sobersides agreed to you taking charge." Zach used their name for the family lawyer Mr Cummerford.

"He did not," Dorothy said. "He believed the instructions came from your father."

She almost smiled when she saw the look of shock on their faces.

Chapter 13

Percy Place
Dublin

In the house on Percy Place, Cook looked around the table in the staff dining room and almost sighed – so many empty chairs. They had just completed the midday meal. "The place feels empty with only us here."

"As to that," Georgina tapped a stack of envelopes on the table at her elbow, "I have something I wish to discuss with you." She looked at the bright-eyed youngsters that formed the main body of her staff these days. "You young people may get started on the chores Mrs Chambers and Cook have set for you."

She waited until the soiled dishes had been removed and the youngsters had filed from the room, closing the door at their back.

"I have received a notification from the BOBs." She searched for the letter she needed. "I agreed some time ago to rent rooms to women who needed them." She looked up from the letter at their shocked gasps. "I need income – you both know how I am situated."

"But to turn your home into a boarding house!" Lily

thought she'd had enough shocks already.

"This woman," Georgina consulted the letter, "Mrs Dorothy Lawler – her husband is ill but she is not yet a widow – she wants to rent a room." She looked up from the page and shrugged. "That is what it says here – I don't understand it either. The amount this woman is offering me for room and board is very generous. I would be a fool to turn it down."

"What about any students the BOBs might send us?" Lily asked.

"We have set their rooms up on the third floor." Georgina shook the letter she held. "I am going to remove myself from the master bedroom and rent it to this Mrs Lawler." That room had no happy memories for her.

"I don't know if we can keep going with the staff we have." Lily Chambers considered this house her home. She had been in service here since she was twelve years old.

"I have to agree with Lily," Betty Powell said.

"We will discuss our staff problems. I know what an effort it has been for you both to keep this house running. I will not ask you to continue working so hard – it is folly – you have both earned an easier life than the one you are presently living."

"I'm not ready to be put out to pasture quite yet," Cook said.

"Speaking of pasture," Georgina picked up another letter, "the men who will install our bathrooms have been in touch. They wish to begin immediately. This letter warns of the unavoidable mess that will be made of our front and back gardens as the men lay down pipes."

"It's never dull around this house," Lily said. "If it's not one thing it's another."

"Well, we can't sit here all day," Cook stood. "I've work to be doing."

"I must get on too." Lily followed her friend from the room.

Georgina picked up the letters with a sigh, all the while wondering how her departed charges were getting on.

Chapter 14

The *Oceanic*
Mid-Atlantic

On the sea the ship had finally sailed into calmer waters. The four women were once more standing in line – this time on the steerage-level deck. A man with a clanging bell had passed through that deck, shouting for everyone to present themselves.

"Dear Lord," Mia gasped, "we are to be injected! I must change." She turned to push her way out of the crowd around her.

"Wait ... what are you talking about?" Felicia grabbed hold of Mia's arm before she could escape. The other two moved closer to hear what was being said.

"I saw them when the crowd moved!" Mia gasped. "There is a man up there," she pointed to the head of the line, "injecting people. I am wearing a long-sleeved blouse under my jacket. The only way for me to receive an injection would be either to tear the sleeve or remove the blouse. I will not provide more entertainment for that lot."

She pointed to the crowd of cabin passengers hanging

over the rail and staring down at the steerage passengers gathering. The remarks being shouted would make a navvy blush.

The women were almost pushed off their feet when the people above them started to throw pennies and oranges into the crowd. The frantic rush of children and adults alike to capture some of this bounty caused consternation to the crew and those passengers trying to stand aside.

"You must be vaccinated." A crew member barred their way to the hallway leading to their cabin.

"And so we shall." Mia refused to be cowed. They had paid their passage whatever the crew thought of them. "We were not informed of the reason for our presence on deck. We need to change garments."

"*Oh, la de dah,*" the crewman jeered. "Listen to her ladyship. Lost yer way, have yeh? Need me to help you find your way back to your own kind?"

"*Jenkins!*" the shout had the seaman stiffening. "Kindly allow those women to pass. I will see you later, mister."

"Now see what you've done. Only gone and landed me in it." The seaman glared.

"We did nothing of the sort!" Mia began but her friends had had enough. They grabbed her and almost pulled her along the hallway to their cabin.

Chapter 15

County Louth
Ireland

"Well, what do we have here?" Two strapping young farm workers reeled from side to side on the country lane.

Flora Kilroy almost rolled her eyes. She had been making such good time. Without the heavy restricting garments she'd been wearing for years she felt light as a feather. The ten miles to Dundalk Town were disappearing under her feet with an ease that astonished her. She didn't even slow down as she neared the two drunks preparing to have fun by blocking her way past them. She swung the silver-handled walking cane she carried. She had covered the silver head with one of the seemingly limitless supply of black socks she had found. It wouldn't do to make people think she had money.

"Sorry, lads!" She swung the cane and without breaking stride drove one end into the stomach that was hanging over the belt of one of the drunks. The concealed silver head caught the second unfortunate in his family jewels. She left them both groaning in her wake.

"Amazing what you can learn from a book." She almost

danced along, delighted with the success of her first foray into battle as she saw it. She quickened her steps just in case that pair should pull themselves together and follow her.

She reached the outskirts of town and began to walk with a measured step. She knew what she was looking for – there had to be one along here. She was relieved when she saw a swinging sign advertising 'The Stag and Battle' – that would do. She went in and pulled open the door marked *Snug* when she found it.

"Here, what do you think you're about?" a bloated woman yelled at the sight of the overweight man coming into the section of the pub set aside for female use. The room was crowded – the air thick with smoke from a peat fire and whatever the women were smoking.

"Making meself decent," Flora said with a laugh. She didn't care if news of her actions circled the town. The man who thought he owned her would never speak to people such as these. She was free. She didn't exist and she doubted anyone would be sent to look for her. She unbuttoned the flies of her pants.

"Oh God, he's going to show us his bits!" an old wag with a pipe clenched in the corner of her mouth said. It wasn't in shock but in amusement.

"No bits to show, ladies, sorry," Flora shook the yards of black skirt material she'd had wrapped around her belly loose. She had to wriggle some more to refasten the button of the pants under the skirt.

"Here, if you want to leave that gent's shirt here. I can get a couple of pence for it down the pawn. The jacket as well if you want." The old wag wriggled her wrinkled fingers when she saw Flora begin to remove the shirt to reveal a black boned top.

Flora caught the widow's bonnet before it could hit the sawdust-covered floor. "Sorry, missus, I need the jacket." She had planned to take the shirt with her but in the interest of good neighbourliness she tossed the heavy white cotton garment to the old woman. She held onto one end of the shirt until the woman looked at her. "Where is the train station, please?

"Which one d'yeh want? We got a whole slew of them around here. We got the Newry, the Greenore, the one to Belfast and one to Dublin. Which way you going?"

"Belfast." She had studied *Bradshaw's Railway Guide* in the library. The Dublin to Belfast – Belfast to Dublin line ran through Dundalk.

She listened intently to the old woman's instructions, with shouted corrections from the other women in the snug. She tossed the cap she wore to the old woman. She'd keep the black gents jacket over the dress top. She pulled the battered black veiled widow's hat onto her head. She was as ready as she'd ever be. She pulled open the door of the snug with a shouted goodbye, aware of the buzzing of gossip behind her.

Flora sat in the mail wagon of the train. She had found the station easily. She leaned against a stack of mail that was being carried to Dublin. It was the cheapest way to travel. She had only a small sum of money that she had managed to steal and conceal over the years. She was aware of the looks the guard was giving her out of the corner of his eye. She didn't care. She was free after all these years – she felt she could conquer the world.

The train rattled along at a startling pace. She wished the mail van had a window. She would have enjoyed looking at the passing scenery. She was tired and hungry but that was nothing new. She settled down to endure the journey. Dublin – her heart was beating fast in her chest. What would she find when she reached the address she'd memorised so many years ago. Would the family still be living in the same house? Her granny seemed to think that the house would stay in the same family. Even if they had moved, hopefully the people living in the house would have news of the family. Ah well, no use worrying about that now. She'd see what happened when she got where she was going.

While Flora travelled, Mary Smith was struggling to wake up. The noise of a bell rattled through the house. She tried to shake her husband Tom awake but he lay as if dead. She rolled her heavy body over the bed and almost fell to the floor. She had to do something to stop that noise – it felt as if someone was slicing her head open. She pushed her feet into her house shoes and, shaking out her skirts, left the room. She hurried down the stairs, shouting at whoever was pulling on that bell to stop for God's sake.

She unlocked one half of the wide front door and pulled it open. She stared in open-mouthed amazement at the horse and cart standing on the gravel in front of the house. How had they opened the tall gates that remained locked at all times? She didn't have time to think about that now.

"Are yeh going to stand there all day, woman?" a deep voice demanded. "I have this bloody piano to deliver – and glad I'll be to get rid of the thing. Where do you want it?"

"In here." Mary tried to clear the fog from her mind.

"Well, we'll never get it in that narrow opening," the

driver said, wondering if the woman was simple the way she was staring at him. "You'll have to open the two halves of the doors, missus."

"Oh, of course." Mary began to unlock the second of the tall doors of the main entrance to the house.

"Here." The man rudely shoved a thick envelope at her.

She grabbed it close to her chest before it could fall to the floor.

"Get those ropes off this bloody thing!" the driver called to his young assistant. "The sooner I get rid of it the better – a more awkward package I've never delivered."

Mary stood aside as the two men wrestled the piano off the cart and onto the gravel. It took her a while to realise that she needed to run ahead of them and open the music room.

While she was instructing the sweating, cursing men her head was in a spin. What was going on here? How did these men get that gate open? Why was Tom still asleep and why could she not seem to think clearly?

"*Tom! Tom!*" Mary shook her husband, relieved to hear him groan. "*Will you for God's sake wake up! Tom!*"

"I'm awake."

"Here, have a cup of tea – if you feel anything like me, your mouth is like a sewer." Mary pushed the mug of tea into his seeking hand. She waited for him to take the first gulp before saying, "I don't know what's going on around here, Tom, but the gates must be open." She saw his eyes open wide at that. "The men have delivered the piano and gone – they came right up to the front door. The cow is missing and the door to the henhouse was left wide open."

"In the Name of God, woman, what are you talking about?" Tom tried to fight his way out of the fog that seemed to surround his brain.

"I'm thinking your woman has done a runner – I unlocked the door to her room and waited. She didn't unlock it from her side. I knocked and knocked but she didn't answer. Her clothes are still on the chair outside the door."

"Don't talk daft, woman. There is no way out of that room. The poor girl is like a rat in a trap in that place. Besides she wouldn't be running around the countryside naked as the day she was born."

"I need you to wake up, Tom. I'm telling you there is something wrong. I put me ear to your one's door and there was ne'er a sound." Mary had been running around like a mad thing. "The wheelbarrow is gone and so is the bread. I'm telling you, Tom. I don't know how she did it but she's gone. You mark my words."

When they failed to wake their charge Tom brought an axe from outside and broke open the panels top and bottom of the door. He put his hand through the broken panels and unlocked the bolts. The pair stood staring around the empty room.

"I don't know how she's done it but she's gone," Tom remarked needlessly.

"Well, all I can say is, the best of luck to her." Mary was almost weak at the knees with relief. She'd be glad to shake the dust of a very unpleasant job off her heels.

"It'll be us that gets it in the neck." Tom, the axe held loosely in his hand, stared.

"Indeed it will not." Mary turned to leave the room. She grabbed her husband by the elbow when he appeared happy to stand still. "We'll lock up this unhappy house and get ourselves well away before anyone discovers a thing. *Move!*"

They practically ran around the house, locking wooden shutters over the windows. The interior of the house was mostly under dustcloths – anything not covered could look after itself as far as they were concerned.

When they had their personal affairs packed on top of the wheelbarrow which Tom had retrieved, the pair got ready to disappear. They locked the house and gates behind them.

Chapter 16

Dublin

Flora stepped onto the streets of Dublin feeling like a world traveller. The sights, sounds and smells were all foreign to her. She wanted to stand and stare at the gorgeous gas lamps that illuminated the streets. She wanted to kick up her heels and laugh like a fool. She gave herself a stern talking-to and stepped out briskly. She asked and followed the directions from helpful strangers as she walked the streets of Dublin. She had never seen so many people before in her life. Where did they all live? What were they all doing here? She tried not to attract the attention of the red-coated soldiers marching around the streets. She wanted to take in the energy all around her. But she knew that it would be foolish to linger so continued along the road.

She was soon standing on a bridge, staring at the row of houses across from her. The sign on the side of the road assured her she was in the right place. There were barges tied up along the lip of the canal – light and voices drifted to her. She took a deep breath, straightened her shoulders and with her chin in the air marched towards what she hoped would be her future.

"Billy Flint said to tell yeh there's a woman walking up the front steps," Liam fell into the kitchen, shouting. He was delighted with this bit of excitement. "He doesn't know her."

Georgina walked out of the housekeeper's drawing room which opened off the kitchen. She had been discussing tomorrow's chores with the housekeeper and cook.

"Do you want me to go see?" Liam offered eagerly.

"No, thank you."

Georgina, with Lily and Cook on her heels, determined to protect her, went up the stairs to the entrance hall. Ever since the trouble her husband caused they were extra vigilant.

Liam ran to knock on the door of the three young maids' room. They might be needed.

"I wonder if she's knocked yet?" Cook said. They wouldn't have heard downstairs.

"It wouldn't be someone from the BOBs," Lily said. "They would have let you know to expect her."

"Only one way to find out." Georgina opened the door of the porch and prepared to pull back the bolts of the front door.

"*Be careful!*" Lily shouted.

"Best have this stick by you." Cook pulled a walking stick from the hallway stick-stand and shoved it into Georgina's hand. It saddened her to think this house had become an unsafe place.

Georgina pulled open the door. A complete stranger stood in the light leaking out from the hallway.

"I am looking for Mr Corrigan – my name is Flora Kilroy," the stranger offered.

"I am sorry but Mr Corrigan is no longer living." Georgina wondered what this woman wanted with her father.

"Oh, dear!" Flora hadn't thought of that. "I wonder if you could give me directions to a relation of his – I've come a long way, you see." She didn't want to beg but she would if she had to.

"You had better step inside." If she has come such a long way, Georgina wondered, where is her luggage?

"I don't wish to trouble you." Flora was tempted to jump at the offer but she had to find somewhere to stay before it got too late to be out on the streets. "If you have some knowledge of the Corrigans I'd appreciate it if you would tell me."

"I'm Mr Corrigan's daughter Georgina." She held the door open and waited for the stranger to step inside. "Please."

"Thank you," Flora stepped in, almost sagging with relief. She waited while the door was locked at her back.

"Follow me." Georgina turned to lead the way.

"I believe you and I are by way of being cousins," Flora said as she followed the trio. "My grandmother and your father shared grandparents." She wanted that out in the open straight away. This woman was related to her by blood.

"Is that a fact?" Georgina almost tripped. She hadn't known her father had extended family.

"It is." At least Flora hoped her grandmother had been telling her the truth.

"Are you hungry?" Cook asked as soon as they

reached her little kingdom, the kitchen, where the young people had gathered.

"I am but I don't want to put you to any bother." Flora pulled off the widow's hat. She was here now. She wouldn't need that hat again – she hoped. She didn't know what the future held for her – but she'd escaped – dear Lord, she was free! She'd handle whatever life threw at her – but in the morning. The events of the day seemed to have taken the strength from her knees and she longed to sit down.

"Good heavens, what happened to your hair?" Georgina gasped. The other woman's hair was cut to her chin. It exploded around her head in a wanton black cloud, making her white skin look almost translucent.

"Well, you see . . ." Flora looked around the room at the fascinated glances of the group of strangers. They were a strange bunch to her eyes but then, what did she know? It seemed to be a house of women. There was a young boy there too but no men. "I have been by way of being a science experiment for many years." She was going to start out her new life with the truth. It might well sound stranger than fiction but it was the only life she knew.

"In the Name of God, what does that mean?" Cook looked to Georgina for an explanation.

"I have no idea," Georgina said.

"I'll put the kettle on." Cook looked at the strange woman.

"I'll cut the bread." Ruth stepped forward.

"I'll set the table," Bridget offered before she paused. "Sorry, which table will I set?"

"Liam," Lily said, "stoke up the fire in the servant's living room." The upstairs rooms – the best rooms – were kept mainly for company these days. It would be best if this young woman knew from the outset that she hadn't discovered a rich relative.

"Yes, Mrs Chambers." Liam grabbed a bucket and went out the door to fetch more coal. He'd noticed the coal bucket in the living room was empty.

"Cook, if you could organise something to eat, please." Lily looked around at the three young maids. They would be up and at work early in the morning. "Madam, if you take this young lady into the living room, we'll bring a tray through."

She waited until Georgina and the stranger had left the room before ordering the maids back to bed.

"What do you make of that?" Cook waited until she was alone in the kitchen with Lily before commenting. She was making sandwiches while the kettle boiled. That poor young woman looked half starved. Never let it be said that she sent anyone to their bed hungry.

"It's one for the books." Lily was arranging a tray with crockery. "I don't know what she meant by saying she was a science experiment." The two old friends stood waiting for the kettle to boil. The goings-on in this house kept getting stranger. What were they going to be expected to cope with now? "No doubt Georgina will tell us what we need to know. In the meantime, if you'll pass me what you have prepared I'll carry this tray in to them."

Cook transferred the sandwiches to the tray. "I'm going to bed now unless you have need of me." She had been working since early morning.

"I'll be going up myself after I've served this." Lily picked up the laden tray. It had been years since she'd carried a tray but she hadn't forgotten how.

Flora practically fell on the food offered to her. She was tired and hungry, grateful she appeared to have reached a safe haven. She would worry about tomorrow later. For now there was a fire, food and a friendly stranger. That was a vast improvement over the life she had left.

While the two women in the living room discussed their connections, the house in Percy Place settled down for sleep.

Chapter 17

The *Oceanic*
Mid-Atlantic

The women who had left the house on Percy Place were on the high seas, coping with their new circumstances as best they could.

Felicia, sitting on a top bunk, looked up from the book she was reading when the door of the cabin opened. "Jenny, what are you doing? Are you ill?" She stared at the scrubbed bucket her cabin mate was carrying. She was a strange one, Jenny. They had been living cheek by jowl yet the other woman remained a stranger.

"I simply cannot abide the stench any longer." Jenny opened one of the jars of strong scented salve Granny Grunt had prepared for them. "I am going to put salve into this bucket and add hot tea when we go to lunch. I'm hoping it will work as an infusion and scent the air of the dining room. Anything would be better than the stench of unwashed bodies and I include our own in that sentiment."

They had been on board ship for five days now. She was determined to give herself a good standing wash today. She would top up the bucket with sea water and have one of the other females stand outside the cabin door while she stripped and washed. She'd offer to do the same for any that pleased.

"I do not believe it!" Mia slammed into the cabin.

Verity followed on Mia's heels. "They have roped off a section of our deck."

"Apparently the first-class dining room overlooks that section of deck," Mia fumed. "The important people have complained that they can see and hear the Great Unwashed from their large windows – it is ruining their digestion!"

"It's the area where Mia reads to the children," Verity explained.

The passengers had been asked to volunteer any skills they might have to help pass the time on the voyage. Mia had offered to read to the children. Felicia was teaching very basic sewing skills. Verity was helping those with some skill improve their reading and writing. Jenny was instructing the young girls on board who were hoping to be taken on as maids on the social structure of the staff in a big house. A ladies' charity had donated paper, pens and ink for the steerage passengers' use. They had also provided material and sewing implements for those learning to sew.

"Oh Mia, I am sorry!" Felicia jumped down from the top bunk. "The children so enjoy your stories. Why, I've even noticed some adults standing close to listen."

"I've asked the stewardess to try and find me a little alcove where I can continue with my reading. Why should the children be punished?" The success of her stories had come as a pleasant surprise to her. She didn't only read to the children – she also made up action stories and had the children move to her words. It was noisy certainly but children needed to release energy – as did she. The days they had spent on this ship had brought her close to screaming.

"What of your admirer?" Jenny, the bucket in her arms, turned to ask.

"That man!" Mia was being hotly pursued by an attractive young widower travelling with his two small daughters. "He had the temerity to ask me to marry him!"

All three women stared at her.

"He has offered marriage?" Felicia said, astonished – as were the others. The man was travelling first class and judging from the reaction of the ship's company to the man it was obvious that his pockets were very deep indeed. They had worried the man might offer Mia something – but not marriage.

"I know we are supposed to speak the same language as the Americans," Mia sat on a bottom bunk under the fascinated gaze of her companions, "but truthfully I have difficulty understanding a word he says. Do any of you know what a range is or indeed a prairie?"

"Mia," Verity gasped, "did he use those very words – oh my dear – is he a cowboy?"

"He's very handsome," Felicia said with a smile.

"So, Mia," Jenny said. "A handsome, rich young cowboy has proposed marriage to you. What are you going to do?"

"Have you all lost the run of your senses?" Mia stared. "We have not been formally introduced. I know nothing of the man." She stared at Verity. "What is a cowboy?"

"The Dowager Duchess is addicted to the penny

dreadfuls she receives from America. She had me hide the books in my room when I lived with her. I could not resist reading them. They are full of adventures about lawless men riding horses, chasing cows, shooting guns and having range wars. They are wonderful."

"Sounds delightful!" Mia groaned. "What am I to do?" She had never thought something like this would happen when she'd agreed to read to the children on the ship. "He is from the Great State of Texas, he tells everyone with pride. I don't even know where that is!"

"What do you want to do?" Jenny asked.

"How am I to know!" Mia wailed. "I only met the man three days ago. It is far too soon to discuss matrimony."

"The sailors have told me," Felicia put in, "that we have a good tail wind blowing us swiftly before it. They believe we may make land in as little as two more days – three at the outside. That does not give you much time to reach a decision."

"It may well be only a shipboard romance," Verity offered.

"There has been no romance," Mia said with a glare. "What do you think I am?"

"I meant nothing improper," Verity hurried to reassure the other woman.

"If the man's attentions are honourable, you could do a great deal worse. He appears a very pleasant type of man from the little I've observed," Jenny said. "You might give him the address we are staying at in East Hinsdale. He can communicate with you there. Perhaps the lady whose house we will stay in will have some knowledge of him. He did tell you he has a house in New York after all."

"You may be able to further your acquaintance while we await to see what the future holds for us," Felicia suggested.

"Indeed." Verity thought a moment. It might well be a passing fancy but if the man's attentions were sincere it could be the answer to Mia's future. "Why not ask for his address in New York? Then we can consult our hostess as regards the area of New York he inhabits."

"It is too ridiculous for words." Mia stood. "The man has an entire suite of rooms in first class. I saw it when I returned his children to him. The stewardess was too busy to return the children and sent me in her place. What would a man of such wealth want with someone travelling steerage?" She didn't wait for the others to respond but walked towards the cabin door. "The bell has been rung for lunch. Let us go to the dining room and enjoy having our food offered to us as if we were pigs at a trough." She stepped into the hallway.

The others exchanged glances but didn't comment. They followed on Mia's heels, Jenny clutching the bucket with its dollop of highly scented salve, close to her chest.

Chapter 18

Percy Place
Dublin

"Sarah, since you are so familiar with the garments available in this house, would you help our latest addition to some when she awakens?" Georgina looked at the young maid who was turning out to be such a boon to this household of women.

The women and bootboy were gathered around the breakfast table in the servant's dining room. Last evening, her recently arrived new relative fell asleep on the sofa in the living room after devouring the food offered. Georgina had hated to disturb her. The poor woman looked exhausted. She had covered her with a lap rug and left her with the light of the fire for company.

"Yes, ma'am." Sarah hadn't really noticed the woman's figure last night. She would wait until she was up and about before worrying about clothes for her.

"Lily, if you can spare Bridget to help me move my affairs from the master bedroom, I can start on that this morning." Georgina didn't think it would take her very long to move into one of the guest bedrooms. She wondered which room and what assistance she should offer her newfound relative.

"Good morning." Flora stood shyly in the doorway of the dining room. She was horrified she'd fallen asleep last night without offering a word of explanation about her sudden appearance at this house.

"Flora," Georgina gestured the woman into the room, "Come in, let me introduce you to everyone properly."

"I need the necessary, please." Flora tried not to dance in place.

"I'll show you." Bridget smiled and led the woman out the back to the W.C.

Ruth jumped to set a place at the table for the newcomer.

Sarah tried to think what she might have to hand that would fit the woman.

Cook and Lily smiled politely and waited to hear what the young woman had to say for herself.

"I am afraid that if you were hoping to come to the home of a rich relative," Georgina said to Flora when everyone was seated, "you will be much disappointed."

Flora looked around her at the mistress dining with her servants in the basement – even she knew that was peculiar.

"I had ... I suppose I should say have, since my husband is alive but living elsewhere . . ." Georgina waved a hand at her own meanderings. "Sorry, I have a husband who is trying to drive me into the poorhouse. I won't go into the details at this moment in time – you will discover them over time I daresay. I am living, as you find me, with . . .' she pointed to the three wide-eyed young maids and

Liam in turn, 'Sarah . . . Bridget . . . Ruth . . . Liam . . ."
She gestured towards Lily. "Mrs Chambers, my
housekeeper, has been with my family since before my
birth as has Mrs Powell, our cook. I would be lost without
them."

"How do you do – I am Flora." She didn't know what
else to say.

"Why don't we eat this good food before we try to
discover everything about everybody?" Cook suggested.

"Yes," the others chorused.

"Flora, I don't quite know what to do with you,"
Georgina said when the first pangs of hunger had been
satisfied by all at the table.

"If you have time I would like to tell you my story."
Flora wasn't going to conceal anything from this woman.
"But it is not suitable for all." She used her eyes to
indicate the younger members of their group.

"That shouldn't be a problem." Georgina was curious
as to what had driven this young woman to her door.
"Liam, have you cleaned out the grate in the living
room?"

"Yes ma'am." He smiled at Flora. "I've cleaned and set
it. I was quiet as a mouse. You didn't even move when I
was going in and out of that room."

Flora felt her blood run cold at the thought of someone
walking around her while she slept. She fought to hide her
reaction.

"Liam, as soon as breakfast is over I want you to light
the fire in the living room, please." Georgina looked
around the table. "I'll go upstairs with Bridget and get her
started on moving my affairs. Ruth, you can clear the

121

table and wash the dishes. Sarah, do you need to measure Flora before you can pick something for her to wear?"

"No, ma'am, I've seen her clearly now. I'll have to spend some time in the attic selecting items. I'll bring what I find to the lady's room … ah, which room would that be?"

"I'm not sure yet." Georgina hadn't decided where to place this relative. "Just put anything you find in one of the students' rooms. We'll sort something out later."

"Yes, ma'am."

"I wonder if you would mind my housekeeper and cook joining us, Flora?" Georgina said. "They are more friends than employees and I will share what you tell me with them anyway."

"I have no problem with that." In fact, it would suit her not to have to explain herself to the other women. They might as well hear her tale all at once.

"I was eight years old when I first met the master – he was twenty-two," Flora began when the four women had gathered around the fire in the living room.

"My dear," Lily said, shocked.

"No, no, it isn't what I think you're thinking. My story is – I believe – rather strange. Please allow me to tell it to the best of my ability." She smiled at the other women. "I've been practising this speech for years, you see."

"Very well, we will just listen." Georgina sat back.

"I was born on an estate in County Louth belonging to one of the many Anglo-Irish families. Our cottage was small but sufficient to our needs, with mud flooring. I didn't know any different and was quite happy. My mother, however, wanted something different for me – her

122

only child. My mother wanted me to receive the same education as the better-off boys in the village. She begged the vicar to take me on as a student – which he did. I was given a good basic education. It was a matter of pride to my mother that I began to put some of the boys to shame."

Flora stared into the glowing fire – remembering.

"The vicar happened to mention me when he was taking tea at the Big House. It was a matter of curiosity to see a girl being given a boy's education. He meant no harm I am sure but whatever he said aroused the Master's curiosity. He came to the vicarage to see me at my lessons. That was the beginning. For the next two years this young nobleman would ride up on his shining steed, question me about my studies and demand that I receive a treat for being such a good student. The treat was always food-related and always welcome."

Flora looked up to see her audience paying close attention.

"I enjoyed his attention, considered myself something rather special." She smiled sadly. "I was confused, however, by the fact that when the master and the vicar spoke I could not understand a word they said. I asked the vicar and he informed me they spoke in Latin, a language far beyond the understanding of a lowborn person such as myself." She shook her head at her younger self. "I determined to learn this Latin and prove them wrong." She looked up. "I should say here that I find book learning extremely easy. Anyway, the publican's son wanted to become a priest – well, it was really his mother who wanted that, for him to make something of himself – so it happened that he, a boy I had grown up with, was learning Latin. I begged him to teach me. I kept these lessons a secret from all, having great notions of suddenly revealing to everyone how very clever I was." Flora shook her head.

"You were only a child," Cook said into the silence.

"I almost got the publican's son into a lot of trouble." Flora giggled at the memory. "He went from being a poor scholar to overnight being considered brilliant. It didn't take him long to talk me into doing all of his Latin homework for him. It took years of study but I became rather proficient at what the vicar called 'the language of the learned'."

"Your work was considered brilliant?" Georgina asked.

"Yes, indeed, in all the subjects I studied – but I kept my knowledge of Latin to myself, waiting for the perfect moment to reveal all – and that is how I found out what the Master and the vicar really thought of me. I constantly overheard them discuss me – I was an experiment to them – a human laboratory experiment – an amusement."

"Did you ever tell them of your Latin studies?" Lily asked.

"No – thankfully I had learned to keep my teeth firmly locked on the matter. When I turned ten the master decided to purchase me from my parents. Oh, they didn't speak of it like that but that is in effect what they did. They gave my parents a sum of money and I was moved into the Big House. I was neither fish nor fowl there. The Master's parents encouraged his interest in what they called the sciences. A group of like-minded social equals in the neighbourhood were gathered and for the next five years I was a performing monkey for this group."

"Really!" Georgina didn't know what to say.

"I was not unhappy. I had the kind of clothing I had only ever seen others wear. It was passed down from the master's younger sister but I didn't care. I felt like a queen. I had plenty to eat. I was sleeping in a soft bed and I was warm in the winter and cool in the summer. I didn't consider I had any reason to complain. I hid my knowledge to a great extent. I understood what the group were saying – people will speak very frankly in front of you if they are assured you can't understand what is being said – I listened and learned. I gave them exactly what they wanted." She paused to think of that time in her life.

"What happened?" Cook asked as she was sure something had.

"We all grew up," Flora said. "The two women in the group who had been considered bluestockings had offers of marriage. They were the first to leave the group. Then one by one the others lost interest. The Master's family moved back to England on the death of the grandfather. I remained in the house and to a large extent I think I was forgotten. The Master would send lessons and demands by post to the vicar, for me to accomplish one task or another."

She shrugged, and the others were dismayed to see her eyes fill with tears.

"The master married," she continued with obvious difficulty. "He was given the house in Louth to use as his own. He returned to check out his property. I was seventeen." She looked into the fire, ignoring the tears sliding down her cheeks. "Need I say more?"

"You had become a woman?" Lily said softly.

"My body may have developed but I don't believe my

emotions had – I had been locked away, you see."

She looked to see only sympathy on her listeners' faces.

"The master became someone I had never known. He set about closing down the house. He sold off the livestock – got rid of staff – it was a terrible time. People who depended on the estate for their livelihood were thrown out. I could only watch in horror, too lost in my own nightmare existence to help."

"You were a child," Lily said. "What could you have done?"

"Perhaps nothing. But I should have run then." She sighed. "Hindsight is a wonderful thing, is it not?" When nothing was said, she continued. "For three years I have been imprisoned in that house in Louth in the care of a man and his wife who locked me in my bedroom every night. The master would visit and demand I dress in silks and satins. I was there to amuse him. He used and abused my body and mind. He delighted in perversions. He had me read from a revolting book he carried with him. Then he would force me to enact passages from the book. He seemed to truly believe that I was his creation – his creature. That he could do anything he pleased with me. Then he would leave and truthfully I do not know if I was glad or sad. I was then left with my gaolers."

She would not tell them of the tools he used to inflict pain. She had said enough. Instead she spoke of her life with the Smiths. Her discovery of the attics and hidden servants' passages – she told them everything up to the time she escaped.

"That is how I ended up here." She held her hands out to the fire's warmth. "I have no idea what I will do or where I will go. I just knew I had to get away from that place."

"Looks to me like you found the perfect place," Cook said. "We are turning it into a home for lost lambs it seems to me."

"Thank you for sharing your story with us." Lily Chambers stood and shook out her black bombazine skirts. "I need to get on. I have to check on our three young maids." She looked at Georgina. "We are leaving those youngsters to muddle through on their own much too often, madam. They need supervision and instruction."

"I need to be getting a shopping list started." Cook too stood. "It's a blessing that Billy always has a man willing to take care of my shopping. I don't know what we'd do without that young man, ma'am."

"Wait a moment. One more matter . . . let us get my name sorted." Georgina had noticed the difficulty her staff seemed to be having on settling on a title for her, ever since she had abandoned the name 'Whitmore'. She would never use her husband's name again, divorce or no divorce. She knew the two old family retainers would never call her simply Georgina. "I do not enjoy being addressed as 'ma'am' – it may well be good enough for the queen but I can't like it. 'Madam' makes me feel like an old woman. Why not simplify the whole thing and address me as Miss Georgina again as you did when I was young?"

Flora saw that the two old dears blushed to be permitted such familiarity.

"Very well, Miss Georgina." Lily gave a brisk nod of her head.

"I'll be getting about my business then." Cook turned and walked towards the door. She'd think about this name business while in her kitchen – everything made sense there.

Georgina looked across the fire at Flora when the two older women had left the room. "What am I going to do with you? We will have to choose a room for you to use. Sarah will help you find suitable clothing – we can hope." She studied the younger woman closely. "You are welcome to stay for the present at least . . . but you cannot simply float around the house all day getting in everyone's way." She clapped one hand to her mouth. "I'm sorry, that sounds incredibly rude."

"Not in the least." Flora laughed. "I think it would be best if we start as we mean to go on and tell each other the truth – no matter how unpleasant. I am glad of a roof over my head. I would be willing to turn my hand to anything you might ask of me." She needed to feel she was paying her way.

"Flora, I am struggling to survive." Georgina liked this young woman. Putting a roof over her head would be no problem but keeping this house warm and food on the table cost money. What was one more person to worry about in the scheme of things? "I have no idea from one day to the next what is going to occur. My main problem, as I'm sure it is with most of the country, is money. I have to keep this house running and support those who work to help me."

"Why don't we start with small steps?" Flora could see the other woman was feeling overwhelmed. "Show me where you want me to be and let me think about what I can do to help you and your household."

"Yes, you're right – let's get you settled in."

"Do you mind . . . I would like your permission to

explore the house." She shrugged. "I like to know every inch of a place – would that be a problem?"

"I can't see why it would be." Georgina didn't know half of the contents of the rooms in this house. If this woman wanted to explore, she would welcome anything she might discover. "I have never taken the time to investigate each room of this house. The thought never occurred to me. Now!" She clapped her hands. "Let us find Sarah and with luck she will have something for you to wear. That very ancient dress and the gentleman's pants you are wearing underneath it need to go." She laughed and stood, offering her hand to pull the young woman from her seat. "Sarah has a very clever way of arranging short hair. We should ask her about it."

The two women left the room together.

"It is very kind of you to seek out a fashionable outfit for me, Sarah." Flora looked at the garments spread over one of the beds in a room on the third floor. "I will enjoy wearing something like that when you have made the alterations you've mentioned on your sewing machine." She pointed to a pile of violet satin. "That will be ideal when and if I walk out about town – but, for everyday wear, are there any black skirts and simple blouses and jackets? I have no intention to sitting sewing a fine seam in fancy clothes." She saw the disappointment on the young maid's face. "I like to be active. If at all possible I would chose clothing that allows me to move freely. Am I a great disappointment to you, Sarah?"

"No, miss." Sarah rooted among the clothes on the bed.

She tried to hide her feelings but the changes in this

129

house were making her dizzy. The nuns had placed her in this house until she turned sixteen. The money she earned here was paid to the nuns. She had to pay them back for their care of her in the orphanage. What would become of her after that she'd like to know? Would any upper-class house be willing to hire her, knowing she'd been trained in such an unusual house? The worry kept her awake at night.

"Something like these." She passed white linen underskirts over to the other woman. There had been no time to air the garments out but the clothing in the attic was packed in cedar boxes which everyone knew kept the cloth fresh – or so she'd been told. "If you would put these on and come down to the sewing room," she added a black heavy linen skirt and one of the white long-sleeved blouses she'd run up on the sewing machine to the pile, "I can see if they need to be altered." She looked from the clothes to Flora. She thought she'd picked out items that should fit.

"Thank you, Sarah. I'll dress and come downstairs when I'm ready."

She watched the maid leave the room before dropping onto one of the stripped beds in the room. What a very strange house she'd come to! She raised her chin, staring around her with wild eyes for a moment. So many changes in such a short space of time – still she'd adapt. It was a blessing they hadn't asked her to leave when she revealed her past.

Chapter 19

"Liam, see if Mr Flint is at home, please." Georgina was holding a note that had been delivered. She smiled as she watched Liam sprint to obey her order. The boy did love any excuse to visit the men living in the carriage house at the bottom of her property.

"Ruth, will you find the rest of the household, please, and ask them to come to the kitchen?" She preferred to tell everyone the news at once. "Cook, may I have a pot of tea?"

"Sit yerself down, out from under me feet." Betty pulled the heavy black kettle over to the hottest part of the range. She supposed she had better make a big enough pot for everyone. She selected the largest teapot for warming and waited while the members of the household assembled. She had a fruit cake in the pantry she could serve. It would keep them going until lunch.

"Am I now suitably clothed and shod?" Flora, with Sarah, walked from the sewing room into the kitchen. She was wearing a black skirt made voluminous by the many white underskirts Sarah had altered to fit. The white blouse with its high neckline felt very smart to her. Thankfully the garments had only needed a nip and tuck. The young maid had a good eye for size. Her hair was shaped around a stuffed cloth circle that Sarah had cleverly designed and made to conceal her short hair.

"You look very smart," Georgina said to nods of agreement from the others.

"You sent for me?" Billy Flint stepped into the kitchen with a grinning Liam on his heels.

"Yes, thank you for coming. Billy, this is Flora, an addition to our household. Flora, this is Billy Flint. I'm not quite sure how to describe Billy's position within this strange household of mine." Georgina shrugged. "Perhaps solver of problems and protector?"

"I'll take that!" Billy greeted Flora with a nod and a smile.

Flora watched the rest of the household appear.

"Everyone grab a mug of tea and a slice of that delicious fruit cake Cook is taking from the pantry."

Cook, Lily and Flora joined Georgina at the table in the alcove. Ruth and Bridget served everyone tea and cake. Billy, the three young maids and Liam stood with their cake and tea in hand, waiting to hear the reason they had been summoned.

Georgina picked up the note from where she'd put it on the table in front of her.

"A man from the building company will be here tomorrow." She consulted the note. "He wants to walk around the front and back gardens and generally make a study of the area being set aside for the new bathrooms."

"Does it give a name?" Billy had recommended the building company.

Georgina consulted the note. "Tommy Spencer."

"A good chap," Billy said. "He won't be here doing the work but will oversee the workers."

"Is he the one who will put in my gas cooker?" Cook had been promised a new gas cooker. She was nervous about learning to use the new cooker but at the same time the thought of not having to constantly check the heat when she baked was very attractive.

"His company will." Billy chewed rapidly to remove the traces of delicious fruit cake in his mouth.

The three maids ate and drank, saying nothing. Liam too was all ears.

"This is going to turn the running of this house on its head." Lily Chambers looked around the room.

Flora didn't know what they were talking about, but she ate her cake and drank her tea, sure she'd understand eventually. If she didn't – she'd ask.

"Billy," Georgina said, "I asked you to come over because I believe we should put a bathroom and toilet in the carriage house at the same time. The men will be here and underfoot. We may as well get all of the work done together." She looked around the company. "We must move with the times." The money for the additions to the house was coming from a fund set up by her forebears for the upkeep of the building.

"That sounds like a fine idea." Billy didn't try to hide his pleasure. Imagine him living in what was essentially his own house with an indoor toilet and bathroom! He was coming up in the world.

"What time does this man say he is calling?" Lily asked.

"Eleven tomorrow morning."

"Good." Lily nodded. "That will give us time to brush down the house and have our breakfast out of the way."

"Tomorrow is one of the days that Ruth and me go out." Sarah raised her hand like a child.

"That's fine, girls," said Georgina. "Ruth and Sarah are both training outside the house, Flora, developing their special talents – cooking and sewing."

"Lucky girls," said Flora.

"Cook and Lily – I think we should follow this Mr Spencer around tomorrow. We can listen to what he has to say and ask any questions while he is here to answer."

"I'll make sure I am there." Lily needed to know the exact details of the disturbance the installation of four toilets and bathrooms would bring to her domain.

"I'd like to ask about the gas being piped into the house." Cook was frantically trying to think of the food she could prepare in advance so that her charges would be fed.

"I'll be here too," Billy said. "I want to know what is going on."

"Bridget, pour more tea," Cook ordered. "Ruth, slice more of that cake."

Sarah and Liam stood out of the way.

"We can't make any plans," Georgina said. "None of us know what is going to happen. We will meet with this man and try to keep the turmoil to a minimum." She sighed. "Since we will have bathrooms and toilets on every floor – which will be a great boon to everyone here – that means that the entire house will be affected. We can only do our best to keep everything ticking over."

"If I can help in any way, please tell me." Flora accepted another slice of cake from the plate Ruth held out. "As I said, I am willing to turn my hand to most things."

The company settled down to discuss the upheaval that was sure to follow with a group of workmen around the place. Billy stood and listened, having nothing to offer. He would wait to see what Tommy Spencer had to say.

The four youngsters thought it all very exciting. It would change their lives for the better. It would mean they didn't have to haul water around the house. There would no longer be a need to empty slop buckets every morning. The installation of the bathrooms would reduce the amount of work each of them had to do – not a bad thing in this house – and they were excited to see the changes.

Chapter 20

"Richard, I wasn't expecting you!" Georgina said the following morning as her friend Richard Wilson stepped into the kitchen, accompanied by Billy Flint.

Richard had begun entering these premises by the back gate. He hoped to avoid causing gossip.

"I invited myself for breakfast, Cook. I hope you don't mind." He smiled charmingly at Betty Powell.

"What's one more?" Betty muttered. "I suppose you want to stay and all?" She looked at Billy.

"Thank you, Mrs Powell, yer blood should be bottled," Billy said, giving Cook the Dublin compliment for someone you admire.

"Get out from under me feet. Yez can go into the dining room. I've work to be doing." She examined the food she was preparing, adding more rashers of bacon and sausage to the pans sizzling away on top of the range. Two men ate a lot. She sighed inwardly. She did enjoy feeding people but she would be glad of a bit of advance warning from time to time.

"You had both better come with me into the servants' dining room," Georgina said with a laugh and led the way.

"Ruth, we'll need more toast." Cook noticed the young maid was already slicing an extra loaf of bread. "That bread was fresh from the bakery this morning." Liam had been sent to wait for the bread to come out of the ovens. "We'll leave some of it sliced on a charger. Not everyone wants toast with their breakfast."

"Yes, Cook." Ruth kept slicing – ten people ate a lot of bread.

Bridget stepped into the kitchen from the dining room where she had been laying the table. "Bridget, fill those kettles back up again and put them on the range," Cook ordered the young maid.

"Yes, Cook." Bridget jumped to obey.

"We have two extra for breakfast, Bridget – you'll need to set more places at the table." Cook looked around her domain, checking she had everything in hand. She didn't know what the world was coming to when the gentry sat down with the staff. Still, it wasn't her place to question her betters.

Sarah and Flora had been giving a final polish to the company rooms on the first floor. They could be heard hurrying down the stairs. They entered the kitchen and each took a moment to put away the cleaning supplies.

"Miss Flora," Cook called as soon as Flora closed the broom cupboard, "we have company for breakfast! You will need to be introduced. You go into the dining room. Sarah – give the other two a hand."

"Yes, Cook," they chorused.

"You'll have your work cut out for you getting this house ready for the workmen." Tommy Spencer felt like the Pied

Piper with the crowd of people following in his footsteps. The two men he didn't mind – but three women!

"I beg your pardon?" Georgina was standing by his side.

They had walked through the house and had now reached the attic and the list of things that needed to be accomplished before the men began work on the house kept growing. Georgina tried not to glare at the little barrel of a man turning her home upside down. Flora had accompanied the group to take notes. Richard and Billy were asking excited questions while the three women, Georgina, Flora and Lily were tight-lipped at the thought of the work ahead of them. Cook and the four young people were in the kitchen carrying on the working of the house.

"If I had my way I'd move the lot of you out while the work is being done on the house." Tommy rocked back on his heels. "The extension to the rear of the house will be messy. There's no two ways around that."

"I thought the bathrooms would be built separately." Lily's head was spinning at the thought of the work that had to be done."

"Now, missus," Tommy almost glared at poor Lily, "yez have gone with the best way of doing this thing – there's no two ways about that – but yeh can't make an omelette without smashing eggs." He looked over at Richard. That man was paying for all of this – why was he letting these women interfere?

"Ladies," Richard stepped forward slightly. "While the fixtures and fittings for the bathrooms and toilets will be in the extension to be constructed at the rear of the building – there will have to be access to the extension from inside the house on each floor. Then I'm afraid you

138

will have the mess of the water pipes, waste pipes and gas lines going down in the garden."

"Oh, my Lord," Georgina groaned.

Tommy sucked on his lips. "Yez are wanting an extension from ground to roof – yez have to know that will take a lot of time and effort. There will be work going on inside and outside the house. Yez are wanting four bathrooms and toilets installed – one for each floor. There will be structural changes to be made inside and out. The men will be coming in and out of the house." He ignored the groans from his listeners. He was well aware of the shock he was delivering but it couldn't be helped. That was progress.

Afterwards Georgina and Richard sat in the living room that had once been used only by senior servants but was now used by all of the household – how things had changed! The fire was glowing in the hearth. Georgina had no intention of lighting a fire in her private sitting room just to speak to her friend – coal was expensive.

"Now, Richard, tell me why you have invited yourself to my home today."

"I don't know if you are aware," Richard crossed one leg over the other and sat back in the comfortable armchair, "but my father's company collects the rent on a lot of the houses in this terrace." In point of fact his father owned a great many of the houses in the terrace. "I wanted to be on hand to listen and learn how much work is involved in updating one of these houses."

"Glad to be of service." Georgina was exhausted just thinking about the work that needed to be done to prepare her house for the workmen.

"No knowledge is ever wasted." He had also wanted to be here for Georgina. He knew she was counting off the days, waiting to hear from her four charges travelling across the sea. If the weather had been favourable, today was the day they should reach their destination.

"May I join you?"

"Miss Flora." Lily Chambers moved to stand.

"Please," Flora put her hand on the other woman's shoulder, keeping her in place. "I am just Flora – the poor relation – don't they usually disappear into the furniture?" She smiled as she sat at the table in the alcove with Cook and Lily.

"Not in this house," Lily replied.

"We are teaching women to stand up for themselves," Cook said proudly. "*Especially* poor relations!"

"I wanted to offer my help in preparing this house for the workmen." Flora accepted the cup and saucer Ruth put in front of her. She waited while the maid poured tea and moved back to her chores. "I have untold experience in how to shut up a house." She put a little milk in her tea. "When the Master visited the house I lived in, everything would be uncovered, maids from the village would be called in to dust and polish. Then when he left everything was put back under shrouds. I think, if you don't mind me saying – that is what we need to do here – knocking out walls and such is going to cause dust to fly everywhere."

"You're so right. I am trying to make a list." Lily pointed to the paper in front of her. She was using her precious fountain pen to write down everything she could think of. "It is the lack of servants that is concerning me the most. We ask so much of the youngsters."

"You have a whole team of available muscle at the bottom of the garden," Flora said with a laugh. "I have been reviewing their potential!"

"How and when?" Cook demanded.

"I asked Georgina's permission to explore the house and grounds." Flora was glad she'd told these women her story. "I need to know everything that surrounds me. I have walked this house and the mews while the rest of the house slept. I am sorry but it is something I began to do as soon as I learned to escape my locked room in the Master's house. I needed to know what was around me." She shrugged. "It made me feel I had some power over my own life."

"We will have to find you something to do that will exhaust you so." Lily didn't like the idea of anyone walking around the house while everyone slept. Though at least this poor relation of Georgina's didn't mean anyone any harm.

"May I borrow your pen and paper?" Flora gestured to the items. When Lily pushed them towards her, she turned to a clean page and began to draw. "This is the rear of the house." She drew a quick outline. "This is the area the extension will cover." She'd asked to have a look at the builder's plans. You would have thought she'd asked him to sell his mother he was so horrified. But she'd seen the plans and now tried to explain them to the other two women.

"It's like a carbuncle on the back of the house." Cook wasn't sure she liked the look of it. A great big ugly thing stuck onto the back of the house – still nobody had asked her.

"My word!" Lily looked at Cook. "How do we prepare for something like that?"

"It will be a lot of work but I am sure we can do it. I'll help in any way I can." Flora looked up from her design. "With all of the workmen in and out of the house I think we should lock the rooms, don't you?" She didn't wait for an answer. "I noticed all of the doors have locks – who has the keys?"

"I do," Lily answered. "Well, that is to say there is a hook-board with all of the house keys numbered on it. It's in my sitting room."

"Good." Flora looked at the two women. "I wonder if you would allow me to take charge of your young helpers." These two women were the heart of this household as far as Flora could tell but they were getting on in years and shouldn't have to run around this big house. "I could organise them to clear the rooms that need clearing before the workmen arrive – anything heavy, well, I'll call on the men in the mews. We can use some rooms for storage and lock the doors on those."

"I'm getting a headache just thinking of the problems in front of us." Lily did look pale.

"Mrs Chambers," Flora said, "your bedroom is one of the rooms that needs to be cleared. I think you should be the one to pack up your own room." She had noticed when they all examined the rooms with the building advisor that Lily's room was full of little personal touches – things a woman might want to keep private."

"Where will I sleep?" Lily almost wailed.

"We don't have to decide everything at one sitting." Cook reached over to pat her friend's hand.

"If I am not overstepping my place," Flora wanted to take the burden off this woman's shoulders, "I will organise the shutting down of the rooms. Perhaps your

142

belongings, Mrs Chambers, could be put into storage in the attics for the moment? With anything else of value? I will be sure to lock the attic rooms up tight."

"There," Cook smiled at Flora. "you take care of your own things, Lily. Let Flora take charge of the rest."

"I could do that, I suppose." Lily didn't like to hand control of her house over to this young woman but she simply wasn't up to the task. It was overpowering to think of how much needed to be done.

"There is one other thing . . ." Flora lightly tapped the closed fountain pen on the sketch.

"There always is!" Lily groaned.

"Oh whist, Lily," Cook said. "You're turning into a misery guts."

"This room here . . ." Flora pointed down the long corridor towards the front of the house. "I noticed it last night. The door is locked tight and there is a wooden shutter over the window from the outside. I paced it out. It is a large room. If you have to move from the attics, would that not be an ideal space to set up as a bedroom and sitting room for you – just until the work is completed?" Flora had hoped to ask for that room for her own use but Lily's need was greater.

"No, no," Lily protested. "That room shares a wall with the room we put the young maids in. It wouldn't be at all suitable for the housekeeper to sleep so close to young maids. Not at all the thing."

"Lily . . ." Cook started to protest.

"Well, we will have to find a room that suits you." Flora wanted to smile. She really wanted that room for her own use. It had a window that opened out over the front garden and towards the Grand Canal. It was close to the door that led from under the tall granite steps of the entry into this basement. It would be like having her own home. "What is in that room anyway?"

"Now there's a question!" Cook laughed.

"We don't know." Lily hadn't thought about that room in years.

"You will have to ask Miss Georgina," Cook said. "If I remember correctly it was used exclusively by Miss Georgina's father. He liked to say he was escaping from the women of the house in there."

"Miss Georgina's husband never came down here," Lily said. "Well, why would he? This is the servants' area. The old master – Miss Georgina's father, that is – used his key to the door under the entrance steps when he wanted to use that room. It kept his comings and goings private."

"I'll have to ask Georgina if I may go into that room." Flora wondered what she might uncover. She felt a tingle in her fingers. It was exciting not knowing what might be revealed.

Chapter 21

The *Oceanic*
Mid-Atlantic

"*Mia! Mia!*" Two sweet voices rang out.

Mia, walking with her friends on the steerage passenger deck, heard her name being called. She looked around, then up, and was frozen in horror. On the deck over their heads two little girls were trying to climb through the spaces in the railing that separated the cabin-class deck from steerage. There was a sheer drop below their feet.

"*Stay right there!*" Mia screamed while running in the direction of the ladder that would take her up to their level. "*Do not move! I promise I will spank you hard if you dare to move even an inch!*" She was grateful to be once more wearing her divided skirt.

Felicia, Jenny and Verity were close on Mia's heels. "*Help!*" they screamed as they ran. They raced at dangerous speed, dodging around people wondering what the fuss was all about.

Mia climbed the steep ladder, desperate to reach the two little girls. Where was the multitude of staff that

145

normally patrolled these decks? Why was no one close to hand?

The other women scrambled up after her.

"*Mia!*" Hope clapped her hands to see the story lady rush towards them.

"*Mia!*" Grace, at three years of age two years younger than her sister, held her little starfish hands out, wriggling her fingers. She wanted to hear a story.

"*You two stay right where you are!*" Mia threw one leg over the rail of the barrier. She almost fell to the deck below but caught herself in time. The women at her heels gasped. Mia couldn't believe no one had noticed the little girls' absence. Their father had a nanny and nursery maid on board with the children. Where were they? Why could two adults not keep better watch on two little girls? The children were still in their night attire. It was so cold. They could easily take a chill.

"*Land!*" A sudden shout rang out. "*Land ahoy!*"

Felicia stepped onto the cabin-class deck. She looked to where her friend stood with the two little girls. "*Mia!*" she screamed and pointed. The situation had turned even more dangerous as passengers and crew poured onto the decks, each impatient to spot land. Who would notice two little girls pressed dangerously close to the barrier?

Mia dropped to her knees and with only moments to spare pulled the two shivering little girls to her chest.

"Let me have one." Felicia knelt beside her. "We can turn our backs to the crowd and hold onto the barrier. Quickly – we will be swept along otherwise."

They were only just in time – the crowd of people frantic to catch their first glimpse of New York pressed forward with their eyes locked on the horizon. The two women with their precious cargo were forced to drop to the deck and wrap their legs around one of the metal supports of the rail. Their hands gripped the barrier as they tried desperately to keep the children safe. Their feet hung in the empty air over steerage. There too the passengers pressed to the sides of the ship hoping for a glimpse of land. It was pandemonium, the noise from so many throats almost deafening.

Verity and Jenny stood over the two women on the deck and attempted to protect them from all comers.

"*Here, you, what are you doing there?*" a ship's officer barked and pointed at the two standing figures. "You do not belong here – return to your own class immediately." The man, muttering polite words of apology, pushed and shoved his way across the deck. He knew they didn't belong on this deck. He'd seen their like before putting on airs and graces. The hussies belonged below with others of their class.

"What are we doing here, sir?" Jenny snapped when the man stood over her, glaring. She had the bit well and truly between her teeth. All signs of disappearing into the background had left her. She raised her chin and glared at the man when he tried to reach for her. "Do not, sir, attempt to lay a hand on me." She used two stiffened fingers to poke the officer in the chest. "How dare you, *sir*, approach ladies in such a fashion." Her accent could have cut glass and with each '*sir*' she poked the man in his uniform shirt. "My companions, *sir*, have been saving the life of two vulnerable children – children whose father paid a great deal of money to travel on this benighted vessel."

The man stepped back and opened his mouth, but

Jenny was having none of it. She continued to harangue him.

"I want two warm blankets and a hot drink found for these children." She glanced around. "That is, as soon as this rabble," she gave a disparaging glance at the crowd of cabin passengers lost to everything but being the first to sight land, "allow us space to rescue our companions and their charges. Now, sir, go and see to my demands." She turned her back on the stunned officer. "We will keep the little ones safe."

It was some time before the officer returned with several stewards. The men formed a circle of protection around the four females and their charges and, with many polite remarks muttered through clenched teeth, began to move them towards the infirmary.

"Someone needs to inform Mr Bridges that his children are in the infirmary." Mia was battered and shaken – her back and shoulders ached. She almost fell onto one of the beds in the treatment room they had been taken to.

The little girl she held refused to let loose of her choking grip around Mia's neck.

"Grace, dear," Mia croaked, "please release me. You are safe here. These men will bring your daddy to you." The little girl shook her head of blonde hair and her little face remained buried in Mia's neck.

"Hope, you're safe now." Felicia too tried to get the child she held to release her tight grip.

"Someone go and get the father." The ship's doctor tried to pull the child from Felicia which caused the little one to tighten her grip, almost choking Felicia in the process. "This child is frozen."

"Then might it not be a good idea to find blankets to wrap around them and something warming to drink!" Jenny barked. "As I have already stated! I'm sure that would serve everyone better than trying to inflict harm on the woman who saved the child's life."

She glared at the men in the room. She watched while two stewards almost ran from the room to fetch the suggested items. One came back in a short space of time and almost threw two blankets in Jenny's direction. She sighed and shook her head while covering each child with a blanket and tucking them in as best she could.

"*Where are my children?*" a male voice shouted in the outer room.

The two girls lifted their heads from their hiding place and in voices that hurt the ear screamed for their daddy.

Josiah Huffington-Bridges exploded into the room. His blond hair was almost standing on end, his bright blue eyes manic. He took in the scene before him and the breath he released on first sight of his children could be plainly heard.

"*Someone better tell me what the hell is going on around here!*" Josiah stood with his hands on his hips, all six feet four inches of him expressing extreme displeasure.

The ship's staff present in the room almost tripped over their own tongues trying to provide explanations and excuses. Josiah ignored them all.

"Miss Mia," Josiah asked, knowing that she would give him the bare truth. This was a woman not impressed by anyone or anything. He liked that about her. She'd been reading stories to the little ones on board. He loved to watch her sit on deck with little children spread around her listening intently.

"Your children, sir," Mia raised her head to glare at him, "have managed to escape their carers – yet again! Your girls, sir, were running loose around this ship in freezing cold – *still in their night attire!* I simply cannot express the terror I felt when I saw them attempting to climb the barrier over a sheer and deadly drop! It is all very well to say – as you have done – that your girls are full of go and gallop – but this time their actions could have had fatal consequences, sir, and I do not exaggerate. You simply must employ people who tend to your children with greater vigilance." Mia was almost in tears as she tried not to think of what might have happened if she hadn't reached the little ones in time.

She stood and tried to pass the child to her father, but Grace refused to leave her arms.

"I really must protest," the ship's officer who had first noticed the women said. "These women do not belong on this deck. It would serve us all better, sir, if you removed your children from their care and allowed us to see them back to steerage where they belong."

There was a murmur of agreement from the other males. The doctor, a sour-faced individual, going so far as to sniff and grimace at the presence of these women in his infirmary.

"We will be docking this afternoon," the officer continued. "There is a great deal to do. I would imagine you need to have your bags packed and your children ready to disembark."

"Did you hear that, Grace?" Mia whispered to the child she still held. "You have to go with your daddy now. You have to get dressed so you can get off this ship. Won't that be good?"

"Come on, Hope." Felicia too tried to release the child who clung to her like a limpet. "You have to go to your nanny and get ready to get off the ship."

"Perhaps you ladies could accompany us to our state room?" Josiah said when it became obvious his children were unwilling to leave the women.

"That would not be at all suitable," the ship's officer said. "These women need to return where they belong." He'd make sure they wouldn't get out of steerage again until the ship was clear of the lot of them down there.

"Jenny and I will return to our cabin and pack our bags," Verity offered. "You two could remain with the children. We will all need to be ready to leave."

"Steerage class will not be allowed off this ship with the cabin-class passengers." The doctor sniffed in his annoying fashion. "The steerage passengers will remain in lockdown overnight. Tomorrow a barge will take you all from this ship and sail you to Ellis Island. All of you will be handed over to the authorities for examination." The shipping company would be penalised if any of the steerage passengers were allowed to set foot in New York before they had been duly processed.

"One more night on board this vessel," Jenny said. "What joy."

"I could pay the difference in cost for their tickets," Josiah said. "They can stay with my children until it is time to disembark."

"Well ..." The ship's officer thought of the money he could pocket.

"Thank you but we have to decline." Verity stepped forward. "We four boarded this ship as steerage passengers in order to conduct a social experiment for our

151

journal." She was making it up as she went along. "It would be folly for us to leave the ship at this stage. We must complete our study. We thank you for the offer." She crossed her fingers behind her back, hoping the others wouldn't contradict her words.

"Hope, honey," Josiah stepped close to Felicia. "come to Daddy." He gently removed his child from the woman who had protected her – heads would roll when he had the full story behind this debacle. "Miss Mia," he said when Hope was clinging to him, "if you would be kind enough to carry Grace to our state room." He glared at the officer who opened his mouth to object. "I will see that Miss Mia returns safely to her friends." He looked around, making a note of all there. "I will stay with the ladies until they are safely down onto the bottom deck." He didn't trust the treatment these women would receive from the men glaring at them.

"Why on earth did you say we were conducting a social study?" Felicia asked as soon as they had closed the cabin door behind them.

"We have been an oddity ever since we stepped on this ship, you would agree?" Verity waited until the other two nodded. "I saw the way that man looked at Mia. We have all noticed his attentions – he has offered marriage, for goodness' sake. I have been around the highest level of society for years. Should Mia choose to accept his offer, she will never be allowed to forget she travelled to America in steerage. The news of our social study will be all over this ship like wildfire." She shrugged and looked at the other two, waiting for their opinion. "That doctor will be the first one to complain to all willing to listen."

"You clever thing!" Jenny said with a laugh.

"Yes, should Mia stay in New York she can now look down her nose at anyone who dares suggest she is anything but a diamond of the first water," said Felicia.

The three women looked at each other for a moment before their almost hysterical laughter rang around the cabin.

Mia returned to their cabin, accompanied by a stewardess they had never seen before. By her uniform they knew she served first-class passengers.

"Ladies," the stewardess said as soon as the door had closed at their back, "I need you to pack your belongings and be prepared to move. I shall return shortly." She began to leave then turned back. "Are you all really conducting an experiment? I think you are all awfully brave. My parents quite despaired of me when I told them what I wanted to do." She didn't wait for a reaction, leaving before they could say a word.

"Mia, what is going on?" Verity demanded.

"Mr Bridges had a word with the captain." Mia was pulling the rough blanket from her bunk as she spoke. "He demanded that we four be protected." She turned to look at her friends. "He thinks we will be in danger while the ship remains tied up alongside the North River pier. He insisted on paying for us to be moved to first-class cabins overnight. We will leave with the other passengers tomorrow. I intend to leave this cabin as we found it." She continued to pull her bedding apart.

"Why on earth would he do such a thing?" Jenny asked.

"I may have mentioned the bother we women have

experienced from the 'foreign' louts in steerage," Mia said over her shoulder.

"What foreign louts?" Felicia stood with her hands on her hips, glaring around the cabin. "I know we have all been touched inappropriately by far too many men – crew and passengers both – on this voyage – but I have never remarked on their nationality!"

"Of course, we have all being victims of the type," Verity started to laugh as she understood what Mia meant. "The men with Russian hands and Roman fingers – foreigners!"

The four women sniggered for a moment.

"We will have to thank the man." Jenny began to pull her bedding apart. "In all seriousness, I don't like the way the men on this ship have been looking at us. It has made me very uncomfortable."

The four women exchanged uneasy glances. They had all been subjected to groping hands and whispered threats of a sexual nature while on this ship.

Chapter 22

Percy Place
Dublin

In Dublin the house on Percy Place was being pulled apart.

Lily was in her rooms packing a lifetime of little treasures into a wooden crate Billy Flint had secured for her use. She looked around sadly at her little eerie. She had been so proud when she'd been given these rooms in the attic for her own use. She never thought of complaining of the pain in her knees when she had to climb all of those stairs, morning and night.

Georgina was alone on the family level, organising the master suite for the occupation of her first renter. She wondered about the woman who had asked the BOBs to arrange for these rooms. She hoped she fit into their unusual household. Would she still be willing to stay here with workmen underfoot?

"Did these people never throw anything out?" Flora stood with her hands on her hips, staring around at yet one more of the small attic rooms. She looked at her helpers. Bridget and Sarah wore mob caps and heavy hessian aprons over their black dresses. Liam too wore a hessian apron, much to his disgust. She had insisted they all put cloths around their nose and mouths. The dust up here would choke you. They had passed a busy morning trying to remove decades of dust and clutter.

"Do you think Miss Georgina would let us throw any of this aul' rubbish out?" Bridget's green eyes were bright over the white cloth tied around her face.

"Biddy, mind your tongue!" Sarah wanted to return to her sewing room. She hated dusting and shoving articles around these old rooms. It was scary up here to her mind. Lucky old Ruth, in the kitchen with Cook, she thought.

Bridget stuck her tongue out at her friend, thinking the cloth would cover her movement. It didn't if the glare from Sarah's blue eyes was anything to go by.

"Let us go down to the next floor," Flora said. She had opened all of the windows and dampened down the dust. It would be best to let that settle. She would have to consult Georgina about throwing out some of this rubbish. Bridget had the right of it there. She led her little band from the attic level.

"It doesn't seem any time at all since we were arranging these rooms for the first of the ladies." Bridget stood on the third-floor landing, waiting for instruction. "Flora," she had been given permission to address the woman by her first name, "where are we going to put any ladies the BOBs might send us?"

"Honestly, Biddy," Sarah snapped, "that is none of our concern."

Flora paid no attention to the bickering servants. "I think it would be best if we get the men to take the beds apart." She had been walking from room to room. "Liam, you will have to clean the fires in each room completely. Then we will remove the loose parts and store them." She spun on her heels, thinking. "We will store beds and such in one room, on this level, keeping two or three rooms set up in case we need them." She clapped her hands. She wished Mrs Chambers had made up her mind as to which room she would take for the duration of the build. "The beds have been stripped, which makes our chore easier." She looked at her young helpers. The three youngsters stood surrounded by brooms and cleaning products. They had done a marvellous job this morning. "You three run down to the kitchen and ask Cook for a cup of tea. We have been eating dust up here. There is nothing you can do here for the moment. Liam, if you would ask Mr Flint to find me men who can take these beds apart and shift heavy furniture, that would be most useful." She turned back towards the attic stairs. "I'll have a word with Mrs Chambers."

Chapter 23

New York

On board ship the women passed an uncomfortable afternoon and night. The stewardess had led them from steerage to first class, using the staff's hidden hallways.

An hour after sunset, when the ship tied up alongside her pier in the North River the shouting had been deafening and downright frightening. The steerage passengers had been locked down while the cabin passengers left the ship. The howls of disappointment, curses, wailing and threats echoed around the ship and into the first-class cabins where the four ladies were.

The women had passed the night in two cabins that were the epitome of luxury after their time spent in steerage.

Felicia and Verity joined the others in their cabin that morning.

"I believe if Mr Bridges were still aboard," Felicia said, "I would kiss his feet."

"I doubt the man would care for that." Mia was sitting on one of the comfortable beds in the large cabin. "I do admit he has been kindness itself." She shook the large brown envelope from Mr Bridges that the stewardess had given to her. "He has stuffed this envelope with dollar bills. I have no idea of their value but in his note he did mention the staff would fall over their feet to serve us upon the presentation of one of these bills."

"That is kind," said Verity. "We are going to have to wait longer, I'm afraid. There is a steamer leaving port and this ship is unable to move until it has cleared the harbour.

"Well, we could be in a worse spot," Jenny said and all four women sighed.

They were ready for this sea voyage to be over.

The steerage passengers were allowed, in groups, to leave the ship and stand on the pier while custom house officials tore apart their luggage. Each group was then herded onto a barge that would carry them to Ellis Island. There, the four women had to struggle to keep contact with each other while they were inspected by a doctor, required to show what money they had and closely questioned concerning their, past, present and future lives. They were finally allowed to board the barge again for the short trip to what they were told was the Battery.

They each felt, after the struggle and turmoil of the processing, as if they were spit out onto American soil. They had to jump out of the way of their fellow travellers who were greeted by family and pulled along among much wailing and welcoming.

"Excuse me." A well-groomed man had approached without them noticing. "Would you be the four ladies visiting Mrs Caleb Anderson?" He doffed his hat. "I am Cruikshank, Mr Anderson's man of affairs, at your service."

"Thank you." Jenny as the oldest stepped forward.

She introduced her companions and they followed the gentleman to a waiting carriage.

"This equipage belongs to Mr Anderson. The driver will take you to the railway station. The postern will assist you onto the correct train. It is a short train ride from here to the home of Mrs Anderson. That good lady will greet you when you reach your final destination." He again doffed his hat and prepared to leave. He had done what he had been asked to do. He wondered briefly why there were so many maidservants standing around paying a mite too much attention to the women he had greeted. He'd mention it to Mr Anderson.

"Does anyone else feel as if they are still aboard ship?" Felicia asked when all four were in the first-class railway carriage the postern had procured for them. He'd informed them Mr Anderson had covered the cost. They hadn't argued, glad of the chance to sit and take stock.

"I believe that will pass." Verity looked around her with interest.

The area around the dock had been cluttered as it would be in any port. The train chugged through vast areas of buildings before, almost in the blink of an eye, they were in open country.

Jenny jumped when she heard East Hinsdale being shouted by the ticket collector. "I believe this is our stop."

"My word, that was quick!" Felicia stood.

All four women grabbed their luggage. Verity ran to open the carriage door. She stood on the station platform, holding the door open. They had a lot of luggage to move after all.

"Here!" The ticket collector and a gentleman passenger helped remove the luggage from the train.

The foursome stood in a haze of steam watching the train depart.

"Ladies –"

They turned to see a very attractive well-dressed woman standing smiling at them.

"My name is Eleanor. I have been expecting you."

"How do you do?" Again it was Jenny who performed the introductions.

"I thought we could walk to my home." Eleanor turned to greet the gentleman of colour who had joined them. "This is Samuel – I call him my general factotum because thankfully he is willing to turn his hand to anything. He will load your luggage onto our horse and cart, leaving us free to stroll. Does this suit you?"

"I think we would all be glad to stretch our legs," Verity said. "Is your home very far?"

"Not at all," Eleanor replied. "There is little in East Hinsdale, a few houses, this railway station and a post office. But if you have a longing for city streets the train can carry you to New York in a short space of time."

While they were talking Samuel began to carry the luggage out of the station to the waiting horse and cart. The women picked up what they could carry and hurried to lend a hand. Eleanor watched their actions in surprise.

"If any of you ladies want to jump up on the back of this cart," Samuel said when he had the luggage loaded, "you would be welcome."

After a hasty glance amongst them the ladies declined the offer.

"I can't think of anything I would enjoy more than

walking in the countryside," Felicia said. "I long to blow the smell of the ship out of my nostrils, if the truth be told."

The other three muttered agreement and it was a bevy of five attractive women who strolled along the country lanes under the watchful eye of men more used to seeing livestock there than attractive young females.

"My husband will have sent a telegram to Dublin to inform them of your safe arrival," Eleanor said as they strolled. "I hope you do not mind us taking charge of that, but it is so much more convenient for him to send an international telegram from New York."

"I am glad someone is thinking clearly," Verity said.

"Yes, indeed, it hadn't even occurred to me," Jenny agreed.

Mia remained silent, thinking of a tall, blue-eyed gentleman who had been so kind to her.

"Well, now we are free to get ourselves settled and begin looking for work." Felicia couldn't wait to get started.

"As to that," Eleanor said. "I have been making some enquiries …"

Chapter 24

Percy Place
Dublin

"*Telegram!*" The post office boy, proudly wearing his navy-blue post-office uniform, tipped his hat and waited.

Georgina stared at the small envelope in her hand, her heart beating so hard in her chest it was almost painful. What could be so important that someone had paid the exorbitant cost of sending a telegram!

"Here you go." Lily Chambers stepped forward to press a large brown penny into the youngster's open hand. "There will be no reply." She pulled her mistress gently in and closed the door.

"A tip, I didn't even think of it." Georgina was staring at the envelope.

"The butler used to keep pennies in the drawer of the hall tallboy, for just such a purpose." Lily too was distracted. She wanted to tear the envelope out of Georgina's hands and open it.

"It is from America." Georgina pressed a hand to her heart. She opened the envelope and read, then looked at Lily with tears in her eyes. "The girls have arrived safely!

So good of them to let us know so quickly."

"Well, that is a piece of good news we can share with everyone." Lily took Georgina by the elbow and gently towed her out of the vestibule and into her private sitting room. The fire wasn't lit but her mistress looked like she needed to sit down.

"Silly of me to get in a tizzy because a telegram arrives at the house." Georgina stared into the cold grate for a moment.

"It's only to be expected! It's such a relief to hear they are safe and well."

"It is! Let's go and tell the others."

The two women left the chilly room.

"It's good to know that our girls have arrived safely," Cook said when they were gathered around the table in the servants' dining room. "We will have to wait for their letters to learn more."

The meal had been eaten and the younger members of staff had cleared the table. They were in the kitchen washing the dishes and restoring order while the older women sat sharing a pot of tea.

"Have the BOBs given you any more information about the lady who will lodge with us?" Lily didn't know what needed to be done for a lodger – honestly – were they now to run a boarding house? "I have no experience of serving someone who rents a room."

"We were all nervous before the students arrived." Georgina had had no news of new women being sent from the BOBs so the money the woman would pay in rent would be very welcome. She needed a regular income. The money she'd earned from housing the students was being eked out but wouldn't last for much longer. She had a large house to run and people to support.

"I would like to have a word." Flora walked over and closed the door of the dining room before returning to take her seat. "Cook, if you would bring your tea and move closer, please."

Cook joined them at the end of the table furthest from the door.

"I hope I am not speaking out of turn." Flora was nervous about putting herself forward in this company. "I know I am the newcomer but, perhaps because of that, I see things differently."

"We're listening," Georgina said when Flora fell silent.

"It seems to me that this is a perfect time for change – what with the workmen and all."

"We've had nothing but change around here lately, it seems to me," Cook said.

"Mrs Chambers, I think you should move into the room that the youngest servants are presently using." Flora had noticed how difficult it was becoming for the other woman to climb the many stairs in this house. She had seen her wince with pain when she thought no one was looking. "We could arrange that room to be a comfortable place for you. It is quite large and you and Cook could relax before the fire in the living room of an evening when the day's work is done."

"That does sound attractive, Lily." Cook too had noticed her old friend slowing down. She wouldn't like to have to climb them bloody stairs – not for any price.

"I had originally put the maids in the room down here out of fear for their safety." Georgina exchanged a glance with her old retainers. They would understand. "Those

165

worries no longer exist."

"We have to clear the back rooms of the house for the builders." Flora had been giving this a lot of thought. "Since the household is being turned on its head anyway – surely now is the time to institute change for your own convenience?"

"You would be a lot cosier down here, Lily, don't you think?" Georgina thought the move downstairs would suit her.

"I want to move the maids and young Liam up to the attic rooms," said Flora. "There will be a great deal involved in clearing years of junk out of the attic. This will give us the incentive to clear the rooms and use them for the purpose they were intended." She looked around the table. "I noticed there were a few rooms without junk in them. If we clear those first the youngest members of staff could be moved quickly."

"The male staff used those rooms." Georgina didn't feel the need to explain that her husband had fired all of the household staff except the youngest. Betty and Lily had refused to leave her.

Flora didn't comment on the lack of male staff. It was none of her business. She had been offered a safe haven. She would take what she had been given with gratitude.

"Lord knows there are days when I don't know if I'm coming or going," Cook said.

"I'll think about what you've said. With the way this house is being turned on its head who knows where we'll all end up?" Lily was feeling her age. She had planned to retire but how could she leave Miss Georgina now?

The four women were silent for a while, each thinking her own thoughts.

"Would you say you had received a superior education, Flora?" Georgina suddenly asked. She'd had a brainwave while her mind had been wandering. "When you were being a science project, I mean."

"Better than most men ever receive," Flora said without vanity. She had paid for that education in blood and tears.

"Would you undertake to educate Bridget?" Georgina had planned to set up a course of study for Bridget but life – as it often did – got in the way of her plans. "The child is desperate to learn French. Jenny had been helping her but they can't have got very far with the subject. You could continue those studies. On the days the other two go to their studies you could take Bridget out and about. There are museums, libraries and musical events all over Dublin. You could take Bridget to any and all of those events." She would borrow money from Richard if she had to. Billy Flint had kept her informed of the movements of the Earl of Castlewellan. The beauty of dealing with someone like Billy was he didn't ask questions – simply completed the task you had set him. Clive Henderson, the Earl, had returned north to his estates. Bridget would be safe walking the streets of Dublin.

"I would be delighted to share my knowledge with Bridget." Flora had grown very fond of the young maid. "Very well – we can begin organising the attic rooms. You are willing to be housed here in the basement, Mrs Chambers?"

"A change is as good as a rest." Lily had been giving the matter some thought. "Young Liam will be like a dog with two tails having a room for himself."

"A room for the bootboy?" Cook didn't object – it was just unusual.

"Well, when these bathrooms and toilets are put in," Lily smiled at Betty, "you and me will be able to walk around the place in our bathrobes without having a young boy underfoot."

"You clever old thing!" Cook laughed at the very thought of taking a bath close to her own bedroom. Imagine, the luxury! Talk about coming up in the world. "There will be no flies on us."

"So, we'll arrange the attic rooms for the maids and Liam." Flora wanted to be sure Mrs Chambers was happy with the plan.

"Let us go and see what needs to be done." Georgina stood up.

She put her hand on Lily's shoulder, keeping her in her seat. She wasn't quite as blind as everyone seemed to think she was. She had noticed the grimace of pain on her housekeeper's face whenever she climbed the stairs. She simply hadn't known what to do to move the stubborn woman.

"Lily, you stay here with Betty and plan the wild times you will have in the evening when you have this place to yourselves." She pushed her chair back under the table. "Flora, you come with me. Ladies, I'll send Ruth in with a fresh pot of tea."

The two women swept out of the room and into the kitchen.

"Ruth, please arrange fresh tea for Cook and Mrs Chambers." Georgina was checking the area for any sign of neglect.

"Biddy –" Ruth began.

"No, Ruth," Georgina snapped, "I asked you to serve the two senior servants in this house. Should you need assistance have Sarah help you. Bridget will be busy with other chores. Bridget, come with me." Georgina, with Flora at her heels, swept from the kitchen and up the stairs.

Bridget, with a quick glance at her friends, ran after the mistress and Flora.

"Do you have a notebook, Bridget?" Georgina asked when they stood in the entrance hall. She knew the child didn't but felt she should ask.

"No, Miss Georgina." Bridget didn't have one of those lovely red-leather-covered notebooks that the housekeeper had given to her two friends. She wished she did.

"I noticed you write a beautiful hand." Georgina stepped into her sitting room. She knew she had a new spiral notebook somewhere. She found the items she needed and returned to the hallway, pulling the door closed at her back. She spent very little time in this room these days. "We will need to take notes as we plan the changes in the house. Flora will show you how to draw diagrams if needed." She passed the notebook and two lead pencils to Bridget. "I doubt we will need to make the notes in ink. There will be too many changes." She didn't fail to notice the delight on the young maid's face at being given something as simple as a notebook and pencil.

"I plan to teach you French as we work around the house, Bridget," Flora said as the three began to climb the stairs. "It's a shame to waste your brain when your hands are busy."

"That's what Miss Jenny used to say," said Biddy.

Georgina wondered if she missed the woman who gave

birth to her but dared not ask.

"You will have to count me in, Flora, for the French lessons." Georgina smiled. "It has been many years since I practised my French."

The two women were aware of the beaming maid who followed in their footsteps.

Chapter 25

"Morning, Billy – looks to me as if the women have you and your men hard at work." Richard Wilson, once more slipping in the back gates of Percy Place, stared around the crushed lawn and winced at the thought of the disorder yet to come.

"Morning, Richard." Billy shouted to one of his men to take over before walking to where Richard stood. "What brings you here this freezing cold morning?"

"I wanted a word with you." Richard watched the men place broken and cracked items on a flatbed trailer. "Are you taking all of this to the dump?"

"Not at all," Billy replied. "I know a lad with a market stall. He's handy at fixing things up. He'll have this lot fixed and on his stall before yeh can spit." He turned his back on his workers. "What did you need to see me about?"

"My father is thinking of having bathrooms installed in some of his rental properties. I wanted to know if you would be interested in putting a crew together to handle the work involved in preparing the properties?"

"Well, now you're talking my language!" Billy rubbed his hands together. He was always interested in finding ways his men could earn a few bob.

"I haven't told Georgie yet but I've arranged for a man named Bertie Fielding to meet with us here. The man's a plumber. He's setting himself up as some kind of expert in the installation of sanitary ware." Richard wanted Billy's opinion of the man. "I thought you could join us?"

"Just let me know when and where," Billy said.

"Oh, I expect him shortly." Richard liked putting business Billy's way. He was grateful for all the help the younger man gave Georgie.

"Grand."

The two men began to walk towards the kitchen door.

"Billy Flint," Cook was flushed and bad-tempered, "will yeh for God's sake tell yer men to wipe their feet? Me kitchen floor is awash with mud. How does anyone think I can prepare meals with men constantly under me feet?"

Georgina appeared in the kitchen as if by magic. She was wearing a mob cap and a hessian sacking apron over a black skirt and white blouse. She noticed Richard and gave a jerk of her chin to acknowledge his presence while pulling the cap from her head. She brushed impatiently at her hair, hoping it had remained in place. "Betty, I told you to put your feet up while the men carried out all this rubbish." She put her arm around Cook's shoulders. "No one expects you to turn out one of your fabulous meals under these circumstances."

"I suppose I could sacrifice me stockpot," Betty said. "If I fill it with pearl barley and lentils, throw in a load of potatoes, it will stick to our ribs at least but it's not what I like to serve yeh, Miss Georgina."

"Betty, everyone here knows you're an angel in the kitchen." Georgina bit back a sigh. She'd had more problems since she got out of bed this morning than she felt capable of dealing with. "You get your stockpot stew on the go. We can buy bread from the baker and dip it if need be. I won't have you upsetting yourself like this."

"I won't let you down, Miss Georgina." Betty put her shoulders back and pushed up her sleeves, ready to box the ears of any man who bothered her.

"I knew I could count on you." Georgina tightened her arm around the other woman's shoulders in a brief hug before turning to the men watching her. "Billy, Richard, what can I do for you?"

"If I could have a private word with you, Georgie?" Richard said.

Georgina wondered what this was about. "Give me a moment to wash my hands and face and I'll join you in my sitting room." She hurried off.

"I won't have me best girl reduced to tears." Billy put his arm around Cook's shoulders. "There's a tripe kitchen in a lane over the way. I can have one of me men run over there and fetch food for all of us, if you don't mind." He shook her shoulders gently. "And, in an emergency, there's always the Penny Dinners." He was referring to a soup kitchen run by nuns at a nearby convent.

"The cheek of yeh, Billy Flint!" Cook shook his arm away. "As if I'd serve anything of the sort to my lady – away with yeh before I box yer ears!"

Billy laughed and left to oversee his men.

Georgina noticed Richard had put a match to the fire. Liam kept the fires in all of the rooms set in case of need.

She thought of the price of coal and tried not to sigh.

"Richard, what can I do for you?" She hadn't time to stand on ceremony.

"It is more what I can do for you, Georgie." Richard remained standing while reaching to take his wallet from his inside coat pocket. He removed several white five-pound notes from his wallet before returning it to his pocket.

"While the work is being carried out on the house it would be perfectly legal for you to ask for money from the house-maintenance account, Georgie." He and his father had discussed the matter. They believed they had found a way to give Georgina funds from the monies placed in his father's care by her family – funds set up in such a way that they were legally denied her husband – unfortunately, Georgina too was prevented from accessing these funds while she remained married to Whitmore.

Georgina swallowed tears. She could not afford pride. She'd been worrying and wondering how she was to pay Billy and his men for all of their work. The household accounts too needed an infusion of cash. She stared at the notes in her hands with glittering eyes.

"Thank you," she said simply. Having the worry of paying her way removed from her shoulders – for the moment – gave her a boost of energy she badly needed.

"I hope you will not be angry with me, Georgie, but I have asked someone to meet me here." Richard said quickly when a knock sounded on the front door. He stifled a sigh, he wanted to take her away from all this but how could he make an offer? She was a married woman and so she would remain until Whitmore either carried through with his threat of divorce or died. All he could do was try and help her, as much as she would allow. "I'll answer that, shall I?"

"Why not?" Georgie quickly locked the money in her desk before settling in front of the fire – since it had been lit.

At the door Richard greeted Bertie Fielding. "Ah, Fielding – thank you for agreeing to meet me here."

Richard liked the look of the little man standing before him. He was dressed as a wealthy tradesman but had obviously lost some weight – his suit hung loosely on his frame. His shoes were well polished which spoke well of the man. He was unaware of his own visual examination of the man – judging others came naturally to him.

"Ideally what you should do," Bertie Fielding was in his element, "is have a large gas water heater that will pump hot water around the house – not individual gas heaters as your builder has suggested." He took a catalogue from his briefcase and set it on the small round table in the room. "The kitchen should have continuous hot running water."

"Won't Cook be made up with that!" said Billy.

"Now, for your ladies' retiring room on the first floor . . ." Bertie mentally crossed his fingers praying he'd get the contract – he'd returned to Ireland to set up his own business but times were tough." He passed the catalogue he'd opened to Georgina, stopping just short of placing it in her lap. "I thought something like this ..."

Georgina gasped at the beauty of the engraved and painted sanitary ware displayed on the open page.

"Something like this is elegant and attractive while being functional at the same time," Bertie said.

"I believe you are correct, Mr Fielding." Georgina was

thinking of the ladies of the BOBs using her facilities. A W.C. furnished with this sanitary ware would be superior.

Richard knew by the look on Georgie's face that she had realised what a boon this man's knowledge would be to her. He could take a great deal of the pressure off her already over-burdened shoulders.

"I thought, Georgina, with your permission," he said, "that Mr Fielding could be in charge of the plumbing in of all the bathrooms."

"What about Spencer?" Billy asked before Georgie could answer.

"Spencer works for a building company," Richard said. "Plumbing is a different area of expertise. For that we need Mr Fielding."

"Please, call me Bertie."

"Mr Fielding – Bertie," Georgina stood with the catalogue in hand, "would you show me more, please?" She walked over to the small table near his armchair and placed the heavy catalogue, still open at the page he'd been showing her, on it.

"Thinking of becoming a silent partner?" Richard asked Billy softly while Georgie and Fielding were absorbed in talk of washbasins and baths. He was aware of Billy's fascination with all this talk of an opening field of opportunity. He might be interested in investing in Fielding's company. It seemed to him that everyone would want a bathroom and W.C. when they saw what was available.

"Something like that." Billy didn't know what a silent partner was – he'd never been one for keeping his opinion to himself. But he thought he might just take a chance on investing some of his money with Fielding.

Meanwhile, Bertie Fielding had everything crossed, praying he was going to get the contract for the work on this house. He had no idea that with the help of the two men present he was well on his way to becoming a very wealthy man.

Chapter 26

East Hinsdale
Queens County
New York

Caleb Anderson was sitting in the living room with his wife's guests. The fire in the grate blazed. The logs being burned gave out a pleasing aroma and from time to time spat out bright sparks of colour. It was the gathering place of the house, being the warmest room.

Jenny sat in one chair, a borrowed writing slope on her lap. It was her turn to write to the people in Dublin. They had decided to take turns writing to reduce the cost of postage. She played with the fountain pen in her hand and for the first time in years she longed to paint. Everything was so different here. She longed to make note of everything she saw.

Verity and Felicia were rolling a skein of yarn for Eleanor. Mia sat staring into the distance.

"Ladies, I must tell you." Caleb's voice broke the comfortable silence. He crossed one leg over the other, not at all uncomfortable at being in ladies' company. "I am fascinated by everything I learn about this Harvey." He had made it his business to find out as much as he could about the company these women hoped to work for. It was providing him with much amusement.

"What have you learned, Caleb?" Eleanor, sitting in a chair across the fire from him, leaned forward to ask. She too had been making enquiries but perhaps of a different nature. She looked around her crowded living room. It was nice to have company.

"The man has the most innovative way of doing business," Caleb said. "I'd like to meet him." Unfortunately, the company founder was in bad health.

"What do you mean?" Verity asked.

"The Harvey Company is heavily subsidized by the ATSF – the Atchison, Topeka and the Santa Fe company." Caleb explained that the ATSF used the Harvey hotels and the more famous Harvey girls in their publicity. Harvey had farms and dairies supplying the ATSF railway line. The increase in tourism to the Southwest was accredited a great deal to his vision. He put his name on a lot of the goods sold from the Harvey restaurants and hotels – from postcards of the Harvey Girls to tea and coffee. "It is a dashed clever way of operating. The man is truly a visionary." Caleb had been fascinated to read what had been written about the man, good and bad. "The women and men who work for him have nothing but praise for him." He had made a point of finding people who would know. "One thing he does ask and I hope you ladies are aware – you must agree to enter into no romantic liaison for the first full year of your employment."

Felicia looked up from the ball of yarn in her hand to say, "Mia, you have a decision to make."

Caleb and Eleanor exchanged glances. They had heard nothing of Mia's dilemma.

"I have told you already." Mia glared. "It is too ridiculous for words."

"Perhaps you might explain?" Caleb liked these women. They were willing to take responsibility for their own lives. They weren't waiting around for some man to rescue them.

"I made the acquaintance of a gentleman aboard ship." Mia blushed to tell it. "But there was nothing improper between us, I do assure you."

"You don't need to say that, my dear," Caleb was quick to reassure her. "We would never doubt you."

"Thank you." Mia bowed her head in his direction. "The man is a widower – from Texas – wherever that is – he made me an offer of marriage before he left the ship."

"Are we allowed to know his name?" Eleanor asked.

"Mr Josiah Huffington-Bridges, from the Great State of Texas as he informed all who asked," Felicia laughed.

Caleb stared for a moment. "Is he a tall blond man with two young girls, that Josiah Huffington-Bridges?" At Mia's nod, he took a deep breath. "My dear, the man is wealthy beyond the dreams of avarice."

"I do not mean to dismiss his money or its importance," Mia almost whispered. "But I am afraid." She looked around the company. "I have been left destitute by the actions of my brother. I have found myself without a home or the means to earn a living." Tears came into her big blue eyes. "I wanted to learn to earn my own living. I am terrified of placing my fate in a man's hands again."

"Oh, my dear," Eleanor said in sympathy, while the other women surrounded her in an effort to give her comfort.

Caleb watched them, considering this development. "I think there is another way of looking at this." Caleb was suddenly the focus of all eyes. He wished he had a cigar in his hand. It helped a man think. "I know Josiah – he is a good man." He looked closely at Mia. "Could you develop feelings for him?"

"I like him." Mia could admit that much. "I admired his relationship with his two daughters." She smiled. "Even if they do have the man wrapped around their little fingers."

"Then why not think of this matter from a business viewpoint?" It was standard procedure to enter into a contract when a man was setting up a long-term mistress. He doubted these women knew anything of that but why not apply the same rules here? He kept his eyes well away from Eleanor as he spoke. No one knew of their bargain and he intended to keep it that way.

"I'm not sure I understand your meaning, sir?" Mia would take any help offered.

"You all came to America to improve your lot in life. Josiah is a good man in desperate need of a wife. He needs help with his children as you have noted – he has no need of money – what he truly needs is a helpmate. To my knowledge he does not go around offering marriage to every woman he meets." The first wife had been a weak weed that cried and trembled at every passing breeze, as Caleb remembered. She had died giving birth to their second child.

"You mean," Verity said slowly, her mind whirling as she tried to understand, "Mia has something Josiah wants – she simply has to put a price on it?"

"That sounds rather unsavoury," Mia gasped.

"Look where being nice and understanding has got us!" Felicia said bitterly.

"Then we need to make a pros and cons list – do we not?" Jenny went to turn the page of the pad she'd been trying to write on.

"Wait." Caleb put a hand out to stop her. "May I see?" He took the pad from her without waiting for permission. "These are wonderful." He admired the quick strokes of an experienced pen that had sketched the house they were in, the flowers in the garden, the fruit trees, the horses and the few buildings of this little town.

"I was just scribbling while trying to think of what to write to the people back home." Jenny reached out for the pad.

"If I might make a suggestion?" Caleb didn't return the pad. "I have some letters from an ancestor who left to explore the West. They are treasured family possessions. The man sketched everything he saw. He put fish, cowboys, stampeding cattle and anything else he saw that might amuse the folks back home into the margins of his letters. He even drew on the envelopes. It was very much the fashion at the time. Why don't you do that and show the folks back home the world you've come to?"

"That is a wonderful idea, Caleb!" Felicia almost clapped her hands in delight.

"Yes, but it doesn't help me!" Mia cried.

"Ah yes." Caleb returned the pad to Jenny. "We were going to make a list of your requirements." He looked around at the company. "Then I suggest we begin."

Chapter 27

Percy Place
Dublin

In Georgina's home the work was well under way. They were becoming accustomed to the almost constant noise, dust, yelling and demands. The daily routine of the house on Percy Place was destroyed.

It was into this chaos that Dorothy Lawler arrived. The woman had been offered a chance to change her tenancy by the BOBs but she had insisted the house on Percy Place was ideal for her circumstances – much to Georgina's relief.

"Mrs Lawler, it is a pleasure to meet you," Georgina said to the woman dressed in widow's weeds standing on her doorstep. "Please come in."

She had received a telegram telling her of the widow's expected time of arrival. The fire in her private sitting room was burning brightly. She had done everything she could think of to make this woman want to stay in her home.

"May I take your coat and bonnet?" Georgina offered. She was determined to start as she meant to go on. She had no butler or male servants. The mistress of the house would not normally open the door to visitors nor would she take the guests' hats and coats. Mrs Lawler had been given the information about the lack of male servants but seeing was believing.

"Thank you." Dorothy watched her outer wear being placed on a freestanding hall unit.

Georgina then opened the door to her living room. The heat from the fire was welcome on such a bitterly cold day.

"Come into my parlour," she said. "I shall ring for tea."

"That would be very welcome."

Dorothy had travelled to this house directly from her husband's funeral, as planned. The barge had been waiting for her at the canal dock in Kildare as ordered. She had stepped on board and, with fingers crossed, disappeared – for all intents and purposes – from her old life.

"Did my valise arrive?" she enquired. She had sent a bag ahead of her arrival, with the affairs she would need to see her through a week. She hoped and prayed she had thought of everything she might need in the future. She would never willingly return to her husband's family home as long as her brother-in-law remained its master.

"Yes, it did." Georgina gestured towards one of the two chairs pulled close to the fire, inviting her guest to sit. She rang the tapestry bell to signal that tea should be served. "I had it placed in your room. I did not, however, ask the maid to unpack it, being unsure of your requirements." She smiled as she took her seat across the fire from Dorothy. "This is my first venture as a landlady, you see."

"Then we should get along famously," Dorothy replied with a smile. "This is my first experience as a tenant."

A knock on the door interrupted them. Georgina called out permission to enter and Bridget pushed the door open and with difficulty manoeuvred a tea trolley in.

"Thank you, Bridget." Georgina wondered why Sarah hadn't brought the trolley or even helped Bridget but didn't ask. It appeared that Bridget still was always the maid on call for any and all tasks. "We will serve ourselves."

"Yes, ma'am." Bridget bobbed a knee. "Cook thought your guest might enjoy some of her scones – they are straight from the oven."

"Tell Cook thank you." Georgina waited until Bridget had left the room before saying, "I do hope the BOBs warned you of my unusual situation, Mrs Lawlor."

"They did." Dorothy eyed the items on the trolley. She was hungry and thirsty.

The two women settled down to enjoy what was on offer. They chatted politely while consuming the tea and scones.

"The death of your husband was recent?" Georgina asked as they drank a second cup of tea.

"The funeral was today."

Georgina tried to conceal her astonishment. "I am sorry for your loss," she said.

"Thank you." Dorothy nodded her head slightly. "It was expected." She waited a moment before asking, "How much did the BOBs tell you of my circumstances?"

"Nothing at all." Georgina wondered again what had driven a woman – obviously wealthy judging by her garments – to rent a room in Dublin.

"I am sure we will discuss my situation over the coming weeks and months but, at this moment in time, could I please be shown to my room?" She was exhausted, having had very little sleep over recent days while her husband's body had lain in state in the front parlour of their home while neighbours and friends had come to the viewing. It had been made more stressful by the obnoxious behaviour of her brother-in-law. She thanked God for the assistance her sons had given her.

"Of course." Georgina got to her feet. "Let me show you the way."

They exited the room and, with her guest at her heels, Georgina climbed the stairs. "I have workmen putting in bathrooms and water closets. I hope you have been told of this." She didn't wait for a reply. "The work is being done to the back of the house and your rooms are situated at the front, overlooking the canal. The noise however seems to creep into every nook and cranny. I do hope you will be able to rest." She opened the door to the master bedroom suite.

"Thank you." Dorothy stepped into a well-proportioned sitting room with relief. The blazing fire welcomed her. "I will be having more of my belongings delivered to your home. I hope this will not inconvenience you?"

"Not at all." Georgina looked around the room. Lily and the girls had done a wonderful job of making it welcoming. "The bedroom is through here." She opened a door off the room they stood in.

"Would you think me very rude if I took to my bed?" To Dorothy's eyes the large bed with its rich hangings and pristine sheets looked more than welcoming.

"Make yourself at home." Georgina walked towards

the door leading to the hallway. "There is a bell-pull." She waved towards the bell that would call a servant, hoping the woman wasn't going to be too demanding. "Do let me know if you need anything."

"Thank you." Dorothy couldn't wait to pull off her widow's clothing and seek the arms of sleep. She would be better able to deal with everything when she was rested – she hoped.

Chapter 28

Bridget opened her eyes. It was early, she knew. The birds weren't even singing yet. She waited for the clock at the side of her bed to ring the alarm. She had been given the clock because she was always the first one up. Imagine, she had her own room, a clock to tell the time and a desk. She smiled into the darkness. Miss Flora had told her to take time every morning to count her blessings and plan the day ahead if possible. She stretched her body out. Miss Flora said the body was the best machine ever invented and it was up to each person to keep their machine running efficiently. She had many strange ideas, Miss Flora.

Bridget heard the cogs in the clock change. She turned off the alarm before the loud ringing noise it made could sound. She put her bare feet onto the square of carpet by the side of her bed. In the dark she put out a hand to feel for the Vesta box Cook had entrusted her with – with great care she struck a match and lit the candle stub. She blew out the match and put the blackened match in the base of the candle holder – time to wake the house.

"*Ruth! Sarah!*" She beat on the door of the room next to hers. "*Time to get up!*"

The door across the narrow hallway opened and Liam stuck his head out, his blond hair standing on end. "I'm up. Gi's a light, will yeh? It's black as night up here." He used the flame from Bridget's candle to light his own. They didn't trust him with matches.

Bridget set light to the candles in their glass covered holders on the walls of the hallway. She would have to be sure to blow them out when they were all ready to go downstairs.

"Good morning, everyone," Dorothy Lawler stood in the open doorway of the dining room. "May I join you?"

"Oh, Mrs Lawler," Bridget turned from the sideboard to stare at the woman – it was the first time she'd joined them for breakfast since she'd arrived, "I'm sorry – did you want me to bring your breakfast earlier this morning?"

"Please come in, Mrs Lawler," Georgina called from her place at the head of the table. "You are very welcome. I hope this is not too early for you. We have brought forward the time of first meal in this house. We hope to have something to eat and drink before the workmen cause havoc."

"This time suits me very well," Dorothy took the chair Georgina indicated. "It will give me time to eat something before I leave for work."

Work? The others were shocked by this statement.

"We serve ourselves." Mrs Chambers was uncomfortable. Should she order the maids to serve the woman?

"So I see." Dorothy stood and walked over to the sideboard. She accepted the plate that Bridget passed to her and made a selection from the food laid out. "I can adapt. If you will simply tell me what I must do."

She was so happy to be out from the constant tension of her marital home that she would stand on her head and whistle if that was called for. She had spent the last week grieving for chances lost and planning her future. It had been a time of reflection. She was grateful to the people in this house who had allowed her that time.

"You mentioned work?" Georgina had begun to worry that the woman was going to hide herself away upstairs forever. She only came downstairs to accept the many packages and furnishings that had been delivered here for her.

"Yes." Dorothy accepted a cup of tea from Ruth. "My family have a factory along the Grand Canal. You will have heard of it – Beaulyons." She smiled at the gasps of recognition.

"My sisters work there." Liam buried his nose in his cup and blushed at maybe talking out of turn.

"Do they?" Dorothy said. "I believe we are one of the largest employers in this area." She looked around at the motley crew around the table. How much more pleasant this was than her stately dining room where every mouthful of food seemed to lodge itself in your throat. "I have been running the company through managers from afar since the death of my father." She closed her eyes briefly. She still missed that big gruff man so much. "I intend to be more hands-on in the future." She smiled at Georgina. "The fact that your home is just a stroll from the factory seemed a good sign. I will walk to work every morning. I don't know what time I will return. Will that be a problem for you, Cook?"

"Not at all." Cook prided herself in being able to provide meals at a moment's notice. "We can see how we go and work something out between us."

"That is good of you, Cook, thank you." Dorothy was going to enjoy living in this strange household.

"These managers, are they men?" Georgina didn't think it was going to be quite as easy as Dorothy was making it out to be.

"Yes, indeed, why do you ask?"

"I don't think they'll be very happy to see a woman arrive to boss them around." Georgina had some experience of men, having through the years of her marriage had to deal with her husband and his five sons.

"I don't doubt it." Dorothy was looking forward to their consternation when she turned up. "My father's office has been empty for long enough. I intend to take it over, starting this morning." She would in time bring the twins by the factory to allow them to familiarise themselves with that part of their inheritance.

"I don't know what we can do to assist you," Georgina said, "but if you need a shoulder to cry on or simply someone to listen, well, we are here."

"Thank you." Dorothy applied herself to her food.

"The workmen will be turning off the water and gas supply again today," Cook sighed. "I don't know what we can get done without water. I only thank God that my old range burns coal or we would all be going hungry."

"It is very inconvenient," Georgina agreed.

"Could we not ask the men to set up a standing tap that is off the main water line?" Flora had been thinking about this problem. It was difficult to get anything done without water.

"We can certainly ask them." Lily felt a headache coming on.

Chapter 29

"That's a handsome equipage." Flora, with Bridget by her side, was standing in the front garden. She was greasing the latch on the wooden shutters that covered the window of the room she coveted. The latches had rusted and locked into place from lack of use. Today was the first time she had been free to investigate the room and its contents. She couldn't wait to get started. She wanted natural light when the room was revealed.

"That's the Dowager Duchess of Westbrooke's carriage." Bridget had turned her head at the sound of carriage wheels and horse's hooves on the cobbled street. She recognised the coat of arms on the side of the carriage. "I'd better run inside and tell them who is at the door."

She ran down the long dark corridor. She knocked on the housekeeper's door and almost before Mrs Chambers had finished saying "Come in" she opened the door and stuck her head through a small gap. "The carriage of the Dowager Duchess has just pulled up in the street."

"Thank you, Bridget." Lily had been doing the household

accounts and sighing mightily. A break from paperwork would be a blessing. She stood and walked out to the kitchen.

"Cook," she said as she walked swiftly towards the basement stairs, "you might want to set a kettle to boiling. The Dowager Duchess's carriage is outside. Send Liam to fetch Miss Georgina. I'll keep you informed. Bridget, come with me."

Lily closed the doors at the bottom and top of the staircase behind them. She was hoping that would reduce the level of noise that seemed to shake the house at times.

She stood in the porch behind the front door, waiting for the expected knock. When it came she almost jumped at the noise of a heavy fist pounding.

She pulled open the door and tried not to glare at the uniformed servant standing there.

"*A visit from the household of the Dowager Duchess of Westbrooke!*" the man shouted in a voice more suited to announcing guests to a ballroom. Without waiting for a response he turned and ran down the granite steps.

Flora, standing in the front garden, stopped her work on the shutter and watched the unusual goings-on.

"I am mortified," Erma Willowbee said to Lily in the hall, referring to the loud announcement of her arrival, as ordered by the Dowager. "Such a fuss – but there was a reason for it – I will explain!"

"Erma!" Georgina had dashed from where she was watching the workmen in the rear garden. She was vastly relieved to note it wasn't the Dowager herself who had come to call.

"Could we get Billy or one of his men to carry that

194

downstairs?" Erma pointed to the large box the uniformed servant had carried in and left on the floor. "It is rather heavy and an awkward size." Erma smiled at the woman who had changed her life. "I have a great deal to tell you."

"Of course." Georgina thought there was a vast improvement in the appearance of a woman who had been one of her first students sent to her by the BOBs. "Bridget, run and ask Billy for help." She waited until the girl had disappeared into the stairwell. "What's going on, Erma?"

"I have so much to tell you, Georgina." Erma began to remove her hat and gloves – with familiarity she placed her outer garments on the hallstand. "Perhaps Cook could serve us tea in the servants' dining room?" She lowered her voice. "I don't think the younger house servants need be present but you will want Cook and Lily to hear what I have to say."

"You sent for me, missus?" Billy stepped into the hallway.

"Billy, thanks for coming." Georgina gestured towards the box. "Can you carry that box downstairs and put it in the servants' dining room, please."

"Not a problem." Billy smiled at the little woman who had left this house at the beginning of the year. "Morning, Erma – it's fresh and well you're looking."

"Morning, Billy." Erma had missed the lack of social pretension in this house.

"First, let me apologise," Erma said when the women, including Flora at Georgina's request, were gathered in the staff dining room.

The five women were seated at the end of the table furthest from the door. Tea and some of Cook's delicious fruit cake had been served.

"That ostentatious arrival was the brain-child of the Dowager. I had no say in the matter." She cast her eyes around the table. "I would have preferred to slip in the back way."

"You're welcome here, Erma," Cook said, "however you arrive. The kettle is always on."

"Thank you, Cook." Erma glanced briefly at Georgina, Lily, Flora and Cook. She took a deep breath. She might as well get the unpleasant business out of the way. "The Dowager wanted anyone watching this house to be aware of her carriage. She wanted to publicly show her support of you, Georgina. I daresay anyone who cares noticed our little drama."

"Why?" Georgina asked.

"I am sorry, Georgie." Erma wished someone else had brought this news. "The Dowager has discovered that your husband is planning yet more problems for you."

"That man," Georgina sighed. "What is he doing now?"

"He has approached the courts about suing you for income to maintain him while he recovers from his injuries." Erma couldn't look at Georgina when she said this. "It has come to his attention that you are accepting paying guests and spending money improving your house. He claims that as your husband he has a right to any income you earn."

"I have no money." Georgina had been expecting the man to continue creating problems for her. It was almost a relief to know what he was planning.

"The Dowager suggests that you consult with Richard Wilson." Erma's hand was shaking as she tried to lift her teacup to her lips. She hated bringing anyone distress. "The Dowager wants you to be ready to defend yourself. She believes you need to consult a barrister."

"In the Name of God!" Cook gasped.

"What is the world coming to?" Lily briefly wondered if Billy Flint knew how to employ someone to do murder.

"I have already been informed by Richard," Georgina said, "that no barrister will support a woman defying her lawful husband. It would take a man of very high standing and strong convictions to enter into dispute with my husband." She would not cry – what use were tears?

"The Dowager also suggests that you contact the Earl of Camlough – the man is after all grandfather to three of your stepsons – the Dowager believes he would enjoy entering into battle with your husband." The Dowager had in fact been quite insistent – she was convinced the Earl had a bone to pick with Georgina's husband. The man had been previously married to the Earl's only child. It was only when the Earl witnessed Georgina's husband's brutality to her that he'd come to understand his own daughter's decline and early death.

Georgina looked around the company. The women were practically melting with sympathy for her – lovely to see – but she would need help of the masculine persuasion, she feared.

"The Dowager believes that Billy Flint may also be of assistance in this matter." Erma stood and walked along the table to where Billy had left the box she'd brought with her. She removed a thin file of paperwork and tapped it with her hand. "This is all the information the Dowager was able to gather on the matter of your husband's intentions. There is not much, I'm afraid. I'll leave it here for you to read later." She put the folder on the table before withdrawing another. This one was much fatter. "This folder contains details of two women the BOBs are sending to you."

"More students!" Georgina almost dropped her head onto the table. She didn't feel up to accommodating strangers but she must. She needed the income she would earn from the BOBs.

"They are not in the same category as the original five that were sent to you." Erma had been one of those women. "I doubt either of these women would care to be sent out to the Americas to earn a living with Mr Harvey." She looked down a moment. "I may be wrong about one of them. We shall see."

"Will we have to hide every trace of them?" Georgina was thinking of her friend Eugenie – she had been a challenge to house.

"I don't know." Erma put the folder on the table and returned to her seat. "Let me tell you a little of their background."

She sighed and looked around at the women who were hanging on her every word. She had wanted a position that would allow her to fade into the background. That was not the case in her present position but she intended to do the work to the best of her ability.

"These two women," she gestured towards the folder, "have been employed for many years in the main house on a large country estate. They are both countrywomen so Dublin will come as a shock to them, I dare say."

"Did it to you?" Flora knew a little about the women

who had been trained in this house to go out into the world and earn their living.

"It still does." Erma shrugged. What couldn't be cured must be endured, she thought.

"What positions did they hold?" Lily asked, thinking it was strange for the servant class to ask the BOBs for assistance. But perhaps it wasn't – maybe the women helped all classes of society unbeknownst to her.

"Mrs Hancock – the title is earned – the lady has never married – she was housekeeper on the estate." Erma ignored the gasps of shock. A servant reaching the level of housekeeper seldom sought to leave that position.

"If you tell me the second one was the cook I'll get up and dance," Betty Powell said when the silence lingered.

"No, I'm sorry, Cook," Erma smiled. "The second is a young woman – Helen Butcher is her name. She has been in service to the family since she was ten years old. She has risen through the ranks and become head housemaid."

"Why on earth are they coming here then?" Lily was confused. The two women had good positions within what sounded like a fine house.

"Miss Butcher is with child." Erma blushed to say. She held up her hand when she noticed the others preparing to question her further. "The master of the house took advantage of her."

"Sad to say, that is not unusual." Cook looked at Lily. They had worked very hard together through the years to see that the same thing didn't happen here. "I suppose the mistress of the house threw her out. It is always the woman's fault."

"I don't have those details," Erma said. "I only know that Mrs Hancock has left her position and sought the assistance of the BOBs because she can no longer bear to remain in a position of esteem in such a household."

"I don't know what I would do in such a position," Lily said. All eyes turned to her. "Thankfully I have never been called upon to make such a decision."

"When do they arrive?" Georgina would wait until she met the two women before passing judgement on this situation.

"They are travelling mainly by canal boat and barge. I have no exact date for their arrival, I'm afraid." Erma was glad to pass that problem over.

"Well, we will do what we can to help." Cook looked at Lily, wondering if she was as wide-eyed as herself at this development. What were they going to do with a young maidservant left in an interesting condition?

"Now that the unpleasant business is out of the way . . ." Erma again stood. "I have left the best till last as it were." She pulled another folder from the box. "I have news from America."

Georgina, Cook and Lily clapped their hands in delight. They jumped to their feet and gathered around Erma as she began to draw envelopes from the box on the table.

"I will go and oversee the youngsters." Flora would have loved to hear what was written from America but she did not know the senders and someone needed to check on the youngest members of staff.

"Oh!" Cook slapped a hand to her face. "Lunch! I need to get a casserole in the oven."

"I should check on the workmen," Lily said.

"Nonsense!" Georgina was holding a six-inch square envelope in her hands. She resisted the urge to run her fingers over the drawings that decorated the paper. "Cook, we can have sandwiches. It won't kill us. Lily, leave the door open – if the workmen need us they have but to call." She wanted to clutch the precious envelope to her chest and dance. She couldn't wait to hear what had happened to the women who had left this house. She laid the envelope on the table. "Look how that is decorated with drawings." She grabbed the files. "I am going to put these in my office." She was rushing from the room as she spoke. "I need a letter opener and my father's magnifying glass! I shan't be long."

"I am almost afraid to touch it." Georgina stood with the silver letter opener in hand. She carefully slit the top of the envelope and removed the contents – there was a general sigh of contentment from the four women at the number of pages revealed. "There are more drawings on the pages!" She looked up in delight. "What a clever way of sharing their new world."

"What do they have to say?" Cook was standing with the other women at Georgina's shoulders.

"Oh my!" Georgina put the first page of the letter on the tabletop. "This has been written as a journal." She pointed to the illustration in the margin. "That is the cabin they shared on the ship." She bent to examine the drawing in more detail with the silver-handled magnifying glass. She would recognise Jenny's work anywhere. The detail in the miniature was astonishing. "That is the dining room on board ship." She passed the glass to Lily and continued reading. "The people they are staying with have been most kind. The ladies have been astonished by the number of people in New York." She glanced at the drawing in the margin. She would give it closer attention later. "There is to be an interview in New York for the Harvey Company next month." She quickly turned the page she held. There was writing on both sides of the paper. "If they are successful at interview they must be ready to travel on immediately." She silently prayed that all of the ladies were successful in finding employment.

"Do you really think the cabin was as small as it appears?" Lily murmured.

"I wouldn't like passing any time in that little cabin," Cook said when it was her turn to hold the magnifying glass. "Still, they do say the food was plain but plentiful. That's something, I suppose."

"Do they say what these images on the envelope represent?" Erma was bent over the table, magnifying glass in hand.

"That is the house and small community they are living in," Georgina said.

"The house is strange to my eyes." Erma didn't know what to think of the strange-looking little building. "They appear to be in the middle of nowhere if this sketch is factual." She tapped the tiny image with the tip of one finger.

"They have gone to a strange new world." Lily too had thought the house peculiar.

"My goodness!" Georgina exclaimed. "Mia has received an offer of marriage!"

Gasps of amazement met this announcement.

Georgina put the second page on the table and continued to read. "A gentleman she met aboard ship."

"Mia would never enter into marriage with someone travelling in steerage," Erma stated surely.

"No, indeed," Georgina continued to read, "the gentleman was travelling in First Class, the most expensive cabin on board ship." She laughed gently. "His children attended Mia's storytelling. Apparently each of our ladies did some such good deed during the voyage. The man is a widower from somewhere called Texas."

"We will need a map of America if we are to follow where our friends travel." Erma put the magnifying glass down gently on the table and stood erect. "We do not have enough knowledge of the country or the places they will be visiting. I have brought with me an atlas from the Dowager's library but I cannot leave it with you." She took a leather-bound book from the box and put it on the tabletop.

"What a good idea," said Georgina. "I do have my father's atlas – it is perhaps not as up to date as the Dowager's but we can use it to give us some idea of the world our ladies have gone to." Georgina put the last page on the table. While the others passed the pages around, she used the magnifying glass to study the drawings in great detail.

"I have received letters for Felicia from her brothers in America." Erma had been delighted by the brief note they had included to her – introducing themselves and thanking her for her efforts to keep them in contact with their sister. "They are someplace called Kentucky, training racehorses. I did not know where Kentucky was in relation to New York. The country is vast."

"Lily," Georgina said, "we will need to set up a place where we can display these letters. They must be protected as so many people will want to read the words and examine the drawings." She thought but didn't say it was ironic that she had been married to a sea captain but he had never shared his travels with her. She intended to share – in as much as she could – in the travels of the women who passed through this house. She would start now. "We must find a space where we can display a large map of America and the letters."

"It is a shame the paper is so flimsy," Erma thought of the many people who might handle the letters. "Perhaps you could pin a notice up reminding people to wash their hands and handle with extreme care?"

"We could put the letters in a glass-topped cabinet that opens at the turn of a key. That would make people stop a moment and think." Lily too wanted to have all the information she could. It would be exciting to share in the life of the ladies as they set out to conquer a world different from her own. "We could put a magnifying glass alongside the letters." She pointed to the one Georgina now held. "Although not one framed in silver." She would not like to put temptation in the way of Billy Flint's men.

"The key could be placed on a hook close to hand – we couldn't be on hand every time someone wants to see the letters – this is so exciting," Georgina said.

"Before you become too involved in planning." Erma needed to get about her business. "I have also received a letter from Clementine Winstanley for you, Georgie." She handed Georgina the letter from the first young lady that had been helped by the women of this household. She then turned the box upside down on the table. She wanted to be sure she had removed all contents. "She has made a very generous donation to the BOBs in thanks for all of our efforts on her behalf."

"This is all very exciting but I need to get on," Lily

said. "I will think about where we can display this letter and any we receive in future while I work."

"I too have things that must be done." Cook waved a hand over the table. "We need to clear this lot up. This room has too much traffic to leave that lot laying around."

The two women left the room, closing the door behind them.

"I also have a cheque for you, Georgie." Erma picked up one of the envelopes on the table. "From the BOBs."

"That is very welcome." Georgina didn't open the envelope but began to put the papers spread over the table back in the box. "Let us tidy up here. I want to hear all about your new life. It is not only the people travelling afar we care about in this house." She looked up to smile at Erma. "We can carry this box into the living room and have Cook supply us with a pot of tea while you tell me about your life in the home of the Dowager."

"It has been very difficult," Erma began when the two women were sitting in the living room, cups of tea in hand. They sat in two chairs across the blazing fire from each other.

"In what way?" Georgina hoped she didn't have to drag the words out of the other woman's mouth. She truly did want to know how Erma was getting on but she had a great deal to do.

"The Dowager's household is very different from my aunt's." Erma had spent years as the unpaid companion and nursemaid to her aging aunt on the understanding that the woman would deed her enough to live on when she died. That had not happened and Erma had found herself homeless and penniless for the second time in her life. "I am trying to be as strong as the women who shared this house with me." She gave a sad smile, knowing she was not as outgoing as the other women. "I find myself unable to sleep worrying about being left homeless and alone again. It is difficult to put the past behind me."

"Have people been unkind to you?"

"Not at all. I was fortunate that Verity was able to give me a great deal of advice." Verity, a distant relation of the Dowager's had served for many years as secretary to the BOBs. "I have no difficulty handling the work involved – the paperwork, that is. It is voicing my opinions that I struggle with."

"But you are in a unique position," Georgina said. "You have been helped by the BOBs. You have experienced at first hand what is involved in escaping from one life and struggling to establish yourself in a new one. Surely that gives you a strong position in which to state your case?"

"I was shocked, as was Verity, by the attitude of many of the people paid to help us on our journey to this house – our escape you might say. Since I have access to the paperwork I now know just how well those people are remunerated for offering aid to runaways. Yet we were treated very shabbily."

"You cannot dwell on the past." Georgina didn't feel qualified to help this timid mouse of a woman. They had all tried to instil some confidence into her when she had been a student in this house. They could not continue to hold her hand. She had to learn to stand up for herself. It was sink or swim when you found yourself alone in the world with no money to cushion your life. "You need to step out of the shadows, Erma. I can't do that for you. No one can. I know it is difficult – easy to say but difficult to achieve – but you must stand on your own two feet."

"I am trying." Erma leaned forward with her empty cup. "The servants in the Dowager's house have been most helpful. I feared I might be rejected and expected to keep to my rooms but that has not been the case. I have not made any particular friends but am welcomed when I enter the servants' dining room." She accepted the fresh cup of tea Georgina had poured. "But it is vastly different from the dining room here."

"I am sure it is."

"I have not needed to know how to boil water or peel vegetables." Erma joked about the problems the ladies who came to this house had had learning basic household chores.

"No knowledge is ever wasted," Georgina said, quoting her great-aunt the Reverend Mother.

Chapter 30

Georgina sat in a comfortable chair by the side of the fire in Richard's office. She watched him at his desk reading the letter from America. She had sent Liam with a note requesting a meeting with him. It was nice to get out of the house – away from the seemingly constant demands on her time and attention.

"Our Jenny is not a skilled letter-writer," Richard was examining the miniatures through a magnifying glass he kept in his desk drawer, "but she is an excellent artist."

"Yes, indeed. The drawings are quite delightful." Georgina, when she had time to think about it, was glad the correspondence had gone to the home of the Dowager. Perhaps it was foolish to imagine Eugenie's husband would be keeping constant watch on the house on the slim chance she would turn up there but one simply couldn't be too careful when dealing with that man. "I had to almost smuggle that letter out of the house." She laughed. "It has been much handled and commented upon."

"It's an exciting adventure they have embarked upon."

Richard returned the letter to its envelope before walking over to take the chair across the fire from Georgina. "What's wrong, Georgie? You didn't have to make an appointment with me to show me the letter. Something is bothering you, my friend. What is it?"

"Captain Charles Whitmore." Georgina let her head fall to the back of the chair and stared at the man across the fire from her. She hated to refer to that man as her husband. "It would appear he is making plans to sue me for what he deems are my earnings. He is claiming he needs funds to support his household while he recovers from his injuries."

"What have you heard?"

"The Dowager ..."

"Ah yes, if anyone would know what is happening in this city it would be that woman." Richard wanted to curse the man his friend had married. What on earth had her family been thinking of to entrust her care to such a man? Ah, well, hindsight was a wonderful thing. "The Dowager does like to involve herself in the lives of people she cares about. You should be flattered she includes you in their numbers." He waited to see if she would respond but when she remained silent he asked, "What has she heard?"

"It would seem that Captain Whitmore has been making enquiries through his acquaintances at the law courts." Georgina closed her eyes a moment. She was so tired. Sleep had been impossible to find with this worry hanging over her head. "He has been requesting information on the action he must take to sue his wife – me – for funding – as it would appear I can afford to make improvements to my house. He wants to bring me up before the courts to justify the income involved." She opened her eyes. "He is stating that I concealed monies from him. Can he do this, Richard?"

"I am afraid he can cause trouble for you." Richard hated to be the one to bring pain to Georgie but the laws of the land supported her husband in this. "The funds for improvements to the house are protected – he can't touch those. My father can produce paperwork that can be shown in the courts if it becomes necessary. Anything you earn from your own efforts however – that he can claim. I will speak with your husband's man of affairs. I doubt Elias Simpson is part of this fandango. I am sorry, Georgie, but it sounds as if this is one more effort on your husband's part to bedevil you."

"The man has a great talent for that, does he not?" She fought back tears.

"It would appear so." Rather too late Georgina's parents had regretted the union they had insisted upon – they had taken steps to protect their fortune from the man their daughter married. Pity they hadn't thought of protecting their only child.

The two friends sat by the fire for a moment, lost in their thoughts.

"Richard," Georgina's voice broke the silence, "I have a cheque from the BOBs." He had offered to be her banker when she had discovered any monies she lodged in the bank were considered to be her husband's. "I need to cash it – will this cause problems for you? What will happen if the courts demand you appear to answer questions on my financial position?" This too worried her. She did not want to put her friend in difficulties on her behalf.

"Georgie," Richard sighed, "we can only deal with what is in front of us. Whitmore is playing games with you. The man very publicly threatened to divorce you. Yet he has done nothing to put that threat into action. Now we hear he plans to sue you for funds. When? I will continue to act as your banker. We will face what the man throws at you – together." He looked across the fire wishing he could state his true feelings aloud. "If you will allow me?"

"Richard, you are my dearest friend – I could not bear to bring trouble to your door," Georgina said into the fire. She was unable to meet his eyes.

"Come." Richard stood. "Give me the cheque. I will cash it. Then I will order tea and you and I, dear friend, will discuss the happenings of the world. We will not allow Whitmore to take the joy from our lives. That would give the man too much importance. Something that would delight him, don't you think?"

Chapter 31

New York

Verity Watson ran along the streets of New York, one hand holding her black bonnet to her head, the other clutching a notebook. She paid no attention to the people she passed, her black boots kicking her long black skirt up, showing an unseemly amount of starched white petticoats.

She reached the coffee house where Eleanor, Mia, Jenny and Felicia were waiting for her. "I have never seen so many women in the one place in all of my life," she gasped, collapsing into a chair. She had been sent to the hotel where the interviews for the Harvey girls were taking place, in the guise of a lady journalist, to check out the situation. Eleanor had told them that there were women who wrote columns in several of the magazines available here – *The Ladies' Home Journal* for example.

The interviews would be conducted over a three-day period.

"Have a cup of tea. The owner of this establishment is from England and assures me her tea is famous." She filled one of the china cups sitting by her elbow from a silver teapot. The others at the table had been served and were waiting to hear from Verity.

"There must have been over a thousand women of all shapes and sizes attending the interviews." Verity gratefully gulped tea before continuing. "I do not exaggerate – truly, I have never in my life seen so many women." She looked at her friends. "What are we to do?" she almost wailed.

"Calm yourself," Eleanor said. "I was expecting this – it is common knowledge that these interviews draw a huge amount of interest." She looked around the table. She knew the women were very concerned about their continued living beneath her roof. "Did you learn anything of interest?"

"I talked to a number of women." Verity was trying not to let her teeth chatter. She was terrified. What would they do if they failed to find employment with the Harvey Company? "I also strolled around, looking very busy taking notes." She touched her notebook lying beside her on the tabletop.

"What of their clothing?" Mia asked.

"It was as different as the women," Verity replied. "The outfits seemed to run from extremely high style to black skirts and blouses and all styles in between. There was no one simple style."

"I still believe a black skirt and white blouse would be the attire to wear for these interviews." Jenny said.

"There is a livelihood to be made here for you, Jenny." Verity held out her teacup for a refill – fear had dried out her mouth. "I spoke with one unfortunate woman who has been attending these interviews for years. I could see why she was being refused – her hands and general appearance spoke against her." She shrugged. "I felt so sorry for her and remembered your talks to the women aboard ship. You were brutally honest with them without ever hurting their feelings – a talent I do not possess, I'm afraid."

"Whatever do you mean?" Eleanor was fascinated by the world that these women were opening up to her.

"I believe women would be willing to pay to learn how to present themselves for a better class of employment," Verity was quick to reply. "Jenny gave talks aboard ship to women travelling to America in search of employment as domestic servants."

Jenny ignored Verity's words. "I've been thinking while we've been sitting here," she said. "I know we discussed investigating this open-day interview system before presenting ourselves – but, I believe we should present ourselves for interview today. There are three of us here praying for employment with Harvey as Mia has that appointment to keep this afternoon. I really don't think we should waste any more time." She looked around the table. "I, for one, will be unable to sleep with this matter hanging over my head."

The women around the table looked at each other, each stricken with fear now that the moment was close to hand.

"I am not dressed for interview." Felicia looked down at her daffodil-yellow dress and sighed. "I believe the amount of frill and lace on this dress will speak against me. I look like a flibbertigibbet."

"You look beautiful," said Eleanor. The young woman was attracting many admiring glances. "The gown is not suitable for interview, however, I do agree."

Jenny, in a dark-brown suit with an apricot blouse, said, "Verity and I will interview today and make an in-depth study of everything that would assist you, Felicia. You can just sit and observe."

"I shall keep you company, Felicia, and act as another pair of eyes and ears," said Eleanor.

Felicia smiled at her gratefully.

Verity put her hand over Felicia's clenched fist on the table. "We'll share what we learn with you, Felicia, and accompany you to tomorrow's interviews."

"I will perhaps be accompanying you tomorrow, Felicia." Mia smiled at the youngest of their group. "It will all depend on how Mr Bridges responds to my interview with him this afternoon."

"Are we agreed?" Eleanor asked.

The women stood and prepared to face their future.

"My word! What a crowd!" Eleanor was seated with Felicia and Mia on either side of her in an area set aside for those accompanying the young women seeking interview with the Harvey Company.

"Even with what Verity told us I never expected so many people." Mia was frantically trying to take everything in. The area was obviously a ballroom but it was struggling to cope with the number of young women present.

"I'm afraid to say it is very similar to the horse fairs back home." Felicia had been to many horse fairs where the best of stock was paraded before judges. She leaned in to the others in an effort not to be overheard. The seats around them were well occupied. "If you watch carefully there is a very clear system in place." She nodded towards five tables placed around the room, each with two people seated behind them. "The women in the black-and-white Harvey Girl uniforms are ushering the women along from one table to the other."

"The table nearest us must be number five." Eleanor whispered. "Not a lot of women are reaching it."

"Yes," Felicia watched carefully. She would have to undergo this ordeal tomorrow. "It would appear they are grading the livestock!"

"Felicia," Mia leaned over and slapped a hand on Felicia's knee, "take your mind out of the farmyard."

"Mia," Eleanor consulted her fob watch, "you need to be getting along."

"I hate to leave." Mia felt torn. She wanted to be there for her friends but she had her own ordeal to face.

While her friends were being processed through the Harvey interview process Mia met with the man who had proposed marriage to her. She was considering his offer. She had spent time in his company. Caleb Anderson had kindly arranged social outings for their group. They had been to the theatre, opera and museums in the company of Josiah Bridges. She had thought long and hard about his proposal. Not in the way of a young girl in the first blush of youth but as a woman who had been forced to view the world through the eyes of an independent lady.

Mia waited until the servants had carried in refreshments before speaking. This large house on 5th Avenue was impressive from the exterior, situated as it was with open green spaces all around. She wondered if she could be happy as the mistress of such a home. It was vastly different to the homes she was accustomed to.

"Mr Bridges . . ."

"Please, call me Josiah – or Joss if you prefer."

Mia had discussed this meeting in detail with the Andersons and her friends. She wished she could consult the notes she had taken but that would appear far too vulgar.

"How do you take your coffee?" she asked. The wheeled trolley had been placed by Mia's hand before the servants withdrew.

"Just black, ma'am." Josiah leaned back and studied this woman who had claimed his attention aboard ship. He had enjoyed her company in the outings they had shared recently. She had a sharp mind and a quick wit. She was a fine-looking woman – tall and sturdy – he needed a woman who could stand up to life. Unlike his poor late wife, he thought guiltily.

Mia busied herself preparing coffee, her mind whirling with what she had come here to do. Would he throw her out into the street? Was she being too daring?

She waited until both had coffee in hand, ignoring the tasty treats that lay attractively presented on the trolley. "Mr Bridges, I requested this meeting because you have done me the honour of proposing marriage." She held up her hand when he looked like interrupting. She needed to get this said. "I am flattered, of course, but I need it made clear that I bring no dowry to this union. In point of fact, sir, I am penniless." He needed to have this information before they could go any further. It was a father's duty to discuss terms with a daughter's suitor – in this Mia stood alone.

"I have no need of a dowry from you." Josiah admired

her honesty. He'd reckoned she and her friends were seeking their fortune in the New World when he'd observed them on board ship. The time spent onboard ship produced an intimacy not found anywhere else in his opinion. This woman had spent a great deal of time with his two daughters and because of them in his company also – he had seen to that.

Mia almost collapsed with relief when he dismissed her lack of a dowry. "I would like us to be honest with each other." She stiffened her spine. She had not said all she needed to say. "Will you tell me, please, what a man such as yourself needs from a wife?"

"A man such as me?" Josiah didn't take insult to his origins lightly. The New York snobs delighted in insulting his way of speaking and his attitude to life. They couldn't mock his fortune though and that stuck in their craw.

"Sir," Mia saw she had given offense somehow, "we come from vastly different worlds. I am endeavouring to find my feet as it were." She waved her hands around. "This world is very new to me. I had no idea," she smiled gently, "where the Great State of Texas was until I had consulted an atlas. I know nothing of your world. I intend no insult. I simply wish to know what it is you seek and if I can provide it."

"That's refreshing." Josiah hadn't expected this. He'd thought the woman would have jumped through hoops for the chance of a ring from him.

"I have come to this country to make a new life for myself." Mia tried not to grimace at the taste of coffee. Oh, what she wouldn't give for a cup of the tea they had enjoyed that morning in the coffee house! "I never thought to find myself in this position. My brother gambled away the family fortune, forcing me from everything familiar." She wanted that known, if only between the two of them. "Your proposal interests me – how could it not – but I do not wish to rush into a marriage without first having serious discussions about what you expect from such a union. Please understand."

"You've been honest with me." Josiah crossed one leg over another and stared. She'd surprised him – something difficult to do. "I need a wife, plain and simple. I have two daughters as you have seen. I love them but they are running wild. I have no wish to clip their wings but they must be raised to know their place in society." He started to laugh, his white teeth gleaming between lush lips, his blue eyes twinkling. "I liked the way you refused to allow anyone to treat you without dignity aboard that ship. Truth to tell, ma'am, you impressed me, you and your friends."

"So you need someone for your daughters – would not a strict and capable governess supply what you require?" She had thought to seek such a position herself.

"No, ma'am." Josiah held out his cup for more coffee. Those darn china cups were too small. "I need someone who can show them society ways." He watched her elegant way of pouring coffee. The woman knew what was what. He had seen that right away aboard ship and since then out and about in the company of New York society. "I want them to be aware of the pleasures and pitfalls of life. I believe you could teach them that."

"So in effect you seek not a wife but a teacher for your children?"

"No, ma'am, I need a wife." Josiah didn't want her to think he was suggesting a cold union. She was a good-looking woman. He liked a comfortable armful. "I want a female to stand by my side. I want a companion, someone who can be a help to me." He pulled at his tight white collar. "I need instructing in understanding the unwritten and underlying rules of society too. I have money – more than most in the city but that isn't enough, is it?"

"No, sir, it is not." Mia gave up on the coffee and returned the delicate china cup and saucer to the trolley. "I can guide you through the shark-infested waters of society. I doubt it is much different here than at home. If any should question my behaviour, I can always look down my nose and put them in their place." She thought of the Dowager Duchess of Westbrooke and laughed. "After all – I am from Europe!" Something she had noticed mattered in the short while they had been out and about in New York.

"So, you think we can deal well together?" Josiah was fascinated. He had not expected anything like this when this meeting had been set up. Looked like he'd found himself a filly with fire in her belly.

"There are matters we need to discuss – in detail – before we can both say we know what we are dealing with." She had no intention of ever finding herself penniless and homeless again. She wanted money in her own name and account. She would never again rely on a man to protect her interests. It would be interesting to see how this man – this cowboy – dealt with her demands.

Chapter 32

"I had forgotten how tiring time spent in the city can be." Eleanor longed to return to her little clapboard house and put her feet up.

The ladies were sitting in the ladies' waiting room of the New York train station.

"So, we have some time now, ladies," said Mia. "Jenny and Verity, do tell us more."

It had been difficult to exchange information walking along the streets. However, they had learned that Jenny had been offered a position with the Harvey Company, but Verity had been asked to call back.

"I was informed that with the vast number of applicants it would be necessary to attend several interviews," Verity felt sick with fear. If Jenny could be offered a position straight away – why hadn't she?

"It was my knowledge of French and years spent in domestic service that secured the place for me," Jenny said. "I was one of very few offered a position today – or so I was informed by one of the women who took my particulars." She turned to Verity. "Did you progress through all of the tables set out?" she asked, crossing her fingers while waiting for a reply.

"Yes." Verity didn't remember what she had said to the different people sitting behind each table. It had been a challenging experience.

"That is excellent if you want my opinion," Jenny said. "I noticed a great many women didn't make it past the third table. I believe they are being careful not to offer positions until they have seen everyone. Does anyone know how many positions are on offer?"

No one did.

"Here is the train." Eleanor stood up swiftly. She had booked first-class tickets. She wanted a seat and privacy.

"Jenny, did you learn anything else you can share?" Mia asked when they were all seated in a private carriage.

"Yes, indeed, and it's not good news. I was shocked to learn that the position is not guaranteed." Jenny waited while the others gasped and muttered. "The women will spend a month in Chicago being trained – without payment – before being judged." She shrugged and sighed. "It would appear a great many women fail to pass the final test after the month of training."

"Good Lord!" Eleanor was shocked. "I had no idea – how awful to get so far and then fail the final test."

"We will just have to make sure we don't fail," Jenny said. "I am praying we will all be together in training so that we can help each other."

"From your lips to God's ears," Verity whispered.

There was silence in the carriage while each thought about the trials ahead of them.

"And, Mia, tell us more about your meeting with Mr

Bridges this afternoon," said Eleanor eventually. Mia had been close-lipped up to now. "Nothing was concluded, you say? So I take it you weren't satisfied with what was on offer?"

"That's not the case," Mia answered. "He asked for time to think about it."

"He asked for time!" Felicia gasped.

"I don't consider that unreasonable," Mia said. "I am asking a great deal of the man."

"It is best to sort matters out before you enter into matrimony, especially on such short acquaintance." Eleanor rubbed her belly gently. "It is too late after the vows have been made."

"It was an interesting experience interviewing a male with a view to matrimony!" Mia was proud of her own achievement. She had entered into that meeting with goals in mind and had managed to cover all matters that concerned her. She had the time she'd spent in the Percy Place house to thank for the education they had given her in putting her own best interests first. She'd felt very shrill and demanding as she'd set out her terms. She'd known however, if she failed, she had no one to blame but herself. She was taking her own destiny into her own hands.

"Oh, don't mention interviews." Verity was sick with nerves after spending a great deal of the day being questioned and scrutinised. "What if I have failed?"

"You must stop worrying about something that hasn't happened yet," Jenny said. The woman was making a nervous wreck of herself.

"You must simply do your best." Eleanor had made enquiries but unfortunately her social class employed the women who left service to work for the Harvey Company.

She had heard a great deal of bitter comments but nothing that would help this group. "We have been invited to take breakfast with Mr Bridges tomorrow morning before Felicia presents herself for interview. I accepted on our behalf. I hope that is to everyone's satisfaction?"

"I, for one, would be delighted to see inside Mr Bridges house," Verity said. "As planned, I shall accompany Felicia to the interviews tomorrow. I shall be able to observe without the worry of an interview. I have been asked to call back on the third day of interview – the last day." She looked at the others.

"I would be delighted to have breakfast with Mr Bridges," Jenny said. "If Felicia would like me to attend the interviews with her, I can do that too. There would be three of us there to try and hear all that we need to know to increase Verity and Felicia's chances."

"Four of us," Mia put in. "I may not want to attend the interviews but I will be by your side to offer any assistance I may."

"Make that five of us." Eleanor was not going to be left out. She was four months along though she didn't yet show and felt quite energetic so far. She would be on hand to offer advice. After all, she knew New York, these women didn't.

"If we each carry notebooks and pencils, as I did this morning," said Verity, "we can claim to be junior female reporters from different ladies' journals."

"So, if you ask questions it will seem natural." Felicia would not be carrying a notebook and pencil. She took a deep gulp of breath, fighting to remain calm – she would be facing the interviewers.

"We can try it," Jenny said.

"You must be careful," Eleanor warned. "It would be better to just listen and observe. The people conducting these interviews know that they are offering a cherished opportunity. They will not be fooled by anyone asking them about the criteria they use in selecting successful candidates. And, after all, you will not be able to name any well-known respected journals – if asked, you would have to invent some obscure ones."

The others looked downcast after Eleanor made this point – but they could not dispute it. Very well, they would listen and observe.

Chapter 33

Caleb Anderson was sitting in Josiah's 5th Avenue study. The two men, at Josiah's invitation, had dined together at their club. At the moment they were enjoying a glass of bourbon and a thick cigar – two men in the prime of their lives with the world at their feet.

Josiah had come to New York in August 1897, eager to observe as the Consolidation Plan came into effect on the first day of 1898. He wanted to be on hand to watch as Manhattan, Brooklyn, Queens, Staten Island and the Bronx were joined together to form the greater area of New York. The amalgamation would affect his business interests. He had not intended to stay this long but the place fascinated him. He'd bought this house on 5th Avenue and had his children join him. It was a great time to be American and he wanted to be a part of the energy and possibilities in this city.

"Well, old chap, what did you think?" Caleb enquired.

"About?" Joss bit his cigar with his pearly white teeth. He'd never thought his meeting with Mia would send him into a spin. He needed advice and Cal was a man in the know. The Irishwomen were staying in his house after all, as guests of his wife.

"Come, come!" Cal had to fight to hide his desire. God, the man was gorgeous and had no idea. A slow-talking, quick-thinking man that epitomised everything masculine – he envied Mia the chance to shred the sheets with him. "We dined together at your insistence. You knew I would ask how things went with Miss Euphemia Locke-Statton. I knew of your meeting with her today and I admit my curiosity has been biting."

"Do you know what the discussion entailed?" He surely did, Joss thought.

"Yes, I do." Cal sat up straight and looked across the fire at a man he wanted as a friend – if that was all he could have, and it was. "You know Mia is staying with my wife. I won't deceive you. I was involved in the long discussions the women had before Mia requested that meeting with you."

"I suspected that." Joss leaned forward. "Truth be told, Cal, I don't know if I was more shocked than surprised. The woman knocked the wind out of me faster than a bucking bronc."

"The ladies from Ireland and indeed my own wife appear to have that effect on a man."

"Do you know she put a price on herself?" Joss was still trying to deal with the shock of that. The darn woman had made a list of her skills and the commercial value to him should she choose to be his wife. "She had it all laid out in black and white. What she would bring to the marriage. What this and that was worth and so on. I'd never seen or heard anything like it."

"I had a very similar conversation with my own lady wife – without the list." Cal wouldn't enter into details. "But think about it, Joss. The boroughs of New York have joined together – the Consolidation has made us a power in the world. We are almost in the year 1900. It is sure to be an exciting time. These women, they know what they want and how to get it." He sipped his bourbon. "You, my friend, as much as me, have been paraded like beef on the hoof before the matchmaking mamas of New York – remember Lady Astor's 1987 New Year Ball." Cal didn't have to fake a shudder. Lady Astor had invited the 400 richest families in New York to a ball to celebrate the first day of the Consolidation Plan going into effect. "I know you too suffered the incessant giggles and blushes of fair young maidens being flung before you."

"I feared for my virtue that night." Josiah grimaced. He'd felt hunted at that gathering of the very rich. "It was that very night that I decided to look for a wife of my own choosing. I don't like to be railroaded."

"Have you noticed the greed in the eyes of the maidens and mamas? I certainly have. With a modern woman like Miss Euphemia Locke-Statton you are getting a woman who speaks the truth, puts her cards on the table. It is a new world and we are going into a new century. Are you man enough for it?"

"I reckon I am." Joss nodded. "I began to think of my own daughters the longer Miss Mia talked. Would I ever want them to find themselves in the same position – depending on some man for the food in their belly? Damn it, no!" He beat the arm of his chair with his fist. "I will not leave my girls with no way to protect themselves financially. Truly, that meeting with Miss Mia gave me an awful lot of thinking to do."

"As I said, these women from Ireland have that effect on a man. I have listened to their individual stories. I've been shocked into thinking about my own attitude to the female of the species. I don't think these women will allow us to continue thinking we are the master of all."

"I didn't reckon on any of this when I offered marriage to a woman travelling steerage." Joss gulped the last of the bourbon in his glass. He stood to refill the glass, bringing the decanter back to the fire with him to offer Cal a refill.

"You thought she would fall to the deck and kiss your feet," Cal held his glass high and watched the golden liquid run into the crystal, "vowing to be grateful to you forever more?"

"Something of that nature, yes." Joss returned the decanter to the drinks trolley, enjoying the subtle mockery.

"You perhaps thought she would see you as some handsome knight riding to her rescue?" Cal said as Joss took his seat across the fire from him.

"Hellfire, Cal, the woman admits she is penniless. I am offering her marriage with a wealthy man. What woman doesn't want that? Do you know she demands – and that is the word here, Cal – she demands to be taken to Texas? – maybe not today or tomorrow but sometime. She wants to see me in what she calls my 'natural environment' – made me feel like a buffalo being chased across the plains."

"They do make life more interesting." Cal laughed. He looked at the other man seriously then. "What is it you fear, Joss? This woman is offering you a partnership in her life. She wants to know you – not use you as an open wallet. You will never have to wonder and worry what she is thinking or feeling. She will tell you to your face. That, to me, my friend – is priceless."

"She wants me to buy a stretch of land out by your wife's place," Joss told him. "She wants the deeds in her name. She says my girls need to be able to run wild and free. She wants to be able to escape what she called the constraints of society." She'd asked his help in setting her up as a woman of independent means. What was he supposed to think about that?

"Are you thinking of doing it?" Cal knew Eleanor would enjoy having Mia as a neighbour. The two women were becoming friends.

"Hell, I don't know, Cal." Joss bit his cigar, leaving his hand free to grip the blond hair on his head in frustration. "It's a lot for a cowboy from Texas to take in."

"Don't give me any of that poor cowpoke talk, Josiah Bridges." Cal could appreciate his friend's confusion. He had felt something very similar when Eleanor had put her proposition before him. He was very glad he'd accepted her offer. The freedom of dealing with someone who knew your secrets was indescribable. "You are sharp enough to cut yourself and we both know it."

"I asked for some time to think about it," Joss admitted, almost shamefaced.

"You need to know that you can deal with a woman who will not allow you to pat her on the head and put her in a corner. I can highly recommend the life with such a woman if that interests you at all."

"I'm looking forward to the ride," Joss laughed. Damned if he wouldn't do it.

Chapter 34

Percy Place
Dublin

While the ladies of New York slept and dreamed, Georgina and company were getting ready to start their day. The dining room was a scene of hustle and bustle as they tried to complete their breakfast and tidy before the arrival of the workmen.

"Wear your green today, Bridget!" Georgina called after the three young maids. "You must be smartly dressed when you accompany Flora around town."

"My best dress, Miss Georgina?" Bridget stopped in her tracks, a tray of dirty dishes in her hands, and stared. She was saving that dress – a dress Sarah created for her to wear at Christmas and on high days and holidays. She wore it to Mass on Sunday before brushing it carefully and returning it to its sheet-shrouded hanger.

Ruth and Sarah stood to listen. Bridget never told them much about her trips out and about in the company of Miss Flora.

"Yes, Bridget," Georgina answered absentmindedly. She was mentally preparing a list of chores she must accomplish that day. "I noticed your dress was becoming a little tight and the hemline was creeping up your legs." She smiled at Bridget's wide-eyed stare. "You may as well get some wear out of it before you grow out of it completely."

"Oh, Miss Georgina, I don't want to grow out of my best dress!" Bridget couldn't imagine anything worse. Sarah had made that dress just for her and she loved it. The nuns would say she was being vain but she felt like a princess when she wore her best green dress.

"Perhaps Sarah made extra seams to allow for a growing young body." Lily Chambers didn't like the glare that Sarah was directing at her friend. The three young maids were all growing. They were filling out too with the good food Cook cooked for everyone. Bridget, however, seemed to be growing faster than her two friends – her parents, whoever they were, must have been tall.

"I'm sorry." Sarah was mortified at the thought that she might appear to have failed to think ahead, but she had never made clothes for people to grow into before. "I didn't know I should add extra seams."

"Sarah, dear," Dorothy stopped on her way out the door to say, "I know that ladies when they are increasing – with child – have additional seams placed in their gowns to allow for the changes in their form. Perhaps you could do something like this for the three of you in future. You are all growing." She smiled and went on her way to face another day of male condescension at the factory.

"Yes, ma'am," Sarah bit out but she was speaking to the lady's back. She'd box Biddy's ears. That one was growing like a weed. How was she supposed to keep up with what Biddy wore? She'd made that dress out of the goodness of her heart. It wasn't her place to dress servants. Ah well, hers not to reason why – better just do what she was told.

"That's neither here nor there." Georgina waved the young maids on their way. The workmen would be here soon. "Wear your green today as I've said, Bridget. Right, let's get busy."

"Yes, Miss Georgina," the three maids chorused politely but if looks could kill Bridget would be gasping her last.

"May we go to the lending library today, Flora?" Bridget skipped along in her green dress, her coat flying open to show the treasure beneath, swinging a cloth bag containing her library books at her side. She'd been granted permission to call Flora by her name when they were out and about. It made her feel very grown up. "I've read the books we borrowed last week."

"We'll go there first and drop your books off." Flora had been learning her way around Dublin with Bridget by her side. They had visited museums, lending libraries, parks and all manner of exciting places. The world they visited was new and exciting for both of them. "We will deposit your books but, Bridget, we are not spending hours there." She looked down at her young friend with a grin. She was as bad as Bridget when she saw the treasure of books available to them at the lending library. "The museum of history has a new exhibit. I read about it in the papers and I am longing to see it. We will get new books to read on our return journey."

"That will be lovely," Bridget was willing to do anything and everything to spend time out of doors and learning. She sighed deeply – it was blissful.

Chapter 35

New York

That same day in what would be afternoon in Dublin but early morning in New York the ladies were standing in a group admiring the façade of Josiah Bridge's 5th Avenue home. It was very impressive to the ladies from Ireland but Eleanor had seen it before. The four-storey edifice loomed over the sidewalk, the most interesting feature being a large glass dome that stretched over a two-storey abutment to the side of the house. They couldn't wait to get inside and have a look around. It wasn't quite the done thing for ladies to accept an invitation to breakfast from a single gentleman. These ladies, however, couldn't be concerned with the social niceties. They had their futures to plan.

"I have arranged for Cal to meet us before we join Josiah," Eleanor said. "I didn't see the point of knocking on Cal's door and going through the social dance with his servants – he lives a few doors down." She pointed to a gleaming edifice along the road while wondering what these women thought of her strange marriage. The arrangement suited Cal and her and, really, that was all that mattered. "Here is Cal now."

The women admired the male figure striding towards them.

When greetings had been exchanged, they walked across the road to knock on the opulent door of Josiah's house.

"I hope you ladies enjoy your meal." Joss, at the head of the table, used his linen napkin to wipe his lips.

Male servants dressed smartly in black-and-white uniforms served breakfast from silver salvers under the keen eye of the butler.

"Everything looks delightful." Mia in her position as hostess – at Josiah's request – was sitting at the opposite end of the table from him.

She gazed around at the heavy mahogany furniture. The gleaming silver locked behind glass in the tall sideboards. The exquisite chandelier that hung over the long table. The room and indeed the house needed colour in her opinion – but it was obviously the home of a very wealthy man. They had practically fallen over servants – women and men who hugged the walls as they passed – while they were being given a guided tour of the house by the housekeeper. She had not been at all impressed by the area on the top floor set aside for Grace and Hope. She would be making changes there. The girls had been unhappy not to be allowed spend more time with Mia and her friends.

"I hope you ladies will not be offended if we discuss serious matters over breakfast?" Joss signalled to the butler to freshen plates and cups. While the servants were carrying out this chore he noticed all of the ladies from Ireland smiled at them. He wondered why. He didn't ask, however, because he had matters to handle before the ladies left in order for Felicia to attend the interviews being held in a nearby hotel.

"What's so important it can't wait until we've eaten?" Cal enquired.

Josh ignored Caleb's question. "Ladies, I believe I've come to know something about you in recent weeks. Listening to you talk has opened my eyes. I am the proud father of two girls and am ashamed I've never thought of their future except in vague terms of marrying them off. In fact, meeting you ladies has changed my way of thinking about a great many things." Joss waved away an offer of cream and sugar. "I know you ladies will never have heard of a man called A.T. Stewart." Joss employed a great many people in New York – people he paid to handle his many business interests. He'd had his New York staff do a lot of digging in the past few days. "He set up a working-women's hotel some years ago – over on 4th Street although I suppose we should call it Park Avenue now. We would only have been kids at the time, Cal."

"I don't know the name," Cal said.

"I remembered because Stewart asked my grandfather to invest in his hotel." Joss sipped his coffee. "The reason I remember is because my grandmother had conniptions – now you had to know my gran – she was the calmest, most peaceful woman I've ever known. I guess that's why this stuck in my memory."

"Do tell," Cal prompted.

"Granddaddy had a survey done." Joss reached into his inside pocket and withdrew a sheaf of papers.

"Don't tell me that's the survey results?" Cal couldn't imagine Joss would have such a thing close to hand.

"Nope, this is mine. See, what I remember is that after reading this survey Granddaddy refused to invest in the hotel. He said that the women Stewart was trying to attract to his hotel wouldn't be able to afford the room charge on the wages they would receive. Granddaddy had a survey done on women's wages – just to be sure – and that's what put my gran into a fit – the difference in wages between male and female. So, I asked my people in New York to prepare something similar for me." He returned the pages to his pocket. "I'll show y'all this later – I'm getting ahead of myself."

"What are you getting at, Joss?" Cal asked.

"Cal, ladies," Joss looked around the company, "I know it's none of my never-mind but, after listening to you ladies talk about your plans for the future, I became concerned. Wondering what would you do if you failed to secure employment with this Harvey fella? It's never a good idea to put all of your eggs in one basket. I thought I'd apply myself to seeking out information that might help y'all." He wanted to help. He'd been shocked rigid by the difference in salary between male and female. "I also have some news that concerns you, Miss Felicia."

"Me?" Felicia returned her teacup to her saucer with care.

"I made it my business to talk to a woman who works for the Harvey company." Joss sipped the last of his coffee. "I was going to make an appointment to speak to Harvey himself but word is the man is not in the best of health. You ladies spoke so strongly about the opportunities he is offering it aroused my curiosity. I thought I might be able to offer you ladies help if I talked to him."

"I've had similar thoughts," Cal said.

"I took a lady to lunch at the Waldorf Astoria one day last week. I had my staff make enquiries about the people Harvey had brought with him to New York. It never does any harm to find out all you can about a man." Joss waved that aside. "Anyway, one of the Harvey women hails from Texas. I invited her to join me for lunch. She is an older lady – been with Harvey since the beginning. In the heel of the hunt, Felicia, after talking to this charming lady – you are a mite too young and a mite too green for Harvey." How could he tell her that she was just too pretty, too soft and innocent to be put before crowds of lonely men?

Joss wished he could light up a cigar – conversation seemed to move along more smoothly while puffing on a fat cigar.

"Why don't we withdraw to one of the other rooms?" Mia looked around the table. It appeared everyone had pushed their plates away from them. "The servants can clear this room and we can look at your papers and talk some more in comfort."

"Willingly." Joss stood, pushing his chair back. "Let's go to the yellow drawing room."

"Joss, why don't you offer Mr Anderson a cigar?" Mia said when the ladies had been seated in the yellow drawing room. She had seen Cal pat his breast pocket in search of what she was sure was his cigar case. "I'm sure the ladies won't mind."

"No, thank you." Cal waved his hand in refusal. He

took his seat in the drawing room only after the ladies were seated. "I wouldn't be so rude."

"Give it up, old man. The way things are going these ladies are likely to ask to join us." Joss instructed his butler to bring the embossed cigar box from his study. A minute later it was in his hands. He offered the open box to Cal.

"Ladies," he laughingly offered.

"You know," Verity said. "I am strangely tempted to try one."

"Why don't you light one for us, Cal?" Eleanor missed the look of shock on the men's faces. She ignored the footmen placing large ashtrays around the room in response to a snap from the butler's fingers. "We can each have a puff – perhaps we will find enjoyment in it." She'd always been curious about men and their cigars and port.

"If we are not careful, Joss, these women will be taking over the world." Cal puffed on a cigar until it was lighting to his satisfaction and passed it to Eleanor. He tried not to laugh as she choked on a mouthful of smoke.

She quickly passed the cigar to Verity.

"I could grow to like these." Verity copied the men's posture, leaning back in the chair and waving the cigar about. "Shame they are probably too expensive for my current pocketbook." She passed the cigar to Felicia who just passed it to Jenny – she had no interest in smelling of smoke as the men did.

Jenny and Mia puffed with obvious experience – clearly it was not the first time the pair had smoked. They enjoyed the look of shock on the men's faces. Well, they had offered. The two continued to share the cigar.

"Will you tell us what you mean about Felicia being,"

Mia waved the cigar around, "whatever it was you said she was, Joss."

"I'll translate," Eleanor was enjoying the smell of the expensive cigars. "Joss meant that Felicia is too young and too inexperienced to suit Mr Harvey's requirements."

Felicia felt as if she had been dropped head first into a vat of ice-cold water. She struggled to hide the trembling that overtook her body. What would she do if she failed to acquire a position with Mr Harvey? Where would she go? She was alone in a strange world. She had to be able to earn enough money to support herself.

"What do you mean, Joss?" Mia sat forward to demand. "The advertisement the Harvey Company ran in the paper clearly stated women from eighteen to thirty years of age. Felicia is nineteen." She had increased the younger woman's age by a year.

"So it says." Joss puffed on his cigar, giving Felicia a look of sympathy through the smoke. "The woman I spoke to informed me that Harvey has been known – in an emergency – to take girls as young as fifteen." He held up his hand when every woman there looked ready to argue. "These young girls are farm girls – they've been working on the family plot from the time they could toddle. They know what hard work is." He bit into the butt of his cigar. "Felicia, I'm sorry but you look like two miles of trouble."

"I beg your pardon?" Mia was ready to do battle – if only she could understand what on earth the words – albeit in English – meant!

"Well, look at her!" Joss waved his cigar in the air outlining Felicia from her head to her feet. "She's young and extremely beautiful," with a body designed for sin but

240

he'd keep that thought to himself. "The kind of woman men behave stupidly over – it would be taking a risk putting someone like her in front of men on the frontier where women are scarce."

"My looks!" Felicia sank back into her chair and closed her eyes to hide the tears. "They have certainly caused me enough problems."

"You are being unfair, Joss." Mia sat forward ready to argue. They needed to move matters along. They were all very aware of the passing of time. Felicia must attend today's interviews. The poor girl didn't need to turn up despondent from having her hopes and dreams knocked out from under her feet.

"No use having words with me," Joss said. "I'm telling you what the woman from Texas told me." He looked around the room and sighed. "It seems that the young girls from New York and Boston have trouble settling into the life of a Harvey Girl. They have been cossetted at home and real life comes as a shock to them. The Harvey Company hasn't got the time to coddle them – they have to hit the ground running. I'm sorry."

"Dear God, Joss," Cal had been reading the report Joss had passed to him when they entered the room, "are these figures factual?"

"Yep, quite an eye-opener, aren't they?" Joss remembered his own disbelief when he'd read the report.

"Felicia will have to get a position with the Harvey Company." Cal tapped the pages in front of him. "No one could be expected to live on the wages mentioned here."

"Yet a lot of women earning that pittance are supporting families," Joss said.

"I have to present myself to the Harvey Company in

such a way that they will want to employ me." Felicia well knew the difficulties women faced in the workplace. She grieved for those women but at this moment in time her own worries took precedence.

"Felicia," Joss said sadly, "looking at you, you've never done a day's work in your life. Now I don't know if that is true or not but that is certainly the impression one gets from your unblemished skin and lilywhite hands."

"I don't know if I should be flattered or angry." Mia took excellent care of herself. She worked hard to present an attractive image. "Are you saying the rest of us look like workers?"

"Mind how you answer, Joss!" Cal said with a laugh.

"I too have noticed what lovely skin you all have – not just Felicia." Eleanor leaned forward to say. She had been slightly jealous of the creamy soft skin of these women from Ireland.

"It seems all that Irish rain is good for something." Verity said with a laugh.

"Not to mention my mother's constant reminders to wear a hat and gloves at all times." Felicia had never been allowed to forget the need to appear as a lady of leisure.

"Look," Joss pushed one hand through his hair, "I talked to you ladies on board ship. I know Miss Verity has been employed as a private secretary. Miss Jenny was an under-housekeeper. You two women have experience of a working woman's life. Miss Felicia, I never heard you talk about work of any kind." The woman had been strangely silent about her past, now he came to think about it.

"Felicia, I don't believe I have either." Jenny remembered her own struggle to fit into the life of a working woman. It had been quite a shock to be ordered to empty the night soil. Learning to take orders without question when one had given orders all of one's life had been a brutal awakening for her. How would someone as young and lovely as Felicia cope with the sudden demand to jump at a barked command?

"You need to tell them, Felicia." Verity knew more about Felicia's life than the others. The women had exchanged secrets when they shared a room at the house on Percy Place.

"I'm sorry," Felicia practically jumped to her feet, "I can't remain seated for this." She began to pace in front of the long windows.

The others in the room exchanged glances but remained silent, allowing her to sort her thoughts out.

"I have never discussed my family situation. I wanted to leave my past firmly behind me." She looked over her shoulder to say. "I suppose you could call us gentry." She gave a bitter laugh. "How I envied the people who worked on my uncle's estate and earned actual money."

She continued to pace in silence.

"What do you mean?" Eleanor asked when the silence lasted too long.

"My mother is one of those weak women who flutter and faint – yet invariably get their own way. My uncle, her brother, owns and runs the large family estate as well as a famous racing stable and stud farm."

"What's it called?" Joss had a great many business interests dealing with horses.

"Glencormac Stud!" Felicia almost spat the name.

"I've done business with them." Joss wondered if the pompous man he'd done business with could be Felicia's uncle – he hoped it wasn't her father. He had tolerated the man because of his superior horseflesh but he wouldn't trust him in the dark.

"Many have." Felicia refused to comment further. She would not allow herself to become one of those women who spit bitter words out and pitied their own existence. She was stronger than that. "My father, as the third son of a gentleman, was destined for the church as so many are." She was aware of the frowns on the gentlemen's faces. "I don't know how things are done here in America," she attempted to explain, "but generally wealthy families have an heir and a spare. The third son, should there be one, is for the church, a fourth for the military." She shrugged. "That is just how things are – I have never questioned it."

Joss tried to turn his laugh into a cough and succeeded only in gasping and turning red in the face. He waved one hand in front of him and forced out, "Sorry, sorry, but I was just imagining my brother Jed's reaction if someone told him he was destined for the church." He slapped his knee, allowing his humour free rein. "I'm so sorry, Miss Felicia." He wiped tears of laughter from his face with a pristine white handkerchief he pulled from his jacket pocket. "Please continue."

"You are fortunate to live in a country that is not burdened with the weight of centuries of expectation," Mia said.

"Indeed we are," Cal agreed.

"I don't want to cause you any pain, Miss Felicia, but I would like to know how your father ended up working for your uncle." Joss knew they were all curious. There was a mystery there – maybe what she was hiding would work in her favour when she went to seek employment.

"My father!" Felicia tried not to sigh. She returned to take her seat, avoiding catching the eye of any of the others. "He is the most gentle of men." It was only as she aged and realised that he did not protect his children that she became aware he was a weak man. The discovery had broken her heart. "His interest in the care and nurturing of horses and dogs from early childhood was encouraged, as it appeared to support the family's belief that he had a calling to the church – dumb beasts don't you know! Without going into too great detail, he married my mother. My uncle pushed the union. My father is the horse expert, he is the one who turned the stud into the flourishing business it is today."

"You can be proud of his achievement." Joss looked around the room. "I bought some of the finest horseflesh I've ever seen from that stable." He tried to bite back the words on his lips but failed. He wanted to know. "I'm sorry if I appear bad-mannered, Miss Felicia, but how in the name of goodness did you end up having to seek employment? Surely the monies your father earns would see you set for life?" He knew how much he had paid for those horses. It had been outrageous but he'd considered it money well spent.

The others in the room leaned forward to hear her answer. They had known nothing of this.

"Oh, my uncle is a dangerously clever man – particularly when it comes to his own best interests." Felicia's smile, had she known it, was bitter. It looked strange on her beautiful face. "My mother at my uncle's – her brother's – strong urging, stated that my father and brothers should never receive a salary – God forbid – as that would make them tradesmen – paid labour – and that would never do. It would lower our social standing, you see." She looked at the people listening to her and sighed. "We were gentry perhaps but living in genteel poverty – the food on the table and the clothes on our backs were donated to us from my uncle's family. In the nicest way possible we were never allowed to forget that fact." She raised her head and almost glared around at the others, who were hanging on her every word. "This was in spite of the fact that we all worked long hard hours in the stables. My father and brothers are superior horse trainers and breeders." She stated this with pride. It hurt to think of her family. "I was my father's shadow from the time I could walk. I cleaned stalls, mended tack, handled accounts, stood at his side as he met with horse owners brought to the stud. I daresay I know almost as much about the stud farm as my father – certainly far more than my uncle – who reaps the benefits from our labours."

She looked at her clasped hands, praying that was all they wanted to know. She did not want to share her uncle's despicable plans. She tried never to allow herself to think of her uncle's glee as he discussed with her his plans to make money by selling her body to his circle of friends. The man was beneath contempt. Her brothers had helped her escape – it was they who had discovered the BOBs. Her brothers' horror at their uncle's plans had acted as a release to all of them. After helping her, her brothers had left to seek their fortune in the race-going fraternity of America. She prayed they had succeeded. They were both excellent at their work. They did worry about her though and she wanted to be able to remove that concern from their shoulders.

"So," said Verity, "if I may be permitted to say . . . Mr

Bridges, you have completely misjudged Felicia and her capacity for work."

Joss looked shamefaced. "I surely did. I apologise." Now he could better understand the lines of her body. She'd been pared down to perfection by hard physical labour. "Miss Felicia, maybe I could find you work at one of my stables."

"Thank you, Joss," Felicia smiled sadly, "but we both know I would never be allowed to show what I know in any stable. The men would cease work in protest at the presence of a woman." She had worked in the stables but always at the side of her father or one of her brothers.

"I'm afraid that's a fact," Joss was forced to agree. He couldn't force his workers to open their eyes to the changing role of women in their world.

"What we must do," Eleanor said, "is make a list of your abilities, Felicia – your work experience. Surely such a thing is possible." She looked around the room enquiringly.

"That's a good idea," Cal said.

"We will make one of your infernal lists, Verity," Mia laughed. Verity's love of list-making had long been a joke amongst the women.

"I think that's an excellent idea," Jenny said.

"Verity has a way with words." Mia had asked Verity and indeed the other ladies for their assistance in compiling the list of her own qualities that she'd presented to Joss while discussing their marital agreement. It made sense for a woman to have a listing of her own qualities surely. "I believe we can compile a list of Felicia's work experience that will appeal to the people at the Harvey Company." She glanced around. "After all, Joss has said the man employs women and girls straight from the farm."

"I would love to see my mother's reaction to her daughter being called a farm worker." Felicia was able to laugh at the mental image of her genteel mother's horror.

"It would appear that you are capable of working very hard without ever showing signs of stress," Verity said. "Surely that can only be a good thing?"

"Well!" Mia slapped the arm of her chair. "Write it down."

"By the way, Miss Jenny," Joss leaned forward to say, "the lady I met with was very interested in your command of the French language. Seems they have one French chef who loses all knowledge of the English language when he is put under pressure. It's causing problems."

"Felicia speaks French fluently," Jenny tried not to think of her daughter and the fun she'd had teaching Bridget French phrases. "We have been practising."

"I came into contact with a great many French people through the horse farm. They were some of our most consistent buyers of horses." Felicia had worked hard at her lessons in order to understand what the men from France were saying about the horses they were viewing. It had been at her uncle's suggestion that she'd been schooled in the language. Strange she might have something to thank that man for. "I also speak German."

"Be sure to put that on your list, Verity." Eleanor clapped her hands. "This is capital – we'll have no trouble at all making a list of Felicia's saleable qualities." She looked at the bright-eyed women whose company she so enjoyed. "I suggest we make such a list for all of you. It would see you in good stead for the future. When asked you will be able to make mention of any skills you may have to further your chances. That will see you through if it be in life or at a job interview. We women will have to learn to sell ourselves. We can no longer blush and titter and disclaim any knowledge of the world at large. Times are changing and we have to change with them."

"That is my darling Eleanor on her soapbox." Cal laughed with genuine appreciation of the fine mind behind the beautiful face of the woman he could call his wife.

"Time is passing." Mia called the room to order. "We must work on Felicia's list now. She should have it in hand and be prepared to answer any and all questions at her upcoming interview. We can make a list for each of us at a later date – with Verity's aid. I do so admire your command of the English language, my dear." She looked at Verity fondly. They had come a long way together.

"Ladies!" Jenny clapped her hands. "There is work to be done."

The two men sat back and watched as the women prepared as if for battle.

Chapter 36

Percy Place
Dublin

"In the Name of God, what's going on out there?" Cook gave a jerk of her head towards Liam. "See what that lot are up to now." She continued to mutter to herself as Liam ran to obey. "It's coming to something when a body can't even put a meal on the table without workmen underfoot. A few weeks they said they would be – months it's been – and it feels more like years. What with all that screaming and shouting going on, me nerves won't take it." Her body continued to move and her skilled hands and eyes checked her pots and pans.

Liam ran back in to report, "There's women coming off one of the barges pulled up outside our door." He stated with fine Irish exaggeration. The canal was indeed close – past the end of the front garden, across the road and you were at the wall that fenced the canal bank but to his eyes that was close enough to be just outside the door.

"That better not be one of those stupid April Fool's jokes, young Liam, or I'll box your ears. I've enough to be putting up with." Cook was bent over, taking her fish pie from the oven. It needed to stand while she organised the rest of the meal. "I don't know what those priests were thinking of making Easter Saturday the first day of April. They should have more sense." She wasn't really conscious of what she was saying – there was work to be done.

"Honest to God, Mrs Powell," Liam didn't want his ears boxed, "Billy Flint sent men out to unload the luggage. There are two women being delivered here – *by barge!*"

"*Bridget, leave them dishes!*" Cook shouted to Bridget who was laying the table in the dining room. "Run find the mistress. Tell her she's needed."

"Yes, Cook!" Bridget appeared and rushed up the stairs.

"Ruth, this food is going to be ruined," Cook sighed. "We will have to put it on platters and keep it in the warming ovens until we see what's what." She wiped her hands in her clean white apron. "It ruins food it does – that warming oven. Liam, go get Flora out of that room."

Liam didn't have to ask which room. Flora had been removing a lifetime of chaos from the newly opened room at the front of the basement. Everyone was enjoying seeing some of the goods she was discovering. The old master had used the room to stash goods he had picked up in his travels.

"Get Sarah out of the sewing room while you're about it – tell her to find Mrs Chambers. I can't do everything."

"Yes, Cook." Liam ran to obey.

"You are very welcome." Georgina stared at the two women standing looking around the chaos of the kitchen.

She didn't know what they could be thinking of the mess the workmen were making outside. The shouts and

251

grunts as they worked almost drowned out her words. The noise was headache-inducing at times.

The women were an eye-catching sight – the tall dark-haired woman who must be the housekeeper and the shivering thin blonde maid almost clinging to her side.

"I am Georgina Corrigan-Whitmore, this is my house."

"Pleased to meet you," the bewildered twosome muttered.

Billy Flint was ordering his men to carry the women's luggage into the kitchen.

"I am just about to serve up the midday meal," said Cook. She wanted this lot out from under her feet.

"Billy, if you could lend us some men to carry the luggage up to the third floor." Lily was looking at the chests now sitting at the women's feet. These two hadn't scarpered with only the clothes on their backs. "Ladies, if you would follow me. I am Mrs Chambers, the housekeeper." She didn't wait for a response but led the way towards the stairs. She was glad they had kept several of what had become known as the students' rooms on the third floor ready for occupants. She couldn't ask these two to share a room. There was too much difference in their social station. A housekeeper should never be asked to share a room with a maid in Lily's opinion. They shouldn't really be housed on the same floor, she thought – still needs must.

"If you would care to wash up, I'll have a meal on the table when you come down!" Cook called after the disappearing women.

"I don't know if I've done the right thing," Agatha Hancock said when the youngsters were ordered to clear the table. The meal had been delicious and well presented, she couldn't deny that – but really! She stared around at the strangest household she'd ever been in. The mistress sat at the table with the servants! Where had she fled to in the Name of God? There was another lady of quality at the table if she wasn't much mistaken. She'd been introduced as Mrs Lawler, a resident, but Agatha knew quality when she saw it. "It was my idea to run … now I'm not sure if that was the right thing to do." That poor little girl, what have I brought her to, she thought.

The younger woman, Helen Butcher, had refused all offers of food, asking only for a bed that didn't move. They had left her upstairs.

"Mrs Hancock," Lily began, intending to say something comforting. The poor woman was too upset to notice she'd just insulted the woman offering them shelter.

"Agatha – I've never been married."

"The title is one of respect," Lily said gently. "I too have never married but I am called Mrs Chambers. It is simply the way things are done, is it not?" She didn't wait for a reply.

"Liam, when the dishes have been washed and the kitchen restored to order I will want you to take a note across to the wise woman. You can visit your family but get back in time for your bath. I want you clean for Mass in the morning."

"Yes, Mrs Chambers." Liam had to fight to keep the smile off his face. He'd be able to see his mam.

"I'll give you a basket to take across when you go, Liam," Cook said. "It will be an Easter Basket for your mother to share."

"Sarah."

Lily's voice halted Sarah in her tracks.

"Did you manage to finish the work on Bridget's dress?"

"Yes, Mrs Chambers." Sarah gave the innocent Bridget, who was returning to the dining room for a fresh batch of stained dishes, a heated glare. Honest to God, she sometimes thought Biddy was more trouble than she was worth. She'd had to take the dress to Lady Sutton's house with her. Mademoiselle Claudine, Lady Sutton's French maid, had suggested inserting panels – only she called them a fancy name – godets.

"Well done, I look forward to seeing it. Flora, if you would check on Miss Butcher. See that she has everything she needs." Lily thought the two women were much of an age. They might be company for each other.

"Yes, Mrs Chambers." Flora hoped Helen Butcher was awake. She'd love to talk to her.

"Come along!" Lily ushered Liam, Ruth, Bridget and Sarah out of the room. "There is much to be done – the four of you need to bathe and wash your hair this afternoon. Ruth, when you three girls have had a bath you may organise a pot of tea and snack for all of you. Serve it in the kitchen alcove."

"Yes, Mrs Chambers." Ruth shared a resentful glare with Sarah. She wasn't meant to serve junior staff. It wasn't fair.

"I'll see to a pot of tea for us." Cook followed the others from the dining room. The sideboard held all she'd need to serve the tea – it just needed a pot of hot tea made. That should settle the poor woman's nerves.

"I didn't mean to drive everyone off." Agatha lifted tired grey eyes and gazed around the room. Her long narrow fingers played with her grey-streaked black hair, checking none of the strands had come loose from the bun her hair was coiled into at her neck.

"You didn't," Georgina was quick to reassure her. She wanted to reach over and touch the poor woman. She looked as if she had the weight of the world on her shoulders. She was a good-looking woman, a tall impressive figure. It was plain she had held a position of some importance in the household she'd left – even if they hadn't already been told that she'd been housekeeper. "You look tired. Why don't you go lie down for a while? I have a great deal to get done yet today. Give yourself time to recover from your journey. We can talk later."

"That is a good idea." Agatha slowly stood. "I am muzzy-headed and that is not the best time to think about anything, is it?" She smiled sadly.

Georgina watched the woman walk slowly from the room. What new problems had this pair brought to her door? Ah well, she'd have to handle it – whatever it was.

Chapter 37

Later in the evening the older females of the house were gathered in the living room, relaxing after another demanding day.

Granny Grunt, the wise woman, had been and gone. She'd spent time with a very distressed Helen Butcher under the watchful eye of Agatha Hancock. She'd recommended a good night's sleep for the young woman. She would return tomorrow to eat Easter dinner with them. She wanted to judge the woman's mental state then. Before leaving she had taken Georgina to one side and suggested she try and get Agatha to talk.

"That one has been holding poison inside her for so long that, if she doesn't spill it, it might well kill her. She's bent over with the pain." Granny had held Georgina's eyes. "Get her drunk – I doubt the woman is a drinker – a glass of sherry in front of the fire, some feminine sympathy and she'll crack like an egg if I'm not mistaken. Get her drunk and talking, Georgina, and we'll help her heal."

Easier said than done, Georgina had thought at the time.

The three maids were in their beds, their damp hair wrapped in rags. Liam had returned with thanks for Cook from his mother and a new jersey his mother had knit for him to wear to Mass in the morning.

Dorothy had accepted the invitation to join the women. Flora, after waiting until Helen had fallen into a deep sleep had joined the group. They were enjoying glasses of sherry before the brightly burning living-room fire. Lily and Cook sat together on a two-seater fabric-covered sofa – Flora shared another such sofa with Dorothy. It was all very pleasant but they were aware – because Georgina had told them what Granny said – that the woman knocking back the dregs in her second glass of sherry needed to talk.

Now the silence in the living room was becoming uncomfortable.

"Would you care to share with us the troubles that have brought you to my door?" Georgina, sitting across the fire from Agatha Hancock, asked.

"I don't know where to start." Agatha put her empty glass on a nearby table before standing. She was overwarm from the fire – her head felt slightly fuzzy. She had to tell these women staring at her so intently something of what had gone before. She began to pace the width of the room furthest from the fire – forcing the women sitting on the two sofas to turn their bodies around to keep her in their line of vision.

"Did all of this start with Helen?" Agatha's heavy black skirts kicked out in front of her with every step. She walked with her head bent, her hands clenched in white-knuckled fists pressed into her stomach. "Or did it start with her father? I don't know." She stopped for a moment and simply stood. She looked at the company and, with a sigh and a nod of her head, began to pace again. The women in the room with her were almost afraid to breathe.

"I was born, grew up and worked on a very large estate in County Limerick – close to the River Shannon. I know no other life."

She seemed to be almost talking to herself. The women watched her pace and settled in to listen.

"The big house is the centre of our world. Everything seems to either start or end there. There is a bakery, a barber shop, a creamery, a saddler, a weaver, even a cobbler shop in the big rooms in the basement of the main house. Everyone for miles around depends on the family who live and rule on that estate. The very roof over your head and the food in your mouth is dependent on your overlords." She stopped pacing for a moment to look at the other women.

"I am afraid you speak of a world we know nothing of," Georgina said when it seemed the woman was waiting for some kind of response. Well, Lily, Cook and Georgina herself were Dublin born and raised. Flora and Dorothy hadn't mentioned a house such as the one Agatha described.

"The master of the house is all-powerful." Agatha began to pace again. "He rules your life. It is his choice who you should marry. If you don't follow his commands in this he will not allow you to have one of the estate cottages." She continued to pace. "If you should try to leave the estate without his permission, he will set the local magistrate on you – the magistrate is of course a crony of the master's. The master has been known to have innocent men imprisoned for defying his commands."

"'*Power tends to corrupt and absolute power corrupts absolutely.*' Baron Acton, a friend to Queen Victoria, wrote that," Flora was moved to say. She bit her lip, hoping she hadn't disturbed the pacing woman's train of thought.

Dorothy, sitting beside her, touched her shoulder and shook her head. They needed to let this woman talk.

But Agatha didn't appear to hear Flora's words. She stood with her eyes closed, lost in thoughts of the past.

"I was fourteen when I met Alwin Butcher. He was seventeen and the most beautiful man I had ever seen. He had thick golden hair and robin's-egg blue eyes. His smile could light up the world." She turned her eyes towards the ceiling. "You are not seeing Helen at her best. She is the very image of her father." She became lost in thought.

"What happened?" Lily dared to ask when the woman seemed to forget their presence.

"The master happened!" Agatha almost spit the words. "Alwin was a skilled painter and illustrator. He had been taught as a child by the vicar when he showed signs of the talent. Teachers were found for him as he grew older. The master ruled his world well. He wanted to know and nurture any natural talent discovered on his estate. Of course, in the master's eyes, any talent discovered belonged to him. He has books of Alwin's paintings and drawings that he shows his company with as much pride as if he had created them." She walked back to the fire and picked up her empty sherry glass. "May I have some more? All of this talking has made me thirsty."

Georgina thought about warning the woman of the danger of drinking too much alcohol but, really, she could sleep in tomorrow. She needed to talk tonight. She refilled the glass and held the decanter aloft to offer a refill to the others but was refused – wise of them, she thought.

"When I was sixteen and Alwin nineteen the master demanded that Alwin pick a bride. It was time, he said. The master had started building work on a three-room cottage – a mansion to most – the cottage was intended for Alwin and his bride." She sipped her sherry, closing her eyes against the painful memories, but clearly the scenes were engraved on her heart and played out behind her closed lids. "Alwin refused. He and I planned to wait until I was older before leaving the estate and making our own way in the world. We were saving every penny we could for our future. We had such plans." She sighed, tears leaking from under her closed eyelids. "To cut a long story short the master tricked Alwin and a girl from one of the many struggling families that live in his estate cottages. Jane Cooper had made her attraction to Alwin known to all who cared to listen. At the Harvest Festival the master slipped some foul concoction into Alwin's drink – something to make him perform like one of the master's bulls – he cried about it in my arms – he felt violated by what had been done to him – but it was too late – Jane was with child – Alwin's child. They were married and moved into the master's fancy new cottage – as if that could recompense for stealing a man's soul!"

"Oh, my dear," Lily said softly.

"We discovered later that the master had learned of our plans to leave the estate." Agatha was panting as if she had run miles. "We were stupid to think we could keep our plans secret. The master insists he knows everything that happens on his estate. Alwin and I were young and stupid."

"Helen is that child?" Georgina was trying to understand.

"*Yes!*" Agatha almost spat the word. "The master planned well. The woman and child and indeed any more children they might have would trap Alwin and keep him on the estate." She looked around. "He was not the kind of man to run from his responsibilities."

"That is so sad." Flora had been a victim of one such man. A man who thought those under his care belonged to him body and soul.

"Indeed. Jane Cooper never bore another child for Alwin. He couldn't bear to touch her! She swore she had nothing to do with the trickery but Alwin could not believe her. When Helen was two years old the Master demanded Alwin capture the image of an unusual bird's nest he had seen on the banks of the Shannon. The Shannon is not always a gently flowing river. A storm blew up as often happens and Alwin – my beautiful Alwin – lost his life." Agatha put a fist to her mouth to hold back her sobs. She took a deep breath and after a moment continued. "Jane married the estate farrier within weeks of the accident. The master threatened to throw her out of her three-room cottage if she didn't. She has given birth to ten burly sons for the farrier."

"I am so very sorry," Georgina said. "But what has that to do with the girl upstairs?"

The other women listened but said nothing. They had never heard the like – sitting here was like having the best seat in the theatre.

"The master has one son." Agatha returned and took her seat by the fire. "Ten years or more ago that son was married off to an English girl. The poor woman had no idea of what she was getting into, I'm sure. She is of good family and her dowry was said to be extremely generous." Agatha let her head fall onto the chair back. "The poor woman has been delivered of five children. The poor little mites last a day or two. The longest lived two weeks. The doctor has said another child would kill her." She closed her eyes. "The young master cares for his wife. He will do nothing to endanger her life." She opened her eyes and said bitterly, "The old master has been heard shouting that one woman is as good as another."

"I am dreadfully sorry for the woman." Georgina did pity the poor woman but what had that to do with the situation they now found themselves in?

"I said the master knew his workers." Agatha stared across the fire at Georgina, a world of pain in her eyes. "Jane comes from a family of females known to be extremely fertile. The females of the Cooper family all have a slew of children born healthy who survive – something to be remarked upon. The master is a renowned stockman – of course the knowledge is someone else's – but the man knows how to use it. He knew what he was doing when he put the very fertile Jane Cooper with my Alwin." She bit back a cry. "Three or four months ago – he did it again – played God as my Alwin called it. He used whatever foul potion he'd used on Alwin on his own son. While the mistress was visiting her family in England, he drugged my poor Helen and put her in the young master's bed. He gambled that Helen was enough of her mother's daughter to fall for a child quickly.

The poor lamb has no memory of the events of that night. But she is with child and has no idea how that came about."

"But how do you know that is what was done?" Georgina was aware of the others leaning forward to hear the rest of this dreadful tale.

"The master boasted of it to me." Agatha wanted to scream. "*To me!*" She beat her chest with a clenched fist. "One morning when Helen became violently ill over the smell of the night stools she was carrying, the old man was almost dancing with glee and gloating at his own cleverness. He said he had to share it with someone – someone like me – who would understand and say nothing." She looked at the other women and they could see the truth on her face. "I knew I had to get away, take Helen away, or as God is my witness I would have swung with a smile on my face for killing the master."

The silence in the living room lasted for a long time. The listeners exchanged stunned glances but no one seemed to want to be the first to speak.

"Does the girl . . . Helen . . ." Dorothy's voice broke the silence, "does she want this baby?"

"No, she does not." Agatha glared into the fire – stunned she had shared her secrets with these women – these strangers – after all the years of holding her silence. She turned and glanced at the company. It would seem none of them were judging her harshly. She met only understanding in their gaze. "That may sound harsh," she said, "but Helen, the poor lamb, has been hauling babies around almost since she could toddle. It was rare to see her without a baby on her hip."

"Her poor mother must be exhausted, I suppose," Cook, who had never borne a child, said.

"Not at all," Agatha replied. "Jane Cooper rules that house of hers with a fist of iron. She never lets anyone forget that it is her house. The farrier tiptoes around her. The lads are her servants. Helen, only a baby herself, was her mother's nursemaid almost from the moment the first son was born." She sighed deeply. "Still, I suppose it's that way in all big families."

"Yet this woman allowed Helen to work at the Big House – she let her come to you." Lily was fascinated.

"Oh yes." Agatha laughed bitterly. "Jane knew how I felt about Alwin – well, everyone did. She knew I would guard his child with my life. So, Jane sent Helen to the Big House for the money she could earn. Every quarter Jane is waiting with her hand out for that child's money. She doesn't leave her sixpence to spend on herself. She is no one's fool, Jane Cooper."

Chapter 38

New York

Mia and Eleanor were lunching – under the watchful eye of the hovering servants – at Caleb Anderson's 5th Avenue home on Easter Saturday. Josiah had been invited to join their company. The four people – two men, two women – sat around the shortened dining-room table listening to the rain outside.

It had been several days since they waved goodbye to Jenny, Felicia and Verity. The three women had secured a placement with the Harvey Company. They were now on their way to Chicago to begin their month of training. After many months of planning and praying, three of the four were on their way to grab at the chance of the new life they had been offered. Mia, left behind, was struggling to find her feet without the other women at her side. She had accepted Mr Bridges' offer of marriage – it served her very well indeed – but, oh, she would miss her friends.

"I had thought to cheer you ladies up by taking you to lunch at the nearby Waldorf Astoria Hotel." Caleb used his linen napkin to wipe his lips. "The roof garden is quite delightful. The weather, however, is not conducive to my plans."

"What a very kind thought, Caleb dear." Eleanor, with Joss by her side, smiled from her place across the table from her husband. "It is rather quiet without the other three ladies, is it not? Mia and I are rattling around my little house. It feels so empty. I do hope we will hear from the ladies soon. I will be almost holding my breath until we receive news of how they get on."

"I don't know quite how to feel about their rapid departure." Mia, sitting by Caleb's side, remarked. "It was silly of me. I knew the Harvey Company insisted that the ladies be ready to leave as soon as they were hired. That did not prepare me, however, for how abrupt their departure would be."

"I was mighty glad all three ladies found work with that Harvey fella." Joss reached across the table and offered his hand to Mia. The poor dear looked so lost. He would have to make certain she didn't regret her decision to remain behind and marry him. He would find out if the hostel the women were roomed at had a telephone. He too would like to know how they were getting on in their new life. He had watched and worried like a proud parent over those women even though they were not much younger than he.

"Felicia was hired on the spot as was Jenny. When Verity arrived at her second interview she had her facts and figures at her fingertips. I am sure that had a great deal to do with her success." Mia smiled at Eleanor. It had been her suggestion they make a detailed list of each ladies' qualifications.

"Eleanor had the right of it. It was a good idea but

nothing new." Joss smiled at his soon-to-be bride and tightened his hand around hers briefly before releasing it. "Men have been doing the same thing for years – why shouldn't women?"

"Why indeed?" Mia blushed to think of the list of her demands and accomplishments she had put before Josiah when discussing their agreement to marry.

Cal wanted to change the subject. They were all sad after the busy days of preparing the three ladies from Ireland for their adventure. He looked at Eleanor. "My dear, what are we to do about the Easter Parade tomorrow?"

"I have been thinking about that." Eleanor smiled. "It is such a shame the other ladies will miss it."

"What is the Easter Parade, please?" Mia asked.

"Oh, my dear," Eleanor gushed, "it is simply splendid. Do you remember last year, Caleb?" The sadness in her eyes was obvious to Caleb if not the others. Nathan had been with them last year. She turned her eyes to the company. "It was the first New York Easter Parade." She blotted her lips with her napkin. "Well, the first since the five boroughs joined – everyone, and I do mean everyone, strolled along the avenues. There were theatre stars and boxers strutting along being admired by the crowd. High Society stepped out booted and gowned. Some rode in carriages but those that wanted to be seen walked. It was quite the spectacle, I do assure you."

"It was the topic of conversation for weeks afterwards," Caleb laughed. "Lady Astor complained about allowing the hoi polloi to gaze upon their betters. She was not alone in her condemnation."

"It was so much fun," Eleanor said. "There were street

vendors selling food and some selling memorabilia to celebrate the day. There were street performers. Truly, it was joyful."

"It sounds like a great deal of fun, but I don't know if I would be brave enough to join the crowds," said Mia. "There are a great many more people in New York than I am used to seeing, I'm afraid. It can be quite intimidating."

"You have not yet seen crowds, Mia," Caleb said. "I thought last year at the Parade that there was not room to take a deep breath in places. The crowd was enormous. They are predicting more people will be present this year."

"I don't fancy walking the streets of New York surrounded by strangers," Joss said. "I was on horseback last year and almost broke my fool neck when the animal spooked." He looked at the other three. "What I suggest is this. We can have my staff serve food and drinks in the atrium." The large glass building known as the atrium had a domed ceiling and covered two storeys of a four-storey addition attached to the side of Josiah's house. It would offer a perfect view over the streets below. "The girls and their nanny will enjoy that and we will be able to look down on all our friends and neighbours stepping out in their finest. We can point out who's who to Mia as they pass. It will give her a notion of what's ahead for her. How does that sound?"

"I think that sounds perfect." Caleb leaned forward to touch Eleanor's hand. "With you in such a delicate condition, my dear, it would perhaps be best not to be shoved and shaken by crowds. What do you think?"

"We can send a footman out to buy any little treats that you ladies fancy," Joss promised.

"I think I will feel quite the monarch of all I survey sitting in your atrium, Joss, while New York passes beneath our feet," said Eleanor. "It is a wonderful idea and I for one will be thrilled to accept your kind invitation." Eleanor hid her pain at Nathan's loss behind her sad eyes – she would remember this time last year when her beloved had been by her side – but her pain she shared with no one. She had a new life growing inside her. A piece of the love she had shared with Nathan remained for her to cherish – she would not fail his child. She could not afford to sink into the dismals.

"I think that is a splendid notion, Joss," Mia said. "Besides, I have nothing to wear to stroll along the streets under the eyes of high society. I would prefer to purchase a new wardrobe before being subjected to the opinion of others." She shrugged. "I packed my bags in Ireland thinking I would be a working woman when I reached the United States. I never dreamed that I would receive a proposal of marriage before I had even stepped foot on American soil." The clothes she had packed for best when leaving home were now somewhere in Sarah's ragbag she didn't doubt – pulled apart to create something for others.

"Mia," Caleb said when coffee was served and all of the servants had withdrawn. "I am glad that you're aware that you will be scrutinised within an inch of your life when you step out into society as the wife of Josiah Huffington-Bridges. Some ladies will not be kind."

"After all, you have had the barefaced presumption to entrap one of New York's premier bachelors," Eleanor said with a laugh.

"I have suggested purchasing a special licence to Mia

and she has agreed." Joss had waited until they were private before sharing this information.

"Did you not dream of a glorious wedding day, Mia?" Eleanor asked. The other woman clearly loved clothes and was not embarrassed by standing out from the crowd. Surely she had planned her wedding day down to the very last detail?

"Everyone here knows my position." Mia refused to apologise yet again for her poverty-stricken state. These people knew of her shame. "I would prefer a simple wedding ceremony with the people here today and Joss's children present. Then perhaps back to Joss's house for a light repast. Something simple will suit me down to the ground. It would not be seemly to expect Joss to pay for my clothing before we marry." She smiled with fondness at her fiancé. She had a gown Sarah had fashioned for her. That would serve as her wedding garment. She had noticed that the ladies she'd seen out and about in New York wore garments that differed greatly from the fashions in Dublin. She needed to make a serious study of American fashion before she created a wardrobe and stepped out as a married woman in polite society. "Although he did offer to pick up the tab for any purchases I might make. I declined his generous offer. There will be time to enter society with all its attendant fuss at a later date. When I am fully prepared and gowned to face society's biddies."

"I think that is very astute of you, Mia." Caleb exchanged a glance with Eleanor. They were still the subject of a great deal of gossip.

"I have agreed to marry Joss. I see no need to subject myself to society's views and opinions before we marry," she had been too conscious of the opinion of others in her past life. She was marrying a very wealthy man. She planned to be a leader of fashion from the moment she stepped out into her new world. "I'd like to get married and get on with learning the ropes of my new life."

The other three clapped their hands at her determination.

Mia, seated, took a mock bow.

Chapter 39

Chicago

"I don't think I have ever been so tired in my life." Felicia groaned as she collapsed onto one of the beds in the room that the three women were sharing.

The hostel housing the trainees for the Harvey Company was homely and welcoming. The house mother, as the chaperone was called, had been very helpful.

"There is so much to learn," Felicia continued, staring at the ceiling. "How can we be expected to serve a full meal in under thirty minutes to crowds of people?"

"We must because that is the Harvey way." Jenny wanted to fall onto her bed and sleep for a week.

They had been on the go since the moment they had arrived in Chicago. There had been no time even to tour the area outside the hostel. Their heads and bodies were being crammed with advice and information.

"I am fascinated by the Harvey Code for serving drinks." Verity was having difficulty in obeying the order to write nothing down. Surely it would be simpler to take notes that one could consult at one's leisure?

"The cup code, I was informed, is part of the growing Harvey mystique." Felicia was still staring at the plain white ceiling over her narrow bed. "Without writing it down, I am having difficulty remembering the sequence. If the cup handle is to the right, does that mean tea or coffee and what if a diner moves the cup?" She sat up and stared at her two companions. "Our first task as new Harvey Girls will be to observe the experienced staff and serve beverages. How are we supposed to remember everything?"

"There are tricks to remembering things," Jenny didn't remove her head from the pillow as she answered. "The tricks differ for everyone – find something that works for you. We can't use our fingers because they will be busy. Use your mind – when the cup is right way up in the saucer that means coffee – upside down the customer is requesting tea. The cup upside down and tilted against the saucer means iced tea and the cup removed from the saucer means milk. If necessary move your body around while chanting the code in the privacy of our room. Whatever works for you – for example, Verity will write the code out a dozen times I have no doubt."

"You make it sound easy but I don't know how to do any of that!" Felicia was terrified of failing the final tests.

"All we can do," Verity said, "is learn and we are fortunate in that we can help each other when we are alone together. If one of us is having difficulties the others will help. We will *not* fail."

There was silence in the room for a moment as each woman struggled with her own thoughts and feelings.

"Do you realise how much we owe to the house on Percy Place?" Felicia whispered into the silence. She didn't think her friends were asleep. "I would not have known how to set a table without Mrs Chamber's teaching. Bridget taught me to polish glass and silver."

Jenny felt a clutch at her heart at the mention of her daughter.

The Harvey Company delivered a complete dining experience. The tables were set with Irish linen, fine china, crystal glass and silver cutlery. It was the job of the Harvey Girls to polish and present these items and it was a sacking offense to present a table that did not live up to Harvey's high standards.

"We do owe a great deal to the women of Percy Place," Verity agreed.

"I, of all of us, have the most experience of not only setting tables but overseeing staff," Jenny said. "I will help in any way I can." She sat up in bed to stare over at the other two women.

They perhaps felt her eyes on them because they turned their heads to face her.

"*We will not fail*," she said. "That is not an option for us. Whatever we have to do in the coming weeks we will do together – and we will do it well."

"Come," Verity pushed herself to her feet, "it is almost time to eat – our problems will be waiting for us when we close our eyes tonight. In the meantime let us enjoy the fine dining that we will be offering in the future."

"The food is most enjoyable." Felicia too stood.

"We need to write letters later." Jenny joined the other two and prepared to leave the room. "We can each choose who we wish to write to."

The three women left their room in the hostel and joined others moving towards the dining room.

Chapter 40

Dublin

Billy Flint was being groomed to step out in polite society as his alter ego William Armstrong.

He was struggling to present an image of a man of the world as fat-bellied old men gathered around – naked as the day they were born – to laugh heartily and discuss the country's economy. He'd never heard of a Turkish bath before but if this was what those Turks did – well, they could keep it – he preferred to keep his clothes on in company and bathe in private!

"Stop squirming," Alfred, Earl of Camlough, seated to the right of Billy on the slatted wooden bench, said out of the side of his mouth.

"Your first time in a steam bath?" Edward Whitmore, the Earl's oldest grandson and one of Georgina's five stepsons, was seated on a bench across the tiled aisle.

"*Silence!*" Alfred hissed when the door to the steam-room opened and a new group of gentlemen entered. "Judge Hartlepool as I live and breathe! I didn't expect to see you here today." He sent a beaming smile of welcome towards one of the men entering the steam room.

Judge Hartlepool stopped in front of Alfred. "The ladies have turned my house into the closest thing to bedlam known to man."

Billy didn't know where to put his eyes. The man was vastly overweight, all of the folds of his body, beginning at his whiskered face, seemed to be trying to drop to his feet. He had his large towel – the one supplied by the bathhouse – thrown over one shoulder. Billy started to stand but a vicious pinch – hidden from view – from the Earl kept him in his place.

"Ah, then we will be seeing you at the castle this evening?" Alfred was all bonhomie. "The judge has five beautiful daughters," he turned to Billy to say. "You will no doubt meet them this evening at the ball. Oh sorry, Judge, do you know William Armstrong?" He gestured to Billy. "I believe you do know my grandson Edward." Another elegant hand gesture across the aisle – the judge and his wife had been trying to interest Edward in any one of their many daughters for years.

"Pleased to meet you, Armstrong." The Judge gave a brisk nod of his head towards Billy then began to scratch fiercely at his balls. "The big event at the castle." He sighed with pleasure at the relief from the itch as his hand continued to scratch. "That blessed evening is all I hear about lately. The ladies are positively agog with excitement." He continued to scratch unashamedly.

Billy didn't want to even think about the ball being held that night at Dublin Castle. The Earl had insisted that Billy accompany him to the event. That was scary enough, but right this minute, all Billy could think about or see were the Judge's hairy balls. The bloody things were almost in Billy's nose as men pushed past the judge to find a vacant bench in the steam room. Billy had pushed back against the tiled walls as far as he could – it didn't help – the Judge's hairy bits were still very much in his line of sight.

"Billy, go over and join Edward, if you don't mind." Alfred tapped Billy's naked sweat-soaked shoulder. "I want to talk to the Judge."

Billy couldn't wait to move. He almost leapt to his feet in his eagerness to escape the unsettling view. He checked the knot in the towel he wore at his waist and with a brisk nod to the two older men stepped across the aisle to join Edward. Before he could sit down Edward stood up.

"Let's step into the cool room, old chap," he said. "You seem a mite overheated."

Billy would have willingly followed the other man onto an iceberg to escape this madhouse.

When the door to the steam room closed at their back Edward almost pushed Billy in front of him. When he was far enough away that he wouldn't be heard he allowed the laughter he'd been supressing with great difficulty to escape. He had to lean against a wall his body was shaking so much. Tears of laughter poured from his eyes.

"I'm sorry!" He tried to control his mirth but the bewildered look on Billy's face set him off again. "I am so sorry . . . but if you could have seen your face!"

"I didn't know where to put my face!" Billy spat out.

"My view wasn't much better, I assure you." Edward was still smiling so widely his face hurt.

"We don't have to go back in there, do we?" Billy almost begged.

"No." Edward laughed again at the expression on

Billy's face. "Come along, we will visit the cool room, soak a while then have a massage."

Billy felt like he was listening to a foreign language but, willing as always to learn, he followed along.

Billy tried not to pull against the brilliant white starched collar that was almost choking him. What the hell was he, Billy Flint, doing wearing a tail suit of all things and standing in the ballroom of Dublin Castle? He was very conscious of the sideways glances he was receiving from his sire and his legitimate family. Did the woman even know that her husband had another family with his mistress or was that something never discussed? He'd bet money the woman knew but preferred to ignore the matter – poor cow – it couldn't be easy married to that man. His half-brother knew who he was alright and was trying to look down his nose in his general direction. Shame the lad was inches shorter than him – it ruined the look entirely. The threesome looked as if they were sucking lemons. Billy tried not to smirk. Here he stood with an Earl and that Earl's heir, chatting with the mother of a Duke. The Dowager Duchess was all charm and sparkle.

"Did you see Hartlepool?" The Dowager hid her lips behind her fan.

"We saw rather more of him than William was comfortable with." Alfred gave his grandson an ungentle nudge when that young man's shoulders began to shake. Edward had been exploding into gales of laughter throughout the day. Every time he looked at Billy his misplaced humour tried to escape. It could not be allowed – not here!

278

"Well?" The Dowager used her fan to slap Alfred's arm.

"Your information was accurate as always, my dear Constance." Alfred bowed slightly from the waist. "The tittle-tattle around the law courts is indeed of Whitmore's intentions to sue his wife for maintenance."

"I would –" Constance bit her lip, suddenly remembering that Whitmore for all his faults was Edward's sire. "Ah, well, no matter." She admired the three fine figures standing before her – she did so admire the masculine figure in tail coats – so elegant, she always thought. "You three need to circulate. I dare to say that each of you can give the uniformed officers a run for their money. Alfred, you have instructed William and Edward in what is required?" Two handsome single young males would be welcome in any society. The Earl as a titled widower was also being apprised by greedy eyes. Constance liked to think that these three men were her secret weapons.

"I have." Alfred again gave an old-fashioned bow. "It will be as you commanded, Constance."

"Very good." She dropped her fan. "Alfred, you may walk with me." As the higher ranked, it fell to her to make the suggestion. "You two, mingle. I want to hear every word of gossip you may pick up." She gave a brisk pat to William's cheek, well aware of the frantic whispers that rushed around the ballroom. No one knew who this young man was but they were deathly curious. Just see the company he kept! She could almost read their minds. "Try not to lose too heavily at the gaming tables, William," she said, loud enough to be overheard. "I promised your dear aunt I would keep an eye on you."

She had to bite her lip at Billy's raised eyebrow and laughing eyes.

"As you command," Billy copied the elegant bow the Earl had given, much to the Dowager's delight.

The two young men took their leave of the Dowager, each with their instructions – each with a plan in mind.

"Do you know what that young man reminds me of?" Constance asked as she accepted the Earl's bent arm.

"I can't begin to imagine." Alfred stepped out to stroll around the walls of the ballroom with the Dowager on his arm.

"Years ago," she waved a hand in the air, "too many years to remember, I saw a play by W.S. Gilbert in the Haymarket Theatre in London. The play was all about some man who fell in love with his own sculpture. It was a jolly romp. The sculpture came to life somehow – I really don't remember the particulars – but looking at Mr Flint tonight – his complete metamorphosis into a gentleman of fashion – for some reason that play came to mind." She shrugged, sending sparkles from her diamonds dancing in the light. "We have made a gentleman from rough clay, have we not?"

"We are certainly working on it." Alfred was delighted to see that William Armstrong's sire was also present tonight with his chinless legitimate heir and longsuffering wife. The man was a fool not to claim such a fine figure as William as his natural son. He would have if he'd been in the same position and would have strutted proudly at the fine son he'd created. It must truly chaff his drawers to see the son he ignored stepping out in such high society.

"How went it with the Judge?" Constance asked when she was sure no ears could overhear. One could never be certain of course, but with the music and the sound of conversation and laughter their words should be private. They were away from the red-coated soldiers who seemed to attract so much attention.

"I sought his advice." Alfred fought to suppress the memory of the expression on young Billy's face when the Judge stood before him. He could not fall prey to unseemly hilarity here. "Do you know, Constance, I believe society has forgotten that Captain Charles Whitmore was ever attached to my family."

"Do tell," Constance prompted. She wanted to hear all.

"I bemoaned the despicable conduct I had witnessed between that man and his current wife. I reminded everyone – politely, of course – that Whitmore is on his third wife. I let it be known that I was horrified by the lack of gentlemanliness I had been forced to endure over the years. I made much of bemoaning the behaviour of a man who had once been attached to my family – my grandsons' sire, don't you know." He smiled widely.

"I am glad to have your support in this, Alfred." Constance nodded slightly to a passing acquaintance while letting it be known by her very body language that she did not want to be disturbed. It gave her a tingle of satisfaction to wonder what the biddies around the room were whispering behind their fans at her continued monopoly of such a worthy marriageable male. "I feel strongly that Georgina Corrigan needs the support of all who know her."

"You can count on me to do all that I can. I will continue to remind people that Whitmore was once married to my own daughter. You should have seen old

Hartlepool stiffen when I reminded him of that fact. I made much of bemoaning the behaviour of such a man towards his own wife – the beloved stepmother to my grandsons. My dear Constance, I practically trowelled on my sorrow at the current state of affairs." Alfred wished it were different times. He would willingly shoot Whitmore, not only for his treatment of Georgina but for the torment the man subjected his own daughter to – how had he never been aware of the suffering inflicted on his own child? He tried not to sigh – hindsight was such a wonderful thing. If helping Georgina Corrigan could in some way make restitution for his failures to protect his own daughter – well, he'd be happy to lend his support.

"Do you think it had the desired effect?" The Dowager's voice interrupted his thoughts.

"If you look towards the dance floor," Alfred prompted, "my grandson is dancing with the eldest of Hartlepool's daughters. Young Armstrong has the second daughter up to dance. The Judge won't want to risk endangering a match between his girl and my grandson – not that there is the slightest chance of one. But hope springs eternal in a father's breast when his daughter catches the eye of a title." He deliberately used the word *title* – it didn't seem to matter to some, what class of man that title was attached to. "I am confident the Judge will have a word with any around the law courts who dare to make much of Georgina and her perilous position." He looked down at the woman on his arm. "Do you know, Constance? It does my old heart good to bring trouble to Whitmore's door. The man is a bounder."

"Less of the old, if you please, Alfred!" Constance too wanted to bring down the wrath of the gods on

Whitmore's head. The man was a disgrace to his gender. "Young Armstrong dances well, does he not?" She had not thought to question if the man could dance when she'd planned this evening.

"I believe, Constance, that that young man will do anything well that he turns his mind to – he is a very determined individual." He had an interest in seeing young Billy Flint prosper. The lad's sire had behaved in a cavalier fashion towards his offspring. Alfred could not admire neglecting one's responsibilities. There was a code to be followed in such matters and a true gentleman would have seen to providing for his issue.

"It will be interesting to follow that young man's progress in life. But that is for the future. Now, my friend, let us see if we can spread more gossip about Whitmore in our wake as we walk along." She turned a trained eye to the crowd. Spotting the very gossips she sought, she applied a little pressure to the arm she held and led the way to the aging biddies gathered around the ballroom floor.

"*Charge!*" Alfred muttered under his breath as he followed along.

Georgina might know nothing of the matter but her friends were taking steps to ensure her husband would not be allowed to ruin the rest of her life. Whitmore might well not care about society but his cronies would think twice before attacking a woman who appeared to be held in high regard by the leading members of society. If they had anything to do with it Georgina would never be forced to make an appearance in the law courts.

Chapter 41

"Do you really believe this will work?" Georgina turned from covering the window in the entrance doorway with a thick blanket.

They needed to darken the area. She stood in the narrow hallway leading from the door under the granite entry steps into the basement. She really didn't have time for this. There was always so much to do – but really, wasn't she allowed some amusement?

"I don't see why it should not." Flora and Bridget had been working for what seemed ages to them, trying to find the best way to fashion a large map of North America. They had painstakingly drawn a large paper map, but this had to be folded over to be stored. It wasn't ideal. Then Flora had found – much to her delight – a very expensive magic lantern machine in the room she was slowly clearing of its treasures. She was positioning that marvel of brass and glass now with Bridget's assistance.

"I remember that machine from my childhood." Georgina smiled at the precious memories. "My father had many wonderful slides of his travels." She laughed softly. "He even had children's stories on slides just for me." She remembered how the large glass hand-painted slides were placed in the machine – a bright lantern light was then illuminated and the image was projected large and bright onto a white screen her father would unroll and hang on a tall stand custom-made for the screen.

"I've seen some of those," Bridget said over her shoulder. "I hope you don't mind."

"Not at all, they were meant to be shared." Georgina stood back and watched the two young women work. She was fascinated to see if they could indeed achieve what they had promised.

"Bridget has made a marvellous slide of the map of America. We discovered a box of blank slides with the machine." Flora wasn't paying much attention to her words. She was intent on positioning the magic lantern to achieve the maximum reflection.

"The hallway is so much brighter since Mr Flint's men whitewashed it." Bridget too was absorbed in their work but didn't want to appear rude by not joining the conversation.

"*Ooohh!*" Georgina clasped both hands to her mouth when a large image of America appeared, beaming onto the whitewashed wall.

"Quick, Bridget!" Flora sat with her back to the wall opposite where Bridget stood ready. She had her knees bent. She and Bridget had been working together trying to discover the best way to do this thing. They thought they had cracked it – fingers crossed. She held the machine firmly using her upraised knees as a steady mount. "Draw the outline!"

Bridget jumped forward to use the narrow brush and pot of green paint the workmen had given her. Trying to keep her body out of the light from the lantern, aware any shadow would break the image, she began to draw the map on the wall – being as careful as possible to capture the image faithfully.

"Good girl, Bridget," Georgina said when Bridget didn't even flinch at the loud explosion of noise coming from deeper in the house.

"The sound of workmen knocking down walls and banging about is becoming almost commonplace," Flora panted. The lantern was big and heavy. She wished now she'd positioned it on a table, but she'd wanted precision placement and you could only achieve that by hand, she'd felt.

Georgina practically held her breath as she watched them work.

"I think I'm finished." Bridget had worked as fast as she could, wanting to capture the outline of the map. They would fill in details over the coming months and years. She placed the paintbrush carefully across the lip of the paint tin before shaking out her hand. It had cramped with the tight grip she'd had on the brush.

"Has Helen disappeared into her room again?" Georgina asked. "She can't be with Mrs Hancock – she is with Mrs Chambers – they are trying to find a way to run the house while the madness of the workmen takes over every inch of the building."

"I've stopped trying to keep our hallways dust-free. It's a thankless task. As to Helen, she is in her room." Flora shared a concerned glance with Georgina.

Helen Butcher was a worry to them both. The young

woman was fading in front of their eyes. In the weeks she had been in the house she had helped with the household chores, but she spoke very little. She crept around the house like a ghost. They had all tried to make her feel welcome, but the girl seemed to exist on a different planet to the rest of them.

"Ruth and Sarah are in town getting Cook supplies." Bridget had been invited to join them but she had wanted to get started on the American map. "Cook said she is going to try and prepare a week's worth of meals today." She looked over her shoulder to smile. "She is completely fed up trying to cook with all of those men underfoot."

"*Miss, miss!*" Liam ran along the hallway, shouting for attention. "Miss Georgina," he panted, "me big sister Molly is here. She's in the kitchen. Cook gave her a mug of tea." He gave a disgusted shake of his head. "She's carrying a message from Granny Grunt and won't tell me what it is."

"I'll be right there," Georgina said and watched Liam turn on his heel and run back the way he came. "At least someone in this house is enjoying the workmen. Thankfully, tomorrow is Sunday. We can all have a day of rest." Georgina's words carried over her shoulder as she hurried down the long hallway towards the kitchen.

A young woman she presumed was Molly was sitting in the kitchen alcove, clutching an enamel mug of tea. At Georgina's appearance the girl dropped the mug to the tabletop. She yelped when the hot tea spilled from the mug over her hand but still managed to stand almost to attention.

"Are you alright, our Molly?" Liam hurried to his sister's side. He might be disgusted at her keeping secrets from him – but all in all she wasn't a bad aul' skin for a sister.

"Yeah, it was just a shock." Molly rubbed her hand against her black wool skirt. "I've had worse."

"Cook, would you give Liam a mug of tea for me, please and a fresh one for Molly?" Georgina took a chair across the table from the girl.

"The things I have to do around here," Liam grumbled as he shuffled over to where Cook was sitting.

"You should have my headaches, young Liam," Cook said as she stood up.

She had been sitting at one end of her long kitchen table making a list of foods that could be prepared in advance and safely kept cool in the pantry. She had a Dublin coddle on the range for today. A coddle was a one-pot meal that could sit for as long as you liked on the back of the range. The longer it cooked the better it tasted. They had no time for sitting down to table today. Everyone could serve themselves from the big pot whenever they got hungry.

"Here." She put two filled enamel mugs of tea on the table. "Carry those over to the mistress and then you can go outside and bother the workmen." If she didn't get him out of the way he'd be trying to hear what was being said in the alcove.

"I do have a message from Granny." Molly finally found the courage to raise her eyes from the table to say. "That wasn't a lie but ..." she swallowed nervously, "I wanted to talk to you, ma'am. I'm sorry. I could have given the message to our Liam but I didn't know any other way to get to speak to you in person."

"I'm right here now, Molly." Georgina sipped her tea

and waited. It felt good to be off her feet for a while. She seemed to spend her days running around this house like a madwoman, checking on everyone under her care.

"I'll give you Granny's message." Molly didn't try to take a sip of tea. She was sure it would choke her. She was that nervous. "She was in too much of a hurry to write the message down. She had delivered a baby and was tidying the place up. I don't know what the message means or what Granny has planned but, ma'am, after I give it to you – could I talk to you – woman to woman like?" When Georgina waved a hand in permission Molly said, "Granny wants to meet with you and someone called Helen. She says the meeting should be in the living room before the fire with a pot of tea close to hand. She wants Mrs Hancock and, it being half day at the factory, she hopes Mrs Lawler can be there." Molly took a deep breath, glad she'd remembered all of the message.

"Did Granny give a time for this meeting?" Georgina asked.

"Sometime this afternoon was all she said." Molly shrugged.

"Thank you for bringing the message." Georgina would wait and see. The only person who needed to be asked to remain in the house was Mrs Lawler. She'd take care of that as soon as she saw the woman.

"Ma'am," Molly's voice shook, "Liam talks about this house but he doesn't gossip." She was quick to defend her little brother and, when Georgina nodded, she continued. "He likes to tell us about the people in this house and what goes on here." She couldn't keep the words back any longer. She had to know. "Ma'am, those women Liam told us about – the ones helping other women – do they only help the rich?"

"I beg your pardon?"

"I'm making a dog's dinner of this." Molly was almost in tears. The most important question of her life and she hadn't even thought about what she needed to say. Well, how could she – she didn't know she was going to be here – Granny had seen her coming into The Lane from her factory work and asked her to run this message. She had to take the chance fate seemed to be giving her.

"Let me get fresh tea." Georgina grabbed the two mugs from the table. Hers was empty and Molly hadn't even touched hers. "You think about what you need to say to me. I'll be right back."

Molly's eyes were as big as saucers. Name of God, the mistress of the house was serving her. What did that mean? She dropped her heavy head into her hands and tried to order her thoughts.

"Here we go." Georgina put the mugs of fresh tea on the tabletop. "There is always tea on the go here." She sat across from Molly and waited.

"I work in a factory – Mrs Lawler's factory – I don't know if you know that?" Molly waved a hand, impatient at herself. "Anyway, I've been working in the factory since I was eleven years old. That's seven years or more now. I was good at school. I enjoyed learning. The nuns, no matter what any might say about them, gave us a good education. I had to leave school to support my family like everyone else." Molly raised big blue eyes to Georgina's face. "I'm sorry, I'm rambling. It's just … there's a man works in the factory … he's been bothering me … he follows me everywhere I go. I don't know what to do. I was content enough working at the factory and handing up the pay to me ma. It's what everyone does after all."

"Content," Georgina said. "Not happy." It wasn't a bad thing to be content with your lot in life.

"No, me da says I'm a dreamer."

Such a sad smile didn't belong on a pretty face, Georgina thought.

"Perhaps I am a dreamer but dreaming costs nothing and I'm harming no one with my dreams of a better life for all of us." Molly's eyes opened wide when she saw the fragile-looking woman walking into the kitchen – her stomach took up most of her body. "I am afraid of ending up like her." She jerked her head in Helen's direction. "This man at the factory – ma'am – he said he was waiting for me to grow up." She dropped her head into her hands for a moment. "He's older than me da. I want nothing to do with him." She raised her head so the truth could be seen on her face.

"Oh my dear!" Georgina's head was in a whirl. If she understood correctly this girl wanted to escape the life she was living. But that cost money. Would the BOBs help her? She had seen how expensive helping the four who had escaped to America had been. The two who found employment in Ireland had been less expensive but it had still cost money to house, clothe and feed them. Would the BOBs be willing to take on that expense for this girl? Georgina simply did not know.

"This man, he forces the girls – he does, missus. He doesn't wait for them to grow up. He said he was saving me because he wants lots of babies out of me – like me ma had. But I don't want to spend my life under that man's fist!" She put her head on the table and cried. She had come to this house praying for a miracle. What would she do if they turned her away? She would not marry that man – she wouldn't!

Georgina put her hand on the sobbing girl's shoulders and let her cry. Sometimes that was all you could do. She saw Liam run back into the kitchen and stand staring at his sister, his mouth open wide.

"Liam, take your sister up to your room." Georgina would have to think. She couldn't send the girl out of the house if she would be in danger. "Let her lie down for a while on your bed."

"Is that another lost lamb we'll be taking in?" Cook whispered when Georgina walked over to stand by her side.

"I don't know," Georgina replied. She would have to think of something to help the girl.

The two women watched Liam lead his sister from the basement.

Chapter 42

Georgina stood outside the closed door of the master bedroom. She avoided looking at the mess the workmen had left behind. At least they now had doorways instead of gaping holes in the exterior wall. Surely it couldn't take too much longer to complete the work? It was beginning to feel as if the workmen had always been underfoot. She turned her back to the mess and waited. Standing in the hallway after knocking on this door brought back memories of her childhood. She had stood like this – waiting – when her parents had been alive – wanting to climb into bed with them after an unsettling dream. She shook her head at her own fancy – what she'd give to climb into protective arms and be assured that 'everything will be alright'.

"Georgina, I'm sorry to keep you waiting." Dorothy opened the bedroom door wide and with a wave of her hand invited her landlady inside. "I was preparing to wash the dust of the office off."

"Sorry to disturb you on your afternoon of rest." Georgina stepped into the room, noting the many changes. Dorothy had turned these rooms into her own. There was additional furniture with bright touches of colour and new paintings on the wall. A roll-top mahogany desk stood against the wall between the two windows. These gave the room a different feel, she was happy to note.

"Please sit down," Dorothy gestured towards two luxurious-looking dark-green leather chairs pulled close to the blazing fire. "I need to change my clothes." She stepped behind a painted Chinese screen and continued speaking while she undressed. "I feel so dirty when I return from the factory." Clothing began to appear over the top rim of the screen. "I can't begin to tell you how much I am looking forward to having a plumbed-in bath to use at the end of each day."

"I sometimes think those workmen have been here forever." Georgina didn't sit but walked over to examine the paintings on the walls. "Thankfully, they have left for the day. We will have peace this afternoon and tomorrow. I am promised daily that," she dropped her voice to growl, "'it will only be a bit longer, missus'." She returned to her normal voice to add, "The bathroom and toilet fittings have been carried into the completed rooms." She didn't know what they would have done without Bertie Fielding and his men. The pipes were laid according to Government rules and regulations thanks to Bertie. The tiling in each room had been completed to Bertie's exacting measurements. The end was in sight. "I cannot wait until I wave goodbye to the last workman." She laughed. "I believe I will have a long hot scented bath to celebrate."

"We have to suffer for progress." The sound of splashing water accompanied Dorothy's words. Bridget had been ready to carry up hot water as soon as Dorothy returned to the house. "I don't wish to be rude but did you want to see me for a reason?"

"We have been summoned." Georgina took a seat. "Granny Grunt asks that we make ourselves available to her this afternoon." She stared into the fire. "It seems to be about Helen Butcher as she wants her to be present too."

"I can't imagine what that has to do with me." Dorothy appeared, tying the belt of a floor-length full-skirted embroidered linen robe around her waist.

"Nor can I but the request has been made and I thought I would give you the option of refusing."

"I wouldn't dream of refusing." Dorothy took the seat across from Georgina, making sure her robe concealed her naked limbs. She laughed softly. "My dear Georgina, you can have no idea of the pleasure I am receiving from living in a house of women. I have spent most of my life in the company of men. I was raised by my father after my mother died – then of course I was married and gave birth to boys. In moving to these rooms I feel the burden of running a home has been removed from my shoulders, allowing me to concentrate on improving my family business. I appreciate that freedom more than I can express. Living here," she looked around the room, pleased with how her treasures fit in, "has been a revelation to me."

"I'm glad to hear that you are settling in comfortably," Georgina was intensely curious about this woman but she hadn't liked to pry. Dorothy Lawler kept her own counsel. She'd accepted that but it looked as if the woman would enjoy feminine company.

"I would like, with your permission of course, to invite my twin sons to visit me here." Dorothy's sons were back in nearby Trinity College. She missed them and wished to have somewhere private where they could visit.

"You have twin sons?"

"Oh! I thought the BOBs would have given you my seed, breed, and generation when they asked you to open your home to me."

"No," Georgina said. "No, the BOBs supply me with background information on what we call my students – women running away from a difficult situation. In your case they asked simply that I rent rooms to a gentlewoman. You have been here long enough to have some idea of my circumstances." She laughed. "It is impossible to keep secrets in a house of women. I needed the income your rent adds to the household funds." She wondered how much she could or should share with this woman. "The women of the house are consumed with curiosity about you – a woman who leaves the house every day to run a factory – you are something of a heroine to the younger members of the household."

"Really?" Dorothy was surprised.

"Yes, indeed, we are all agog to know about your work." Georgina took a deep breath. She had to take the chance. "There is a matter I would like to discuss with you. It concerns the workers at your factory." She should have thought longer about how to broach this subject.

"Yes?" Dorothy could see the other woman was nervous. But she needed to get on, she wanted to dress and have something to eat before this meeting with the wise woman.

"I have a young girl resting at this moment in the

attic." Georgina hoped young Molly had been able to rest. The poor girl was in a dreadful state. "Molly, the young girl, is Liam the bootboy's oldest sister. She works at your factory and . . ."

Georgina proceeded to tell Dorothy all that Molly had shared with her.

"That is outrageous!" Dorothy sat forward and almost spat the words. That this should be going on under her nose – regrettably she knew that the all-male management would willingly ignore something of this nature. It simply would not be allowed under her watch. "Did the girl give you a name? Who is this man pestering my workers?"

"I didn't ask." Georgina shrugged. "I'm sorry, the poor thing was in such a state that I sent her up to rest." She stood and walked around to the back of the chair. She gripped the headrest tightly. "She has asked for assistance from the BOBs. Molly looked me right in the eye and asked if the BOBs helped only the upper classes – I don't know the answer." She beat a fist on the back of the chair. "Yes, I know some of the women sent to me are from the working class, Helen being a case in point." She paused for a moment. "But what is the BOBs criteria? I simply don't know.

"I have supported the BOBs financially for most of my life." Dorothy hated to see Georgina in such a state. "I believe they like to help wherever they can – primarily females it is true but there have been cases of them assisting males." She spread her hands wide. "We can but ask, I suppose."

The women Granny had requested to attend the meeting were gathered in the basement living room – they stood around the room, each wondering what they might be called upon to do. All except Helen Butcher – Flora had gone in search of her.

"I don't know how we are going to deal with this situation." Granny needed to find something to force young Helen into wanting to remain in the land of the living. If they didn't or couldn't, she was afraid the young woman would simply fade away. "I asked Dorothy along, Agatha, since she is aware of the particulars. I hope you don't mind?"

"I don't know what help I will be," Dorothy, dressed in a purple gown and with her hair in a chignon, said.

"I'll accept help from the devil himself," Agatha sobbed. "She is fading away before my very eyes and I don't know what to do!"

"We need to find something to take her mind off her situation," Granny said. "We should all sit down. We don't want it to look like we have been waiting for her."

"Should I order tea?" Georgina asked.

"Let us see how things progress." Granny waved her hands around. "Sit down, all of you. I can hear someone coming."

The women quickly took seats, trying to appear as non-threatening as possible.

"Bridget, do you need more light?" Flora called to the crouching figure of Bridget in the long hallway leading to the front of the house. "You can go into the living room, Helen, they are waiting for you." Flora walked down the hall to join Bridget. She didn't realise that Helen followed on her heels like a silent ghost.

"*Oohh*, Kentucky – did you know Daniel Boone is buried in that state?"

The animated voice carried down the hall and through the open door of the sitting room at the back of the house – because of its situation the room had thankfully escaped the workmen's attention. The voice was unrecognisable to most in the living room. Agatha's body snapped forward in her chair – and she stared white-faced at the other women. She hadn't heard Helen this animated in a very long time.

"They called him King of the Wild Frontier. He explored the American States on foot – fought and died at the Alamo – that's in Texas. Did you know?"

"No, I didn't know." Bridget completed writing in the word Kentucky on the map of America she'd been working on whenever she had a spare moment – there was an atlas open on the floor at her feet as she struggled to name, position and note all of the United States of America.

"And Virginia, the war between the States ended there – did you know?" Helen Butcher put her hand forward to touch the map.

Bridget with a wild-eyed stare at Flora – who had thought Helen joined the ladies in the living room – caught Helen's hand before it could touch the wet paint.

"Do you know where Texas is on this map?" Flora asked. It would save Bridget time finding it and she was curious. This was the most animated she had ever seen the other woman.

"Texas is the biggest state – you will have to be careful drawing it." Helen shook her hand free of Bridget's grasp to point to the area of Texas on the map. "They had outlaws, and rustlers, and range wars, and bank robbers and all sorts in Texas. Did you know?"

"No, I didn't know." Bridget knelt on the floor by the atlas to study the area Helen had pointed to on the map.

"How do you know?" Flora asked Helen. She knew the others were waiting to talk to the girl but she felt it was important to keep her talking.

"I love to read the stories of the Wild West." Helen stared at the map of America outlined on the wall. "My stepfather buys all of the books he can find on it. I spend my Sundays helping my mother." She never removed her eyes from the map. "My stepfather loans me his latest books on Sunday and allows me to carry them back to my room at the Big House. I take very good care of his books, I do assure you. I wouldn't want him to stop loaning them to me. The writers call the Wild Men of the West cowboys – they wear cowboy hats called Stetsons and wear cowboy boots and have guns strapped to their hips. It is so exciting to read about these cowboys. The Texas Rangers are famous. They chase outlaws and hang 'em high!" She sighed deeply and put her fisted hands to her chin as she stared with dream-filled eyes at the map.

Bridget stared at Flora, wondering what to do, while Helen just stood there gazing at the wall.

"Why are you doing this?" Helen suddenly demanded of Bridget.

"Don't you remember, Helen?" Flora stepped forward to answer. "I told you about the women who had gone from this house to America." She had been sure Helen wasn't taking in a word she'd said but had kept speaking to fill the uncomfortable silences that fell around the other woman.

"What has that to do with this map?" Helen gestured at the wall.

"Felicia's two brothers have travelled to Kentucky to train racehorses," Bridget had begun to trace in the state of Texas. "And Mia has accepted an offer of marriage from a gentleman from Texas."

"No! She is to marry a cowboy – a man from Texas – and you know her?" Helen clapped her hands and squealed.

"Why don't you step in here and we will tell you all about it?" Granny had walked down the hallway, unnoticed by the three staring at the map.

"Oh." Helen began to retreat from the world again as they watched.

"The women who have been sent out from this house are going to help settle the Wild West." Georgina came to stand at Granny's shoulder. "We are going to follow their journey, using that map and the letters they send."

"You receive letters?" Helen snapped back into life. "You receive letters," she flung her arms out, "here, from the Wild West?"

"Come, child." Granny took the young woman by the shoulder. She gave a nod of her head to Flora and Bridget as she led Helen down the hall and into the living room. "We will tell you all about the adventures the women from this house have embarked upon." She closed the door at her back with a sigh of relief. Finally, something had managed to break through the wall this young woman had built around herself. Now, if they could just interest her in remaining mentally present – well, she would feel she had won a major battle.

Chapter 43

"Helen, I need you to pay attention to what we say in this room." Granny gently pushed the young woman into a chair by the side of the fire in the living room. She bent forward at the waist to stare at the young woman. "You need to listen to us." The young woman had a way of disappearing inside her own mind when you were talking to her. You could see it in her eyes – there was nobody home.

Helen stared back, completely confused. She was sitting right here – how could she avoid hearing?

"You know everyone here, don't you?" Granny waited for Helen to look at the other women and nod before continuing. "We want to talk to you about the situation you find yourself in. We know you had no part in what happened to you but sadly you have been left to deal with the results of another's actions. We need to ask you about your plans and dreams for the future – can we do that, Helen – help you plan a future?"

"What future do I have?" Helen snapped. Did these

women think she didn't know her life was destroyed – she had no future? "I am a fallen woman – a disgrace – what point is there in even thinking about the future?"

"You need to snap out of this." Dorothy stood and with hands on her hips stared down at the wilting girl. She hadn't had a lot of experience dealing with women, true – however, she had watched what was going on in this house. The women had been melting with sympathy for this poor girl. That wasn't working – time to take off the kid gloves. "You are not a child. Yes, you have been treated disgracefully. You are not the first and sadly you will not be the last. It is time for you to take control of the rest of your life. You have options – people willing and ready to help you – there is no point in them working towards your future if you just waft around the place like a little ghost. Wake up, girl!" She bent to stare into Helen's bewildered blue eyes.

"Dorothy!" Georgina was shocked.

The other women stared, horrified to hear this woman abuse one so delicate.

"I believe I am the only woman here who has borne a child." She looked around at the others for confirmation. "I know just how much a child takes from its mother. If this little girl isn't careful, we are going to lose both of them. There are options and it is time Helen woke up and realised that – she needs to take back control of her life."

"What would you know of anything?" Helen leapt to her feet and glared at the taller woman. "You with your fancy clothes and lilywhite skin! You with hands that are soft as silk – you have never worked hard in your life. What would you know of my life or what it has been like? How dare you think to tell me of my future? I *have* no

303

future." She pointed to her swollen stomach with a gesture of disgust. "I will never again find a place in a decent household. What am I going to do with a baby? I have no means to support it or myself." She screamed into Dorothy's face: "*I don't want this!*"

"Well," Dorothy was pleased to see the hint of fire in the young woman, "That is one decision out of the way. You don't want the child."

"What kind of monster doesn't want her own child?" Helen fell back into the chair, sobbing.

Granny watched and wondered if she should interfere. Agatha clenched her hands. She needed to stay seated and allow the others to deal with Helen – her way wasn't working. Georgina knew nothing about being with child but waited to see if she would be needed.

"That baby you are carrying is innocent." Dorothy still stood over Helen's sobbing figure. "The child is as innocent of any sin as you are yourself." She gestured around the room. "We have been called here to help you. We are all willing to do this but there is simply no point in any of this if you do not begin to accept the situation you find yourself in. We can help – but only with your help."

"How can I help anything?" Helen wanted to go back to her room and pull the bed covers over her head. She wanted to die. "I am destroyed."

"Oh, for heaven's sake, girl, nothing can be achieved if you simply sit and wail about it. Pull your socks up!" Dorothy snapped. "You are in possession of something your old master wants – the man has gone to a great deal of trouble to create this baby – a baby you don't want – but he does – time to make the man pay and pay well for

304

what he has done to you." She returned to her seat and accepted the condemning stares of the other women. Someone had to make this child see what she had before it was too late. There was work to be done. "I think it's time for that tea you mentioned, Georgina."

There was a stunned silence in the living room while they waited for the tea Georgina had requested to be delivered. Granny waited to see what would happen. Agatha wanted to demand an explanation, but she was coming to realise that she couldn't live Helen's life for her. She'd been deathly afraid that she'd brought the girl to this house only for her to die amongst strangers. Georgina was keeping well out of this – she didn't feel she had anything to offer and, besides, Dorothy seemed to have the matter well and truly in hand. Their softly, softly approach simply wasn't working.

"I wouldn't give a sick dog to that man," Helen whispered into the silence.

"I would agree he would not be an ideal guardian." Agatha gave her opinion softly.

"What of the son and his wife – surely they would have some say in this matter?" Dorothy asked.

"The young master and his wife – that would be different. But I don't know what you mean when you say make him pay." Helen was paying attention now. "How?"

The women barely refrained from applauding. They were delighted. Finally, something had made Helen ask a question about her future.

"My late husband ran a stud farm and racing stables." Dorothy sat back in her chair and crossed one leg over the other – the very picture of relaxation but that was not how she was feeling. She knew how important her next words would be. "It is a crime punishable by law to allow your stud to mount a mare without the owner's permission. I suggest we apply that law to this situation."

"Dear Lord above!" Agatha gasped. "What is the world coming to?"

"Explain." Granny was all for making people pay for their crimes.

A knock sounded and Georgina stood to walk over and open the door. The room was silent while Ruth pushed the tea trolley into the room.

"We will serve ourselves, thank you, Ruth," Georgina said.

"Cook put some of her biscuits on the trolley for you all." Ruth gave a quick bob of her knee before leaving the room.

Georgina closed the door at Ruth's back and with a deep breath returned to the subject at hand.

"Dorothy, you were about to explain," she said, as she began to pour the tea.

"I believe we need to send someone to visit this estate to gather information." Dorothy had never heard the man's name. Helen and Agatha referred to him always as 'the master'. "This man – 'the master' as you call him – has dared to treat his son and Helen as possessions. Sad to say, the situation with Helen will not move the gentlemen of the law to act. However, I think if we approach the son we will find that man has a great deal to say about the situation. After all, he too was drugged and forced to behave against his free will."

Dorothy accepted a cup and saucer from Georgina's hand. She waited for the reaction to her words.

"How would we go about contacting the son?" Granny wanted to know.

"It would be very difficult to speak to the young master without his father being present." Agatha's hand holding her cup and saucer shook. "The man is truly master of all he surveys there. He opens his adult son's post for goodness sake. If we were to do this thing, could we not come up with a plan to draw the young master and his wife to Dublin?

"If we lived in the Wild West we could go in all guns blazing." Helen smiled to think of shooting the old master. The man deserved to know pain for what he had done – not just to her but to her father. Agatha had told her all about her late father and the master.

"I think we will leave guns out of it," Georgina said.

"If it's money for Helen we're after, the young master doesn't have any," Agatha put in. "The son is as much of a prisoner of that estate as the rest of us. The master keeps a very tight rein on him and his wife. I've heard the butler and footmen talking. The son can't breathe without his father's permission. After all, the old man holds the purse-strings – and he holds them in an iron fist."

"We need a plan of action," Georgina said. "I believe we need to consult Richard Wilson and Billy Flint. They will be able to assist us in practical matters. I am confident Richard will waive his fee, but Billy must be paid. He has overheads to cover. I think, when it comes to matters of cash in hand, it is time to consult the BOBs." That would give her an opportunity to mention Molly and request assistance for her.

"Then everyone will know of my shame!" Helen wailed.

"It is not your shame," Dorothy said. "Get that idea out of your head right this minute."

"Child," Granny snapped, "you have done nothing to be ashamed of – and so we will make known. Look around you, do you see anyone of great wealth here? No," she answered her own question. "We need practical help but we also need funds. Stick your chin in the air, child, and defy anyone to pass comment on your situation."

"My firstborn son is always up for a lark," Dorothy put in, then held up a hand when the others attempted to speak. "My husband's family are well known in racing circles – just the mention of our name would open doors – a visit from a young man of family would surely be welcome on this estate. Then he could seek an opportunity to speak to the son of this estate in private. But – I will not ask him to risk his person – he must have people with him who know how to protect him."

"The old master is deaf," Agatha offered. "That is why he shouts all the time. He will not admit to this weakness but we who serve him know. If your son should speak softly – even in front of the master – his words would not be heard."

"It would appear we have the start of a viable plan." Georgina offered more tea to those who wanted it.

"I would caution you against allowing your son to stay on the estate." Agatha didn't want to be responsible for a young person's injury. "He could be visiting in the area, I suppose."

"We will not commit to sending Dorothy's son until we have a plan in place." Georgina passed a refilled cup to Granny. "In matters of security we need Billy Flint.

Richard can advise us of the legalities of the situation. We need to consult both men before we go any further."

"That sounds sensible to me." Granny sipped her tea with pleasure. "You can keep me informed but I can't see as I'd have anything to add to this venture."

"Would I have to be part of this discussion?" Helen asked.

"Yes!" Dorothy snapped before anyone else could comment. She doubted very much that the girl would be invited to the meeting, but it was her life … she should bloomin' well be willing to do anything to help herself. It was time to stop all of this softly, softly treatment – it wasn't working. "We will be discussing your life. Surely to God you want to be part of any decision-making?"

"I suppose," Helen sighed with tears in her eyes.

"I may well be asking my son – a young man I love very much – to put his person in danger for you." Dorothy wanted to shake the young woman until her teeth rattled. "The least you can do is supply what information you might have to safeguard him and the others who may be travelling with him. That is not a great deal to ask."

"So," Georgina said, "we are in agreement. I will set up a meeting with the BOBs and invite Billy Flint and Richard Wilson to attend. Surely if we all put our heads together we can come up with a plan of action?"

"I would like to meet the young man and his wife." Granny had been told all about the man and his wife's difficulties in producing a healthy baby. Agatha had been a mine of information. It seemed that once she had begun to talk about the past she was willing and able to share her pain with others. That was a good thing to Granny's way of thinking – she believed that poison was better out than in. Now she had something on her mind when it came to the young couple. "I may very well be able to help them lead a better life." She didn't mention the blessing it would be for the young couple to have a child to care for – it would be a bit insensitive, she thought.

Chapter 44

"Come in!" Georgina responded to a knock on the door. The room had fallen silent, each person lost in her own thoughts.

"I'm sorry to interrupt, ma'am." Bridget entered the room and with a bob of her knee stood ready to give her message.

"What is it, Bridget?" Georgina was tempted to cross her fingers. She had enough problems to deal with.

"It's Molly, Liam's sister. She is in the kitchen getting ready to leave. Cook sent me to tell you."

"Agatha, Helen," Georgina said, "I believe we have discussed all that we can of your situation for the moment. No more can be done until we consult the BOBs. I need to occupy myself now with someone else. Granny, if you could stay please. Dorothy, this matter concerns you too."

"I've things to be doing." Agatha stood and offered her hand to help pull Helen to her feet. "We'll get out of your way."

Georgina watched the two women leave the room. "Bridget, tell Cook I said to give Molly tea and perhaps something to eat. We will send for her soon. Do not allow her to leave until we have spoken to her."

"Yes, ma'am," Bridget gave a bob of her knee and left the room, wondering what all this fuss was about.

"I'm thinking of moving my bed in here," Granny said when the door had closed behind Bridget. "I'm over here that often I'm beginning to feel like I live here."

"Granny, there are times when I wish I could move my bed out!" Georgina leaned forward to put her aching head in her hands. Would she ever know what peace was?

Granny looked at Georgina shrewdly. "So, what's the problem with young Molly Mulvey?" Granny was fond of all of Liam's family.

"When she brought the message from you today she asked me for help."

"What kind of help could she be expecting from you?"

"She is being pestered by a man at the factory – an overseer, I believe –"

"Harry Phelan!" Granny almost spat. "That man should have been gelded years ago!"

"You know this man? You know what he is capable of?" Dorothy felt as if she had walked into the middle of a play. It felt incredible to her that these women knew more about what was happening on her factory floor than she did. She didn't know this Phelan. The demarcation line between the factory workers and those above them was deeply entrenched. She had been unable to change that attitude so far, but she was working on it! "I believe I need clarification."

"Harry Phelan is overseer of your factory floor alright,

Dorothy. If you'd ever met the man yourself, you'd know all about it – he's a greasy little crawler of a man." She turned to Georgina. "If you don't mind my saying – I don't doubt Molly's word for a minute – but she's a mite old to attract the attention of that reprobate Phelan." She had been forced to deal with the harm that man had visited on many a young girl. He liked them young, did Harry Phelan.

"According to Molly he has been saving her for marriage," Georgina said. "He believes she comes from a fertile line and wishes to get many children from her."

"Ladies," Dorothy snapped, "you are giving me a headache!"

"That Harry Phelan is a bad egg," Granny said. "The men who manage that factory are only interested in profit. They don't care what happens on the factory floor as long as it doesn't interfere with the money in their pockets."

"Dear Lord!" Dorothy closed her eyes and fell back in her chair with a sigh. "I feel as if I've been swimming against the tide ever since I set foot in the factory." She opened her eyes to look at the other two women. "I am not offering that as an excuse. I simply do not know what is happening on the factory floor. I have not succeeded in taking control of the office floor yet. I am struggling to establish myself in my role as owner and manager. I desperately need a qualified assistant that answers only to me."

"I was anxious to know how you were getting on, but I didn't like to ask." Georgina had watched Dorothy leave every day, wondering how she was handling the old guard at the factory.

"I know some of the old men running that factory –

can't imagine they like the idea of answering to a woman," Granny said.

"Those men have been allowed to rule the roost since my father's death," Dorothy said. "I have been kept informed on the financial returns of the factory – I insisted on that – but I have no great idea of the day-to-day running. I want to learn but am meeting with resistance every step of the way. Returning to your home every evening, Georgina, is the only thing that has kept me sane these last months."

"It would appear that once again this house is to be indebted to Billy Flint." Granny smiled with satisfaction. She could help here but if she kept her mouth shut Billy could prove himself useful once again. She had an interest in seeing that young man prosper.

"I'm afraid I don't understand." Dorothy exchanged a confused glance with Georgina.

"If I'm not mistaken, Billy can find you a man to assist you," Granny replied. "It will have to be a man – that lot won't listen to a woman – as you've discovered."

"Before I send Liam to fetch Billy," Georgina hadn't forgotten what had started this discussion, "what are we to do about Molly?"

"Are there any children born from this man's actions?" Dorothy too had been thinking about the young girl.

"No," Granny answered. "I would have heard. I've had to deal with the results of his actions often enough – not in every case I wouldn't think – but enough people know of me to bring me their youngsters when they've been hurt."

"Surely that's unusual," Dorothy said. "That he has begotten no children, I mean."

"It is and it isn't. Harry Phelan had the mumps as a young man. I've noticed that affects a man's ..." Granny

314

paused a moment, trying to find a delicate way to state the indelicate "his … well, his baby-producing faculties."

The three women hurried on with the conversation, none willing to question further.

"What a shame. I had thought to set the Poor Law Guardians on him." Dorothy had been thinking of getting the man's wages held back to support the babies he produced without the mother's consent. Being left short of funds would soon put a halt to his gallop, she was sure. She'd have to think of something else.

"That lot do a good job of chasing fathers that don't pay for their childer and I won't say different." Granny knew the Poor Law Guardians were trying to save money spent on supporting not only bastard children, but the women and children deserted by a husband and father. "That won't work with Harry Phelan though. The rotter has never produced a child from his shenanigans, at least not to my knowledge."

"As you said, Granny," Dorothy stated, "the man needs to be gelded."

"None of this helps Molly," Georgina reminded them.

"We need to speak with the girl." Dorothy had an idea of how she could help but didn't know if it were feasible.

"I'll send Molly in on my way out." Granny groaned at the pain in her knees as she stood. "I don't think I'll be able to add anything to the conversation and I've things to be doing."

"Thanks, Granny." Georgina began to place the soiled crockery on the wheeled tea trolley. "I'll return this to the kitchen and ask Liam to take a message to Billy while I'm about it."

"So, Molly, you're saying that even in your home you're

not safe from this man?" Dorothy had listened in horror to what this young girl had to tell her. How dare this man treat the women she employed as his personal harem! That this same man was welcome in Molly's home – shocking! He had to be stopped.

"I'm not, no, missus." Molly didn't think she could protect herself from his hurting hands and foul comments.

"So you haven't told your parents?" Georgina knew the Mulveys – they were a decent family.

"Oh yes, missus, I have!" Molly's laugh was a sob. "I told them. Me ma thinks I should be delighted. Harry is older than me – well, he's older than me da. He has a good steady job and his own room on Henrietta Street. Me da thinks Harry is a sound lad because he always stands him a pint at the pub. They think I should be flattered he wants to walk out with me." She looked at the other two women with tears in her eyes. "They can't see he is a street angel and a house devil – I want nothing to do with him."

There was silence in the room while each woman struggled with her thoughts.

Dorothy broke the silence. "I need to ask, Molly – would your parents allow you to leave home?"

"What do you mean, missus?" Molly had no money and nowhere to go.

"Well, are your family dependent on your wages?" Dorothy felt adrift in this situation. She really needed to learn more about her workers and their lives outside the factory. "Do you think they could manage if you were not bringing home your wages to them?"

"I don't mean to be hard-hearted, missus, but I've been paying into that house for seven years. I'm not the one having the babies every five minutes. Me ma and da are the grown-ups. I figure I've paid them back for me upbringing. After all, if I married like they want I wouldn't be paying into the house, now would I?"

"Dorothy, why are you asking?" Georgina leaned forward to ask.

"Molly, I'm sorry. I need to speak to Georgina in private." Dorothy stood and with a wave of her hand indicated that Molly should leave. "Please wait for us to call you. Do not leave the house. I may have an idea of how to help you, but I must first speak with Georgina." She practically pushed Molly out of the room, closing the door firmly at her back.

She turned to Georgina.

"Georgina, I don't want to send Molly out into danger if I can prevent it." Dorothy couldn't allow the young woman who had worked for her for years to be put in danger's way if she could prevent it. In these modern times she felt it was up to women to help each other – no matter their social class. "I wondered if Molly should come and live here – I know it is your home and I am a lodger – but I would be willing to pay for Molly's board and lodging."

"That's all very well and good, Dorothy," Georgina would be glad of more income, "but to what purpose?"

"My head is swirling with ideas." Dorothy walked to lean on the mantelpiece and stared into the fire for a moment. "Molly is of an age with Helen." She turned to look at Georgina. "Listening to Molly speak, it would appear she has the same background as Helen, both being the oldest in a large family. We need someone to push Helen along. Flora is too polite and sympathetic. I somehow can't see young Molly allowing Helen to wander like a ghost around the place, can you?"

"We cannot offer Molly the role of nursemaid to Helen." Georgina stared at Dorothy, wondering if she'd lost the run of her senses.

"No," Dorothy waved her arms around, "no, that is not what I am proposing." She pushed her long, lean fingers into her forehead as if to push thoughts out. "Molly wants a chance at a new life. She has been brave enough to come here and ask for help." She waved Georgina to silence when the other woman opened her mouth. "Helen, if everything goes to plan, should have enough money to support herself for some time but not for a lifetime. What I am wondering," she spun in a circle, unable to believe she was even thinking in such a fashion, "while we wait for Helen's baby to be born – could you teach both young women to appear genteel? Is it possible? Could we send both of them to America, to this Mr Harvey, to become Harvey Girls?"

"Jesus," Georgina stared, "you don't think small, do you?"

"But is it possible?"

"Anything is possible," Georgina said. "But it will take a lot of planning and funds I simply do not have."

"I will fund Molly." Dorothy was excited at the chance to change even one woman's life for the better. "I support the BOBs financially – send in my donation regularly – but I have never involved myself in the working of the society. Well, I never even thought about becoming involved, truthfully. But now I can make a difference. Can we do this?"

"We can but try." Georgina had long since passed the point of being surprised. "We can but try."

Chapter 45

"You need to talk to Dulcie Mortimer." Billy Flint was sitting in the living room with Dorothy. Georgina had excused herself, believing she had nothing she could add to the conversation between these two.

Billy had almost run into the house when Granny told him what was going on. He'd known what he was going to be asked – good aul' Granny had tipped him the wink. He'd listened while Dorothy explained her needs, all the while planning how best to turn this situation to his advantage. A man had to look after his own interests after all.

"Dulcie Mortimer? I don't know who that is." Dorothy felt her eyes had been opened since coming to this house. There was so much native intelligence and talent available in places she had never thought to look before. The man in front of her was a prime example of her new admiration and appreciation for the lower classes.

"Dulcie works in your factory office. She's secretary to

your manager, Mr Fox. She was one of the first women to go to night school and learn that new way of writing – I believe it's called shorthand – that and typing on one of those typewriter machines."

"I think I've seen her about the place. A little grey mouse of a woman."

Dorothy had often been in her manager's office. The man might well be called Fox but he was a toad in her eyes. The attitude to women in the workplace came directly from that man's office. He dismissed her presence at the factory as a woman's fleeting fancy. He would learn differently when she was ready to act. The unfortunate woman who served as his secretary was like a rabbit in a fox's mouth. She had thought so every time she visited that office.

"That little mouse could run your factory if aul' Fox were to drop dead." Billy had made it his business to discover all he could about that factory when he learned the owner was to live in this house. He'd had a pint with some of the men who worked there – flirted with the girls who worked on the floor. The top men were just as loose-lipped. It was amazing to him what you could hear while sharing a cigar and whiskey with the big boys. Those men loved to boast about their success and money-making ability. He listened and learned.

"You do surprise me." Dorothy tried to bring a clearer picture of the woman into her mind's eye but failed. The woman appeared to be part of the office furniture.

"Dulcie is one of those women born to be burdened – life has treated her very badly. She's the only girl in the family – her brothers left home and made their own lives, so Dulcie was left with the father and mother to take care of – she is not the only woman in that position. I daresay when the parents finally kick the bucket the little house on Appian Way will be left to one of the sons in spite of Dulcie wasting her life waiting on her parents hand and foot."

Dorothy knew too many women in the same position to express much surprise. "You are telling me all of this for a reason, Mr Flint."

"I feel sorry for the poor woman. She has a difficult life and, to hear it told, that Fox does nothing but verbally abuse her at the factory. A boss shouldn't be allowed talk to his workers in that way." Billy's life hadn't started out ideally but he was working on changing his future.

"You seem to know a lot about what goes on in my factory," Dorothy said. He certainly knew more than she did. She looked at him thoughtfully for a moment before saying. "Mr Flint, I want to employ you."

"I'm sorry but I have no intention of ever being a hired man. I'll make my own way in life." Besides he'd go mad shut up inside a factory all day.

"Not in that way." Dorothy smiled. "I want to pay you for the work I'll ask of you. In the case of finding workers I will pay you the same fee as a domestic agency is paid – a percentage of the workers' yearly salary."

Billy was glad he was sitting down. He'd never heard of such a thing. Yes, he charged for the information he gave out – sometimes in actual money, sometimes in favours – but to receive a percentage of a body's yearly wage – now that was money.

"Fair enough." He managed not to sound as stunned as he felt and continued in a business-like tone. "I've been giving the matter of an assistant to you some thought."

He felt his mouth go dry as he tried to mentally calculate how much money he could earn from this bit of knowledge. "There is a young man lives with his mother in a little house further along the canal. He used to work for you. In fact, your father thought a lot of him."

"Are you speaking of Myles Roach?" Dorothy sat forward to ask.

"Yes – you know him then?"

"I've been looking for him." Dorothy had been surprised by that man's absence when she'd arrived at the factory. She'd made enquiries of management at the factory without success.

"Aul' Fox laid him off." Billy was pleased to see the look of disgust on the woman's face. It was a bloody disgrace and so he'd say to aul' Fox's face if he ever met the man. "Myles took time off to nurse his mother through a bad illness. Aul' Fox told him to pick up his cards and not to come back."

"Did he indeed?" Dorothy bit out through gritted teeth – she'd been trying to play nice with management while she learned the ropes of running the factory. It would appear it was time to take the gloves off. That factory was her inheritance and she would run it as she saw fit. There was no need to treat the workers with the kind of frigid disregard for their dignity that she had observed. Yes, indeed, time to put the boot in as her late father would have said.

"They are having a hard time making ends meet without Myles's wages." Billy had sold a few items for him and his mother in the past. It was obvious to all that they were struggling to survive.

"You are earning your fee already, Mr Flint." Dorothy

felt the blood flow hot in her veins. "I will want to meet with Myles if you can arrange it. I don't want to turn up on his doorstep and cause embarrassment to him and his mother. Then I want you to advise me of a way to meet with Dulcie Mortimer in secret. If, as you say, the woman is capable of running my factory she is someone I need to have a long discussion with. Can you do this?"

"Not a problem." Billy would stand on his head for anyone who talked of paying him fees. It sounded so upper-class to his ears.

"I will, of course, pay you for your efforts on my behalf." Dorothy knew this man was going to be worth his weight in gold to her. There was no point in penny-pinching.

While Billy talked with Dorothy, Georgina was in the kitchen meeting with Molly. They were seated in the alcove out of Cook's way.

"Me, come and live here?" Molly couldn't believe her own ears. She was all eyes as she stared at her brother's employer. She'd come asking for help but deep in her heart she hadn't really believed it would be possible to change her life. "But what would I do? How would I earn my keep? I don't mean to sound ungrateful, missus, but I never wanted to go into service." She might have been raised poor, but she'd not been raised to pull her forelock to anyone. Her da wouldn't allow it.

"Molly, you've told me you have heard Liam talk about this house." Georgina wondered how much to reveal. "I doubt he knows the half of it. You will have seen Helen . . ." she waved her hand in front of her stomach.

"Yes." Molly thought you couldn't fail to notice the

woman. She looked like Misery's Mother creeping around the place. She'd been sick afraid that she'd end up like that herself.

"Well, she's not doing so well." Georgina sighed and looked across the table at the young woman. Here was no innocent in the ways of the world. "She was forced. She does not want to keep the baby." She waited to see the other's reaction.

"I can't say I blame her." Molly nodded, not in the least shocked.

"What we are suggesting is that you come and live here in this house. You would share a room with Helen and we would ask you to treat her as a sister. We don't want you to cater to her, but it would help us if you could keep an eye on her." She leaned over to whisper, "We are afraid she is going to fade away – everything we have tried so far to help her has failed."

"I'd be sharing a room with her?" Molly had thought Liam's little room all to himself in the attic was a palace. She tried to imagine what it would be like to have a bedroom for only two people and live in a fancy house like this – she wouldn't know herself. "I wouldn't be a servant?"

"You would indeed share a room but while living here you will be asked to help with the household chores. Everyone is asked to lend a hand from time to time. While you are here, we will teach you what we feel you need to know. You have said that you enjoyed school but the lessons we will give you are in presenting yourself to the world. We will need to dress you, not as a young woman of means but of a woman sure of her place in the world. Would you like that?" Georgina thought that was a rather simplistic way of describing the changes they planned for the girl.

"I love to learn. I'd live in the lending library if they'd let me. I didn't want to leave school but what can you do? My family needed my wages." Molly didn't consider that strange. It was the same for everyone she knew.

"We will test you in reading, writing and arithmetic. We will have to see what standard you have achieved. Will that upset you?"

"Not at all." Molly looked around at the warm kitchen with wonderful smells floating on the air. Liam had told her all about the bathrooms and W.C.s they were adding to this house. Well, she'd seen the workmen herself. What would it be like to live in a little palace like this? Was it possible that she might actually find out?

"Mrs Lawler has offered to pay your room and board at this house." Georgina didn't mention the cost of dressing the girl. "We will endeavour to turn you into a young lady –" She stopped talking when Molly started to laugh. "I mean it, Molly. We will teach you many things before we send you out into the world to seek your fortune." They would have a little time while they waited for Helen's baby to be born.

"That sounds like a fairy tale, missus." Molly prayed they weren't having a joke at her expense.

"Not at all." Georgina leaned forward to stare at the young girl. "What about your family? Will they allow you to accept this offer?" She held up her hand when Molly opened her mouth to answer. "You need to think about this carefully, Molly. You will not want to fall out with your family. You have said you feel you have paid back the cost of your rearing – but will they agree with you?"

"Me da will be all for it," Molly surprised Georgina by saying. "It will be me ma who causes problems." Her mother firmly believed in the old ways – you gave birth to children to look after you – she wouldn't be willing to do without Molly's wages and her help around the house with the little ones.

"We will need to set up a meeting with your parents to discuss this." Georgina wondered what she could say or do to make the couple allow their daughter this chance. It was asking a lot of any parent living in poverty.

The pair sat in silence for a while, each lost in her own thoughts. Georgina leaned forward to ask again about Molly's safety. "Molly, is there some way you can protect yourself until we have a plan in place for you?" She'd never forgive herself if she sent this young woman out of her house and into danger. If this Phelan fellow lived in Henrietta Street it was only a few minutes' walk away from The Lane – where doors were never locked. He could lay his hands on Molly at any time. He wouldn't be the first man to pull a young woman down an alley to have his way with her.

"I don't know and that's the God's honest truth," Molly answered softly. She didn't think he would physically harm her – not when he was trying to impress her ma and da – but he took every opportunity of touching her – which she hated. At Mass the man was impossible to avoid. It didn't matter what service she attended, he turned up beside her. He made her cringe. Would she be able to bear it for a little longer? What would happen if she did move into this house? Would he still follow her?

"You need to stay here for a little longer today while

we think of a way to protect you from this man." She'd have to talk to Billy Flint when he completed his meeting with Dorothy. She blessed the day that man was introduced into this house. What would they have done without him and his men to turn to? She dreaded to think.

Chapter 46

"*Here, Liam!*"

Liam thought his heart would jump out of his chest when the large heavy hand landed on his shoulder. He squirmed and tried to escape. "I was only looking."

He'd been climbing over the bricks and pipes the workmen had left lying out.

"Don't be daft!"

"*Da!*" Liam's mouth fell open in shock. His da never came here. "What are you doing here?"

"I'm looking for your sister."

"Which one?" Liam had more than one sister.

"Don't you box clever with me, young man!" Matthew Mulvey shook Liam's entire body, using the grip he had on his young son's shoulder. "Your sister Molly. Someone told me she was seen talking with Granny Grunt – to hear you tell it, that woman's over here more than in her own home." He shook Liam again. "Now, tell me truthfully – *is your sister inside?*" He jerked his head towards the nearby house.

"Everything alright, Liam?" One of the men living in the carriage house had come out to check what was going on. "This man isn't bothering you, is he?"

"It's me da." Liam puffed up his chest. His da wasn't a tall man but he was muscled and powerful-looking to the young boy's eyes. His da was his hero.

"Sorry, sir!" The other man returned to his post inside the carriage house. What went on between a father and his child was none of his business.

"Now, our Liam," Matthew hadn't released his tight grip on his lad's shoulder, "is your sister about?"

"She's inside talking to me lady." Liam couldn't lie to his da – besides, he didn't know what Molly was up to – she wouldn't tell him.

"Run in and tell her I want her," Matthew ordered.

"Da, I can't interrupt our Molly when she's talking to the lady of the house," Liam objected. "It wouldn't be right."

"I can't go in there, our Liam." Matthew looked down at himself. "I'm in me work clothes. Yer ma wouldn't even let me stop for a cup of tea. I couldn't tramp me dirt all over their clean floors here." He shook his son. "Now do as I say and run inside and get your sister." He released his grip.

Liam took off but he wasn't going to bother Miss Georgina – he'd ask Cook – that woman would know what he needed to do. He ran into the kitchen and stood for a moment. Miss Georgina and their Molly were sitting in the alcove. What was he supposed to do? He mentally took his courage in both hands.

"Beggin' yer pardon, Miss Georgina," he said as he walked towards the table. He didn't want to take them by surprise. They might think he was trying to overhear their conversation.

"Liam," Georgina turned, "what is it?" The young lad looked disturbed.

"Me da is outside, Miss Georgina. He wants to talk to our Molly."

Molly couldn't believe it. Had her ma sent him to fetch her home?

"Have him come in," Georgina said.

"He won't come inside, Miss Georgina. He's in his work clothes and he doesn't want to walk the dirt through the house."

"I'll have to go talk to him, Miss Georgina." Molly pushed her chair back. She felt sick to her stomach. If her da insisted on her going with him she'd have little to say about it.

"In the Name of God, our Molly," Matthew pushed his flat cap back on his head when he saw his eldest girl exit the back door of the fancy house, "what are you doing here? Your mother is frantic. She says you never came home from work. The little ones are crying their eyes out because you never brought them their sweets. What were you thinking of? I'd be still looking for you if someone hadn't seen you talking to Granny."

"Da . . ." Molly didn't know what to say or do. She didn't want to fall out with her family but there was no way she was going back to a place Harry Phelan was welcome.

"Come along home now, our Molly." Matthew draped one arm around the shivering girl's shoulders. "There's trouble. Your mother needs you."

"What trouble is that, Matthew?" Billy Flint stepped out of the kitchen doorway. Georgina had knocked on the living-room door and asked him to help Molly if he could. She hadn't had time to explain the situation to him. He'd been in a rush to get outside. "Maybe I can help."

"Is it yerself, Billy Flint?" Matthew turned to face a young man who was making a name for himself in and around Dublin.

"What trouble, Matthew?" Billy repeated. He didn't like to see a young girl shivering in fear around her father. He'd never heard that Matthew Mulvey was a bad sort but who knew what went on behind closed doors?

"It's Harry Phelan, Billy," Matthew began.

"*What!*" Molly pulled away from her father. She stood, hands on hips, and stared at her father. "What has that man done now?"

"It's not him, Molly." Matthew didn't understand what was going on. His Molly was looking at him as if she hated him. It hurt his heart. "The man's been hurt bad – the redcoats are all over The Lane asking questions. Your poor mother is frantic. She can't leave the childer to go see him – she feels she should be by his side in his hour of need – what with him being your promised and all."

"*He's her what?*" Billy shouted.

"*He's no such thing, Da!*" Molly wanted to kick something. "I've told yeh and told yeh I'll have nothing to do with that man!"

"Molly, go into the house." Billy Flint stepped down to join them. "Take Liam with you and all. His ears are almost flapping."

Liam had sidled out of the house, hoping to hear what was going on.

"Billy, fair dues to yeh, but this is none of your business." Matthew took Molly by the elbow. "We'll be getting on our way. You leave me to know how to deal with me and mine."

"Da –" Molly began.

"I want a word with your father, Molly." Billy didn't know Matthew Mulvey that well but surely the man couldn't know what Harry Phelan was really like – no man in his right mind would let that low life anywhere need his female children.

"Billy –" Matthew tried to object.

"There are things I don't think you know, Mr Mulvey." Billy was politely insistent. "Let your children go inside to the kitchen. They won't go farther than that and what I have to say isn't suitable for young ears."

"I'll talk to you another time, Billy." Matthew began to tow Molly towards the back gate. She dug in her heels but she was no match for her powerful father. "There is a man who has been a friend to my family who is in a bad way and in need of his friends. I won't let our Molly disgrace her family by not being by his side."

"Those aren't your words, Da!" Molly struggled. "They're me ma's!"

"Don't you back talk me, young lady." Matthew couldn't believe Molly would talk to him like this in company. "I'll show yeh the back of me hand!" It was an empty threat. He could never hurt his childer. He left that kind of thing to the wife.

"In the Name of God, man!" said Billy. "I was trying to be polite – talk to you man to man." He was aware of his men coming out of the carriage house. He didn't want this to descend into fisticuffs. "Harry Phelan is the lowest form of life. I cannot believe that you would allow your daughter to be in his company. Are you the only man in Dublin who doesn't know what he is?"

"Harry makes sure that me ma and da never hear any bad about him," Molly said softly. "What man or woman would risk their jobs by telling me da what that man is really like?"

"What are the pair of you talking about?" Matthew looked from one to the other. He too was aware of the men gathering around.

"There isn't a young girl over the age of nine working at that factory that Harry Phelan hasn't forced himself on," one of the men stepped forward to say. "I'd shoot him down like a dog in the street if he ever came sniffing around a daughter of mine."

"Molly," Matthew stared at his daughter, "is this true?" She'd tried to tell them he was a bad 'un but her mother insisted it was only a maiden's fear talking.

"It's true alright, Da." Molly had tears flowing down her face. Her poor da. He was a good man but he was said and led by her mother.

"What's happened to him anyway?" Billy waved the men away.

"I haven't got the full story." Matthew felt sick to his stomach. "It seems some woman in The Lane let a pot of boiling tea drop on his nether regions."

"Waste of good tea," one of Billy's men muttered.

"Couldn't happen to a nicer chap," came another voice.

"Does everyone hate the man?" Matthew looked to the men standing around.

"*Yes, Da!*" Molly screamed. "*And with good reason.*

That's what I've been trying to tell yeh but you never listen to me!"

"I'll have a talk with your mother – explain things like," Matthew promised weakly. His woman was determined Molly would marry Harry Phelan. What was she going to think of all this? "Come away home now, our Molly. Your mother needs you."

"I'm not going, Da." If she had a chance of a better life – then by heck she was going to take it. Imagine anyone thinking they could make a lady out of her! It would be like making a silk purse out of a sow's ear. But if the thing were possible …

"Molly, love, your mother can't manage on her own." Matthew was sure that was all he needed to say. What girl would refuse to help her mother?

"There are plenty more to take my place. Da, I've been promised a better job here in this house. I haven't all the particulars yet. I'll be home when I know more."

"Why didn't you tell me you were after a job?" Matthew almost sighed with relief. The missus would be happy if Molly was bringing more money into the house. With so many childer there was always someone needing something. "I'll tell your mother you'll be along later." He fixed his flat cap on his head and with a nod took his leave. He'd done what he'd been sent to do.

"Liam," Billy spotted the lad hanging around at the back of his men, "take your sister into the house." He waited until the lad had obeyed him before turning to his men. "Someone needs to find out what happened to that Phelan fella and why."

"Ah Jaysus, Billy!" one of them groaned.

"We don't want some poor woman being punished for

334

delivering justice to that fella!" Billy snapped. "We need to know the facts. Stretch, you and one other go ask around. See if anyone needs help escaping the law. I need to know more before I offer my help. Get away now. There's a good chap."

Billy stood gazing around while his orders were being carried out. He had a lot of thinking and planning to do.

"*Where is she?*" Lettie Mulvey roared as soon as her husband stepped into their two-room home. "*What have you done with her, you useless article! Didn't I tell yeh to drag her home by the hair if you had to?*"

"Now, Lettie . . ." Matthew tried to block out the noise of crying children. There always seemed to be one or two of the childer screaming over something.

"*Don't you 'now Lettie' me, Matthew Mulvey. You're too soft on them girls and so I've told you time and again.*"

"Why are you all done up in your Sunday best?" He sniffed the air, trying to smell food cooking. He was hungry after a morning's work.

"I am not likely to turn up at the hospital in me dirt, now am I, man?" Lettie was ready to pull her hair out. "*If you kids don't shut up I'll leather ye!*" How was a person supposed to think with all that noise going on?

"It's not your place to go to the hospital," Matthew objected weakly. He knew his Lettie would do whatever she thought right – didn't matter what he said.

"Who else is going to go and see poor Harry Phelan?" Lettie would scratch their Molly bald-headed when she got her hands on her. "There is talk that the priest has been sent for – their talking Last Rites, Matthew."

"Is he that bad?" Matthew hadn't heard. In fact, now that he came to think about it, there was very little being said in The Lane about the man. A juicy bit of gossip like this would normally have the place buzzing.

"Who knows?" Lettie needed to get on her way. She had to be nearby in case Harry Phelan really was dying. The man had no family as far as she knew. Surely anything he had should be left to the girl he'd planned to marry? She needed to be at the hospital to make sure their Molly got what was coming to her. Harry Phelan must be well set. Come to think of it, she might get more out of the man dead than alive. She crossed herself frantically, thinking God would strike her down for thinking such a terrible thing. "I need to be on me way." She pulled her woollen shawl over her head. "You'll have to send one of the kids out to the Penny Dinners for a bucket of stew. Who knows when I'll be back?" She didn't wait for anyone to object. She was a woman on a mission. If there was money coming to anyone, she'd make sure it was coming to her.

Chapter 47

The Dowager Duchess of Westbrooke smiled around at the company. "I declare, Georgina, since you joined our Dublin Chapter there has been more excitement than ever before. I don't know if I'm coming or going."

Georgina hadn't expected the appearance of these particular women when she'd sent out her appeal for help with what she considered the 'Helen' situation. These women were the leaders of the BOBs. She had expected someone further down the ranks, not the cream of the crop. But now the Dowager Duchess of Westbrooke, Lady Beatrice Constable and Lady Arabella Sutton – despite Arabella being in the family way – graced her dining room in all of their glory. The bejewelled and bedecked ladies were sipping from the cups of tea Bridget had served to them and gazing around in obvious delight.

Georgina was flattered they had decided to attend this meeting in person. She was torn, however, because she wanted to be in the kitchen with her two ex-students Tavi and Erma, listening to all of their gossip. She almost sighed aloud. She couldn't be in two places at once.

Bridget, in her best dress uniform, stood against the sideboard ready to serve – praying they would forget her presence. She was hoping to hear more about the Harvey Girls. She had her secret dream to become one of them in time – and, besides, she did love to be in the know.

"I have asked Richard Wilson and William Armstrong to join us." Georgina had planned to meet first with whichever lady the BOBs sent and so had issued the invitation to the men for a later time. "They will join us shortly."

"I will look forward to hearing what they have to say. But before we begin to discuss the reason you sent for us, Georgina," the Dowager was almost grinning, "I simply have to share the latest with all of you." She snapped her fingers in Bridget's general direction. "You there, run downstairs and ask my secretary for the file she is carrying." Bridget jumped to obey. "I have news from America."

"How exciting, Constance!" Lady Arabella Sutton tried to find a comfortable position for her swollen body. It was considered the height of bad taste to appear in public in such a condition, but she would be blessed if she retired to their country estates to wait for this baby to appear – she would not miss the fun she found in the city – whatever anyone else might think.

"I feel out of the loop of information as far as our ladies in America are concerned," Beatrice leaned forward to say. "Arabella, you have Tavi close at hand and I'm sure she has exchanged letters with her former roommate." Octavia and Mia had shared a room in the Percy Place house while they learned what they needed to know to go out into the world and earn their bread. "Constance, you too will have news through Erma that I miss. I declare myself quite put out – I too should have demanded a secretary from our first batch of students!" She sat back with a smile.

"The situation with the first of the ladies we placed with you is so much more positive than any in the past." Arabella had been the one who discovered the existence of the Harvey Company. She allowed herself to feel pride in having brought this chance for the women they helped to the attention of the BOBs.

"Yes, indeed." Beatrice didn't like to think of the number of women who had been unable to accept their new position in life and had sought the unthinkable – suicide.

"I believe I have the best source of information from the Americas," Constance said as Bridget stepped back into the room and placed a brown folder in her hand. "My distant relative, Verity." She pulled a diamond-encrusted chain from her bosom and held the lorgnette that dangled from it. She looked up to find the others staring in her direction – positively hanging on her every word – she so loved to be in control. "As you are all aware, I was vastly displeased when my relative decided to leave my employ to seek a position with this Harvey fellow." She didn't wait for the others to acknowledge her words before continuing, "I will confess myself in error." She removed a thick sheaf of paper from the folder and shook it in the air. "I had no idea Verity would be such an interesting correspondent. Her words and images practically jump off the page. She brings the world around her to life. I now attend the postman's arrival at my home with bated breath, praying for a letter from America.”

Bridget, again standing at the sideboard, was listening avidly. She wanted to hear every word spoken about America.

“Do get on with it, Constance,” Beatrice laughed. “You do so love to be the centre of attention.”

“Very well.” The Dowager picked up the first page of the letter from the table, raised her lorgnette to her eyes and began to read.

She could not have been more pleased by her audience reaction. They gasped, they muttered, they exclaimed but no one interrupted. Bridget wanted to clap her hands and dance in place. The words on the paper were coming alive in her imagination. What skill the letter writer had – it was as good as a book! With the news of Mia’s romance she almost gasped aloud.

There was an awed silence when the Dowager laid the final page of the letter on the table.

“Is that not too extraordinary?” she said as she looked at her audience.

“I am almost breathless!” Arabella applauded lightly. “So much has happened to our ladies since they left us. I am quite determined to visit New York and check out the wonders mentioned in the letter for myself.”

“Imagine one of our first-ever ladies sent to America has accepted an offer of marriage from a gentleman of wealth!” Beatrice exclaimed in delight. “Someone she met on the ship travelling to America! It passes all of our expectations. Mia will be set up for life! I feel full of admiration for the ladies.”

“I was so pleased to hear that all who wished had been employed by the Harvey Company.” Georgina felt weak with relief. "I have no doubt that each and every one has worked hard at this training the women are offered. They will not fail at this, the last hurdle." The girls were on their way to a new life and she'd had some small part in their success. She felt a glow of achievement.

"Can you believe Mia discovered a man in New York who teaches women to fight with walking sticks?" Arabella said.

"It would appear she wishes to continue with the training offered to the women here by Mr Flint and his men." Georgina was happy to know Mia would continue to learn how to protect herself.

"The world Verity writes about seems very different to our own," Constance said. "I too have been making plans to visit New York and perhaps places beyond. I find it frustrating that I have no knowledge of the places Verity mentions. I have consulted our library atlas but the information for the Americas is so dense that I have difficulty finding what I seek on the page – in spite of a very efficient index. Where is this Texas for example?"

"Bridget and Flora have created a large map of America in the basement. They are using my father's atlas to fill in the states of America so that we may know where our ladies are visiting and talking about." Georgina was proud of what the two young women had achieved under difficult circumstances.

"I want to see it!" Constance snapped. "Bring it to me."

"That would be impossible, Your Grace." Georgina used the Dowager's title despite the many times she had been asked to call the woman Constance. It was impossible to think of her so when she snapped out orders as she just had. "They have used the wall of the basement entrance for the map. It is very large and detailed."

"In that case, take me to it!" Constance stood.

"I too would like to see this map – if that would not be too inconvenient for you, Georgina?" Beatrice had the grace to ask.

"I will not be left out." Arabella began to struggle to her feet.

Bridget was by her side in a trice ready to offer assistance.

"Ladies!" Georgina pressed her fingers into her forehead as she stood trying to think of the best plan of action. The Dowager would never make it down the stairs to the basement – her skirts were far too wide. Arabella too would be better not trying to walk down that steep staircase. "If we take the outside steps down to ground level we can enter the basement from the front of the house – directly into the hallway that bears the map. Bridget, you run down the inside staircase." She glared in a fashion she hoped the young woman understood. The occupants of the basement needed to be warned of the presence of the titled ladies in the hallway. "You can open the basement door and, if necessary to illuminate the map, light the gas lamps." The day, in spite of it being warm, was overcast and damp.

"Yes, ma'am." Bridget waited a moment to be sure Lady Sutton was firmly on her feet then bobbed a curtsey and left the room.

She ran down the steep narrow staircase to the basement, jumping down the last three steps.

"Merciful heavens, Bridget!" Cook put a hand to her chest in shock when the maid appeared suddenly at the foot of the stairs. "Whatever is the matter?"

Cook was not in the best of moods. She was longing to enjoy the company of the two ladies who had once lived there and hear all of Tavi and Erma's news but she hadn't had time to sit – not with quality in the house demanding service.

"Where is everyone?" Bridget looked around as if expecting the others to be hiding nearby.

"In the staff dining room catching up on all the news," Cook said sourly.

"I am to open the basement door for the Dowager and the other ladies. *They want to see our map!*" Bridget raised her voice so it would carry to the women in the nearby staff room. "Miss Georgina is taking them down the front steps and into the hall."

"*What!*" came from several voices at once.

"Can we never escape those darn women?" Tavi appeared in the open door of the dining room.

"They're all coming down here?" Cook felt quite faint. What was the world coming to when the gentry went places they didn't belong?

"I have to open the door." Bridget ran down the hallway.

"Everyone," Lily Chambers took charge, "into the dining room." She clapped her hands. "Quickly, you too, Cook – I'll stand at the bottom of the hall in case of need." She tried to think of what needed to be done. "Liam, run and tell Billy Flint he needs to meet with Mr Wilson outside and take him in through the front door. I have no doubt it is standing wide open if all of those ladies are coming down here."

"This is a wonderful achievement! Splendid!" The Dowager, lorgnette firmly in front of her eyes, examined the map.

"I had thought to have a cabinet created to hold the letters we receive from America." Georgina gestured to the far side of the hallway. The area wasn't wide but it was seldom used to enter the basement so a lack of space should not be a problem.

"I know the names of some of these areas from my reading." The Dowager practically pushed her nose into the wall holding the map. She wouldn't dream of admitting she read the penny dreadfuls about the cowboys of America but this map fascinated her – so many places she had read about! Imagine, the Wild West and Verity was going to live there!

"What is this line?" Arabella pointed to an area of the map.

"Bridget?" Georgina turned to her maid for an answer.

"We are drawing in the Atchison, Topeka and Santa Fe railway and the part of America it covers." Bridget pointed to New Mexico on the map.

"Where is this Chicago that Verity writes about?" the Dowager lowered her lorgnette to demand.

Bridget waited to receive a nod of permission from Georgina before she spoke. "I believe it is in Illinois, Your Grace." She remembered that from Verity's letter. The women would be training – without pay – for a month in Chicago before being sent out to one of the many Harvey hotels and restaurants. She pointed to the state itself, having no real idea where Chicago was until she looked it up in the atlas.

"I must say, this is all terrifically exciting," Beatrice said. "A window onto a new world."

"Yes, indeed, Beatrice," the Dowager lowered her lorgnette to say. "I feel sure that this Mr Harvey and his restaurants are going to add a great deal of excitement to our world over the coming months and years."

"I am more determined than ever to travel to America and see this world for myself." Arabella rubbed her swollen stomach as she stared dreamily at the large map in front of her. "If Mia's future husband could travel with his children than surely I too could manage the feat."

"Are we the only ones here?" Richard stood in Georgina's dining room, staring around.

"No, indeed," Billy Flint, once more in the persona of William Armstrong, said. "The hens are in the basement cackling over the map of America. I was asked to keep an eye out for you and let you in."

"What map of America?"

"Oh, not you too!" Billy couldn't understand this fascination with a place almost on the other side of the world. There was enough to keep him busy here at home. "The women have a giant map of America painted up on the wall downstairs. As I understand it, they're going to follow the travels of the ones that left as they work their way around America."

"I wouldn't mind a trip to America myself," Richard said. "It only takes between seven and ten days by ship to reach New York. I'd like the chance to check out business opportunities for myself."

"More power to you." Billy would make his fortune here in Ireland first before he could think of taking on America.

"I dislike hearing of members of the better classes abusing those in their care." The Dowager sat back in her chair with an air of disgust. "We of the upper class have a duty of care to those less fortunate than ourselves."

The group had returned to the dining room and joined Richard and Billy. Tea and coffee with light pastries had been served while the tale of Helen and Agatha was shared with the group as were their tentative plans to send someone to the Limerick estate to check out the possibility of contacting the father of Helen's child.

"It would be nice if everyone thought like you, Your Grace," said Billy. The story Georgina had shared with them hadn't come as a surprise to him. He knew many a one who thought others were put on this earth to serve them.

"These ladies came to us through a contact of yours." Lady Arabella rubbed her stomach gently, trying not to think of how she would feel if this child had been forced upon her. "Did they not, Beatrice?"

Bridget, ready to serve, wondered if that was how she had come about, when a man forced a woman? What about her friends Sarah and Ruth – was that why their mothers had given them to the nuns to raise? She tried not to think about the circumstances of her birth but it was difficult not to.

"They did indeed, Arabella." Beatrice looked around the table while leaning slightly to the side to allow Bridget to refill her teacup. "I know the Limerick estate and its master well. Miss Judith Babington-Hawthorn – first cousin to the man these ladies call 'the master' – is my godmother – and my hero. I have always wanted to be just like Aunt Judith when I grew up." She shared a smile with the people at the table before continuing. "There will be no need to involve Mrs Lawler's son in this matter. Aunt Judith will be all the help we will need."

"Beatrice!" the Dowager exclaimed. "You *are* a dark horse. Do tell!"

"Hawthorn Manor – as Aunt Judith's home is called – is a major staging post for the BOBs," Beatrice explained. "Because of its location in Limerick we can often make arrangements for women from Cork, Galway, Waterford and other areas of the country to be stashed there until we can make arrangements for them."

"I had no idea the lady was a connection of yours, Beatrice!" Arabella said. "She is one of our most generous benefactors."

"Aunt Judith is the reason I became involved with the BOBs," Beatrice said. "I had long been aware of the work she carried out for the organisation."

Georgina didn't want the ladies to become involved in patting each other on the back. She had things to do even if they didn't. And she could see Billy and Richard becoming uncomfortable with this chatter.

"I'm sorry," she said. "How can this woman be of assistance to us in the matter of Helen?"

"Miss Babington-Hawthorn is the only child of Hawthorn's eldest brother – the man Helen calls 'the master' insists on being addressed as Hawthorn. Family legend maintains that Judith blackmailed her grandfather into granting her Hawthorn Manor free and clear. It is a large estate that abuts the much larger estate that Hawthorn manages. Judith has turned Hawthorn Manor into a showplace. She maintains control of all areas of its management."

"Does this mean my help will not be needed?" Billy tried to bring the conversation into an area that interested him.

GEMMA JACKSON

"I think not, Mr Armstrong," Beatrice said. "If we need the young master – Mr Ethan Babington-Hawthorn – and his wife to visit Dublin it only needs for me to issue the invitation through my godmother. I will send a letter privately to her home and trust her to manage the matter."

"Then, if you ladies will excuse me, I have matters to attend to." Billy got to his feet.

Richard also stood. "Ladies, please keep me informed of anything I may do to help – but it appears you have everything in hand and my presence is no longer required here." He hesitated. It wasn't socially correct to leave before the Dowager granted permission.

"You have my permission to withdraw," Constance said grandly.

The two men escaped the room of females with matching feelings of relief. "That lot will be twittering on half the day." Billy pulled at his tight collar.

"But they get things done."

They ran down the stairs to the basement.

"Are that lot about ready to leave or do I need to keep these kettles on the boil?" Cook asked when the two men stepped into her kitchen.

"Keep the kettles on by all means, Cook," Richard replied. "That lot will send Bridget down if they need anything, I'm sure. I can't imagine what else they have to discuss but one never knows when a group of ladies gets together."

"What is all the fuss about up there, Richard?" Tavi stood in the open door of the servants' dining room to ask.

Richard stepped over to join her and glanced over her

348

shoulder to see who else was in the room. Erma was by the fire while Helen and Agatha were sitting at the table polishing silver.

"They are trying to work out a plan of action, I believe," he said. "Something to do with you, Helen."

"Miss Georgina told me they might send for me." Helen dropped the fork she held. She dreaded the very thought of appearing before the ladies of the BOB's. She didn't want to think about what had been done to her, let alone talk about it. She just wanted it all to go away.

"I doubt they will need you – that lot have got the bit well and truly between their teeth." Richard put his hand on Tavi's shoulder and turned her back into the room. "Do you plan to join us, Cook?" he called over his shoulder.

"Yes, I'll get as much done there as here, I suppose," Cook sighed.

Billy wanted to get out of his good clothes but hated to miss anything. He followed along.

"My day is all turned around with that lot," Cook grumbled as she took a seat at the table. "But at least Ruth and Sarah are out from under me feet." It was one of the days the two young maids went out of the house to study. "Poor Bridget has been dancing attendance on that crowd all alone. The child must be fair starving." She'd put a covered dish in the warming oven for Bridget.

"Where is Flora?" Richard looked around the room.

"Where she always seems to be these days – in the old master's storeroom sorting years of what she calls treasure." Mrs Chambers walked into the room to join the others.

"Richard and Billy were just about to share what has

been going on upstairs with us," Tavi said.

"Were we?" Richard leaned against the wall. Billy copied his movements and leaned alongside.

"It's only fair we know what is going on." Agatha wondered what they had planned for Helen.

"It seems Lady Constable is very familiar with the estate you lived on, Agatha." Richard didn't know how much he could tell her. "I believe she is about the take the situation in hand. It looks like I will not need to be involved."

"Nor I by the sound of things." Billy didn't know if he was glad of that or sad at the prospect of losing a little extra income.

"Do you know a Miss Babington-Hawthorn, Agatha?" Richard asked.

"Miss Judith!" Agatha put a hand to her breast, shocked to hear that name mentioned here. She had gone to Miss Judith for help in removing Helen from the master's estate. There was no love lost between the cousins but Miss Judith was the only person for miles that didn't fear the master. She had told that good lady that Helen had been forced but had not shared the particulars – not wanting to upset the lady. Had she made a mistake not taking Miss Judith into her confidence?

"It would appear the lady is a connection of Lady Constable's," Richard said.

"Well, I never!" Agatha had never had much to do with Miss Judith. The master would have heard about it and made Agatha's life a misery.

"I know that name." Erma pulled one of the large Gladstone bags she'd carried into the house over closer to her. She removed a pair of wire-rimmed spectacles from the bag and busied herself folding the wire earpieces behind her ears.

"Spectacles, Erma?" Tavi remarked.

"The Dowager discovered I need them for close work." Erma had been terrified she could not hold down her position with her failing eyesight. The Dowager had sent her to an eye specialist she knew and Erma's world had opened up – dealing with correspondence was so much easier when one did not have to struggle to see the letters on the page.

"They become you," Tavi said.

"I have it here – Miss Babington-Hawthorn," Erma said, ignoring Tavi's compliment. "I knew I recognised that name." She looked around the room, her eyes appearing impossibly large behind her glasses. "I passed through her home on my way to Dublin. It was one of the nicer homes I stayed in on my travels to reach this house." Erma had not been impressed with most of the people who were paid to assist the women under the BOBs' protection. "Miss Judith, as she insisted I call her, made quite an impression – a formidable lady."

Agatha and Helen were dismayed. They had been asked to mention anything that might help their situation – why had they never thought of mentioning Miss Judith?

"Lady Constable seems to think that whatever this Miss Judith wants, she gets." Billy looked at the two women from Limerick. "Would you say that was right?"

"She does seem to have a way of getting her own way." Lord knows the master screamed and cursed the poor woman's name on a regular basis, Agatha thought.

"Well," Billy shrugged, "we'll leave the matter with her then and see what's what." He'd enough to be doing.

351

"So, Cook, have you made a decision about your range?"

"I don't know what to do." Cook had been asked by Bertie Fielding if she wanted the men to remove her big black range from the kitchen. The men were about ready to install her lovely new gas cooker. She'd been to the gas showroom to select the oven herself. It was a marvel. She'd been told by the salesman that all of the fancy hotels had the same cooker installed. Imagine, her – Betty Powell – using the same cooker as some fancy French chef! "I know I'll have my new gas cooker but that aul' range has been me friend for years. I hate to throw it away."

"*No!*" Erma almost shouted. "Don't do that, Cook! You'll be lost without somewhere to hang the wet laundry and leave your stews."

"What are you talking about, Erma?" Tavi looked at the other woman. She'd had no idea Erma was so interested in domestic life.

"Sorry!" Erma waved her hands around. "Sorry, Mrs Powell, it's just something the Dowager's cook has said over and over again." She looked around to find everyone was listening to her. She blushed to be the centre of attention but carried on. "Mrs Hodgekins is the lady employed as cook to the Dowager. She prepares breakfast and lunch for the family and staff – if there are guests invited to lunch the French chef cooks but that is the exception rather than the rule. The poor woman bemoans the loss of her black range daily. She is lost without it."

"Well, fancy that!" Betty said. "I well knew the Dowager would be one of them that insisted on having a fancy French chef, but I'd never have believed the man didn't prepare all of the food for the family." It was one thing to have a good cook for the servants but surely to

God if you employed a fancy chef he should be the one preparing the family's meals? Still, it was none of her never mind what the better class of person did in their own homes, but it was strange and that was all she had to say about the matter.

"It's all very different from your kitchen," Erma said. "There's a great number of staff to be fed and it is Mrs Hodgekins who does most of the cooking of everyday meals. The chef is a different kettle of fish altogether. He insists on visiting the food markets very early every morning and selecting what he says is the best of the produce available. He orders what he needs from the market to be delivered. Then he goes back to bed when he returns from the market!" She looked around the table and shrugged. "He states often that his genius needs rest." She tried not to snigger as she thought of the pompous man.

"Isn't it well for him!" Billy remarked.

"Well, I've heard it all now." Cook said shaking her head.

"You keep your black range, Cook," Erma insisted. "I'm sure it won't be in your way and come the winter you'll be glad of it I'm sure despite having the new gas cooker."

"Well, now," Cook nodded her head wildly, "I'll be keeping me range so. I'll tell that nice Mr Fielding." She hadn't wanted to get rid of what at times seemed an old friend.

"Now that that has been decided, Mrs Chambers, the workmen tell me they are about ready to leave." Richard wondered how it had come about that he was becoming so comfortable standing with the staff discussing household matters. This house and these women had certainly changed his world. "It will be up to you to see that everything that needs doing is done. Would you like me to walk around the house with you and check that the work has been completed to your satisfaction?"

"Ready to leave, Mr Richard!" Lily clasped a hand to her breast. "I don't think so. Have you seen the mess these men have left behind them? What am I supposed to do about plastering the walls they damaged?"

"Billy, why don't you come with us while Mrs Chambers shows us what needs doing?" Richard wasn't a building contractor but he knew that workmen sometimes tried to escape without finishing up a job. He would not pay the final bill until the Percy Place house had been completed to his satisfaction.

"I'd be happy to," Billy said. The men had installed a bathroom and W.C. in the carriage house. He had thought it looked half-finished but didn't like to say. If there was more that needed to be done, best he find out what it was.

Chapter 48

Chicago

In America three women stared at each other with tears in their eyes. They were Harvey Girls. Their uniforms had been delivered and they stood in their room at the hostel wearing the black dress and white apron of their new profession.

"We made it!" Felicia didn't know whether to laugh or cry.

"It is not the end of our journey but the beginning." Verity too felt quite choked. She examined her image in the mirror.

"We are to find out today where we will be sent," Jenny said. "But it is unlikely we will be sent to the same restaurant or hotel."

She hadn't told the other two but she'd been offered a higher-paying position within the company. It seemed Mr Harvey had a shortage of women who could handle the position of head waitress. The head waitress it would appear was responsible for the welfare of the women she worked with and for the smooth running of the restaurant, answering directly to the manager. Jenny was older than most of the women she'd trained with here in Chicago. She'd been questioned closely about her work as under-housekeeper at a large country house. A position as head waitress had been tentatively offered to her. She would be expected to complete three months as a Harvey Girl before she would receive a firm offer of the more responsible position and higher wage. It would be up to her to succeed or fail and she had no plans to fail. She would be sad to say goodbye to these two women.

"I feel quite sick at the thought of stepping out on my own." Felicia pressed one hand to her nervous stomach. "Which is stupid – when I left home I had no one to rely on but myself." She stuck her chest out. "I can and will do this."

"It will be easy for us to keep in touch." Verity too was heartsick, but they had trained and planned for this moment. Now it was time to put all of their work into effect. "The Harvey Company will see to it that our letters are delivered by train to our place of business. We will not lose touch." She reached for Felicia's hand. The two of them had shared this journey from the first. It would be hard to say goodbye.

"Shall we go down and see what is our destiny?" Jenny asked before the other two could dissolve into tears.

Chapter 49

Shelbourne Hotel
Dublin

"Mr Roach, thank you so much for agreeing to meet with me."

Dorothy was meeting with the man she hoped would assist her in wresting power from the hands of the men currently in control of her company. The lounge of the Shelbourne Hotel was comfortable and discreet. She'd ordered coffee to be served as soon as her guest arrived.

"Please accept my condolences on the death of your mother." She'd had to wait to meet with the man. Billy Flint had informed her the man's mother was at death's door.

"Thank you." Myles Roach pushed his fine mouse-brown hair out of his watering eyes. It wasn't easy to talk about his beloved mother. "In many ways it was a blessing. My mother was in a great deal of pain."

"That doesn't make it any easier on the ones left behind," Dorothy said with sincere sympathy.

"No." Myles didn't want to make a show of himself by breaking down in tears in the lobby of one of the fanciest hotels in Dublin.

"I had hoped to talk to you about returning to work." Dorothy watched the waiter approach with a laden tray. "I didn't like to approach you while your mother was ill." She was slightly uncomfortable with the younger man's apparent distress.

"Billy Flint said you had come to Dublin to take control of the factory." Myles allowed the waiter to serve him coffee. He waited until the man had left before saying, "They won't let you."

"So I have discovered." Dorothy appraised the young man. Her father had thought a great deal of Myles Roach. She'd expected someone older and more impressive-looking. The weedy young man with his flyaway hair and tearful eyes did not align with the impression her father had given when he spoke of Myles.

"Mr Roach …"

"Please call me Myles."

"Thank you, Myles, and I am Dorothy. I asked for this meeting because quite frankly I need help." Dorothy had no time for false pride.

"You have been beating your head against the brick wall that is the management of your factory." Myles sipped coffee, his pale-blue eyes staring at the woman across from him.

"That is it exactly!"

"I had the same problem after your father's death. I was pushed to one side and firmly excluded from any decision-making." He put the cup back on its saucer and spread his arms. "Look at me – I am not an impressive figure." He held up one hand when Dorothy opened her mouth to object. "I have a mirror, Mrs … Dorothy. Your father was a very impressive figure. He walked into a room and commanded the space. You have that same air of command about you – if you don't mind me saying, however, you are female. Those men will never listen to you or respect you."

"I own the bloody business!" Dorothy beat her open palm against the table.

"So you do." Myles looked at the spilled coffee in his saucer, not shocked by her swearing. He could understand the woman's frustration. "Fox and company will treat you with politeness to your face while expecting you to go away and leave the men to do the work. Sadly they treated me the same way."

"I have considered firing the lot of them."

"You could do that," Myles looked at her in sympathy, "but you'd be cutting off your nose to spite your face. The men your father employed are good at their work. He did not employ fools. You also have to consider that any man you employ will have the same attitude. You cannot change society all on your own."

"Myles, will you come work for me?" Dorothy was prepared to beg. She needed information and support. "You would answer only to me. I need you by my side. I can't achieve anything with the situation as it stands."

"I would be happy to come back to work. It's not healthy for a person to sit around the house all day staring at the walls." Myles had nursed his mother with loving care but he felt less of a man than ever. He needed to make his own life. "But what are you hoping to do? Do you have a plan of action?"

"I want to walk every inch of the factory –" Dorothy stopped when Myles started to laugh.

"I do beg your pardon, Dorothy." Myles was mortified

at his inappropriate reaction. "I was imagining your reaction to your father's overseer Harry Rotten Phelan. The man's an animal and treats the women under his charge disgracefully."

"You haven't heard?"

"Has something changed – you haven't tried to fire Phelan surely? The man would burn the factory down around you."

"Phelan was involved in an accident." Dorothy knew she had to be careful in what she said. "It seems a woman ... the mother of several girls who work in the factory ..." She stared at Myles and realised he understood what she was trying not to say. "It would appear that this woman was offering Phelan a cup of tea when the large teapot she held fell out of her hand scalding the man very badly in his ..." she paused to search for words, "in his masculine area."

"I haven't heard a word." Myles was shocked. This news should have run around the streets like wildfire. "When did this happen?"

"I'm not quite sure – ten days – two weeks ago?" Dorothy had noticed a change in the energy around the factory. She had been fighting against naming another man to be put in charge of the women. She wanted to know what the job entailed and who would be best suited to hire or promote from the factory floor to oversee her workforce. She hoped Myles Roach might be able to help her with that decision.

"This changes everything." His mind was running in circles at this news. The factory would be a different place with that man out of the picture. "Will he be returning to work at any time?"

"It doesn't appear so." Dorothy had Billy Flint keeping her informed. The man had been active in helping the woman accused of harming Phelan prove the scalding was a tragic accident. "It seems infection has set in." More people died from infection received from an injury than the injury itself.

"Then it seems we may have a chance of changing your factory from the ground floor up!" Myles couldn't express any sympathy for Phelan – the man made life a misery for all around him.

"Will you help me?"

Yes, Phelan's accident changed everything.

"Dorothy," Myles said with a huge smile on his face, "I would love to."

"Here you, Billy Flint, I want a word in your ear." Lettie Mulvey stood in the lane outside the carriage house, her arms folded over her chest holding her black woollen shawl in place. She wasn't moving from this spot until someone told her what was going on. She'd left that young upstart Molly in charge of the youngsters. The day was still light even at this time of the evening. It being the end of June, the summer evenings were long and bright.

Billy turned from where he was inspecting the ground. The workmen would be leaving in the next few days. He was determined that the house and grounds would be returned to normal before that crowd left. They had promised to replace the turf they had torn up to place the pipes. The flowers were dead – nothing they could have done about that, he supposed. He stifled a sigh and turned to walk over and join the woman who looked ready to scream at him.

"Mrs Mulvey, what can I do for you?"

"You can tell me what the heck is going on!" Lettie almost spat. "I want to know what was said that put airs and graces on my eldest. I can't do a thing with the girl since she came over here. I won't have it, I tell yeh. She is my daughter and I say what's what."

"How would I know what's going on with your daughter?" Billy didn't feel it was his place to get between parents and their child. He'd enough of his own problems to be going on with.

"Don't give me that flannel, Billy Flint – you think you know everything." Lettie wasn't going to be brushed off.

"Lettie –"

"That's Mrs Mulvey to you, you upstart!" Lettie tightened her grip on her shawl. "You think I don't know it's you helping that woman get away with murder?" She forced a tear. "I'm up at that hospital morning, noon and night. That unnatural daughter of mine can't be budged. She refuses to visit the man she was promised to. How will that look to the neighbours?"

"Mrs Mulvey, I don't know what you're talking about." Billy couldn't afford for this woman to spread rumours. She could be dangerous. He had kept his face and name well away from what was going on with Phelan. Yes, he was involved in seeing that a miscarriage of justice didn't take place but he preferred to stay away from being noticed by the red coats. There was no shortage of witnesses willing to swear that the poor woman dropped the teapot by accident. He'd had to do very little to help the woman.

"Oh, don't yeh now, me fine young fella!" Lettie pushed stiffened fingers into Billy's chest.

"I'd advise you not to touch my person, Mrs Mulvey." Billy stepped back.

The look on his face gave Lettie pause. She wasn't fool enough to upset Billy Flint. He had too many friends about the place.

"That's none of my never-mind." Lettie let the matter drop. "I came here to find out what was said to turn my daughter from a loving helpful girl into a little vixen I can do nothing with!" she wailed, looking for sympathy. "The girl has given her notice at the factory and packed her bag. What am I going to do without her money coming in every week?" She wailed louder, wanting to attract the attention of the men she knew lived in the carriage house. Surely they would be on her side? "She has her bag packed and says she is moving in here!" She pointed dramatically at the big house in the distance.

"I suggest you go home and talk to your husband and daughter." Billy knew what the woman was trying to do but his men knew better than to interfere in a woman's business. That was a sure way to get hurt.

"There is no talking to the pair of them!" Lettie wailed. "Isn't that what I've been saying?"

"What goes on in your home, missus, is none of my business." Billy turned away. "Now good day to you – I've matters to attend to." He walked away, half expecting the woman to throw something at his back.

Lettie stood open-mouthed in shock. She always got her own way. How dare that man think he could leave her standing here? She waited to see what would happen but finally admitted defeat and turned away. She'd scratch their Molly bald-headed for putting her in this position. A woman on a mission, she left.

"*You are not going, I said!*" Lettie was ready to do violence to her headstrong daughter. She'd stormed back to The Lane determined to take matters into her own hands.

"Yes, I am, Ma." Molly was sick of the same argument. She had stayed with her family for two weeks, feeling safe now that Harry Phelan was out of the picture. She'd given her mother every penny she'd earned in that two weeks but enough was enough. She wanted to start her new life.

"You'll not be taking anything out of this house." Lettie ignored the crying children watching their mother and sister fight. Matthew had gone to the pub, knowing there was no talking to his Lettie when she was like this. "Everything in here," she waved her hand around the miserable space grandly, "belongs to me."

Molly had thought her mother would pull something like this. She was wearing her Sunday clothes and best shoes and stockings. She had a spare set of clothes underneath the one she wore. But if she had to walk out of the house naked she was going to grab at this chance of a better life. Her mother had made her own choices – now it was time for Molly to make hers.

"You are an ungrateful young whelp!" Lettie slapped Molly across her face with the flat of her hand. "Now see what you've done! Me hand hurts!" She shook the hand in question. "Never has a mother given birth to such an ungrateful child. If you walk out that door you'll not be coming back." She grabbed at the brown-paper-and-twine-wrapped package sitting at Molly's feet. "I'll be keeping hold of this too. Who knows what you've taken as your own."

Molly didn't bother to cover her stinging cheek with her hand. It wasn't the first time her mother had hit her but by God it would be the last.

"You do what you think best, Ma." Molly wouldn't break down in tears. She had to be strong. She had a chance at a better life. One she'd never dreamed possible. She was off to seek her fortune and no one was going to stop her.

"Jimmy, run get your da from the pub." Lettie couldn't believe what was happening. How dare this young madam defy her?

"Don't bother, Jimmy," Molly said to her young brother. "I'll be gone before he gets here." She pulled away from her mother's grabbing fingers and stepped towards the door. "Goodbye." She stepped outside, pulling the door closed behind her. She ignored her mother's screams and the neighbours who suddenly appeared in the long hallway asking questions. Her mother could tell them what was going on.

"This is Molly," Georgina stood in the open doorway of one of the rooms on the third floor. "She will be sharing this room with you. Molly, this is Helen." She pointed to the figure stretched across one of the beds in the room.

She hoped she was doing the right thing. Molly had appeared at her door without even a shawl to keep her warm. Billy had told her of the unpleasant scene in the laneway with Molly's mother. Georgina tried not to sigh. She had one more person under her roof. She could only wait and see what would happen.

"I'll leave you two to get acquainted." She turned away. "Cook will have something for you to eat, Molly, if you haven't eaten. Just go down to the kitchen. Helen can show you the way."

"What happened to your face?" Helen moved to sit up on the side of the bed.

"My mother." Molly took a seat on the bed opposite. She had been so looking forward to moving into this house. She was determined not to let her mother spoil this for her.

Chapter 50

"Ladies, you may enter." Madame Arliss, a sour-faced retired governess who had been employed to teach at the Percy Place house three times a week, stood in the open first floor dining-room doorway. "Elegantly." The voice was soft but cracked like a whip over the heads of her students.

Flora, Bridget, Helen and Molly lined up against one of the dining-room sideboards and without being requested held out their hands.

"While I realise you ladies perform tasks of a menial nature," Madame Arliss walked along the row examining each hand, "there is no excuse for neglecting the appearance of your hands." She held one of Flora's hands and glared. "You will be judged before you open your mouth – your hands speak of the nature of your position in society." She dropped the hand she held and continued on.

Flora tried not to gasp as her hands passed inspection.

"Each of you should be in possession of a clean white

linen handkerchief." She continued to examine hands as she spoke. "You should carry this item about your person in case of need. It is acceptable to carry your handkerchief in your sleeve," She paused to catch the eye of each student. "I advise it only when the trim is of a superior nature. It is perfectly acceptable to silently boast of your position by showing a trim of Belgian lace or extra fine Irish Carrickmacross trim. This item demonstrates that you have the funds to spend on expensive trivialities."

The four students were examined from head to toe before being allowed to take a seat.

"Miss Mulvey, we do not drop down into a chair."

Bridget bowed her head, glad that the woman was – for once – not lecturing her. The woman was determined to force the four young women under her charge into some semblance of gently reared females.

"Miss O'Brien, chin up, shoulders back. You are not at your prayers now." Madame Arliss glared around at her four charges. Really, what was she supposed to do with such a motley group? Still, she had turned out some of the finest young ladies on the Dublin social scene. She would not fail in the task put before her.

Bridget snapped her body into the required shape. Molly, Flora and a greatly enlarged Helen followed the directive too.

"You may open your notebooks."

The dining room on the first floor of the Percy Place house had been turned into a temporary schoolroom. The four young women took lessons for two hours three times a week.

"Today, for the first hour, we will study the social order of the elite of society." She tried not to sniff in disgust as she observed her students. "I doubt you will ever be in need of this knowledge, but no knowledge is ever wasted."

Bridget wondered if the woman was related to Reverend Mother at the convent where she grew up. She often used the same phrases as the old nun as she tried to force knowledge into her students' heads.

"In the second hour you will learn to serve tea and coffee – not as a servant – but as a young lady of good family. There is an art to serving while seated. I will begin your education in this art today."

"Cook, any chance of a pot of tea?" Georgina walked into the kitchen, a batch of envelopes and a letter opener in her hands. "Where is everyone?"

"The four young women are in class." Cook watched the blue flame ignite under her new lightweight kettle.

"Good Lord, is today one of their days?" Georgina was opening envelopes but not removing the contents.

"I thought you'd be wantin' to take tea with yer one." Cook jerked her chin towards the ceiling in the general direction of the dining room.

"Don't tell anyone, Cook," Georgina smiled, "but that woman intimidates me. I don't know where the Dowager Duchess found her but I am sure she is mentally passing comment on every move I make. I find myself almost petrified in her presence, terrified of making an unladylike move."

"You and the rest of the house." Cook sniggered.

"Speaking of which," Georgina again asked, "where are the others?"

"Ruth and Sarah are out at their fancy lessons. Then

there's a one giving lectures at the Gresham Hotel if you can believe it," Cook was busying herself preparing tea for Georgina and herself, "and Agatha and Lily have gone along to listen to what she has to say."

"A lecture in what?"

"Bathrooms."

The two women looked at each other and started laughing.

"Agatha and Lily are determined we will have every modern convenience on hand." Betty put the cups and saucers, milk jug and sugar bowl on the table and stood for a moment, laughing. "The pair are like to drive themselves mad."

"I am still in awe of the convenience of indoor bathrooms, Cook." Georgina tried not to think of the expense involved in kitting out the bathrooms – not to mention the constant supply of running hot water.

"I just threw young Liam into the bath." Cook carried the cosy-covered teapot to the table before taking a seat. "He was away with the pig farmer and I don't want to know what he fell in – but he fair stank to high heaven." She began to pour the tea. "I was that glad that I didn't have to boil pots and put the bath in the middle of the room."

"Ah," Georgina had opened one of the envelopes and removed the contents. "A thank-you note for the gift we sent – from Lady Sutton." Arabella had been delivered of a healthy baby girl – after three sons the lady was said to be delighted.

"Isn't that nice," Cook said with a smile.

"This one is from Erma. She has included a letter to us from America." Georgina examined the envelope. "It seems to have travelled around the world from the impress stamps on here. It has taken an age to reach us."

Cook waited impatiently for her to get on with it – the whole house was enjoying living vicariously through the women in America.

"Oh, our three ladies are now Harvey Girls!" Georgina looked up to share her delight with a beaming Cook. There were tears in her eyes. She had worried so in case any one of them had failed their final test. She should never have doubted them. "Flora and Bridget will have to get busy with their map. I have the name of their postings here." She was rapidly reading the tightly packed writing. "Not that they will mean anything to us . . ." Then she gasped.

"What is it?" Cook leaned forward to demand.

"*Verity has been assigned to Dodge City!*"

"*Never!*"

"The girls will be so excited." Georgina was beaming. You could not live in this house and not know of the reputation of Dodge City. There wasn't a lending library within walking distance of the house that hadn't been searched for books on the Wild West.

"There will be no living with them now." Cook laughed. "If they're not careful I'm going to start serving beans at every meal. That seems to be all cowboys eat in them books."

"Cook," Georgina gasped mockingly, "not you too! Has everyone in this house been infected with Wild West fever?"

"Now, now, Miss Georgina – don't you come the innocent with me – I've seen you reading them books meself!"

"I know, Cook, but they are so outrageously entertaining!"

The two women laughed together as Cook stood up.

"I better check young Liam hasn't fallen down the plughole."

"No rest for the wicked, Cook." Georgina returned to the beginning of the letter from America, preparing to enjoy a leisurely read of the contents. She had rushed through it the first time, very aware of Cook hanging on her every word.

"Miss Georgina," Billy Flint stood in the open kitchen doorway, "Granny Grunt is out in the front garden. She asks that you join her."

"Do you know why?"

"Who knows anything with that woman?"

"Thanks, Billy." Georgina shook the letter. "We've had news from America!" It was understood she was offering it to him to read. Everyone in and around the house read the letters from America avidly.

"That's grand!"

Billy stepped into the kitchen as Georgie left to walk down the hallway towards the front of the house. She pulled open the door, squinting slightly against the bright sunlight.

"Granny, you wanted to see me?"

"It's easier to show you than tell you." Granny turned and walked towards the Grand Canal.

"I'll be just a moment," Georgina turned back into the house. She needed to fetch her summer hat and jacket.

Chapter 51

"Thank you so much for joining us." A smiling suntanned man greeted Georgina as soon as she'd stepped onto the deck of the gently bobbing canal barge moored against the section of the Grand Canal nearest to her house. "I am Ethan Babington-Hawthorn – please forgive my appearance but I was under orders." He flashed gleaming white teeth. He was dressed in the manner of a barge sailor with loose canvas trousers in a sun-bleached shade of white. His flowing shirt matched the trousers.

"How do you do?" The name was familiar to Georgina but for the life of her she couldn't remember from where.

"They are here because of Helen," Granny whispered as the man began to unfold deckchairs onto the gleaming surface of the deck.

"Won't you sit down?" Ethan gestured towards one of the four chairs he'd unfolded and placed in a close grouping. "My wife will join us shortly."

"*EXTRA, EXTRA, READ ALL ABOUT IT!*" the cry of the local newsboy echoed over the water. "*TRAIN*

CRASH IN THE NORTH! READ ALL ABOUT IT!"

"Excuse me." Ethan's hand went to his head to tip the hat he wasn't wearing. He dropped his hand and jumped from the deck.

"Please excuse my husband." A woman stepped from the living area of the barge. She was tanned and glowing with health, her black hair falling loose around her shoulders in abundant curls. She wore a flowing white blouse over a black skirt quite without petticoats. "We live in the country so do not have many occasions to read news hot off the press." She extended a hand to Georgina. "I am Lavender Babington-Hawthorn, Mrs Whitmore. It is a pleasure to meet you. Granny has told us so much about you."

"Call me Georgina." Georgina accepted the outstretched hand in a daze. Surely this wasn't the woman Agatha had told them about – the woman who had suffered the loss of all her babies? What in the name of goodness was going on?

"Let's sit down and talk." Granny took the two younger women by the arms to lead them towards the deckchairs.

"Should we not wait for my husband?" Lavender looked over her shoulder to where the newsboy had been surrounded by a crowd of men and what appeared to be servants all shouting for a copy of the newspaper.

Granny took a seat. "I know men – they won't be able to resist reading the news at once and giving their opinion on the latest."

"In the street!" Lavender lowered her body carefully onto the deckchair. They could sometimes snap closed, pinching the unwary.

"This is terribly awkward," Lavender said when the women

were seated and had been served refreshments. The cheerful wife of the owner of the barge had served them juice and delicious fresh fruit before going to join her husband in the crowd around the newsboy. "I had not expected to be so abandoned by my husband." She looked to where the crowds of people stood around – some reading the newspaper and others shouting for a copy to read.

"I have to ask . . ." Georgina had been waiting for a letter from the father of Helen's baby. She certainly hadn't expected a visit from him and his wife! "How have you come to be here?" And dressed so strangely, she thought, in the casual fashion of barge owners and workers.

"Let me begin at the beginning – well, the beginning of the story for my husband. You should know . . ." Lavender was mortified at being left to deal with this matter on her own. "my husband has no memory of the night in question." She blushed. "The first we knew of the matter was when my husband's relation Miss Judith Babington-Hawthorn sent for him ... that was unusual enough to gain our attention, I do assure you ... my father-in-law is a difficult man ... he has never encouraged my husband to know his near-relative."

"I contacted Lady Constable." Granny was enjoying sitting here on the water with a cool drink and sections of fresh fruit to hand. "I asked her to allow me to communicate with her godmother – this Miss Judith."

"How blessed we are that you did!" Lavender almost whispered.

"I sent along a selection of my tisanes and suggested a course of treatment for Mrs Babington-Hawthorn." Granny knew all about women enduring multiple births and losses. This woman might not be poor as many of

Granny's patients were but nonetheless they were all made the same way. She had been sure she could treat this woman even if only from afar. "Lady Constance was sending a rider from her own home with a package for Miss Judith. I included my tisanes and written instructions with that package."

"You saved my life." Lavender leaned over to place a hand on top of Granny's. "We were ordered," she turned to Georgina to say with a smile, "to shake off our restrictive clothing – our rigid lifestyle – and take to the waterways! We were even instructed in what to eat and when to eat it!"

"Well, I knew this Miss Judith had contacts with barges." Granny was thrilled to see the results of her work. "After all, Helen and Agatha arrived by barge, did they not?"

"I am so terribly sorry, my darling. Please excuse me, ladies." Ethan Babington-Hawthorn joined them, shaking the paper he held in his hand. "A terrible train wreck in the north of the country – it's reported that many have lost their lives – quite puts one's own problems into perspective."

Chapter 52

Georgina punched the pillow and sighed. She flopped over onto her back and stared at the ceiling. The noise from the house informed her everyone else was on the move. She closed her eyes and clenched her fists. She wasn't ready to face the day. Would it be too much to ask to be allowed to lie here in her bed and simply rest! The wants and needs of everyone in the house sometimes felt like an actual physical weight attached to her shoulders. She wasn't ready to pick up that burden yet. She wanted time – time to herself – time to think – was that too much to ask! Tears of self-pity ran down her face into her hair. She brushed them away impatiently.

Helen was going around the house smiling – finally taking part in the world around her. Georgina only hoped her change in attitude hadn't come too late. She had received an abject apology from a man who had no memories of his crime against her – the fact that Ethan was as much a victim as she seemed to have released some of the poison that had been brewing in her system. She was in daily talks with the pair. The couple were to take the baby into their home and claim it as their own. Granny had been in meetings with them, laying down her rules and regulations. Georgina hadn't been party to these meetings – she had enough problems of her own to be going on with.

The week since the arrival of the Babington-Hawthorns had been a hive of activity and decision-making. The news that they had received a letter from America on the same day added to the almost festive glee within the house. Tavi and Erma had visited to discuss and pick apart every little shred of information.

"Nature calls." Georgina could no longer deny the demands of her body. She threw back the white linen sheet that was all that covered her. The weather had been glorious for several weeks now. In her cotton nightgown, without donning a dressing gown, she walked from the bedroom. She missed her bedroom at the front of the house – missed standing at the window watching the waters of the canal flow past.

The bathrooms were still a source of delight and wonder to her and, as she always did, she said a little prayer of thanks for the convenience. She met no one on her way and almost scurried back to her bedroom and jumped back into bed. She was determined to take time for her own thoughts and needs this morning.

Money, she thought, staring at the ceiling. It always seemed to come back to that one thing – money – or her lack of it. She had Molly, Helen and Agatha on the third floor – she received money for their keep – Dorothy too paid her a sum of money. But she had so many people who relied on her for their living.

"Who do I blame for the state I find myself in?" she asked the uninterested ceiling. Her parents who had insisted she marry the very upstanding Captain Charles Whitmore – or that man himself for the mental and physical torture he had subjected her to? "*Yes, torture!*" she hissed at the ceiling. "For that is what it was and is." The fear of what her husband would do next was like an anvil hanging over her head, constantly swinging and in danger of dropping and flattening her. "Or was it my fault? I should have demanded to be heard."

A knock on the bedroom door sounded and Georgina bit back the scream of frustration she longed to let rip. Could she not have even one morning to herself?

"I'm sorry, Miss Georgina," Lily opened the bedroom door without waiting for permission, carrying a cup and saucer in her hand. "You need to get up and dressed."

"Why?" What had happened now? What earthshattering catastrophe had occurred that only she could take care of?

"The Earl of Camlough and his grandson have come calling." Lily was opening the wardrobe to find a suitable dress for her mistress to wear.

"*At this hour of the morning!*" Georgina pulled a pillow over her head and groaned.

"Yes – and Mr Richard and Mr Elias Simpson have also chosen this time to pay a morning visit."

"Has the world gone mad because I decided to spend the morning in bed?"

Then Georgina slowly sat up. This was very odd. Elias Simpson – her husband's man of affairs? Could this have something to do with the attempt to claim her 'earnings'. Surely not, not at such an early hour of the morning!

Hurriedly she got out of bed and with Lily's help began to dress. She needed to know what new catastrophe could be responsible for bring these men to her door – at such an unfashionable hour of the morning.

"Gentlemen!" Georgina, wearing a light flowered cotton dress walked into the drawing room.

Four men jumped to their feet.

"To what do I own the honour of this visit – at such an *ungodly* hour of the morning?"

Richard stepped forward. "Georgie, come sit down."

All four men remained standing and appeared uncomfortable.

Georgina remained standing. "Just tell me what it is that has brought you all to my door," she demanded.

"Georgie, my dear . . ." Richard knew by the raised chin, the sparks of fire that seemed to be shooting from her eyes and the clenched fists that his dear friend was about to explode. He couldn't have that. "Georgie . . . it would appear you are dead!"

"*What?* It is too early in the morning for jests, Richard. I'm not in the mood."

"Madam," Elias Simpson pulled at his collar, "I was approached ... I didn't know ... I hope ..." How he hated to be the one to bring bad news to this poor woman. Hadn't she enough to contend with? He had seen for himself the disgraceful way her husband had treated her. He wished himself anywhere but here, but felt it his duty to be present.

"Georgina," Alfred was very much the Earl of Camlough this morning, "I was informed of this matter after Mr Simpson supplied my grandson's name as next of kin ... I'm sorry to be the one to tell you that your husband Captain Charles Whitmore is dead."

Georgina fell into a chair, her movement allowing the men to also take seats.

"Richard . . . what is going on?"

Richard pulled the cord to call for a servant. He remained standing, looking intently at his friend. "Elias has given me what details he is in possession of ... it would appear that Whitmore, while undergoing treatment in the north, was a guest of the Earl of Castlewellan." He coughed loudly to hopefully cover Georgina's gasp – he'd been expecting it. "They took the Earl's private railway carriage and set out for a day's enjoyment of the delights of the north coast."

"That dreadful train crash in the north!" Georgina reached for Richard's hand. The news of the railway crash had been reported in the newspapers. A carriage with a wheel gauge that could not be carried on a stretch of track was in the process of being removed from a train when another approached at speed. The resultant crash had knocked both trains and the loosened carriage from the track. "Charles was in that carriage!"

"Yes, he was," said Richard. "Initially, the identities of the Earl and his party were kept secret from the press."

"I had no idea he even knew the Earl of Castlewellan!"

"They are or indeed *were* friends of long standing," Edward Whitmore said.

Georgina clasped Richard's hand and tried not to show her dismay. What did it mean that Georgina's husband knew Eugenie's husband on such close terms – why hadn't she known? Had Charles Whitmore actually been spying on his wife for his good friend the Earl? It didn't bear thinking about – not now.

"Indeed, they had many business ventures together," Elias Simpson said.

"I'm sorry to have to tell you, Georgie, that the carriage was completely destroyed and all within it killed."

Richard's voice seemed to echo around the room.

Into the silence a knock on the door sounded.

"You rang, ma'am?" Bridget came inside and dipped a knee.

"Have Cook . . . prepare a tray of tea . . . for five, please, Bridget." Georgina struggled to get the words out.

"Yes, ma'am."

Georgina waited until the maid had left before asking, "Was the Earl in the carriage?"

"Yes." Richard patted the hand he held, giving and receiving comfort. "The Earl, Whitmore and what servants they had with them were all killed. Georgie, a woman identified by the authorities as Mrs Whitmore was also killed."

"What!"

"The authorities must be made aware that Captain Charles Whitmore's widow is alive." Elias Simpson was determined to correct the case of mistaken identity. This woman had paid dearly in her time as that man's wife. He would not see her suffer further.

"Surely no one here believed that was me!"

"No – no – of course not!" they all hastened to assure her.

"Edward!" She released Richard's hand and stood, aware of the men standing as she did. She walked to her stepson and put one hand on his arm. "I am desperately sorry for your loss." What else could she do or say? The deceased had been far from a well-loved figure.

"Thank you." Edward kissed her cheek. He didn't offer his condolences to her. He didn't feel it would be appropriate. The man who had sired him had treated the woman before him disgracefully.

"What on earth do I do about this?" She returned to take her seat. All of the men would remain standing as long as she did. She looked around the room into the concerned faces of males who had supported her in her time of need. She had never wished harm on the man she married. She'd merely wished he wouldn't behave so brutally towards her. Why then did she feel like kicking up her heels and dancing? She was free ... dear God ... she was free.

Eugenie and Bridget, their lives too would be affected by this news. What would they do? What should they do?

"You will need to contact the authorities and correct the mistaken impression of your death." Richard wanted to grab Georgina in his arms and carry her away. She was free!

"The family of the female on that train have a right to know what has happened to her," Alfred said. "Does anyone know the actual name of the unfortunate?"

"If it is the woman seen on his arm in Dublin," Georgina said, "I seem to recall having received notice of her name and particulars at one time. I would have to search my papers."

"I will undertake to inform my brothers of our father's death," Edward said.

"The most pressing matter as I see it is correcting the mistaken identity that the authorities have made – Mrs

Captain Charles Whitmore is not dead – such an error cannot be allowed to stand," Elias Simpson insisted.

Georgina lowered her head to her knees. She felt faint. She was free.

FREE.

THE END

ALSO BY POOLBEG

Through Streets Broad and Narrow

GEMMA JACKSON

On New Year's Day 1925 Ivy Rose Murphy awakes to find her world changed forever. Her irresponsible Da is dead. She is grief-stricken and alone – but for the first time in her life she is free to please herself.

After her mother deserted the family, Ivy became the sole provider for her Da and three brothers. Pushing a pram around the well-to-do areas of Dublin, she begged for the discards of the wealthy which she then turned into items she could sell around Dublin's markets.

As she visits the morgue to pay her respects to her Da, a chance meeting introduces Ivy to a new world of money and privilege, her mother's world. Ivy is suddenly a woman on a mission to improve herself and her lot in life.

Jem Ryan is the owner of a livery near Ivy's tenement. When an accident occurs in one of his carriages, leaving a young girl homeless, it is Ivy he turns to. With Jem and the people she meets in her travels around Dublin, Ivy begins to break out of the poverty-ridden world that is all she has ever known.

Through Streets Broad and Narrow is a story of strength and determination in the unrelenting world that was Dublin tenement life.

ISBN 978-184223-6147

ALSO BY POOLBEG

Ha'penny Chance

GEMMA JACKSON

Ivy Rose Murphy dreams of a better future. For years she has set out daily from the tenements known as 'The Lane' to beg for discards from the homes of the wealthy – discards she turns into items to sell around the Dublin markets. And now she has grander schemes afoot.

But, as her fortunes take a turn for the better, there are eyes on Ivy – and she is vulnerable as she carries her earnings home through the dark winter streets. And, to add to her fears, a well-dressed stranger begins to stalk her.

Ann Marie Gannon, a wealthy young woman who has struck up an unlikely friendship with Ivy, wants to protect her. But will the stubborn woman she admires allow her to do so?

Jem Ryan, who owns the local livery, longs to make Ivy his wife, but she is reluctant to give up her fierce independence.

Then a sudden astonishing event turns Ivy's world upside down. A dazzling future beckons and she must decide where her loyalties lie.

ISBN 978-178199-9547

ALSO BY POOLBEG

The Ha'penny Place

GEMMA JACKSON

Through hard work and determination, Ivy Rose Murphy has come up in the world. She still begs for discards from the homes of the wealthy which lie only a stone's throw from The Lane, the poverty-ridden tenements where she lives. These discards she repairs and sells around the Dublin markets.

But being in the ha'penny place may soon be a thing of the past for Ivy. She is fast turning herself into 'Miss Ivy Rose', successful businesswoman. With her talent for needlework and a team of neighbourhood helpers, she has begun to supply an upmarket shop in Grafton Street with beautifully dressed dolls.

Her fiancé Jem's livery business is going from strength to strength, and Emmy, the little girl Jem is raising, is thriving and happy.

Then Ivy's wealthy friend Ann Marie Gannon, with her beloved camera, spends a day at the airport photographing planes.

Little does she know that her visit can destroy all Ivy's hopes for the future.

ISBN 978-178199-9455

ALSO BY POOLBEG

Ha'penny Schemes

GEMMA JACKSON

In 1920's inner-city Dublin tenements, Ivy Rose Murphy struggles to survive and thrive in the harsh poverty-stricken environment she was born into. She is trying to adapt to her new role as a married woman. There are those jealous of the improvements she has managed to make in her life. To Ivy it seems everyone wants a piece of her. She is stretched to breaking point.

Ivy's old enemy Father Leary keeps a close watch on her comings and goings. She has attracted the attention of people willing to profit from the efforts of others. She needs help. Ivy's friends gather around to offer support – but somehow Ivy is the one who gives hope to them.

Ivy's husband, Jem Ryan, is a forward-thinking man. He is busy making a better life for the family he longs for – but can he protect Ivy when her enemies begin to close in?

If you liked *Strumpet City*, you'll be riveted by this authentic story of Dublin tenement life.

ISBN 978-178199-8229

ALSO BY POOLBEG

Impossible Dream

GEMMA JACKSON

In 1898 three young girls leave a Dublin orphanage to enter a life of domestic service. They are placed in the home of Captain Charles Whitmore but soon discover that the household is in turmoil. Charles, hoping to amass a fortune, is preparing to set off on a long sea voyage, deliberately leaving his wife Georgina almost penniless to fend for herself and the servants.

Georgina, who has been desperate to break free from a life of violent marital abuse, is relieved that he will be gone for some years, but nevertheless the future is frightening.

Then help comes from an unexpected quarter. An organisation that helps women escape lives of abuse or genteel poverty makes Georgina an offer. They propose that her house should become a school designed to train such women to seek employment in the American West. The very idea is at once shocking and appealing.

Can Georgina step into the unknown and lead the women under her care into the future?

The orphan maids listen and wonder. Can they too dare to dream of a better life for themselves?

ISBN 978-178199-8298